ECHOES OF
SHERLOCK HOLMES

ECHOES OF
SHERLOCK HOLMES

STORIES INSPIRED
by the HOLMES CANON

EDITED BY **LAURIE R. KING**
AND **LESLIE S. KLINGER**

PEGASUS CRIME
NEW YORK LONDON

ECHOES OF SHERLOCK HOLMES

Pegasus Books Ltd.
148 West 37th Street, 13th Floor
New York, NY 10018

First Pegasus Books cloth edition October 2016

Interior design by Maria Fernandez

Library of Congress Cataloging-in-Publication Data is available.

ISBN: 978-1-68177-225-7

10 9 8 7 6 5 4 3 2 1

Printed in the United States of America
Distributed by W. W. Norton & Company

To Sir Arthur Conan Doyle: Steel true, blade straight.

CONTENTS

ECHOES OF
SHERLOCK HOLMES

INTRODUCTION

by Laurie R. King and Leslie S. Klinger

A man on a mountainside shouts . . . and his words return, tumbled and shaped by the granite and grass they have encountered. A man in a too-quiet doctor's office sets pen to paper . . . and generations later, the reverberations of his words are still felt.

Echoes of Sherlock Holmes is the third volume of short stories that are, as we requested from our writers, "inspired by the world of Holmes." We did not ask for "Sherlock Holmes" stories—pastiches—or modern adaptations or commentaries: simply that the authors allow themselves to be *inspired by Holmes*. Then we stood back in awe.

Sherlock Holmes first appeared in 1887, the product of a young and not terribly successful Scottish doctor named Arthur Conan Doyle. Holmes was a man of his times: London in Victoria's Golden Jubilee year was a city of glittering jewels and silk hats, diseases and starving children, impenetrable fogs and millions of gaslights. Crossings-sweepers fought back the tide of dung from 300,000 horses. Boundless determination and energy were forging an empire.

Through this setting walked a "consulting detective" and his companions, solving crimes, setting lives back into order, defining not only an era but an entire genre of storytelling. The fifty-six short stories and four novels Conan Doyle wrote about Holmes continued to be published well into the twentieth century, but even in the later stories, there remains a whiff of the gaslight, the faint clop of horses' hooves in the background.

An echo only results from a sharp and powerful source. A tentative noise will not bounce back against those hard surfaces; soft fiction never reverberates. A century and a half after Dr. Watson met an apparently mad young potential flat-mate in the laboratory of St. Bart's Hospital, the echoes from that scene are still bouncing through the world of fiction. And to prove that the human imagination is more powerful than the laws of physics, the seventeen echoes contained in this volume stand on their own, miraculously undimmed by any distance from the origin.

New stories using the characters of Holmes and Watson are no longer, as a matter of law, controlled by the Conan Doyle Estate Limited (a company that holds the remaining copyrights for ten of the original stories). So long as creators don't rely overly much on "protected elements" of those late stories, they are free to make up their own adventures. This was conclusively established in November 2014 when the U.S. Supreme Court declined to overturn the decision of the 7th Circuit Court of Appeals in *Klinger v. Conan Doyle Estate Limited.* Not that this seems to have slowed down the business practices of the Estate (which the 7th Circuit described as "a form of extortion"). For example, they attempted to block the elegiac *Mr. Holmes* (starring Sir Ian McKellen, based on Mitch Cullin's *A Slight Trick of the Mind*) by arguing that Holmes's retirement was a "protected element," since it is mentioned in a copyrighted story—even though Holmes's retirement is also prominent in an unprotected story. (The case was resolved on undisclosed terms.)

Legal matters aside, one wonders what Conan Doyle would have made of the stories in the present volume. Some of them would confirm his beliefs as a Spiritualist: surely only automatic writing during a series of trances could explain his having forgotten Watson's meeting with M. Dupin, Irene Adler's unsuspected history, various prominent crimes, or the fact that Holmes's fascination with bees began with a gun battle? As for these visitations of embodied characters—proof of ectoplasmic emanations given voice!

Others of these stories might speak more intimately to Conan Doyle's non-Holmesian writing: a tale of evil on a remote and windswept island, 100 years in his future; a child who imagines himself a great detective.

Some, however, might have shocked even this Victorian author's vivid imagination. Yes, he was a proponent of women's rights (some of them, at any rate) but—a jeans-wearing young woman detective? Actresses in moving pictures? A detecting ladies' maid? And what might he make of a detective story peopled by members of a black-power movement? Or a London that could snatch away law-abiding citizens—children, even—in the name of security? As for these revelations about Mrs. Hudson . . . ?

Sir Arthur would have put his foot down at *that*, to be sure.

All of which only goes to prove that when one is dealing with Sherlock Holmes, a man "who never lived and so can never die," physics goes out the window. Rather than thinning out and fading, the Holmesian form is invigorated and made stronger with each reflecting surface (for remember, the word "inspire" means "breathe into").

These stories prove that sometimes, echoes take on a life of their own.

HOLMES ON THE RANGE

A TALE OF THE CAXTON PRIVATE LENDING LIBRARY & BOOK DEPOSITORY

by John Connolly

The history of the Caxton Private Lending Library & Book Depository has not been entirely without incident, as befits an institution of seemingly infinite space inhabited largely by fictional characters who have found their way into the physical realm.

For those unfamiliar with the institution, the Caxton came into being after its founder, William Caxton, woke up one morning in 1477 to find a number of characters from Geoffrey Chaucer's *Canterbury Tales* arguing in his garden. Caxton quickly realized that these characters—the Miller, the Reeve, The Knight, the Second Nun, and the Wife of Bath—had become so fixed in the public imagination that they had transcended their literary origins and assumed an objective reality, which was problematical

1

for all concerned. Somewhere had to be found for them to live, and thus the Caxton Private Lending Library & Book Depository was established as a kind of rest home for the great, the good, and, occasionally, the not-so-good-but-definitely-memorable, of literature, all supported by rounding up the prices on books by a ha'penny a time.

The death of Charles Dickens in June 1870 precipitated the single greatest mass arrival of such characters in the Caxton's history. Mr. Torrans, the librarian at the time, at least had a little warning of the impending influx, for—as was traditional when new characters were about to join the Caxton—he had recently received a large quantity of pristine Dickens first editions in the post, each carefully wrapped in brown paper and string, and without a return address. No librarian had ever quite managed to figure out how the books came to be sent; old George Scott, Mr. Torrans's predecessor, had come to the conclusion that the books simply wrapped and posted themselves, although by that stage Scott was quite mad, and spent most of his time engrossed in increasingly circular conversations with Tristram Shandy's Uncle Toby, of which no good could possibly have come.

Of course, Mr. Torrans had been anticipating the appearance of the Dickens characters long before the death of the author himself and the subsequent arrival of the first editions. Some characters were simply destined for the Caxton from the moment that they first appeared in print, and Mr. Torrans would occasionally wander into the darker realms of the Caxton, where rooms were still in the process of formation, and try to guess which figures were likely to inhabit them. In the case of Dickens, the presence of a guide to the old coaching inns of Britain provided a clue to the future home of Samuel Pickwick, and a cheap bowl and toasting fork would serve as a reminder to Oliver Twist of the terrible early start to life that he had overcome. (Mr. Torrans was of the opinion that such a nudge was unnecessary under the circumstances, but the Caxton was mysterious in its ways.)

In fact, Mr. Torrans's only concern was that the characters might include rather more of the unsavory sort than he might have preferred—he was not sure what he would do if forced to deal with a Quilp, or a Uriah Heep—so it came as a great relief to him when, for the most part, the influx was largely restricted to the more pleasant types, with the exception of old Fagin, who appeared to have been mellowed somewhat by the action of the noose. Hanging, thought Mr. Torrans, will do that to a man.

But the tale of the Dickens characters is for another time. For the present, we are concerned with one of the stranger stories from the Caxton's annals, an occurrence that broke many of the library's long-established rules and seemed destined, at one point, to undermine the entire delicate edifice of the institution.

In December 1893, the collective imagination of the British reading public suffered a shock unlike any in recent memory with the publication in the *Strand Magazine* of "The Final Problem," in which Arthur Conan Doyle killed off his beloved Sherlock Holmes, sending him over a cliff at the Reichenbach Falls following a struggle with his nemesis, Professor Moriarty. The illustrator Sidney Paget captured the hero's final moments for readers, freezing him in a grapple with Moriarty, the two men leaning to the right, clearly on the verge of falling, Moriarty's hat already disappearing into the void, foreshadowing the inevitable descent of the two men.

The result was a disaster for the *Strand*. Many readers immediately canceled their subscriptions in outrage, almost causing the collapse of the periodical, and for years after, staff would refer to Holmes's death only as "a dreadful event." Black armbands were allegedly worn by readers in mourning. Conan Doyle was shocked by the vehemence of the public's reaction, but remained unrepentant.

It's fair to say that Mr. Headley, who by that point had succeeded Mr. Torrans as the librarian upon the latter's retirement, was just as shocked as anyone else. He was a regular subscriber to the *Strand*, and had followed the adventures of Holmes and Watson with both personal and professional interest: personal in the sense that he was an admiring, engrossed reader, and professional because he knew that, upon Conan Doyle's death, Sherlock Holmes and Dr. Watson would inevitably find their way to the Caxton. Still, he had been looking forward to many more years of their adventures, and so it was with no small amount of regret that he set aside the *Strand* after finishing "The Final Problem," and wondered what could have possessed Conan Doyle to do such a thing to the character who had brought him both fame and fortune.

But Mr. Headley was no writer, and did not profess to understand the ways of a writer's mind.

Let us step away from the Caxton for a moment, and consider the predicament of Arthur Conan Doyle in the year of publication for "The Final Problem." In 1891, he had written to his mother, Mary Foley Doyle, confessing that "I think of slaying Holmes . . . and winding him up for good and all. He takes my mind from better things." In Conan Doyle's case, those "better things" were historical novels, which he believed more worthy of his time and talents than what he described as the "elementary" Holmes stories, the choice of that word lending an unpleasing ambiguity to Holmes's own use of the term in the tales.

Here, then, was the apparent reason for killing off Holmes, but upon Conan Doyle's death a peculiar piece of manuscript was delivered to the Caxton Private Lending Library, tucked into the 1894 first edition of *The Memoirs of Sherlock Holmes*, the volume that concluded with "The Final Problem." It was written in a hand similar to Conan Doyle's own, although with discernible differences in capitalization, and with an extensive footnote relating to the etymology of the word *professor* that was untypical of the author.

Attached to the manuscript was a letter, clearly written by Conan Doyle, detailing how he woke one morning in April 1893 to find this fragment lying on his desk. According to the letter, he wondered if it might not be the product of some form of automatic writing, for he was fascinated by the possibility of the subconscious—or even some supernatural agency—taking control of the writer in order to produce work. Perhaps, he went on to speculate, he had arisen in the night in a semiconscious state and commenced writing, for aspects of the script resembled his own. Upon the discovery of the manuscript he examined his right hand and discerned no trace of ink upon it, but was astounded to glance at his left and find that both the fingers and the edge of his palm were smudged with black, a revelation which forced him to seek the comfort and security of the nearest chair.

Good Lord, he thought, what can this mean? And, worse, what consequences might it have for his batting? Could he somehow be transforming into an ambidexter or, God forbid, a favorer of the left hand: a sinister? Left-handed bowlers on the cricket field were one thing—they were largely harmless—but left-handed batsmen were a nuisance, necessitating the rearrangement of the field and causing all kinds of fuss, bother, and boredom. His mind reeled at the awful possibilities should his body somehow be rebelling against him. He would never be able to take the crease for Marylebone again!

Gradually Conan Doyle calmed himself, and fear gave way to fascination, although this lasted only for as long as it took him to read the manuscript itself. Detailed on its closely written pages was a conversation between Sherlock Holmes and Professor Moriarty, who had apparently taken it upon themselves to meet at Benekey's in High Holborn, a hostelry noted for the privacy offered by its booths and the quality of its wines. According to the manuscript, Moriarty had instigated the meeting by way of a note delivered to 221B Baker Street, and Holmes, intrigued, had consented to sit down with the master criminal.

In his letter, Conan Doyle explained what he found most troubling about the contents upon first perusal: he had only begun writing about Moriarty days earlier, and had barely mentioned him in the course of the as-yet-untitled story. Yet here was Moriarty, seated in Benekey's, about to have the most extraordinary conversation with Sherlock Holmes.

Extract from the manuscript (Caxton CD/ MSH 94: MS)

Holmes regarded Moriarty intensely, his every nerve aquiver. Before him sat the most dangerous man in England, a calculating, cold-blooded, criminal mastermind. For the first time in many years, Holmes felt real fear, even with a revolver cocked in his lap and concealed by a napkin.

"I hope the wine is to your liking," said Moriarty.

"Have you poisoned it?" asked Holmes. "I hesitate even to touch the glass, in case you have treated it with some infernal compound of your own devising."

"Why would I do that?" asked Moriarty. He appeared genuinely puzzled by the suggestion.

"You are my archnemesis," Holmes replied. "You have hereditary tendencies of the most diabolical kind. A criminal strain runs in your blood. Could I but free society of you, I should feel that my career had reached its summit."

"Yes, about that archnemesis business . . ."

"What about it?" asked Holmes.

"Well, isn't it a bit strange that it's never come up before? I mean, if I'm your archnemesis, the Napoleon of crime, a spider at the heart of an infernal web with a thousand radiations, responsible for half that is evil in London—all that kind of thing—and you've been tracking me for years, then why haven't you mentioned me before? You know, it would surely have popped up in conversation at some point. It's not the kind of thing one tends to forget, really, is it, a criminal mastermind at the heart of some great conspiracy? If I were in your shoes, I'd never stop talking about me."

"I—" Holmes paused. "I've never really thought about it in that way. I must admit that you did pop into my mind quite recently, and distinctly fully formed. Perhaps I took a blow to the head at some stage, although I'm sure Doctor Watson would have noted such an injury."

"He writes down everything else," said Moriarty. "Hard to see him missing something like that."

"Indeed. I am lucky to have him."

"I'd find it a little annoying myself," said Moriarty. "It's rather like being Samuel Johnson and finding that, every time you lift a coffee cup, Boswell is scribbling details of the position of your fingers and asking you to say something witty about it all."

"Well, that is where we differ. It's why I am not a scoundrel."

"Hard to be a scoundrel when someone is always writing down what one is doing," said Moriarty. "One might as well just toddle along to Scotland Yard and make a full confession, thus saving the forces of law and order a lot of fuss. But that's beside the point. We need to return to the matter in hand, which is my sudden arrival on the scene."

"It is somewhat perturbing," agreed Holmes.

"You should see it from my side," said Moriarty. "Perturbing isn't the half of it. For a start, I have an awareness of being mathematically gifted."

"Indeed you are," said Holmes. "At the age of twenty-one you wrote a treatise on the binomial theorem, which has had a European vogue."

"Look, I don't even know what the binomial theorem is, never mind what it might resemble with a European vogue—a description that makes no sense at all, by the way, when you think about it. Surely it's either the binomial theorem or it isn't, even if it's described in a French accent."

"But on the strength of it you won a chair at one of our smaller universities!" Holmes protested.

"If I did, then name the university," said Moriarty.

Holmes shifted in his chair. He was clearly struggling. "The identity of the institution doesn't immediately spring to mind," he admitted.

"That's because I was never chair of anything," said Moriarty. "I'm not even very good at basic addition. I struggle to pay the milkman."

Holmes frowned. "That can't be right."

"My point exactly. Maybe that's how I became an ex-professor, although even that doesn't sound plausible, given that I can't remember how I was supposed to have become a professor in the first place, especially in a subject about which I know absolutely nothing. Which brings me to the next matter: how did you come to be so expert in all that stuff about poisons and types of dirt and whatnot? Did you take a course?"

Holmes considered the question.

"I don't profess to be an expert in every field," he replied. "I have little interest in literature, philosophy, or astronomy, and a negligible regard for the political sphere. I remain confident in the fields of chemistry and the anatomical sciences, and, as you have pointed out, can hold my own in geology and botany, with particular reference to poisons."

"That's all well and good," said Moriarty. "The question remains: how did you come by this knowledge?"

"I own a lot of books," said Holmes, awkwardly. He thought that he could almost hear a slight question mark at the end of his answer, which caused him to wince involuntarily.

"Have you read them all, then?"

"Must have done, I suppose."

"Either you did or you didn't. You have to recall reading them."

"Er, not so much."

"You don't just pick up that kind of knowledge off the street. There are people who've studied dirt for decades who don't know as much about it as you seem to."

"What are you implying?"

"That you don't actually know anything about dirt and poisons at all."

"But I must, if I can solve crimes based entirely on this expertise."

"Oh, *somebody* knows about this stuff—or gives a good impression of it—but it's not you. It's like me being a criminal mastermind. Last night, I decided that I was going to try to commit a perfectly simple crime: jeweler's shop, window, brick. I walk to jeweler's, break window with brick, run away with jewels, and Bob's your uncle."

"And what happened?" asked Holmes.

"I couldn't do it. I stood there, brick in hand, but I couldn't throw it. Instead I went home and constructed an elaborate plan for tunneling into the jeweler's involving six dwarfs, a bald man with a stoop, and an airship."

"What has an airship got to do with digging a tunnel?" asked Holmes.

"Exactly!" Moriarty exclaimed. "More importantly, why do I need six dwarfs, never mind the bald man with the stoop? I can't think of any situation in life where the necessity of acquiring six men of diminished stature might arise, or none that I care to bring up in public."

"On close examination, it does seem to be excessively complicating what would otherwise be a fairly simple act of theft."

"But I was completely unable just to break the window and steal the jewels," said Moriarty. "It wasn't possible."

"Why not?"

"Because I'm not written that way."

"Excuse me?"

"It's not the way I was written. I'm written as a criminal mastermind who comes up with baroque, fiendish plots. It's against my nature even to walk down the street in a straight line. Believe me, I've tried. I have to duck and dive so much that I get dizzy."

Holmes sat back, stunned, almost dropping the revolver from his hand at the realization of his own true nature. Suddenly, it all made sense: his absence of anything resembling a past; his lack of a close familial bond with his brother, Mycroft; the sometimes extraordinary deductive leaps that he made, which baffled even himself.

"I'm a literary invention," he said.

"Precisely," said Moriarty. "Don't get me wrong: you're a good one— certainly better than I am—but you're still a character."

"So I'm not real?"

"I didn't say that. I think you have a kind of reality, but you didn't start out that way."

"But what of my fate?" said Holmes. "What of free will? If all this is true, then my destiny lies in the hands of another. My actions are prede-termined by an outside agency."

"No," said Moriarty, "we wouldn't be having this conversation if that were the case. My guess is that you're becoming more real with every word that the author writes, and a little of that has rubbed off on me."

"But what are we going to do about it?" asked Holmes.

"It's not entirely in our hands," said Moriarty.

And with that he looked up from the page.

And that was where the manuscript ended, with a fictional character engaged in a virtual staring contest with his creator. In his letter, Conan Doyle described letting the papers fall to the floor, and in that moment Sherlock Holmes's fate was sealed.

Holmes was a dead man.

Thus began the extraordinary sequence of events that would come to imperil the Caxton Private Lending Library & Book Depository. Conan Doyle completed "The Last Problem," consigning Holmes to the Reichenbach Falls and leaving only his trusty Alpinestock and silver cigarette case as a sign that he had ever been there at all. The public seethed and mourned, and Conan Doyle set out to immerse himself in the historical fictions that he believed would truly make his reputation.

Mr. Headley, meanwhile, went about the business of the Caxton which, for the most part, consisted of making pots of tea, dusting, reading, and ensuring that any of the characters who wandered off—as some of them were inclined to do—returned before nightfall. Mr. Headley had once been forced to explain to an unimpressed policeman why an elderly gent in homemade armor seemed intent upon damaging a small ornamental windmill that stood at the heart of Glossom Green, and had no intention of having to go through all that again. It was difficult enough trying to understand how Don Quixote had ended up in the Caxton to begin with, given that his parent book had been written in Spanish. Mr. Headley suspected that it was something to do with the proximity of the first English translations of Cervantes's work in 1612 and 1620 to their original publication in Spanish in 1605 and 1615. Then again, the Caxton might simply have got confused. It did that, sometimes.

So it came as some surprise to him when, one Wednesday morning, a small, flat parcel arrived at the Caxton, inexpertly wrapped in brown paper, and with its string poorly knotted. He opened it to find a copy of that month's *Strand* containing "The Final Problem."

"Now that can't be right," said Mr. Headley, aloud. He had already received his subscription copy, and had no use for a second. But the nature of the parcel, with its brown paper and string, gave him pause for thought. He examined the materials and concluded that, yes, they were the same as those used to deliver first editions to the Caxton for as long as anyone could remember. Never before, though, had they protected a journal or magazine.

"Oh dear," said Mr. Headley.

He began to feel distinctly uneasy. He took a lamp and moved through the library, descending—or ascending; he was never sure which, for the

Caxton's architectural nature was as individual and peculiar as everything else about it—into its depths (or heights) where the new rooms typically started to form upon the arrival of a first edition. No signs of activity were apparent. Mr. Headley was relieved. It was all clearly some mistake on the part of the *Strand*, and the paper and string involved in the magazine's delivery only coincidentally resembled those with which he was most familiar. He returned to his office, poured himself a mug of tea, and twisted up the newly arrived copy of the *Strand* for use in the fireplace. He then read a little of Samuel Richardson's epistolary epic *Clarissa*, which he always found conducive to drowsiness, and settled down in his chair for a nap.

He slept for longer than intended, for when he woke it was already growing dark outside. He set kindling for the fire, but noticed that the twisted copy of the *Strand* was no longer in the storage basket and was instead lying on his desk, entirely intact and without crease.

"Ah," said Mr. Headley. "Well."

But he got no further in his ruminations, for the small brass bell above the office door trilled once. The Caxton Private Lending Library didn't have a doorbell, and it had taken Mr. Headley a little time to get used to the fact that a door without a doorbell could still ring. The sound of the bell could mean only one thing: the library was about to welcome a new arrival.

Mr. Headley opened the door. Standing on the step was a tall, lean man, with a high brow and a long nose, dressed in a deerstalker hat and a caped coat. Behind him was an athletic-looking gent with a mustache, who seemed more confused than his companion. A slightly oversized bowler hat rested on his head.

"'Holmes gave me a sketch of events,'" said Mr. Headley.

"I beg your pardon?" said the man in the bowler, now looking even more confused.

"Paget," said Mr. Headley. "'The Adventure of Silver Blaze,' 1892." For the two men could have stepped straight from that particular illustration.

"Still not following."

"You're not supposed to be here," said Mr. Headley.

"Yet here we are," said the thinner of the two.

"I think there's been a mistake," said Mr. Headley.

"If so, it won't be resolved by forcing us to stand out in the cold," came the reply.

Mr. Headley's shoulders slumped.

"Yes, you're right. You'd better come in, then. Mr. Holmes, Doctor Watson: welcome to the Caxton Private Lending Library and Book Depository."

Mr. Headley lit the fire, and while doing so tried to give Holmes and Watson a brief introduction to the library. Initially there was often a certain amount of shock among new arrivals, who sometimes struggled to grasp the reality both of their own physicality and their fictional existence, as one should, in theory, have contradicted the other, but didn't. Holmes and Watson seemed to have little trouble with the whole business, though. As we have already seen, Holmes had been made aware of the possibility of his own fictional nature thanks to the efforts of ex-Professor Moriarty, and had done his best to share something of this understanding with Watson before his untimely demise at the hands of his creator.

"By the way, is my archnemesis here?" asked Holmes.

"I'm not expecting him," said Mr. Headley. "You know, he never seemed entirely real."

"No, he didn't, did he?" agreed Holmes.

"To be honest," Mr. Headley went on, "and as you may have gathered, I wasn't expecting you two gentlemen either. Characters usually only arrive when their authors die. I suspect it's because they then become fixed objects, as it were. You two are the first to come here while their author is still alive and well. It's most unusual."

Mr. Headley wished that there was someone he could call, but old Torrans was long dead, and the Caxton operated without the assistance of lawyers, bankers, or the institutions of government, or at least not with the active involvement of any of the above. Bills were paid, leases occasionally secured, and rates duly handed over to the authorities, but it was all done without Mr. Headley having to lift a finger. The workings of the Caxton were so deeply ingrained in British society that everyone had simply ceased to notice them.

Mr. Headley poured the two guests some more tea, and offered them biscuits. He then returned to the bowels—or attic—of the library, and found that it had begun to create suitable living quarters for Holmes and Watson based on Paget's illustrations, and Watson's descriptions, of the rooms at 221B Baker Street. Mr. Headley was immensely relieved, as otherwise he might have been forced to make up beds for them in his office, and he wasn't sure how well Holmes might have taken to such sleeping arrangements.

Shortly after midnight, the library finished its work on 221B, complete with a lively Victorian streetscape beyond the windows. The Caxton occupied an indeterminate space between reality and fiction, and the library was not above permitting characters access to their own larger fictional universes, should they choose to step outside their rooms for a time. Many, though, preferred either to nap—sometimes for decades—or take the occasional constitutional around Glossom village and its environs, which at least had the merit of being somewhere new and different. The inhabitants of the village tended not to notice the characters unless, of course, they started tilting at windmills, talking about witches in a Scottish accent, or inquiring about the possibility of making a suitable marriage to entirely respectable single, or even married, gentlemen.

Once Holmes and Watson were ensconced in their quarters, Mr. Headley returned to his office, poured himself a large brandy, and detailed the events of the day in the Caxton's records, so that future librarians might be made aware of what he had gone through. He then retired to his bed, and dreamed that he was holding on by his fingertips to the edge of a precipice while the Reichenbach Falls tumbled thunderously beneath him.

After this mild hiccup, the life of the library proceeded largely without incident over the following years, although the activities of Holmes and Watson were not entirely unproblematic for Mr. Headley. They were fond of making forays into Glossom and beyond, offering to assist bemused officers of the law with investigations into missing kittens, damaged milk churns, and the possible theft of a bag of penny buns from the noon train to Penbury. Their characters having ingrained themselves in the literary affections of the public, Holmes and Watson were treated as genial eccentrics. They were not alone in dressing up as the great detective and his amanuensis, for it was a popular activity among gentlemen of varying degrees of sanity, but they were unique in actually being Holmes and Watson, although obviously nobody realized that at the time.

There was also the small matter of the opium that found its way into the library on a regular basis. Mr. Headley couldn't pin down the source of the drug, and could only conclude that the library itself was providing it, but it worried him nonetheless. God forbid that some olfactorily gifted policeman might smell traces of the narcotic on Holmes, and contrive to follow him back to the Caxton. Mr. Headley wasn't sure what the punishment might be for running a narcotics operation, and had no desire to find out, so he begged Holmes to be discreet about his intake, and to reserve it for the peace and quiet of his own rooms.

Otherwise, Mr. Headley was rather delighted to have as residents of the library two characters of whom he was so enamored, and spent many happy evenings in their company, listening as they discussed the details of cases about which he had read, or testing Holmes's knowledge of obscure poisons and types of tobacco. Mr. Headley also continued to subscribe to the *Strand*, for he generally found its contents most delightful, and had no animosity toward it for publishing Holmes's last adventure since he was privileged to have the man himself beneath his roof. He tended to be a month or two behind in his *Strand* reading, though, for his preference remained books.

Then, in August 1901, this placid existence was disturbed by a most extraordinary development. Mr. Headley had taken himself away to Cleckheaton to visit his sister Dolly, and upon his return found Holmes and Watson in a terrible state. Holmes was brandishing the latest copy of the *Strand* and demanding loudly, "What's this? What's this?"

Mr. Headley pleaded, first for calm, and then for the offending journal, which was duly handed over to him. Mr. Headley sat and, once he had recovered from his surprise, read the first installment of *The Hound of the Baskervilles*.

"It doesn't mention my previous demise," said Holmes. "There's not a word about it. I mean, I fell over a waterfall, and I'm not even wet!"

"We'll have to wait and see," said Mr. Headley. "From my reading, it seems to be set prior to the events at the Reichenbach Falls, as otherwise Conan Doyle would surely have been forced to explain your reappearance. Don't you have any memory of this case, Holmes—or you, Doctor Watson, of recording its details?"

Both Holmes and Watson told him that the only details of the *Hound* of which they were aware were those they had read, but then admitted that they were no longer entirely certain whether those memories were the result of reading the first installment, or if their own personalities were being altered to accommodate the new story. Mr. Headley counseled caution, and advised Holmes and Watson not to overreact until they learned more about the tale. Mr. Headley made some discreet inquiries of the *Strand*, but the magazine's proprietors were tight-lipped about the return of Holmes to their pages, grateful only for the spike in subscriptions brought by his reappearance, and Mr. Headley's efforts were all for naught.

So he, along with Holmes, Watson, and the British reading public, was forced to wait for the arrival of each new monthly instalment of the story in order to try to discern Conan Doyle's intentions for his creations. As time went on, though, it became clear that the story was indeed historical in nature, preceding the events of "The Final Problem." As an experiment, Mr. Headley withheld the conclusion from Holmes, and then questioned him about its contents. Holmes was able to describe in detail how Rodger Baskerville had embezzled money in South America, taken the name Vandeleur, and opened a school in Yorkshire that closed following its descent into infamy, all of which was revealed in the final part of the story that Holmes had yet to read. From this they were able to establish that Conan Doyle, by revisiting his characters, was effectively creating new memories for Holmes and Watson which, although mildly troubling for them, was not a disaster.

Nevertheless, Mr. Headley was unable to assuage a growing sense of impending doom. He began to keep a very close eye on the *Strand*, and he paid particular attention to any and all rumors about Conan Doyle's literary activities.

The rumblings began in the autumn of 1903. Mr. Headley did his best to keep them from Holmes until, at last, the October edition of the *Strand* was delivered to the Caxton, and Mr. Headley's worst fears were realized. There, handsomely illustrated by Paget, was "The Adventure of the Empty House," marking the return of Sherlock Holmes, albeit initially disguised as an elderly book collector. Mr. Headley read the story in the back office of the Caxton, with the door locked and a desk pushed against it for added security, locked doors being no obstacle to any number of the library's residents, Holmes among them. (Mr. Headley had endured a number of awkward conversations with the Artful Dodger, who the librarian was convinced was stealing his biscuits.)

To be perfectly honest, the explanation of how Holmes had survived the incident at the Reichenbach Falls rather strained Mr. Headley's credulity, involving, as it did, the martial art Baritsu and a gravitationally unlikely ability to topple from a cliff yet somehow land on a path, or perhaps not fall and just appear to land on a path, or appear to fall and—

Never mind. Some business about Tibet, Lhasa, and Khartoum followed, and dressing up as a Norwegian, and it all made Mr. Headley's head hurt, although he admitted to himself that this was due in part to the potential consequences of Sherlock Holmes's return for the Caxton's Holmes. He would have to be told, of course, unless he was already aware of it due to a sudden change in his memories, and a previously unsuspected ability to speak Norwegian.

Mr. Headley felt that he had no choice but to visit the rooms of Holmes and Watson to find out the truth for himself. He moved the desk, unlocked the door, and headed into the library, stopping off in the dictionary section along the way. He found Watson napping on a couch, and Holmes doing something with phials and a Bunsen burner that Mr. Headley suspected might not be entirely unrelated to the production of narcotics.

Mr. Headley took in the dozing figure of Watson. One additional unpleasant piece of information contained in "The Adventure of the Empty House" was that Watson's wife, Mary, appeared to have died.

This might have been more awkward had it not been for the fact that the Watson living in the Caxton had no memory of being married at all, perhaps because his wife hadn't figured much in the stories, or not in any very consequential way, and therefore hadn't made much of an impact on anyone involved. Still, Mr. Headley would have to mention Mary's demise to him. It wasn't the sort of thing one could brush under the carpet.

For now, though, his main concern was Holmes.

"Everything all right, Mr. Holmes?" asked Mr. Headley.

"Is there any reason why it shouldn't be?" Holmes replied.

He didn't even look up from his workbench. A sweet, slightly spicy scent hung in the room. It made Mr. Headley's head swim.

"No, no, none at all. Um, is that some kind of narcotic I smell?"

"I'm experimenting," said Holmes, quite tartly, and, thought Mr. Headley, not a little defensively.

"Right, of course. Just, er, be careful, please."

There was a vent in the wall behind Holmes's head. Mr. Headley wasn't entirely certain where it led, exactly, but he still lived in fear of that mythical policeman sniffing the air and organizing a raid, once he'd recovered his senses.

Mr. Headley cleared his throat and enunciated, as clearly as he could:

"Goddag, hvor er du?"

Holmes looked at him peculiarly.

"What?"

"Lenge siden sist," said Mr. Headley.

"Are you feeling all right?"

Mr. Headley glanced at the small Norwegian phrase book in his hand.

"Jo takk, bare bra. Og du?"

"Are you speaking . . . Norwegian?"

Watson woke.

"What's all this?" he asked.

"Headley appears to have struck his head," Holmes explained, "and is now under the impression that he's Norwegian."

"Good Lord," said Watson. "Tell him to sit down."

Mr. Headley closed his phrase book.

"I haven't hit my head, and I don't need to sit down," he said. "I was just wondering, Mr. Holmes, if by any chance you spoke Norwegian?"

"I have never had any cause to learn the language," said Holmes. "I did wrestle with *Beowulf* in my youth, though, and obviously there are certain similarities between Old English and Norwegian."

"Have you ever heard of a Norwegian explorer named Sigerson?" asked Mr. Headley.

"I can't say that I have," said Holmes. He was now regarding Mr. Headley with a degree of suspicion. "Why do you ask?"

Mr. Headley decided to sit down after all. He wasn't sure if it was good or bad news that the Caxton's Holmes had not begun producing new memories due to the return of his literary self. Whichever it was, he could not hide the existence of the new story from Holmes. Sooner or later, he was bound to find out.

Mr. Headley reached beneath his jacket and removed the latest edition of the *Strand*.

"I think you should read it," he told Holmes.

He then turned to Dr. Watson.

"I'm sorry to have to tell you this," said Mr. Headley, "but your wife has died."

Watson considered the news for a moment.

"What wife?"

The three men sat in Mr. Headley's office, the copy of the *Strand* lying on the table before them. The occasion called for something stronger than coffee, so Mr. Headley had broken out his bottle of brandy and poured each of them a snifter.

"If he's me," said Holmes, not for the first time, "and I'm him, then I should have his memories."

"Agreed," said Mr. Headley.

"But I don't, so I can't be this Holmes."

"No."

"Which means that there are now two Holmeses."

"It would appear so."

"So what happens when Conan Doyle eventually dies? Will this second Holmes also show up here?"

"And the second Doctor Watson," added Watson, who was still perturbed to have discovered that he was once married, an arrangement about which he struggled to dredge up any but the vaguest of memories after all this time, as though he had dreamed the whole affair. "I mean, we can't have two of us—er, four of us—trotting about. It will just be disconcerting."

"And which of us would be the real Holmes and Watson?" added Holmes. "Obviously, we're the originals, so it should be us, but it could be a messy business explaining that to the rival incumbents for the positions, so to speak. Worse, what if this new Holmes and Watson usurp us in the public imagination? Will we just cease to exist?"

They all looked rightly shocked at this possibility. Mr. Headley was very fond of this Holmes and Watson. He didn't want to see them gradually fade away, to be replaced at some future date by alternative versions of themselves. But he was also concerned about what the arrival of a new Holmes and Watson might mean for the Caxton. It could potentially open the way to all kinds of calamitous conjunctions. Suppose noncanonical versions of characters began to appear on the doorstep, making claims for their own reality and sowing unrest? The result would be chaos.

And what about the library itself? Mr. Headley understood that an institution as complex and mysterious as the Caxton must also, on some level, be extraordinarily delicate. For centuries, reality and unreality had remained perfectly balanced within its walls. That equilibrium might now be threatened by Conan Doyle's decision to resurrect Holmes.

"There's nothing else for it," said Holmes. "We shall have to go to Conan Doyle and tell him to stop writing these stories."

Mr. Headley blanched.

"Oh no," he said. "You can't do that."

"Why ever not?"

"Because the Caxton is a secret institution, and has to remain that way," said Mr. Headley. "No writers can ever know of its existence, otherwise they'd start clamoring for immortality for their characters and themselves. That has to be earned, and can only come after the author's death. Writers are terrible judges of these things, and if they knew that there was a kind of pantheon for characters here in Glossom, then we'd never hear the end of it.

"Worse, imagine what might happen if the Caxton's existence became public knowledge? It would be like London Zoo. We'd have people knocking on the doors day and night, asking for a peek at Heathcliff—and you know what he's like—or, God forbid, a conversation with David Copperfield."

There was a collective sigh. It was widely known in the Caxton that to ask David Copperfield even the simplest of questions required one to set aside a good portion of one's day to listen to the answer.

"Nevertheless," said Holmes, "I can see no other option for us. This is our existence that is at stake—and, perhaps, that of the Caxton too."

Mr. Headley drained his glass, and paused for only a moment before pouring himself another generous measure.

Oh dear, he thought. Oh dear, oh dear, oh dear.

Preparations for the journey were quickly made. Mr. Headley locked up the library, having first informed a few of the more balanced residents of the reason for the trip, even though he knew that his absence would barely be noticed by most of others. They could spend weeks and months—even years—napping, only waking when a publisher reissued their parent book in a new edition, or when a critical study caused a renewal of interest in their existence.

"Please try not to attract too much attention," pleaded Mr. Headley, as he paid for three first class tickets to London, although even as the words left his mouth he realized how pointless they were. After all, he was boarding a train with two men, one of whom was wearing a caped coat, a deerstalker hat, and shiny new shoes with white spats, and could not have looked more like Sherlock Holmes if he had started declaring loudly that—

"The game is afoot, Watson!" shouted a cheery voice from nearby. "The game is afoot!"

"God give me strength," said Mr. Headley.

"Your friend," said the ticket clerk. "Does he think he's, you know . . . ?"

"Yes," said Mr. Headley. "In a way."

"Harmless, is he?"

"I believe so."

"He won't go bothering the other passengers, will he?"

"Not unless they've committed a crime," replied Mr. Headley.

The ticket clerk looked as though he were seriously considering summoning some stout chaps in white coats to manage the situation, but Mr. Headley grabbed the tickets before he could act and hustled his charges in the direction of the carriage. They took their seats, and it was with some relief that Mr. Headley felt the train lurch and move off without anyone appearing to haul them away.

Many years later, when he had retired from the Caxton in favor of Mr. Gedeon, the new librarian, Mr. Headley would recall that journey as one of the happiest of his life, despite his nervousness at the impending encounter with Conan Doyle. As he watched Holmes and Watson from his seat by the door—Holmes on the right, leaning forward animatedly, the index finger of his right hand tapping the palm of his left when he wished to emphasize a point, Watson to the left, cigar in hand, one leg folded over the other—Mr. Headley felt as though he were part of one of Paget's illustrations for the *Strand*, so that he might have stepped from his own life into the pages of one of Conan Doyle's adventures. All readers lose themselves in great books, and what could be more wonderful for a reader than to find himself in the company of characters that he has long loved, their lives colliding with his own, and all being altered by the encounter? Mr. Headley's heart beat in time with the rhythm of the rails, and the morning sun shone its blessings upon him.

Sir Arthur Conan Doyle stepped from the crease at Marylebone Cricket Club, his bat cradled beneath his right arm. He had enjoyed the afternoon's out-of-season practice, and felt that he had acquitted himself well, all things considered. He was by no means good enough for England, a fact that troubled him only a little, but he could hit hard, and his slow bowls were capable of disconcerting batsmen far more capable than he.

Conan Doyle had also largely forgotten the shock caused some years earlier by the apparent somnambulistic use of his left hand to write a scrap of Holmesian manuscript. For many months after, he had approached the cricket field with a sense of trepidation, fearing that, at some inopportune moment, his left hand, as though possessed, might attempt to take control of his bat, like some horror out of a story by Hauff or Marsh. Thankfully, he had been spared any such embarrassment, but he still occasionally cast his left hand a suspicious glance when his batting went awry.

He changed, made his farewells, and prepared to return to his hotel for he had work to do. Initially he had returned with a hint of resignation and a mild sense of annoyance to writing about Sherlock Holmes, but "The Adventure of the Empty House" had turned out better than anticipated: in fact, he had already begun to regard it as one of the best of the Holmes stories, and the joy and acclaim that greeted its appearance in the *Strand*, combined with the honor of a knighthood the previous year, had reinvigorated Conan Doyle. Only the continued ill health of his beloved Touie still troubled him. She remained at Undershaw, their Surrey residence, to which he would travel the following day in order to spend the weekend with her and the children. He had found another specialist to consult about her condition, but secretly he held out little hope. The tuberculosis was killing her, and he could do nothing to save her.

Conan Doyle had just turned onto Wellington Place when a small, thin man approached him. He had the look of a clerk, but was well dressed, and his shoes shone in the sunlight. Conan Doyle liked to see a man taking care of his shoes.

"Sir Arthur?" inquired the man.

Conan Doyle nodded, but didn't break his stride. He had never quite grown used to the fame brought upon him by Holmes, and had learned at an early stage of his literary career never to stop walking. Once you stopped, you were done for.

"Yes?"

"My name is Headley," said the man. "I'm a librarian."

"A noble profession," said Conan Doyle heartily, quickening his pace. Good God, a librarian. If this chap had his way, they might be here all day.

"I have some, er, colleagues who are most anxious to make your acquaintance," said Mr. Headley.

"Can't dawdle, I'm afraid," said Conan Doyle. "Very busy. If you drop a line to the *Strand*, I'm sure they'll see what they can do."

He made a sharp turn to the left, wrong-footing Mr. Headley, and quickly crossed the road to Cochrane Street, trying to give the impression of a man with life or death business to contract. He was almost at the corner when two figures stepped into his path, one of them wearing a deerstalker hat, the other a bowler.

"Oh Lord," said Conan Doyle. It was worse than he thought. The librarian had brought along a pair of idiots who fancied themselves as Holmes and Watson. Such men were the bane of his life. Most, though, had the common decency not to accost him on the street.

"Ha ha," he said, without mirth. "Very good, gentlemen, very good."

He tried to sidestep them, but the one dressed as Holmes was too quick for him, and blocked his way.

"What the devil do you think you're doing?" said Conan Doyle. "I'll call a policeman."

"We really do need to talk, Sir Arthur," said Holmes—or "Holmes," as Conan Doyle instinctively branded him in his mind. One had to nip these things in the bud. It was why quotation marks had been invented.

"We really do not," said Conan Doyle. "Out of my way."

He brandished his walking stick at his tormentor in a vaguely threatening manner.

"My name is Sherlock Holmes—" said "Holmes."

"No, it isn't," said Conan Doyle.

"And this is Doctor Watson."

"No, it's not. Look, I'm warning you, you'll feel my stick."

"How is your left hand, Sir Arthur?"

Conan Doyle froze.

"What did you say?"

"I asked after your left hand. I see no traces of ink upon it. You have not found yourself writing with it again, then?"

"How could you know of that?" asked Conan Doyle, for he had told no one about that unfortunate experience in August 1893.

"Because I was at Benekey's. You put me there, along with Moriarty." "Holmes"—or now, perhaps, Holmes—stretched out a hand.

"I'm very pleased to meet you at last, Sir Arthur. Without you, I wouldn't exist."

The four men sat at a quiet table in Ye Olde Cheshire Cheese off Fleet Street, to which they had traveled together in a hansom cab. Mr. Headley had done his best to explain the situation to Conan Doyle along the way, but the great man was clearly still struggling with the revelations about the Caxton and his characters. Mr. Headley could hardly blame him. He himself had needed a long lie-down after old Torrans had first revealed the nature of the Caxton to him, and he could only imagine how much more traumatic it might be for Conan Doyle with the added complication of witnessing his two most famous creations lunching before him on pea soup. Conan Doyle had settled for a single malt Scotch, but it looked like another might be required before long.

At Conan Doyle's request, Holmes had dispensed with the deerstalker hat, which now hung on a hook alongside his long coat. Without it, he might simply have been a regular client of Ye Olde Cheshire Cheese, albeit one with a certain intensity to his regard.

"I must admit, gentlemen, that I'm struggling with these revelations," said Conan Doyle. He looked from Holmes to Watson and back again. Almost involuntarily, his right hand moved, the index finger extended, as though he wished to poke them to confirm their corporeal reality, the sound of Watson slurping his soup notwithstanding.

"It's hardly surprising," said Mr. Headley. "In a way, they're a testament to the power of your imagination, and the depth of your creations. Never before in the Caxton's history has a writer lived to see his own characters come to life."

Conan Doyle took another sip of his whisky.

"If more writers did," he replied, "it might well be the death of them."

Holmes set aside his soup.

"Sir Arthur," he said, "Mr. Headley has explained the situation to you as best he can. It's most difficult and delicate, and we can see only one solution to the problem. I appreciate that it might place you in an awkward position, but you must stop writing about Sherlock Holmes."

Conan Doyle shook his head.

"I can't," he said. "I've reached an agreement with *Collier's Weekly*. Not only that, but the public will see me hanged if I've raised their hopes of more adventures only to shatter them within a month. And then, gentlemen, there is the small matter of my finances. I have a sick wife, two young children, and houses to maintain. Would that my other literary endeavors had brought me greater success, but no one mentions Rodney Stone in the same breath as Holmes and Watson, and I cannot think of the reviews for *A Duet* without wanting to hide in my cellar."

"But the more Holmes stories you write, the more likely it is that you'll bring a second Holmes—oh, and Watson—"

"Thank you, Holmes."

"—into being," said Holmes. "Would you want a second Sir Arthur wandering the streets, or worse, moving into your home? Think of William Wilson. You might end up stabbing yourself with a sword!"

Mr. Headley leaned forward.

"Sir Arthur, you now know that the fabric of reality is far more delicate than you imagined," he said. "It may be that the consequences of two versions of Holmes and Watson having a physical reality might not be so terrible, whatever the personal or professional difficulties for the characters involved, but there is also the possibility that the entire existence of the Caxton might be undermined. The more the reading public starts to believe in this new incarnation of Holmes, the greater the chance of trouble for all of us."

Conan Doyle nodded. He suddenly looked tired, and older than his years.

"Then it seems that I have no choice," he said. "Holmes must fall again, and this time he cannot return."

Dr. Watson coughed meaningfully. The others looked at him. The good doctor had finished his soup, for it was a pea-based delicacy of the highest order, but all the while he had been listening to what was being said. Dr. Watson was much wiser than was often credited. His lesser light simply did not shine as brightly next to the fierce glow of Holmes.

"It seems to me," he said, "that the issue is one of belief. You said it yourself, Mr. Headley: it is readers as much as writers who bring characters alive. So the solution . . ."

He let the ending hang.

"Is to make the new Holmes less believable than the old," Holmes concluded. He patted Watson hard on the back, almost causing his friend to regurgitate some soup. "Watson, you're a marvel."

"Much obliged, Holmes," said Watson. "Now, how about pudding?"

Sir Arthur Conan Doyle never visited the Caxton Private Lending Library, although an open invitation was extended to him. He felt that it was probably for the best that he kept his distance from it for, as he told Mr. Headley, if he needed to spend time with the great characters of literature, he could simply pick up a book. Neither did he ever again meet Holmes and Watson, for they had their own life in his imagination.

Instead he carefully set out to undermine the second incarnation of his inventions, deliberately interspersing his better later stories with tales that were either so improbable in their plots and solutions as to test the credulity of readers to breaking point—"The Adventure of the Sussex Vampire" being among the most notable—or simply not terribly good, including "The Adventure of the Missing Three-Quarter," "The Adventure of the Golden Pince-Nez," or "The Adventure of the Blanched Soldier." He even dropped in hints of more wives for Watson, whom he didn't actually bother to name. The publication of such tales troubled him less than it might once have done, for even as he tired of his creations he understood that, with each inconsequential tale, he was ensuring the survival of the Caxton, and the continued happiness of his original characters.

Yet his strange encounter with the Caxton had also given Conan Doyle a kind of quiet comfort. In the years following his meeting with Holmes and Watson, he lost his first wife, and, in the final weeks of The Great War, his son Kingsley. He spent many years seeking proof of life after death, and found none, but his knowledge of the Caxton's existence, and the power of belief to incarnate fictional characters, to imbue them with another reality outside the pages of books, gave him the hope that the same might be possible for those who had been taken from him in this life. The Caxton was a world beyond this one, complete and of itself, and if one such world could exist, then so might others.

Shortly after Conan Doyle's death in July 1930, copies of the first editions of his later collections duly arrived at the library, as well as another copy of *The Memoirs of Sherlock Holmes* with its enlightening manuscript addition. By then Mr. Gedeon was the librarian, and he, Holmes, and Watson endured a slightly nervous couple of days, just in case the plan hatched by Watson and enacted by Conan Doyle had not worked, but no new incarnations of Holmes and Watson appeared on their doorstep, and a strange warm gust of wind blew through the Caxton, as though the great old edifice had just breathed its own sigh of relief.

A small blue plaque now stands on the wall of the Caxton, just above the shelf containing the Conan Doyle collection. It reads: "In Memory of Sir Arthur Conan Doyle, 1859-1930: For Services to the Caxton Private Lending Library & Book Depository."

IRREGULAR

by Meg Gardiner

Suicide, they say. She hears them outside as she leans towards the open window.

The woman in pearls mumbles it, sitting on the curb under city lights. Her face scratched by fragments of safety glass, posh frock bloody. She waves away the paramedic again, insisting she's fine, but refuses to look *there*.

The footballer spits it, pacing the pavement, mobile to his ear, speaking to his agent. Pausing to beg a cigarette from a cop guarding the scene. Still so shaky ninety minutes after the thing, he doesn't care if onlookers snap him smoking. He'd just pulled up in the Merc when it happened. *Jesus. Nearly killed us.*

The dog walker sobs it. *Yes, I saw*, she tells the detective, wiping her eyes. She had no warning. The woman simply plunged from the night sky into the windshield of the Mercedes outside the Mayfair

Capital Bank. Straight down into the glass, from . . . she looks up at the window.

Shaz jerks back into the shadows.

Under the flashing lights of the ambulance, the silver Merc is a bier. The young woman is embedded in the sunken windshield, like she's lying in a bed of shattered ice. Glittery mini-dress blown up around her hips. Long legs askew, as pale as curdled cream. A strappy sandal dangling from her foot. Her face is turned away.

So much sparkle. It burns Shaz's eyes, puts a buzz in her ears. Why would the girl take hours to glam up, just to Superman out a fourth-story window?

Blue lights strobe the office ceiling. Shaz calls a number, the private mobile. "As advertised. Victim took a bloody long drop. She had no chance."

"Witnesses?"

"Say she jumped."

But none of them saw her take the leap.

"Get snaps and stop by the office," he says. "Fallon will have your fee." He rings off.

Fallon will have her fee, in cash. They could transfer the money with the swipe of a thumb—she's sixteen, she has a bank account. And fifty pounds for this nighttime reconnaisance, it's a trifle to them. But they want her to spend time coming by. Showing obeisance.

Her word of the day, *obeisance.*

They know she needs the dosh. Fifty quid: She'll put it away. For university. Someday.

Around the corner, from the lifts, come footsteps and radio static. Shaz darts out of the office into the hallway. The detective and a uniformed PC round the corner.

The PC points his flashlight at her. "Oi. Step away from that door."

She widens her eyes, deerlike. "What's wrong?"

The detective reads the logo on her uniform shirt. *CLEAN-TEQ.* She's wearing rubber gloves, holding a dust rag.

"Did you enter that office? Touch anything?"

"No, sir. What's the emergency?"

"Have you seen anybody on this floor tonight?"

Behind him, the door to the stairs cracks open. A little face peeps out. Shaz shakes her head, like she's answering the question. The door shuts.

"The building's closed," the detective says. "You're off the clock."

The PC escorts her downstairs. As the lift doors open she sees a thin boy skitter out of the stairwell and slip through a side door before the cop spots him. *Well done, Harry.*

Beyond the lobby windows a crowd clusters, wraithlike under the strobing lights.

"Was it an accident?"

"Not your concern." The PC points at the exit.

Outside, Shaz jams the rubber gloves in her back pocket. Her real shift, at a Euston office tower, starts at midnight. Harry waits for her in the crowd, watching a police photographer shoot the Mercedes. The camera flash reflects from his eyes like lightning.

Outside the Marylebone headquarters of Croft Security, the surveillance camera swivels and the door buzzes open. Shaz snakes through. Harry shadows her, silent as a stone.

Richard Fallon greets them at the top of the stairs. Croft's second in command is florid and bright eyed. "Here you are. Brilliant."

Fallon escorts them towards the corner office. Through its open door Shaz sees Michael Croft. He sits tapping his mobile against the arm of a Saxon leather chair. His face is brooding beneath the blue flicker of the flatscreen, tuned to Sky News. His client paces.

"Stay calm," Croft says. "Gathering information takes time. The incident happened only two hours ago."

"I can't. I have to know what happened to her. You're the security consultant—I've retained *you* to stay calm and find the truth."

Nic Ramsey is in his early thirties, dressed in a banker's sharp black suit but jittering like a nervy teenager. At least like the nervy teenagers Shaz knows. Fallon raps on the door.

Croft waves them in. "Report. You got access to the roof?"

Harry's cheeks shine with heat. "No, sir. Door's deadbolted. No way to open it. Brand new keypad, but it ain't hooked up. Press the buttons and the display says, 'seek assistance.'"

Croft processes that. "Did you find anything noteworthy in Miss Kendrick's office?"

Ramsey stops, taken aback. "This is your street team? Are you having a laugh?" He points at Harry. "This kid can't be ten."

"We needed intelligence from the scene," Croft says. "That meant getting inside despite the presence of the police. And nobody slips past the cops better than these two."

"Except the boy's wrong. Somebody threw Holly off MCB's roof," Ramsey says.

His words land like a smack. Shaz pauses, and says, "The window in her office was open."

Ramsey spins on her. "No, it wasn't."

Croft's eyes narrow. "Why do you say that?"

"She never opened it," Ramsey stammers. "Street noise. It was practically painted shut."

Croft's voice is a needle prick. "If you lie, I can't help you. Garbage in, garbage out."

"You want to strap me to a polygraph machine? *I* came to *you*."

"Polygraphs are unreliable. But your flushed face, the visible throbbing of your pulse in your carotid artery, and the whiteness of your knuckles reveal everything such a test would." Croft waves at the room. "Moreover, infrared cameras register changes in body heat. High-def audio equipment analyzes vocal tics for deception and dishonesty. It's most sophisticated."

Ramsey seems to shrink.

"Tell me again what happened, this time sparing the fabrications," Croft says.

Ramsey shuts his eyes. "Dammit. Oh, Holly. Calling it suicide is a way of destroying her twice."

Croft looks at Fallon. "Pour Ramsey a whisky."

At the sideboard, Fallon splashes Macallan into a tumbler. Ramsey takes it. "I feel like I'm being interrogated at 221B Baker Street." He raises the glass to Fallon. "So, thanks, Watson."

Fallon's brow knits. Croft smiles fleetingly. His voice turns soothing.

"You didn't actually learn of Miss Kendrick's death this evening from your colleagues."

Ramsey sighs and tosses back the drink. "No. Though I did attend the bank's summer party. At the Royal Academy. So did Holly."

Party, Shaz thinks. That's why Ramsey's suit is speckled with glitter, like Holly's dress.

Croft says, "You and Miss Kendrick detoured on the way there for an assignation?"

Ramsey blinks. "How . . ."

"You're repeatedly rubbing your pocket handkerchief. I presume she helped—" He cuts a glance at Harry. "—ah, put you back together, before going to the Royal Academy."

Ramsey's hand hovers near the pocket square. He lowers it. "We were seeing each other. I need another drink."

He heads to the sideboard. Shaz thinks: For a grieving boyfriend, he hardly seems torn up.

"We were at the party barely half an hour when Holly got a phone call and left. Abruptly." He shakes his head. "That call is the key to what happened. It has to be related to the allegations."

"Allegations?" Fallon turns to peer more closely at him.

"There was a breach in the computer system at the bank. Customer account data was stolen. There was . . . innuendo . . ."

Croft nods at Fallon, who brings up information on the desktop computer. "Mayfair Capital Bank manages twenty billion pounds in assets for its private clients. The breach has been traced to MCB's Investment Management Division—where Holly Kendrick worked." He looks up, eyes avid. "She was suspected of the theft."

"She didn't do it," Ramsey says.

Croft says, "You followed her to the bank."

Ramsey hesitates, then admits, "Yes. I was worried. Because she was *afraid.*"

"Of whom?" Croft's face darkens. "You entered via the back door to avoid the guard at the front desk. But now you fear that when the police review the CCTV footage, they'll spot you."

"No. Holly took a cab to the side entrance and went in the back. And the security cameras are being upgraded. They're offline. As you—"

"So the rollover of security systems was the perfect time for her to destroy evidence and cover her tracks."

"She *didn't do it*. And she didn't jump."

Shaz clears her throat. "The Mercedes was parked directly below her office window."

Ramsey throws his hands up. "Expert testimony from Baby Spice."

"And pitch perfect." She bites back, *Idiot*.

Croft flicks a remote at the flatscreen, bringing up the photos Shaz had snapped. "Ramsey. The Mercedes. Do you recognize the woman and man?"

Ramsey collects himself. "That's Amelia Gordon-Lennox. Managing Director. And—"

"Crikey." Fallon approaches the TV. "It's Jeroen Dijkstra. The Chelsea striker."

Croft steeples his fingers. "Why do you insist Miss Kendrick went off the roof?"

Ramsey deflates. "All right. I went up to Holly's office. It was dark. No sign of her. And the window was *shut*." He glares at Shaz. "Then I heard footsteps in the stairwell."

"Describe the footsteps," Croft says.

"Clicking heels. Light. Hers."

"What did you do?"

"Opened the stairwell door. Called her name, got no answer. Climbed a flight and called again. Then . . ." He chokes up. "I heard the screaming from the street. I ran down."

"And came directly here."

"No, I wanted to help but she . . . Holly was . . . I couldn't . . ." He scrapes his fingers through his hair. "There was nothing I could do."

Fallon says, "Except beat it before the cops saw you."

Ramsey's fists close. "I know I'm in trouble. Amelia Gordon-Lennox saw me. She'll tell the police. But I'm not here just to save my own skin. Holly's office window was shut. If your street team didn't open it themselves, somebody else did. *After* Holly fell." He pinches the bridge of his nose. "Mr. Croft, I don't know who else to turn to. Help me. And Holly. Please."

"You have every assurance." Croft stands and shakes Ramsey's hand. Then he nods at Shaz and Harry. "All right. Good work."

Harry is staring at the photos on the flatscreen, transfixed. Shaz nudges him from the office and they follow Fallon downstairs. Her fifty quid is in an envelope on the front desk. At the door, Harry hesitates.

He gazes up at Fallon. Whispers: "The car looked like a wrecking ball dropped on the windshield. The lady, she was proper smashed."

Fallon sets a hand on Harry's shoulder. "Never intended for you to see such a sight. The police should have put up a screen. Hold in your mind, though—it was over in an instant." He hands him a twenty pound note. "Chin up."

Harry slips from under his grip and out the door. Shaz follows. On the street, Harry pauses under a streetlight. The twenty is crushed in his small fist. Though he tries to act hard, he rubs a hand across his eyes.

The streetlight illuminates a shiny smudge he's left on his cheek. Shaz wipes it off with her thumb. Harry sniffs and says, "I'm not a baby."

"Of course you're not, love."

From the doorway, Fallon gives them a sad gaze. The door clicks shut.

Shaz steps outside the Euston office tower at 7:30 A.M. The sun blazes in a blue sky. She stretches her back and removes her earbuds, the ones she found in a rubbish bin in the HSBC canteen. Birds sing in the chestnut trees.

At the bus stop shelter, the video screen plays a news update. The Mayfair bank. The Mercedes, a yellow tarp spread across its windshield. *Suspected suicide . . . Holly Kendrick . . . security breach at MCB . . .*

Her bus rolls up, a red wall. She hesitates. She has taken assignments from Michael Croft for two years. Been happy for the money. But this one—glitter and glass brilliance and twisted death. And the look in Harry's eyes. Her throat thickens.

The bus pulls away without her.

She walks through the gleaming morning to the Marylebone Flyover. On the elevated roadway, rush hour traffic drones past. The trailer park sits beneath it. She jogs across the roundabout.

The Whalens' trailer huddles on a rough patch of asphalt. A dog rises at her approach, chain clinking. Inside, teacups and spoons clatter. Shaz knocks.

Harry's mum opens the flimsy door. "You missed him. He's off down the road walking the girls to school." Sleepily, Mrs. Whalen nods towards Wormwood Scrubs.

Ten minutes later Shaz rounds the corner across the street from the school. Harry and his sisters are outside the gate. From his lunchbox he hands one girl an apple, the other a juice box. His uniform is rumpled, tie askew. Shaz thinks: He looks spent. He's ten.

She calls and waves. He shoos his sisters through the gate. As Shaz cuts across the street towards him, he checks for traffic and steps off the curb.

The roar of an engine comes out of clear air. A black car speeds up the street, sunlight burning against its windows. It veers over the center line, straight at her.

Shaz lunges across the road. Harry watches the car for a frozen second, and dives for the curb.

The thud is sickening. He spins and lands in a heap. The car squeals away.

"Harry!" Shaz drops to his side. He groans. Fumbling with her phone, she snaps the fleeing car but it rounds the corner, heading for the A40, a roadside fire, or the bottom of the Thames Estuary.

The crossing guard comes running, awkward in her bright yellow coat, lollipop stop sign flailing. "Oh, my God."

Shaz kneels by Harry's side. "Hold still." She rings 999 with trembling fingers.

He sits up, dazed. "It's okay. I think it's okay. It only hit my rucksack."

The rucksack lies in the road, ripped off his back. Shaz wraps shaking arms around him.

◈

At Croft Security, the receptionist looks twice when Shaz storms in. Street team isn't supposed to come through the front door during daylight. The woman says, "Hey, you can't—"

"Hit and bloody run. I can." Shaz sweeps past her.

Marching up the stairs, she hears voices in Croft's office. She slows. Fallon sounds hot.

"Nic Ramsey's a liar. Holly couldn't have accessed the roof. The police confirm that. And 'thrown'—by whom? Jeroen Dijkstra? Holly *landed* on him."

"Dijkstra was an accessory, but not the criminal kind. He was Amelia Gordon-Lennox's arm candy for the party. Boost her profile, let guests rub elbows with a celeb," Croft says. "No. Only one man admits to being in the building when Miss Kendrick fell. Ramsey himself."

"If Ramsey killed her . . ."

Shaz stops.

"If so, he was involved in the account data theft," Croft says. "Either alone or with her. But there were no signs of a struggle in her office. Have the police found her phone?"

"No."

No phone. *No signs of a struggle in her office.*

Shaz knocks. At his desk, Croft frowns, surprised.

She walks in. "A car just tried to run me down. And nearly killed Harry."

"Good God," Fallon says.

She fills them in. "The cops think it was a careless driver, or a drunk."

Croft says, "You don't believe that."

"Not a chance."

"Why would someone target you? Because of this case? Really, Shaz."

She bears their stares, and approaches the desk. "If you're saying I need to find out, then all right. I will."

The library closes at eight. Shaz is there until they turn off the lights. She walks home down the weedy lane, rattles her key into the lock, and squeezes into the flat, past her sister's partner and kids. She drops onto her bed. Her notebook is crammed with information from a *Dummies* book and company records she found online. The noise from the other room, laughter and arguments and the TV, skates over her as she reads her notes.

Her little niece pokes her head around the door to say good-night, then asks Shaz what she's doing.

"Deducing."

"Ick."

Shaz feigns throwing her library book at the girl. *The Complete Sherlock Holmes*, which has proved enlightening. She smiles, but thinks: It was no accident. Not the hit-and-run. Not Holly plunging from the MCB building.

She looks at the time; it's late. She grabs her things and runs out of the flat. Hurrying towards the tube station in the twilight, she sends a text, then rings Harry. Over the phone she hears traffic on the flyover.

"Glad you're okay, sprog. Get your mum, I need to talk to her," she says.

Not long afterwards, she gets off the tube and jogs through Mayfair. The wind is rising and her nerves hum. Harry is in danger.

The hit-and-run was aimed at him, not her. Because he can provide evidence that somebody killed Holly Kendrick.

The Mayfair Capital Bank is quiet this evening. The Mercedes is gone. From across the street Shaz watches the bright lobby. Fluorescents, marble, a guard at the desk, looking alert. Her courage falters. This op doesn't have Croft's blessing. If they nick her, she's toast.

But she thinks of Holly. Broken, forever stilled. Shaz knows now—she thinks—why Holly died. But she has to find proof. To do that, she has to get into the bank.

When she sweeps through the door, the guard looks up. "Who're you?"

"Cleaner." She gestures at her *CLEAN-TEQ* shirt.

His glasses shine. And his polyester company blazer. And his suspicion. He purses his lips. "You're late. They're on the third floor."

She hustles to the lift. The guard says, "Three, mind. Don't let me catch you sniffing around the floor where that bird jumped."

Shaz nods with a servile expression. *Servile*, word of the day. "Yessir." She steps into the lift and pushes Three. When the doors open again, she dashes to the stairs and climbs to the top of the building.

She catches her breath in the echoing stairwell. The door to the roof is dead ahead. Locked. Just like Harry, and the cops, said it would be. Brand-new keypad.

She presses a few keys. The display flashes. *Seek assistance.*

The building's security upgrade hasn't been activated. Holly couldn't have entered a passcode to unlock this door, since *there is no passcode—* not yet. The door's locked. Period.

Except that can't be right. She scrutinizes the keypad. Runs her fingers along its edges. Rises on tiptoe.

Yes. At the top nestled where the keypad screws into the wall is a thin slot for a keycard. A master key. Or a maid's key.

From her pocket she takes the keycard she palmed from Croft's desk earlier. She inserts it. The lock flips.

She pushes the door open and steps outside. The wind hits her in the face.

She props the door open. The roof is a jumble of pipes and ventilation units. Why would Holly come up here, except to jump?

Because she was lured here, to meet somebody. Somebody who betrayed her.

Holly hadn't stolen from the bank. She'd uncovered the breach. She discovered that an intruder had compromised MCB's computer system, and she wanted to expose it. She was killed before she could reveal the truth.

She came up here in secret to meet the person she thought she could confide in.

Not MCB's Managing Director, Amelia Gordon-Lennox. Not her boyfriend, Nic Ramsey. She may have suspected him, or may have wanted to protect him.

Holly came up here on her own, and she opened the door. How?

Shaz thinks: There's a master keycard. There's probably a master code for the keypad too. A code somebody gave Holly.

The cops haven't found a master code, though. And they haven't found the device that would logically contain one—Holly's phone.

Carefully, Shaz walks the roof. The killer could have taken the phone from Holly and got rid of it, but . . . she stops.

Near the edge of the roof is a rain gutter, and a drainage grate. Shaz crouches down. Under the grate is a mobile.

She pulls on rubber gloves and pries up the grate. When she presses a button, the phone lights up. A message is on the home screen.

4321#

The master code. She lets out a breath.

The voice comes from behind her. "I'll take that from you now."

She's a foot from the edge. She grits her teeth to keep her voice steady. "If you throw me off the roof, you can't make it look like a second suicide. Not this soon, Fallon."

She rises. Fallon kicks the door shut.

All his jolly enthusiasm is gone. His eyes are flat. "Don't be daft. Hand over the phone."

Don't cry. Don't beg. Don't let him see your hands shake. She stuffs the phone in her front pocket. "Throw me off and it goes with me. You'd have to retrieve it from the street, in full view."

"Of whom? The guard in the lobby? Who do you think alerted me?"

"You're the one who breached the bank," she says. "But Holly only figured that out once you lured her up here to meet you."

"*Brava*, my little urchin. Now come with me."

"She didn't know who to blow the whistle to. She worried the breach was an inside job, and she was afraid to go to the police. Why? Because the thief used her login credentials?"

"I said, come with me. Or it won't be you who suffers. It'll be Harry."

A chill washes through her. Fallon's phone rings.

He smiles thinly. "As I was saying." He answers with a curt, "Hold on."

Shaz frantically scans the rooftop. Looking for weapons, at the locked door, at various pieces of security kit half-installed. All of it labeled *Croft Security*. Like the door lock. Like the guard's company blazer.

Play for time. "Yeah, Holly's login accessed the data, pointing the blame at her. So she called the person she thought could help her handle the nightmare of going public. You."

"You're a right little genius. Come with me or Harry will pay." He raises his phone. "Put Harry on."

Shaz's back tingles. The edge is so, so close behind her.

Phone to his ear, Fallon steps towards her. Stops. "What do you mean, gone?"

Shaz's pulse pounds as she says, "Harry. And his family. They're gone."

He glances at her sharply. She thinks: *Thank God.* Her warning to Harry's mum took hold. *"Get out of central London. Leave now."*

She says, "When you live in a trailer, you can turn it into a safe house as easy as hitching it to your car and driving off."

Fallon's voice roughens. "You'll never prove it. So you need to come with me and—"

"Let you disappear me?"

"Let me employ you. I have plans, and you're clearly clever enough to be part of them."

Inching sideways, she takes out her own phone to ring 999. The sensation of air and nothingness expands behind her. "What plans? Taking over Croft Security?"

"That's stage one. Stage two is using that platform to expand my influence over every business in London that has a connection to Croft. And you can join me. You have something. Brains. Pluck. Disregard for the law."

He creeps closer. She's so near the edge that he seems leery of charging at her. He might want to shove her off, but he doesn't want to go over himself. She hits speed dial on her phone.

Nothing happens.

Fallon smirks. "You're smart, but only street smart. You don't know about devices such as this." He holds up a black case the size of a cigarette pack. "Mobile phone jammer."

Her knees soften. Fallon's shoulders bunch, like a wrestler preparing to lunge.

"But I don't need to phone the police." The wind threads her hair across her face. "They're coming."

"Bollocks."

She nods at the security camera above the doorway. "CCTV."

"Is inactive."

"*Was.* Before I came here I texted Croft. I told him activate it remotely. He's watching this, live."

From the stairwell, voices sound. Footsteps pound on the concrete.

Fallon reddens like a boil. "Stupid girl." In his eyes, she sees him prepare to attack. "They won't get it open in time."

She throws herself flat on the roof and grabs a pipe. *"Help."*

Fallon charges and grabs her. Though she fights him, he rips her loose and tries to dig Holly's phone from her pocket.

The lock rattles. She yells, *"Four-three-two"*—kicking, punching— *"one-hash."*

The lock beeps and the door flies open. Cops swarm through, followed by Croft.

Fallon hauls Shaz to her feet and shouts, "I captured the killer."

Croft says, "We have everything on video, Richard. It's over. Let her go."

Shaz braces herself. Fallon grips her arms. Then, abruptly, she's free. She spins to see his coat flapping as he leaps from the lip of the roof. The cops shout and dash for him, but he plunges silently from view.

The sound comes a moment later from the street.

It's hours before the cops let her leave. She sits in MCB's marble lobby, staring at the screen set up in the street by the Scenes of Crime team. She nurses a cup of tea that has cooled to lukewarm.

Croft walks over. He's pale, his assurance splintered. "I should ask how you knew."

"Fallon made a mistake. He sent the car to run Harry down."

"Harry. Not you?"

"The car was waiting outside the school when I got there. Harry had to be the target," she says. "Although I'd probably have been next on his list. After Holly died, Harry and I both came here to MCB. We both came to your offices. Talked to you. But on the way out, only Harry spoke to Fallon, and got a pat on the shoulder, and got handed a twenty direct from Fallon's hands. Which had glitter on them. Glitter Fallon got from grabbing Holly and pitching her off the roof. Glitter that was *not* on the windowsill in Holly's office. Fallon transferred it to Harry. I wiped it off Harry's face. That was the proof."

"Glitter."

"Once glitter touches something you can never get it off. Every cleaner knows it." She sighs. "It had to be Fallon. When you've eliminated the impossible, whatever remains, however improbable, is going to be the truth."

Croft looks unsettled, but eyes her with fresh respect. "Why did you steal the keycard from my desk? Why didn't you simply tell me your suspicions?"

"I had to prove it. Holly told Croft Security about the breach. And look what happened to her."

He nods reluctantly. "Why go to such lengths? Surely not for fifty pounds."

"For Harry," she says. "And because I want in."

He raises an eyebrow.

"Me, working full time for Croft Security. Seems I have an eye for things that are out of place. Such as your name," she says. "I spent the afternoon at the library. The Companies House register lists the owner of Croft Security as Freddy Phelps, 'Trading As Michael Croft.' Mike Croft—as in Mycroft Holmes, the detective's brilliant brother. You deliberately gave your business the Baker Street aura. Sweet." She raises her cup. "Pleased to meet you."

"My word."

She smiles. "Street Team. We can 'go everywhere, see everything, overhear everyone.' *Sherlock Holmes for Dummies*, page one hundred twenty."

He leans back. "All right."

"After I get my degree at university, of course."

"Of course."

"I'll join your staff as a paid intern whilst I do my studies. Unless the firm prefers to directly fund my university fees."

"We'll work it out." He looks stunned, yet ready to smile. He turns to go.

"One other thing."

He turns back. "What's that?"

"Harry. His family is probably safe, though Fallon had confederates."

Word of the . . . well, the hour, *confederates.*

"We'll make sure."

"Harry needs a safe school. He and his sisters. Fairfield Park is ideal. You'll see to their fees and transport. Uniforms, supplies, everything. Lunch."

"Of course."

She searches his face for sincerity or signs of duplicity. Extends her hand. They shake.

A cop strolls over, a Detective Inspector. He nods to her. "I hear you helped close this case. We should be thanking you."

"No call for that. It's done." Done, dusted, gone. Like Holly Kendrick.

"Nevertheless, well spotted, Miss . . ."

"Call me Shaz. It's Sharon, actually. Sharon Hill." She glances at Croft. "But from here on I'll be trading as Shar. Shar Locke."

"That's . . . unexpected," Croft says.

"I think you mean *irregular.*"

Word of the year.

WHERE THERE IS HONEY

by *Dana Cameron*

Writing settles my mind. Getting the thoughts out of my head and onto the page, with the accompanying smell of ink and the scratch of the pen across fresh paper, has become a daily habit, especially when we are working on a case. Once committed to paper, my whirlwind ideas cease to plague me so terribly. I hate the persistence of memory, questioning the actions I took or did not take on a case, what I observed or did not observe—and always, what might have been. These "might have beens" stretch to eternity, a litany of failure. I have observed a marked lowness of spirits when I do not keep to this ritual, and so try to be constant in it. On some occasions, since my discharge from the army, I have found myself unnerved by new worries, and the ordering of my rampaging thoughts, corralling and quieting them, helps.

Indeed, I was busily writing when my friend Sherlock Holmes stalked into the room and hurled himself into a chair that late March evening just a few months after we took up residence together. I had hoped that he would presently close his eyes and doze, as he sometimes did after reviewing the successful completion of the day's work, but it was not to be. He immediately leaped up again and began to pace, ignoring the brandy and gasogene, snapping his long fingers as if counting time in music or attempting to summon up a stray memory.

Many would have seen this as rude, juvenile behavior. But for me, alarm bells began to ring. His tenseness often infected me, even as I worked diligently to keep to a quiet life to stave off those terrible spells that come over me, paralyzing and robbing me of all sense. But only this morning he had been bemoaning the swirling yellow fog and the prosaic dun-colored houses across the street.

"You're writing, Watson."

I remarked that his powers of observation had never been more acute.

Ignoring me, he continued, giving a description of my day up to this point: an empty surgery office, a walk in Regent's Park to settle my thoughts, luncheon at home on veal pie, and how my writing was proceeding well, after some pacing, based on the scuffing of the carpet by the desk. I might as well have been the skull he kept on the mantel for all the attention he paid me. I was merely an audience—no, less than that. I was merely the rocks upon which a great cataract crashes, for a flood must rush freely, or else tear up all the earth and everything in its path.

"—and now you are writing up 'The Clue in Amber'—no, 'The Adventure of the Unquiet Grave.'"

"Yes." This recounting of observations was a habit of his, a plaything for a restless mind.

"I recall seeing the note with your new publisher's address in the hallway this morning. There was a sudden re-stocking of our larder. And Mrs. Hudson was humming; she always hums when she's received the rent. Therefore, you've been paid. May I say, this is a far more satisfactory situation than your previous arrangement."

I grunted in agreement, torn between finishing the words I'd worked so hard to find and my relief at Holmes providing himself any kind of distraction. My first attempts at selling my work—for my medical practice was still in its infancy and Holmes's income from his detective work was, to be generous, erratic—had terminated in a most unsatisfying manner, with my publisher retiring for health reasons. In point of fact, the black-guard had cheated me and, when I demanded he make things right, he laughed, telling me I ought to know when I was well off.

A seething red rage had come over me, followed by a calm I knew all too well. As I methodically went about breaking his jaw, I observed aloud that he could expect more of the same, and worse, if he thought about going to the constabulary. As soon as the publisher could write again (his hand having been broken in three, especially painful, places), he laboriously scribbled a note to his secretary, releasing me from my con-tract and paying me the sum I was owed. His editorial successor, perhaps acquainted with his colleague's experiences, cannily suggested that if I made some trifling adjustments to tone and content, my work would sell well to the higher-stepping readers of the more prestigious *Strand Magazine*. No one likes his work altered, but for a few more bob, I can state with no irony whatsoever that I do in fact know when I am well off.

So, no more penny dreadfuls; with some bowdlerization of our real adventures, I now produce thrilling tales that are brimful of derring-do. Some slight recasting of the details is necessary. I wouldn't want to shock my readers, and often the truth is a good deal more unsavory than they would like. But if I smooth over the rough parts of a case, pretty it up—well, it's good for the general populace to have moral tales and model heroes. Perhaps it's good for me and my friend, too, giving us an ideal to strive for. We so often fall badly short, no matter how hard we try.

That day in our sitting room, I crossed out an errant word and stacked my completed sheets with satisfaction. Since I could not resist the attrac-tions of the great cesspool that is London, I strove to keep my tendency to riotous life at bay. I had not slid into old, bad habits for nearly a week, and between being paid, and frugal living, I was quite pleased with myself. "Quite right, Holmes. I finally paid Mrs. Hudson my share of last month's rent, and better still, have stashed away next month's as well in our strongbox. I hope you have something coming in soon?"

"Sooner than I had expected, it seems." He stood by the window and motioned for me to join him. "You will please tell me what you think of the gentleman who hesitates just beyond our doorstep?"

I gladly obliged him, rising to peer out our window. The fog had cleared. "Well-off, in the first rank of fashion, though perhaps a foreigner—I have not seen that style of boots before, on the high streets or in the more fashionable districts. A gentleman, as you say, of robust health, but perhaps troubled by arthritis recently; his gait is somewhat unsteady, and as he pauses, he seems to rest his weight on his left leg."

"Well done, Watson! You give me hope for the British university system!"

I was so pleased at the idea of getting another case before Holmes that I smothered the retort I had ready regarding my considerable talent for diagnostics *and* a remark regarding his questionable parentage. "Well, then, go ahead. Tell me what I missed."

"Almost everything of importance, that is all." He had the all-too familiar look and tone of a schoolboy's superiority. "Yes, a foreigner, American—those boots are made by the New York firm of Getzler and Son. He walks stiffly, I would suggest, not because he has arthritis, but because he has not gained his land legs—you will notice that he does not have the characteristic scuffing mark on those fine shoes that is often found in chronic patients."

I did not interrupt Holmes with a lecture on the variability of symptoms from case to case. My heart was greatly eased to see that vacant restlessness gone from his face, and his eyes sharp and clear.

"So, he's come directly from the wharves, without even stopping at his hotel. If memory serves—and you can confirm this by handing me the papers—thank you, ah, yes. The private steam yacht *Anna Hoyt* docked earlier today, coming from Boston, in the United States. Therefore he had such a pressing need to see me that he could not wait for the scheduled commercial liner and then, on arrival in London, all but flew from the wharf—but why not cable beforehand? Why not a letter, even, than go to all this trouble and postponed haste of a lengthy ocean voyage? Perhaps—"

"He had a secret too valuable to trust to post or an emissary?"

Holmes shot me an irritated look that suggested I'd hit solid in the gold. "Yes . . . perhaps. And yet, what commands such haste and secrecy in a man so well off? Only two things—"

I mouthed the words as he spoke them, so accustomed were they to me. "Much money or vast power."

The bell rang, and the new maid, Aggie, showed him in. Although she was gone as soon as she'd announced "Mr. Habakkuk Sewall," I couldn't help admiring the trim profile of Aggie's posterior. Mrs. Hudson knew my tastes down to the boot button and was determined to taunt me. A dalliance between us, born of equal parts mutual desire and my occasional tardiness with the rent, had cooled recently, but I soon hoped to find my way back into Margaret's good graces. The rent now caught up, this was now entirely dependent on my ability to resist the temptations she put before me in the shape of our most recent maid of all work. We went through housemaids at an alarming rate, given the eclectic nature of our callers, the irregularity of our hours, and the odors generated by Holmes's chemical experiments. I have been subject to more than one angry lecture on the adverse effects of chemical fumes on damask upholstery.

Mr. Sewall was, as we had observed, of elegantly tall proportions, with fair hair, fine teeth, and shrewd, watchful eyes. His rude good health, as much an American trait as a caricature, was carefully restrained with mannerly movement; he had a reserved and contemplative air.

Having assured us that he had dined, Mr. Sewall did not refuse our offer of brandy. "I've come a very long distance to see you, Mr. Holmes. I hope you can help me."

Holmes and I had agreed early on in our association that, with clients, it was best for him to sink the hook with a display of his not inconsiderable detective acumen, followed by a faint pretense on my part to an overfull schedule, playing the fish before we finally landed the hefty fee. And so, I sat back and listened to Holmes recite what we'd just now observed, with a few embellishments drawn from his immediate assessment of our client. The more I saw of Mr. Sewall's gold cigar case, the quality and weight of his cuff links, and the exquisite taste in buttons, the better I liked him. Rather, the more I liked our odds of getting paid, and handsomely.

Doctors, detectives, and writers of detective fiction—or, semi-fiction— must make a living, you see.

At the end of a scintillating performance, Mr. Sewall's mouth opened and closed. "I had thought to come in here with my broadest Chicago hick accent, playing Eustis Goodfellow, the Corn King of the Midwest, but I see I would have failed almost instantly, Mr. Holmes. My hat is off to you.

"My goal in coming to England is of the utmost importance," he continued, in accents that were polished, by American standards. "I hope you will forgive my doubts and my aspirations to test you."

"You are not the first who has tried," said Holmes, inclining his head. I observed he did not actually accept the proffered apology but our guest seemed not to notice.

"Thank you. I am a good judge of character, sir, but that takes time and observation, and speed is of the essence. A fortune stands in the balance, but more than that, the safety and health of many innocent people."

"Pray, tell me how I may be of assistance." Only I recognized the impatience behind Holmes's request.

"My ancestress many times over, Anna Hoyt, was a woman of some means. It has recently come to light that she had a considerable fortune hidden here in England." At this, his expression became somewhat rueful. "I understand that during the War of Independence, she was known as a true patriot, but it appears she was also careful enough to have money— and possibly friends—in both countries, so that she might find some security no matter the war's outcome. This canny little lady, having started as a lowly tavern keeper, founded the family from which I am proud to be descended. Her caution, however, has placed me in a real bind. She hid the money, as one might during those bad old days, particularly keen not to let anyone find, seize, and tax it."

"How did you discover this?" Holmes sat forward, his fingers steepled.

"An advertisement, published by the law firm that was charged with producing the notice one hundred years after her death. I understand that, in addition to notifying possible family connections, newspapers around the world were hired to advertise that anyone with a claim to the inheritance must produce evidence in order to receive the clue that should lead to the treasure."

"What sort of treasure?" I asked. "Why a clue?"

"As I understand it, the old girl hid a small fortune in jewels and gold."

"Small, portable, universally valuable," Holmes remarked.

"Yes. And offered a clue and not a location as her reasoning was, anyone too stupid to find it, didn't deserve it. Of course, the lawyers said it much fancier than that." Mr. Sewall heaved a sigh. "First one who finds it, keeps it. I aim to be the first."

Holmes frowned. "And has any other family come forward?"

"Only one that can be proved—or rather, the lawyers are unable to *disprove* her credentials."

"'Her' being . . . ?"

"Miss Arabella Hartley. I met her once; the little hussy was running with a bad crowd in Europe. She claims to be a direct descendant through the male line, but I can find no record of any marriage between Anna Hoyt and an Englishman over here. Miss Hartley is nothing more than an adventuress, so far as I can tell."

I cleared my throat. "Forgive me for saying so, Mr. Sewall, but . . . would it be so difficult to lose out to Miss Hartley?" I did not like the way he'd spoken of his ancestress—the reason for his family's wealth—and this young lady.

A smirk on Holmes's face revealed that he thought my weakness for the ladies was showing itself.

"What you mean, in your very polite British way, is if I can afford to keep a private steamship, why do I care so much about a fistful of antique jewels?" He sighed. "If it were up to me, I would not. While I do not approve or know this young person, I have a debt of honor to repay."

He looked very solemn now. "My wife asked me, on her deathbed, to fund a hospital. I had need before that to put all my assets into my business—all the political unrest in Europe has been bad for my shipping trade—but if I can find that inheritance, well, I can honor both my wife and the founder of my family."

"And save innocent lives with the hospital," Sherlock Holmes murmured. "You have given me all the salient points?"

"All saving the lawyer, Mr. Deering's, address, my card and letter of introduction, and the address of my residence in London. If I may count on you, Mr. Holmes, I believe I shall soon be at rights with heaven and earth."

We exchanged farewells, and Mr. Sewall left.

"Well, Watson, what do you think?"

"I don't buy that cock-and-bull story about a wife's dying wish for one minute."

Holmes nodded. "I believe that is a lie, but he told one truth: He needs our help."

"He *needs* a good thrashing," I said warmly, thinking of his unkind words about Miss Hartley.

"So powerful a man? Coming here personally and lying to us? You may well get your wish, Watson."

Our eyes met, and a slow smile spread across my face. It was mirrored by Holmes's own rather feral grin.

A client with deep pockets *and* the promise of violence? Better than plum pudding on Christmas Day.

The next morning, armed with our client's particulars, Holmes wired his contact in Boston, asking him to examine more closely Sewall's family, business, and reputation. Then, we went to the office of Deering and Deering, where we presented our credentials. We were surprised when the senior partner, a round, balding little fellow with a gold pince nez, brought us the clue. It was not some legal document, but a portrait.

"It's all very irregular, of course," Mr. Deering said. "But there's nothing about this bequest that *is* regular!"

The antique portrait was in three-quarter, showing the lady herself in the garb of the previous century. She was perhaps sixty-five or so, I thought, but there was still more gold than silver in her hair and her features were very fine. She was resplendent in a scarlet gown and ribbons, and if I was any judge, the satin was costly and the lace on her cap and fichu very fine. There was a hardness in her eyes that might have been some trick of the light, because that hardness was belied by the slight smile on her lips.

"Copley, I think," Holmes said. His eyes were wide and slightly unfocused, his usual way of drinking in the entirety of a view—usually a crime scene.

I grunted.

"Really, Watson, the National Gallery is free. If you would only spend an afternoon improving yourself—"

"What will seeing this picture do to help us?" I broke in. "A lady, some books, a view overlooking a house—it's all quite ordinary."

It was an unsubtle strategy, but I was eager to see him engaged in this new project. His want of diversion affected me, threatening to unbalance the equilibrium I fought to maintain. Holmes, understanding my intent precisely, scowled at me.

But he took the proffered bait—how could he resist? It was precisely to his taste.

I breathed a sigh of relief as he continued.

"If you'll promise to spend time with the images of the great and the good, you'll soon learn that portraits often show the sitters' most valued possessions—books, maps of their estate, ships, family jewels. Therefore, Anna Hoyt's hand gesturing to the window indicates her land and the source of her wealth; the map behind her suggests that she's here in England. From the books on the table, we see she is literate; that table was new and fashionable at the time, and her dress is also quite rich. Very wealthy indeed, to judge from this picture."

"We know she's wealthy, because she left a *fortune*," I retorted. Sometimes Holmes took the long way round to a point.

"We *also* know she's wealthy because she had this portrait made," he said, with some asperity, "and had it done by a very sought-after artist. She knew people, Watson, and knew how to move through society—if she was able to elevate herself from running a tavern to traveling in these circles."

"Wait—Holmes!" An inspiration took me. "The house she's pointing to! Might that not be the location of the inheritance?"

He smiled absently. "It seems almost too obvious, does it not? But we must not count the house out, though we do not yet know its whereabouts. No, Watson, the thing that is puzzling me is that we see this English house—not her ships. Far more traditional either to show the ships themselves, as her main business, or the expensive goods she traded. No, this is odd . . ."

I turned to examine the picture. "That chatelaine-thingummy she's wearing is entirely too bulky for that dress. She should have fine little sewing implements or a locket or vinaigrette hanging from that hook, all in silver or gold. Not that heavy bunch of keys and such."

Holmes looked up. "What—thingummy?"

"The chatelaine—that hook at her waist?" And then I could not resist. "Honestly Holmes, there was a new embroidery pattern for a chatelaine purse in the *Ladies' New Journal* just last number, I, er, happen to know. If you'd only spend an hour or two educating yourself with the popular press, you would learn a great deal."

"No, no, I know *what* it is. Watson, it's your eye for the ladies that has once again proved so useful, as well as your—"

My pistol, my ability to stitch a wound, or my sangfroid? I wondered which he'd choose. *My companionship, my fists? My contributions to our living situation?*

"—your proclivity for reading Mrs. Hudson's periodicals. You are quite right: the woman who would wear that dress, and be painted by Copley, would not wear an ornament so out of place. I had attributed it to a quirk of colonial taste. But it is a clue."

I sighed. But he put his hand absently on my shoulder; I knew that gesture was all I should expect, in terms of a compliment, and took it as such.

We turned back to Mr. Deering. "Has anyone else been here to see this, apart from Mr. Sewall?"

"Just the other young gentleman," he said. "Sent by Mr. Sewall."

"But we are surely his sole representatives?" I said to Holmes.

"No, this was the paintings expert," Mr. Deering explained. "Or rather, Mr. Attenborough's son."

"Mr. Earnest Attenborough?" came the incredulous response from Holmes.

"His son," repeated the lawyer, who seemed to have no idea of the effect he'd just had on Holmes. "Said that his father was ill and confined to the house, and he was to make a sketch and bring it back to him. I was surprised by this, but Attenborough junior certainly knew what he was talking about and made an excellent copy, quickly, in crayon."

Holmes and I shared a look. "Can you describe this young man?"

Mr. Deering finally understood that something was wrong. A sheen of sweat broke out on his bald pate. "Yes. He was well dressed, quiet, stout, red-haired. One of those soft, studious fellows. I was hoping to hear from Attenborough today—by now in fact."

"You will not."

I looked up from the portrait. "Holmes?"

"Attenborough has no children," Holmes said. "The young man probably forged that letter, and was sent to copy the painting for an interested party. Which means that you are in danger, Mr. Deering, for I am convinced there is wickedness at work. Send a message to Scotland Yard, tell them I said to post a guard of their least inept constables. You must make certain no one else who hasn't the right sees this painting."

"I will, I will!"

Holmes turned to me. "Watson, we need reinforcements."

As we crossed London, it was immediately apparent that we were being followed. That these fellows were so bold was worrying. And yet, almost instantly, I felt my body relax, my brow unfurrow, and my breathing become deep and regular. Knowing there would be a brawl made my heart light. I made as if to check my watch, and assured myself that my cosh was handy.

"The next turning," Holmes said quietly, and a little eagerly. "We shall see what these rough fellows want."

But there was another group of men down the next alley, clearly the confederates of those following us. Their clothing suggested they were foreigners, and I could hear them muttering in some guttural tongue. Four against two, I did not mind so much, but at nine against us . . . We had been very carefully herded to this place, by someone who knew how men of action—indeed, Holmes himself—might think.

Holmes strode up to the man directly in front of us, feinted with a jab, and, whirling, kicked the man in the head. He was using that odd fighting style of his own invention, which he called "baritsu." It was undeniably effective, though not at all gentlemanly.

I let fly with my cosh upside one nasty fellow's head, and caught another with my backhanded return. My legs were knocked out from underneath me and I cracked my head on the cobbles. At least two more fellows joined in to kick me.

Holmes was on his own.

I rolled over to one side, as if to protect my head, but pulled out my revolver. Firing into the leg of one of my attackers had the effect of scattering the men from around me, and eliciting screams from the busy street we'd just left. That would bring the police, I hoped.

One brute running by stopped briefly to land one last kick to my jewels. As I doubled up in inexpressible pain, I watched with horror as he cut the throat of the man I'd shot, before escaping himself.

It took us a moment to realize the fight was really over. Gasping, Holmes pulled himself up, dabbing gingerly at a nasty cut across his chin. "Watson, you have an absurd attachment to your firearms. I would tell you I am surprised you would bring a pistol to one of the most respected law offices in the City, but I suspect you bring it to the opera, as well."

I groaned as I hauled myself to my knees. "You may assume I'm armed when I visit the thunder-mug."

Holmes laughed, wincing as he did. "And I am very glad of it."

I stood, shakily. "Who was that?"

Holmes shook his head. "I am not certain. Based on their dress and speech, I have a dreadful notion they were members of the Chercover gang. They are well organized and so ruthless they leave none of their own alive who might tell their secrets. I have no idea why that lot of anarchists might be interested in us." He spat out a mouthful of blood. "If they are after the same treasure we are, we must be twice as vigilant."

"You take this, then," I said, handing him my pistol. "I have another at home."

Holmes pocketed the gun. "Haste, now, Watson; we don't want to waste time with police questions. The game is afoot."

I will admit to whistling in the street as we continued on our way.

Holmes led me deep into Whitechapel, to a recently burned-down block that resembled one of the great ash heaps that still shame our city. Filthy men, women, and children sifted through the mounds, looking for something to sell.

On the edge of this desolation, we arrived at the house—a shell, awaiting demolition—and from the shadows, an urchin emerged. No more than eight or nine years of age, with the flaxen locks and piercing gray eyes of an angel, this pitifully small child, as filthy a street arab as I had ever seen, was dressed in an outré costume of a faded and patched frock, boy's shoes, and a man's jacket that hung like a tent on her. She greeted us with suspicion.

"Whatchu want?"

"I'm here to see—" my friend began, but the girl had already passed judgment and found us wanting.

"Wiggins, get out 'ere! I don't like the looks of these ones!"

"See here, what's your name?" I asked. Holmes only regarded her with curiosity.

She gazed at me with those wide gray eyes and hawked. Along with a considerable amount of tobacco juice, she spat out a curse so blue, so vile, I felt my face burning. She would have put a seasoned sergeant-major to shame.

Before I could collect my wits, or indeed, close my gaping mouth, ginger-haired Wiggins arrived, the tallest and oldest of the troop of other raggedy children who followed on his heels. No matter how many times I saw them, it never failed to break my heart. In the center of the wealthiest, most powerful nation on earth, children went hungry and turned to the streets for survival. It was a bitter thing to see, returning from war: We wanted to bring peace and civilization to the world, but hardly had it at home.

"All righ' then, Éirinn?" Wiggins said. Then he saw who it was paying a call, and doffed his cap. The others did as well, straightening themselves.

One nudged the poison-tongued little lookout. "Mind your manners, Éirinn Mitchell! That there's Mr. 'Olmes! The Guvnor!"

Miss Mitchell only crossed her arms, never dropping her venomous gaze. My shoulder blades itched; I would keep my back to the wall whenever this one was near.

"What can I do for you, Mr. 'Olmes?" Wiggins asked, in polite tones.

"I need two clerks, several spies, and runners to coordinate communication. Possibly a pickpocket."

The boy nodded. "It'll cost you."

"Usual fee, a shilling per day, of course."

"Plus clothing, plus bribes."

"And a bonus if you get what I need in time."

It was negotiated with the efficiency of business transacted many times between trusted partners; Holmes and Wiggins shook gravely upon completion and stepped aside to discuss the particulars. Rather than be left alone with the little gang of pickpockets, thieves, and (I wouldn't have been surprised to learn) cutthroats, and observing that Miss Mitchell had vanished, I ambled down to the corner and bought one of the racing rags. Holmes met me there, his meeting with the Irregulars concluded, and we were about to turn our steps homeward when I heard a shrill cry.

"Oi! You! Guv—Mr. 'Olmes!"

It was the little wretch from the burned-out house. Holmes paused. "Yes, Miss Mitchell?"

Suddenly shy, she lurched into something along the lines of a curtsy. Perhaps Wiggins had scolded her into manners. Or perhaps she was tottering from drink; there was now the reek of gin emanating from her. "This come for yer. Mr. 'Olmes. Sir."

She handed him a scrap of folded paper. It was fine stock but, once pristine white, was now smudged by her grubby hand.

"Who gave it to you?" Holmes asked, offering her a coin in exchange for the paper.

The coin vanished quickly. "Young bloke. Not so much better off than us, maybe, but . . . in regular employ. Not sure 'e could've wrote it, though. Didn't seem that smart. But he give me a hit off'n his flask, and a shilling besides."

"Thank you, Éirinn, those are excellent observations. Let me know if you see him again. Better yet, follow him, and find out who he works for, without getting caught, and there'll be a guinea in it for you. Do you understand?"

Her eyes lit up at the thought of such a fortune. She nodded, and without a word, ran off.

I felt an overwhelming hopelessness in the face of such misery. "Is it fair, Holmes? To encourage them to spy and sneak and God knows what? They ought to be in school or in respectable service."

"Yes, but they are not. I give them a chance, Watson. To learn that paying attention to detail can be profitable. To learn that work for a wage can be an alternative to begging and thievery. I give them a chance, that is all."

"It is not much of one," I said. How much money did I have in my pocket? Never much, but a king's ransom wouldn't cure what I saw around me.

"It is considerably more than we were given," he said darkly.

"We?" Holmes and I seldom trespassed upon each other's early lives; he took me off-guard, hinting he knew anything of my past or that we shared anything in common.

He held up the note. I could see the tiny, cramped handwriting. It read, "Do not interfere with my investigation of Miss H."

"My brother Mycroft sends his regards."

I stared, agape. I had only met Mycroft Holmes a handful of times. A giant of a man, he had an intellect to scale, and while he claimed to be a minor clerk for the British government, I soon learned that he was a spymaster of the first order, with agents around the world who supplied him with a never-ending stream of information. Mycroft ignored me, for the most part, which made me grateful, for I have no shame in admitting that the man terrified me.

I considered once again the radical ways in which Holmes and his brother lived. If one fairly wallowed in the criminal element and the other preferred to be secreted away, dealing at the highest levels of government, I didn't dare guess what *their* early lives were like.

Holmes pursed his lips, considering. "Watson, I must make inquiries. Clearly, Mr. Deering's stout red-headed copyist is working for Chercover, or possibly Miss Hartley."

"What can I do?"

"Go back to Baker Street. See what you can discover in my files about either of those parties. I suspect Chercover is the reason for Mycroft's attention, so I'm surprised he said anything to us about Miss Hartley. There is much more going on here than we expected."

I nodded and departed. I knew that however obscurely Holmes's brain might work, there was always a reason for his instructions. There was certainly no time to waste, because whatever Mycroft Holmes's interest in Miss Hartley, it suggested danger to us all.

As I rounded the corner on my way to Baker Street, I found myself accosted by two unpleasant, and all too familiar, toughs. One short and stout, the other tall and thin, like something from a music hall act. But they were not clowns.

The short one said, "Doctor Watson. A word, with you."

I slowed, cursing under my breath. "Campbell, tell Dermody—"

"Tell me what, Doctor Watson?" A third tough joined us from around the corner, shorter, leaner, and meaner than his messengers. "That you'll have my money tomorrow? That you're on to a sure thing? I've heard that song from you before."

"I have the money at home," I lied, hoping for a chance to escape.

"Let's go get it," Dermody suggested. "Together."

I had tried outrunning and outfighting his two men before this, and barely made it away. With three of them, I was lost.

"Very well," I said, affecting an air of unconcern. "You'll save me the trip to see you tonight."

"Happy I could be of assistance. Now move."

This was bad. Dermody never showed up in person, had never had to. I had always paid my debts. Eventually. This time was taking a little longer, but still, I was confident we'd maintain our cordial association. His gambling den was by far the most honest of its sort around.

I got to the door and paused. And patted my pocket. The cosh was gone, lost in the alley, and I'd given my pistol to Holmes. My curses of frustration were not an act; I desperately did not want to do what I now knew I must. "Lost my keys."

"Very careless of you. I'm sure you still have a maid?"

"My landlady does."

"So what are we doing out here still?"

I hesitated, then rang the bell, two short, one long.

The new girl, Aggie, opened it, and gasped to see the four of us crowded on the step. "My goodness, Doctor Watson—"

Panic flooded me; it should not have been Aggie at the door.

"Well, well, you're a fine bit of stuff, aren't you?" Dermody pushed forward, prelude to grabbing Aggie and forcing her inside. I felt my blood boil and my vision went to pinpoint, smelling his onion breath as he shoved me aside. The panic that threatened me subsided, replaced by a killing rage. If he should hurt this poor girl . . .

Then I saw the dear, dear face of Mags Hudson—and the even dearer sight of her shotgun. She had not become the astute London businesswoman she was without understanding that not all visitors were the polite sort.

"Aggie, don't you dare move!" came the brisk order.

Aggie quailed; she turned her head and uttered a little shriek when she saw a shotgun resting on her shoulder.

"Shut up, and don't move, girl," Mrs. Hudson growled. Slender, an upright posture, with dark brown hair, she was now the very picture of a Valkyrie. "I don't want you to eat the hot load of birdshot I mean to serve to these gentlemen."

"Whoa, now, Missus," Dermody said, still confident he could get past her. "No call for none of that! We're all friends here."

The steely look in her eye and the equally metallic noise of both triggers being cocked convinced him.

Dermody and his boys froze.

"No, we're not friends," Margaret said. "And I don't like the looks of you, so get yourselves gone."

"We'll be back later," Dermody said. His eyes were filled with rage. "Lads."

They backed off warily, almost falling off the step and onto the pavement, then hastened away.

Only when Mrs. H was satisfied, did she remove the shotgun from the maid's shoulder. "I'm sorry, Aggie, but you got here faster than you should. That's the good doctor's *m'aidez* signal, two shorts and a long. You're new, else you would have known. My fault. I'm sorry, girl."

But Aggie heard nothing, still sobbing hysterically.

Mrs. Hudson sighed. "All right, all right, no harm done. There's a bottle in my desk drawer. Pour yourself a big glass of whisky, and get one for me too. Go on, now."

The girl stumbled away, hiccuping.

Mrs. H's look suggested she wouldn't mind shooting me: Aggie wasn't going to last any longer than the last maid. "John, one day, you'll be the death of us all!"

I stepped toward her, closing the door behind me. "Mags, you're wonderful." I ran a hand along her slender waist. The romantic urge often follows hot on the heels of excitement or danger, I've found.

She slapped me away, but not too hard. "Tch. None of that now. I thought you were behaving yourself. Are you short, again?"

"Oh, no."

She shot me a look, and my grin faded. "Well, yes. A bit, but I have more than enough to keep Dermody happy until we get paid again."

Margaret sighed. She knew me far too well. "Let's go get it, then. And you'll go straight to pay him off, right? No trying to land a long shot on the horses?"

"Of course." I led her to the strongbox Holmes and I share, and found it opened. And empty, save for an IOU note in a familiar scrawl.

"Bloody Sherlock Holmes," she said, finally. "It's a damned good thing I got last month's rent."

I spent several elucidating hours with Holmes's files; Scotland Yard ought to have as comprehensive a library of criminals and cases. Marcus Hannibal Chercover was as black a villain as they came. His criminal gang was the terror of Europe, aiding revolutionaries with guns and men for hire at a very steep price. His cunning was matched only by his unparalleled cruelty, and he grew wealthy on the warfare he helped create.

One interesting addition to these notes was a new cable from Boston that arrived as I read. Among other items of interest, Holmes's Boston investigator had confirmed that Habakkuk Sewall had recently been in Prague, the site of Chercover's headquarters.

When Holmes arrived home, he didn't get two steps into the sitting room before I laid into him. "Where is it? The money you took—?"

His face was vacant; he couldn't understand the reason for my emotion. "I left a note saying I'd replace it."

"That's not the *same as* replacing it. What did you spend it on?"

"Well, there was paying the Irregulars, and holding some aside for rewarding their success."

"There was almost a half month's rent in there!" I said, shocked. "You gave them *all* of it?"

"There was also the bribe to let my 'secretary' take my place in the archives, and more to buy that boy something approximating a suit. I spent a great deal on cables to America last night, after Mr. Sewall left. Then there was the investment in locating Miss Hartley here in London. That was no easy matter, for she didn't want to be found, though the Irregulars always succeed. I've sent a note requesting an hour of her time tomorrow at eleven." He paused, frowning. "She evaded me quite a while. However, one must spend money to get more in, Watson."

He sounded so prim and marmish I would have laughed, if I hadn't been so angry.

"Well," I said, mollified, and not a little relieved. "What have you found out?"

Holmes's eyes glittered like a dragon on a hoard; he loved nothing so much as information. "I've discovered that Mr. Sewall is a first-rate cad. He may have made a promise to his wife, but I doubt he intends to keep it. He certainly never kept any of the other vows he made to her; if my source is correct, Sewall has a string of fancy women from New York to San Francisco. And he is in very dire straits, far worse than he suggested. He's squandered a great deal of his family money, teetering on the brink of bankruptcy, with debts coming in fast."

I grinned; that in and of itself was gratifying. "I suspected as much. What about his claim? Is he legitimately part of the family?"

"That I believe is true, and have confirmed it with records in Boston. The question is, why come to us?"

"You said it yourself. It takes money to make more money, and if time is a factor, then it's well spent to come to you."

"Perhaps. But he's up to something, Watson, and I do not like not knowing what it is."

"What about Miss Hartley?"

"She is more difficult. My instincts are all a-tingle, what with both Sewall and brother Mycroft so set against her. She is something more than a mere 'adventuress.' Her claims to be a descendant seem in order, though I have not satisfactorily determined what Mistress Anna Hoyt might have been doing on this side of the Atlantic."

"Hmm, well, if we find Sewall's inheritance, he'd better pay us. The kitty is now quite empty."

"I always honor my debts," Holmes said, a trifle peevishly.

Then he looked at me, an amused smirk playing about his lips. "You do realize, Watson, that if I decide to dip into the butter and egg money to buy cocaine, I shall probably not leave a note saying I have done so?"

"I never imagined . . ." But I felt my face going red all the same and hastened to tell him of the attack. "There might have been dire consequences, Holmes." I recounted my meeting with Dermody and his boys, Margaret's rescue, and Aggie's initiation into one of the household's peculiar habits.

He frowned. "In that case, my apologies. What should have been a slight inconvenience for you was very nearly something much worse." He clapped me on the shoulder. "I have a friend who owes me dinner at his chop-house; we'll go there tonight, form our battle plans. But you must tell me one thing."

"Of course."

"How does it feel to have your lady friend save your life? Again?"

I shrugged, showing nothing but mild amusement at his jibe. "It's rather wonderful, you know. No end of useful in, er, matters of the boudoir. Better than gin. You should look into it, Holmes—oh, my pardon. You don't *have* a lady friend, do you?"

"I don't require anything so base. Mine is a life of the mind."

He looked so pious, I could not help but laugh, as I reached for my hat. "Ha! You only say that when you *haven't* any lady friend."

Since it was so cheap to dine very well, we could not resist prolonging the evening with a quick drink at a local pub. There, I ran into some old friends from the regiment; drinks led to toasts, which led to cards. I lost track of Holmes at one point—he had done pretty well at cards, as he tends to—but rather than exploit his advantages, he left before anyone could grumble about his winnings. I saw him across the way discussing something with an unsavory-looking Egyptian, just as one of my mates took offense at something a sailor said. As the first punch was thrown, I felt that familiar red haze descend and the calm that came before a good row . . .

The next morning, the curtains were pulled open with a racket I usually associate with locomotives. "Oh, John, the state of you. And you'd been doing so well."

"Mags, please . . ." Razors seemed to fill my eye sockets. "We just need to get our feet under us again . . ."

"No time for that. Drink your tea, and do better next time. You have a letter from a Miss Hartley." Mrs. Hudson raised an eyebrow. "On scented paper."

"A client."

"Hmm."

As Holmes and I set off for our appointment that morning, I was profoundly grateful it was raining, for sunlight would have been unbearable. I did wish, however, the rain would not beat down on my hat with such heavy, echoing blows.

Holmes's aspect was ghastly, showing all the sad characteristics of a recent opium binge.

When we arrived at the hotel, Miss Hartley received us in a small parlor. She was a trifle late, but as we stood to greet her, I could only say that it was time well spent. A stunning petite blonde, she was dressed *de rigueur* in dark green velvet. I was utterly bewitched by the little Silesian iron ornament in her upswept hair, making as charming a figure as could be imagined. As she bade us sit, I could see the deep blue of her eyes, like the sea after a storm.

Holmes, who abhors the untidiness of latecomers and missed appointments, obstinately refused to be charmed. He was politeness itself, as he invariably is in public, but I recognized the slight hardening around his eyes that communicates—to those familiar with it—a disdain. For him, punctuality was a cardinal rule of etiquette, and before even shaking hands, Miss Hartley had blotted her copybook.

I'm sure that from her appearance, her claim, and this breach, he had deduced the whole of her history. I myself noted that, while her movements were graceful, there was an anxiety that informed her smallest gestures. The twisting of a handkerchief, the way her eyes darted around the room, her startlement at the least noise all told me of a lady in trouble.

"Thank you for seeing us, Miss Hartley," Holmes said. "Perhaps you know already why I requested this appointment?"

"My claim to the fortune left by Anna Hoyt." She looked away. "I hardly expected to meet the famous Mr. Sherlock Holmes."

He waved a hand dismissively. "How did you learn about the bequest?"

"I had been traveling in the continent; a friend sent me a letter with the clipping from the paper. I contacted Mr. Deering."

"Why were you abroad?"

"I was visiting friends." She hesitated, then looked up at Holmes directly. "I had formed an . . . attachment there . . . and later learned he was untrue to me. I returned because . . . my health declined."

"And the bequest—" Holmes started.

"I'm a doctor," I broke in. "If I may be of any assistance—?"

She laughed, a lovely sound. "Thank you, I am nearly better now. But if I find Anna Hoyt's bequest, I shall travel to Egypt and let the ancient sun heal me."

Holmes frowned briefly at me. "But to the case at hand. You'll forgive me asking—how is it that no record of your birth exists in the United States?"

"For the simple reason that my family has always been in England. It is my belief that Anna's son—my many-times great-grandfather—was the result of either a hidden marriage or an illicit love affair." She blushed prettily. "But the records for my family are here, even if Anna Hoyt did not remain."

"You met your distant cousin, Habakkuk Sewall, while you were in Prague, correct?"

Suddenly, her features sharpened. "Forgive me, Mr. Holmes, but do you work for Mr. Sewall?"

"It is true." He raised an eyebrow. "One cannot always choose one's clients."

I frowned; it was unlike him to be so indiscreet.

"Then I believe this interview is at an end," Miss Hartley said. "I have no interest in furthering the interests of a gentleman—and I must only use the term in its most general sense—who seeks to rob a young lady of something that is rightfully hers. Good morning."

She rose, and for a moment, I could see in her defiance and disdain a great deal of her ancestress. With the barest of nods to me, Miss Hartley moved past with a rustle of silk satin. At the door, she weakened. We ran to her aid, and she would have fallen had I not caught her.

She thanked me, squeezing my hand with a sad smile, and fled before I could ascertain her illness.

"Bravo, Holmes," I said angrily. "She's clearly still unwell!"

"Watson, please." He patted his pockets, frowning. "She knew that I am working for Mr. Sewall."

"What of it?"

"And yet she waited to bring it up as a way to exit."

"What do you mean?"

"Simply this: Why meet us, if she wants to avoid Mr. Sewall?" He cocked his head. "Much more sensible to make up some excuse to us and hide herself away again. And there's the question of why Mycroft would want me to keep me my distance from her. I think, Watson, she wanted to . . . show herself to me. To let me read her history in her words *and* in her person. Communicate something to me."

One of Wiggins's troop of mercenaries ran in. "Mr. Holmes, come quick!"

"What is it, Mr. Coupe?"

"Mr. Deering's office—it's on fire!"

⊰◈⊱

We got there too late. The conflagration kept everyone far back; it was not known if Mr. Deering was alive or dead.

"There is more at stake here than money," Holmes murmured. "This is an act of rage."

"But how—?"

We were interrupted by a shout. Another of the Irregulars ran across the busy thoroughfare, skillfully dodging omnibuses and hansoms, reaching us, out of breath.

"Mr. Holmes! I came as fast as I could!" It was the young man got up as a clerk doing research for Holmes.

"What have you found, Mr. Morris?"

"*Miss* Morris—my twin brother can't read as well as me," she said; I belatedly realized that her hair was tucked under her collar and cap. "I've found the location of the house!" She held up a scrap of paper with an address. "It's in Sussex! On the South Downs, near Eastbourne."

"Very well done, Miss Morris!"

When I saw the way the young lady's face lit up, I could not help but think Holmes was correct in giving the Irregulars the chances he did. With her ink-stained fingers and third-hand clothing, Miss Morris was as proud as an empress at her achievement.

"Shall I find you a cab, Mr. Holmes?" she said, her breath returning.

"No need. But you've earned this." He handed her a coin. "Go find the others, tell them to keep up the fine work."

"Yes, sir! Thank you, sir!"

We immediately found a cab and rushed to the station. "I'm afraid we've missed the good train to Eastbourne, Watson."

"I'm not sure what we'll do when we get there. Our client is Mr. Sewall, but you're saying that Miss Hartley wants our aid?" I reached into my pocket for a cigarette. My fingers brushed across a small scrap of paper. Frowning, I pulled it and read it. "Isaiah 56:5? Where on earth did this come from?"

Holmes's face cleared, and I knew he'd discovered the solution to some part of our puzzle. "I thought I was wrong about Miss Hartley, when she didn't pass me a note. She put the clue into your pocket, because you were there first."

"What?"

"She's given us the location of the treasure. She is indeed asking for our help."

We barely made the next train to Eastbourne. As I caught my breath, I could not imagine what conclusions Holmes had reached.

"I believe Chercover himself was the unfaithful 'attachment' Miss Hartley formed, or possibly she broke it off when she discovered his true nature. The foreign cut of her garments and particularly the Silesian iron jewelry she wore—I'm much better at identifying contemporary fashion, Watson!—suggests a long stay in central Europe. When she received news of the Hoyt treasure, she realized she might find the means to flee him. That Egyptian fellow I spoke with last night? He is the porter for her hotel; he confirmed her luggage had stamps from Prague."

Holmes continued. "She knew my reputation, and she knew that if I was investigating this case, I might be able to assist her. She relied on me reading her situation from her person, and her version of the story. She could not be plainer about Chercover or the location of the treasure for fear we were spied upon, or might give her up."

"Chercover burned down the law offices," I said, remembering Holmes's mention of "rage."

"Yes. He followed her to London, perhaps having read the letter she'd received. And when we were beset by that ruthless gang, I knew it might not only be Mr. Sewall she hid from. But I think Chercover has another purpose here: meeting Mr. Habakkuk Sewall."

"What!"

"Sewall's interest in the treasure is genuine—he needs the money. But I believe he formed the idea of working with Chercover when he visited Miss Hartley abroad. You remember, he mentioned she was with a bad crowd? I think he's been in negotiations with Chercover to sell space on his reputable ships for whatever Chercover wishes to smuggle—men, gold, guns. In exploring Sewall's claim, my man in Boston observed that he sent a large number of cables to Prague."

"Yes. And it was by watching Chercover that your brother Mycroft learned about Sewall, the legacy, and Miss Hartley," I said. "And our involvement."

"Exactly! He warned me away from Miss Hartley, as he believes he can use her to find and arrest Chercover and his men."

I frowned. "It seems so odd that both of them—relatives from opposite sides of the Atlantic—would be entangled with a monster like Chercover, but you've shown me quite material reasons for it."

Holmes shrugged. "There is also the matter of atavism and hereditary aptitudes, Watson. We observe that Mistress Hoyt was clever, cautious, and canny; she survived a rough era to die peacefully of old age. And yet, she hid money to escape possible political reverses and avoid taxes; my man in Boston suggests a dark history behind her wealth. It is not difficult to imagine that her descendants might have also inherited her clever, perhaps criminal turn of mind, one looking for excitement abroad, the other risking large sums of cash."

"But what about this piece of paper?"

"The location of the treasure. Do you know the Bible verse?"

"If memory serves, something about walls and a house?"

"'*Even unto them will I give in mine house and within my walls a place and a name better than of sons and of daughters.*' I believe if we find a wall or construction of late last century's vintage, we will find the treasure. Or, at least, we'll find Miss Hartley, who wants us to help her escape Chercover, who is no doubt closing in on her."

I nodded. "She is the only one in this case not guilty of anything more than bad judgment, to have fallen in love with an anarchist. I'm happy to help her over Mr. Sewall."

"A race to the treasure." Holmes's face was grim, but his eyes were alight with anticipation. "Watson, do not be mistaken: There will be a bloodbath in Sussex."

It took an excruciatingly long time to reach the farmstead; we had good luck getting a taxi from Eastbourne, but after finding directions to the farm itself, were forced to walk the last mile to the long driveway leading to the front of the house.

The farmstead was quiet when we arrived in the early evening. I had to assume we were not the first ones here. There was little wind in this sheltered spot and I fancied I could almost hear the crash of waves on the nearby coast.

The age of the little farmhouse suggested to us both that it long predated Anna Hoyt's time. We agreed to circle around from opposite sides, I from the left, and Holmes from the right as we faced the house. With any luck, we would find a wall constructed within the past century or meet in the back.

Nearing the rear of the house, past a flanking hedge, I could make out several tea-chest-sized structures staggered inside a stone wall enclosing the yard behind the house. Only prudence born of long experience kept me from racing to it, and it was well I did not: as I approached the hedge, I was surprised by several men. Their shouts were in the same guttural language spoken by the brigands who attacked us in the alley. A flock of my bullets drove them away, but, returning fire, they forced me to take cover on the ground behind the hedge.

As the echo of shots died away, I realized that an angry droning noise had risen up all around me. A rich scent, redolent of alfalfa, burned molasses, and thyme, filled my nose. I saw ranks of beehives in the space between an ancient ruin of a moss-covered wall and a much newer construction. Thousands of dark little bodies flitted through the air, disturbed by our gunplay. There seemed to be no end of them. I'd never been stung by a bee, and never thought about it, but now the sheer number of them, the huge noise they made as they rose up to defend their homes, became a phantasm, a terror that robbed me of my will. I had no idea what to do. . . .

The darkening sky closed down around me and my vision narrowed. I felt as if I was being pressed into the earth. The noise was . . . everywhere. Inside my head, down to the hollow cores of my bones. There was no relief, no cessation. I could feel every vibration of the swarm in the dirt beneath me. The enraged hum screamed "danger," thrilling my every nerve. If I moved, I'd be shot. If I stayed, I would surely die. My heart pounded fit to shatter my ribs.

Only half aware of my surroundings, through the stems of the hedge, I saw Holmes approach the rear of the house, toward the hives. Heard the arrival of other men.

Shouts, then. Followed by gunfire.

Holmes hit and fallen. No noise from him but a muffled groan. He never made noise when he fought. Almost never made a noise when he was hit.

Sewall had come from the right, following Holmes. Somewhere in the distance, more confusion; perhaps Sewall's men engaging with Chercover's.

Holmes down.

A hail of bullets drowned out the horrible buzzing. I found it oddly comforting. *That* noise was a continual part of my existence. The reason I could only be happy in the tumult and confusion of London was knowing that something terrible *would* eventually happen.

I found myself laughing at this carnage in the tranquil Sussex countryside.

And that laughter brought me back to myself. I had conquered fear many times. Bloodlust, always so close to me, and its attendant emotionless calm, were my friends now.

One, two, three deep breaths. I pushed myself up and onto my feet. The thought of action, of volition, was a sweet, raging song in my blood. I drew my pistol—my companion in many a battle—and ran, crouching, along the hedge to where it stopped, just three feet from the corner of the house. I was now directly across from where I had seen Holmes go down. A clear path seemed to spread before me, but some blessed instinct told me to hold. If it was in fact so clear, Holmes himself would have fled.

There. One of Sewall's men was positioned behind the low stone wall that stretched to my left, his rifle seeking potential enemies. In the melee beyond the walls, the shrieks of wounded and dying men were terrible.

I stepped back into the shadows, then glanced at my friend. He was tying a handkerchief around his left forearm, his pistol cast aside, bullets spent. I could see blood, glistening black in the fading light, on his sleeve. Holmes's long legs were tucked up to his chest, and while he had made himself almost invisible, I could not understand why Sewall didn't simply shoot Holmes. He knew his location—

Ah. Sewall was also out of ammunition, his last bullet having found its mark in my friend's arm. He did not dare go find more, for fear of me. And he didn't dare approach Holmes for fear of the bees swarming around the hives between them.

Sewall did not know I only had one bullet left. There had been no time to arm ourselves properly before we left London.

I had to choose between shooting Sewall—and giving away my position to the man with the rifle—or shooting the rifleman and leaving Holmes to Sewall's nonexistent mercies.

There was no choice at all.

I stood up, stepped from behind the wall to find my angle, and raised my pistol. Gunshots filled the air, but they were a secondary concern, now. Once you have a plan in mind, and are fully dedicated to its achievement, it is really no matter at all to disregard your surroundings and get to work. I have found this to be true not only in soldiering and medicine, but in all things in life, except for writing.

Before I could take the shot, Sewall went down, with a blood-curdling screech. A cloaked figure ran toward him from the right, scrambling over the wall. Even more upheaval outside the little farmhouse yard, a skirmish growing into a pitched battle.

I turned and fired on the sharpshooter. I hit him, just as his bullet found my left shoulder.

I felt a sharp blow, biting pain, and the cold rush of air into an open wound in the muscle of my right shoulder; warm blood spilled down my arm. More gunshots, and I ran, keeping as low a profile as I could. An unfortunate familiarity with being shot told me that this, unlike my wound in Afghanistan, did not threaten to be a mortal one. What I'd do when I reached Holmes, I did not know; perhaps I could move him to safety.

Cries from around me, and more gunshots—too many of both. Holmes yelled, "Mycroft, for the love of God almighty, stop firing!"

"This matter is beyond you, Sherlock!"

"It will be a matter bloody well *within* me, if one of your lunatics shoots me!"

Mycroft Holmes—outside of London?

I reached the wall along which Holmes the younger was hiding. Bullets continued whizzing past, shouts increasing, the screams of horses adding to the chaos.

The same cloaked form that shot Sewall was now beside Holmes. A flash of bright metal—someone was trying to cut Holmes's throat!

"Unhand him!" I reached them and seized the cloaked shoulder, pulling for all I was worth, which thanks to the bullet in my shoulder, wasn't much. "Damn it!"

It was Miss Hartley.

While my brain struggled to catch up with my eyes, she shoved me over. I fell hard, momentarily paralyzed by shock and confusion, and watched as she ran toward a horse.

Then I scrambled to my knees. "Are you all right? Did she—?"

But the only wound I could see was where Sewall's bullet hit. I immediately went about stanching it, then paused, realizing that Miss Hartley was escaping.

"Let her go, Watson," Holmes said. "All is well."

"How can that be?"

"I have what we need. Help me up."

I did so.

Suddenly, Mycroft Holmes was beside us, a lantern in one hand, pistol in the other.

"Stop her!" Mycroft bellowed, then raised his pistol, aiming at Miss Hartley.

"Mycroft!" I cried out. "What in God's name—?"

Sherlock hurled himself at his brother. Mycroft lifted a ham-sized fist, and attempted to land a punch, but toppled over as Sherlock tackled him. The pistol flew away, and I watched, astonished. Mycroft's blows were accompanied with bull-like bellows; if they landed, they might have shattered an anvil. I suddenly realized that Sherlock's silent speed and unorthodox fighting style had been developed specifically for fighting his *brother*. The titans of myth might have fought such a battle. Both brothers fanatically, in their own ways, devoted to order. Both crossing each other's purposes now.

Despite the fascination of the horror of brother fighting brother, I picked up Mycroft's discarded pistol and fired it into the air.

Finally, the combatants fell apart. The madness left Mycroft's eyes as he became aware of what one of his lieutenants was calling to him: they were arresting what remained of Chercover's defeated force.

Sherlock, panting and holding his arm, could not leave well enough alone. "Sorry, brother. She was *so* clever—possibly the only woman to best you?"

Mycroft wheeled around on him. "You pestilential little weasel! How dare you?"

"I dare, as I dare everything," Sherlock replied, all insolence.

"No matter. You need not hang for treason. My men will find her. We have Chercover."

"She's fleeing his organization," Sherlock said. "She's no use to you now, and will not trouble you again."

"Hrrmph." Without another word, Mycroft stalked away.

If, at times, I found Sherlock Holmes baffling and Mycroft Holmes entirely beyond my ken, then the two brothers together were a mystery for the ages. I knew there was something of great import being communicated in their bickering, but for the life of me, I could not fathom it.

"Don't worry, Watson," Sherlock Holmes said, seeing my utter confusion. "He threatens me with hanging, or a knighthood, every month or so when we *are* talking. With any luck, he won't speak to me for years. More than likely, though, he'll need me and come crawling. Or rather, stride in imperiously, and I'll make him squirm before I give him whatever he wants."

Holmes looked under his jacket and made a face at the wound above his wrist. "Not so bad as some; my coat saved me worse. Should be a cinch for you to—" He glanced at me holding my shoulder. "Oh! Well, after you have stitched yourself up first, of course."

"What about the rest of the case?" I said helplessly.

"Oh, we don't need Mycroft for that." He smiled and reached into a deep coat pocket. Something clanked, and shone in the lantern light—the object I had believed was a knife at Holmes's throat.

"Anna Hoyt's chatelaine!" I cried. "So now, you can find the treasure!"

"Well . . . not quite. Arabella Hartley got here first."

"But if so, why did she stay so long?"

Holmes was rapt in examining the chatelaine, trinket by trinket individually. Nothing more than might interest an antiquarian, there were the usual scissors, pomander, thimble, seal. There was only one key on the chain now—presumably used to open the treasure's hiding place.

The seal had an engraving: "Isaiah 56:5."

"A hint from Anna Hoyt herself. And Miss Hartley knew," Holmes said. "Somewhere around here, she found the wall hiding the jewels."

Holmes shook the decorative little needle case; there was no rattle of needles inside the narrow cylinder. Invariably curious, he removed the top, and drew a slip of paper from inside the etui. Reading by Mycroft's abandoned lantern, we saw the following:

It is not safe for me here. But I will not leave England before trying to assist you. And if you should live, take this small token, with my thanks—AH.

"She saved you," I said.

"She did. Though it was not in her best interest to do so."

Perhaps he didn't notice the smear of lip rouge on his cheek, but I certainly did. "And left you the chatelaine as a memento?"

"Not only that." He held up a heavy leather sack. A smell of mildew overwhelmed me when he opened it, and the soft sound of clanking coin could be heard from inside. "Quite a lot of gold, actually. And as Sewall is under arrest, Miss Hartley, as the lawful inheritor, has apparently disbursed funds as she's seen fit."

"This will certainly set us right enough," I said. "That much gold will get our feet under us!"

"Indeed, Watson." Holmes looked around the place with such an air of contentment as I had never seen before. His quiet calm affected me similarly. He reached over to a bloom, and, with infinite gentleness, ran his finger along the bee lingering there in the lantern light. *"Ubi mel, ibi apes.* Where there is honey, there are bees. A hive is a kind of utopia, is it not? One could learn much from the study of bees."

And so, in spite of our wounds, and our failure in locating the treasure for our client, it had been a very successful outcome. Sewall, the would-be smuggler, was in prison; a dangerous revolutionary gang was eradicated; and Miss Hartley had safely fled to start a new life.

We found our way to the train and were back in London before midnight. After stitching up our wounds and eating a cold dinner, we retired.

I slept for nearly eighteen hours. The next evening, Holmes and I determined to celebrate our good fortune. The mood was festive, and the wine flowed freely. We shook hands as we parted, I to find Dermody, and Holmes to visit a philosopher friend to discuss bees. We vowed we could now proceed as we'd always planned, live more quietly, and settle into a comfortable life, now that our situation was not so precarious.

It was with a great sense of pride and purpose that I paid off Dermody. He agreed that we were square, and we shared a drink to commemorate the occasion. A good-natured argument broke out and a small wager was placed. Pleased at being found correct, I allowed Dermody to make another, about the color of the scarf of the next gentleman to walk in.

You may imagine what followed. I must, for I have no clear memory of the rest of the evening.

I woke the next afternoon in Margaret Hudson's bed, searing pain behind my eyes and a coppery taste of blood and bile in my mouth. A tooth was loose and my stomach was distinctly unwell. The wallpaper pattern seemed to slither up the wall, and my shame and self-disgust threatened to swallow me once again.

Mags appeared, a cup of tea in her hand. Noble woman, she had laced it heavily with brandy and honey. She didn't say a word, and while I expected to see pursed lips or hear some rebuke from her, I saw only concern and love in her face. "That chaos in your sitting room . . . was that you, too?"

"What chaos?" But a terrible memory, one that had resulted in me finishing off the brandy bottle at home, suddenly emerged from my mental fog. My medical bag up-ended, several vials of morphine gone. "No, no. No, that was Holmes."

My friend had fared no better than I. Sadness, anger, frustration welled up inside me, and there might have been tears, if it had not been for Margaret.

"Bloody Sherlock Holmes," she said. I recognized her ruse of disparaging him so that I might think of something other than my own misery.

"He's just a man, with weaknesses, as any of us," I said. "Oh, Mags—"

"Here, now. None of that." She pulled a pen and paper from her apron pocket. "Write it down. Set yourself your own example. You said it yourself, you're just a man, with weaknesses, same as all of us." She paused at the door. "We can only keep striving to find our better selves."

BEFORE A BOHEMIAN SCANDAL

by *Tasha Alexander*

Although he could not deny its effectiveness, cruelty as an art repulsed him. He viewed it as unbecoming to a gentleman of his status. This status was precisely what had insulated him from, as yet, ever having to employ it. Others could take care of any unpleasantness with which he preferred not to deal. Usually. Tonight, however, as he pressed his back harder against the scarlet silk hanging on the wall of the reception room to which he and his friends had retired, Wilhelm Gottsreich Sigismond von Ormstein, hereditary Crown Prince of Bohemia, feared cruelty would prove the only way out of a most inconvenient predicament.

If only she would stop talking, he thought, chastising himself for ever having found her wide blue eyes beguiling. He had not expected an affair of three days to prove so difficult to end, but his subtle attempts to brush off Magda had made not the slightest impression upon her. Firmly up against the wall, his exit was blocked by an inconvenient buffet table on one side and a large potted palm on the other. He dared not step forward, as doing so would put him even closer to her. She was laughing, a coarse, throaty chortle unsuited to a woman of her profession—opera singers should never sound rough—and suggested, too loudly, that they return to his suite.

"Magda, darling, you do realize, I hope, that this—" Irene Adler, celebrated contralto, stopped mid-sentence as she approached, looked each of them over in turn, and raised a single arched eyebrow before continuing. "—this *dalliance* will never amount to anything. I could see the horror writ on your companion's face from across the room. As he stands a good two heads above you, perhaps you were not in a position to notice."

Magda had spun around to face the newcomer. "Miss Adler, forgive me, I—"

"No need to apologize to me, darling. Run along and drink some hot lemon when you get home. Your voice sounds as if it were in shreds."

Tears filled the younger woman's bright eyes, but she managed to hold them in check as she turned and looked up at the crown prince. "Wilhelm, I am most—"

"No, no, that won't do at all," Miss Adler said, the rich musicality of her voice giving every phrase she spoke the sound of an aria. "Go, Magda, before you make a spectacle of yourself. Crown princes do not permanently ally themselves with girls from the opera chorus, and whatever the two of you shared is clearly over."

The prince shifted his weight awkwardly from one foot to the other. "Magda, my dear, I am most sincerely sorry if I—" The young woman did not stay to hear the rest of his apology—the only fortunate choice she had made since meeting him, as Wilhelm had not the slightest idea what he planned to say next. Even if he had, the sight of Irene Adler, whose performance as Rosina in *The Barber of Seville* had dazzled him earlier in the evening, would have robbed him of his words. Her superb figure, shown off to great effect by a violently fashionable gown cut from emerald green silk, would mesmerize any man, but it was her eyes, identical in color to her dress, that he found irresistible.

"I shan't apologize now she is gone," she said. "I may have been rude, but the situation called for it. Subtlety is lost on Magda."

"I am most heartily grateful," the prince said. "I ought to have handled the situation more deftly."

"Quite right," she said. "Are you generally so hopeless with the ladies?"

"I did not realize while watching you onstage that you are American."

"You did not answer my question."

"I never expected to be rescued by Rosina," he said. "I should have thought she would be the one to require rescuing."

"No. I shall never require rescuing."

"A fact that, if true, makes you all the more astonishing."

"I should like very much to be able to return the compliment, but so far you have revealed yourself to be nothing more than a typical prince, easily seduced by a pretty face—eyes, to be specific—and helpless to take care of himself."

"I am not used to being insulted to my face." He was not smiling, but amusement danced in his eyes.

"Surely you would prefer it to knowing it's done behind your back?"

"Eyes are my weakness, yes," he said. "How did you know?"

"Even when you were trying to rid yourself of Magda you could not stop gazing into hers, and now you are doing the same to me."

"We have not been properly introduced," he said. "I know you, of course, the divine prima donna whose talent is in demand at every opera house in Europe. I am Wilhelm Gottsreich Sigismond von Ormstein, hereditary Crown Prince of Bohemia."

"I have never cared for the name Wilhelm and shall call you Sigi instead. Siegmund is one of my favorite characters in Wagner's *Ring*, and the name derives from Sigismond, does it not?"

"I would not dare contradict you."

"Wagner's greatest hero, Siegfried, is the son of Siegmund, conceived after a single night of grand passion."

"Are you suggesting my own greatness will come through a son, not myself?"

She shrugged. "One can never predict what might come from a grand passion. Although I do sing Erda in *The Ring*, a goddess of infinite wisdom who has the ability to see the future . . ."

The prince stepped closer to her. "Then I ought to take any predictions you make rather seriously, as you perfectly embody every role you play."

"Flattery does not impress me."

"What about grand passion?"

"You believe it can strike so quickly?" she asked.

It could, and it had.

If she were Erda, wise and imperious, he was Hercules, strong and strapping. They made a handsome couple, her beauty and his height both seeming to have come from heaven rather than earth. They twirled through waltzes in ballrooms and stayed in cafés well past midnight arguing about politics. He missed none of her performances at the opera and hired the best photographer in Warsaw to make a cabinet picture of them. He called her Rosina until she reminded him of the sour turn taken in Rosina's marriage to the count in *The Marriage of Figaro*, but she never refused his requests that she sing for him, back in his suite at the hotel. He soon found it impossible to imagine life without Irene. She adored him as no one else ever had, loving the man, not the prince. Nothing mattered more to him than possessing this woman who was a vision of strength and loveliness.

Only a sternly worded telegram from his father reminded him of his true purpose in Warsaw: to persuade a Prussian princess to turn over to him a series of embarrassing love letters written by the Bohemian king during, as his father explained, a lapse in moral judgment. The queen, Wilhelm's mother, generally took this sort of thing in stride. What royal marriage did not benefit from the occasional lover? Unfortunately, however, this particular princess happened to be the queen's bête noir, the daughter of the greatest rival of her youth, and the king, upon learning this, had no desire to further risk his tranquil domesticity. Wilhelm, who was close in age to the princess and had always got along well with her, could readily convince her to see reason—or so the king hoped. However, Princess Anna Elisabeth Victoria proved less pliable than the king had imagined, and on the very night the crown prince had met Irene, Wilhelm had all but given up the task. Ladies, it seemed, were loath to relinquish souvenirs of royal affairs.

"You appear most dejected, Sigi," Irene said, gliding into the sitting room of his suite. The scent of attar of roses followed her, delicate and sweet. She perched on the arm of the settee where he sat.

"I am afraid I have failed my father. He is mercilessly disappointed in me." She pressed him for details, and he held back nothing. The story finished, Irene sighed.

"I should expect better from the King of Bohemia. How foolish of him to stray so indelicately."

"I cannot defend his actions," the prince said, "but I do wish I could protect my mother from being hurt by his carelessness. Yet what more can I do? I begged Anna to see reason. She was unmoved."

"Surely this does not surprise you?" Irene asked. "Cast-aside lovers are not known for their desire to help former paramours."

"Perhaps I was foolish to address the matter so directly."

"Some things, my love, are better dealt with lady to lady. Allow me to assist you."

That afternoon, the Countess Xenia Troitskaya (Irene had always found herself unaccountably fond of the name Xenia) called on Princess Anna Elisabeth Victoria. The two exchanged pleasantries and warmed to each other immediately on discovering a shared adoration of Byron's poetry, but it was the countless troubles stemming from wiry and untamable hair that brought them closest together.

"An absolute nightmare," the countess said. "I know it all too well."

"One would never guess it from looking at you," the princess said. "However did you train your maid? Mine is hopeless."

"Adèle is French and a genius. Are you attending the mayor's ball this evening?"

"I shouldn't dream of missing it."

"I shall send Adèle to you without delay. You won't know yourself—or your hair."

⬦

"But how could you possibly know she would agree?" the crown prince asked later, when he met Irene at her rooms.

"My dear man, you do not understand ladies in the slightest," she said, gently removing the Countess Xenia's enormous wig from her head. "The moment I saw her I identified her hair as her weakness. The texture is difficult, as evidenced from the countless wayward bits sticking up from her scalp in every direction. The number of pins and combs employed told me she does all she can to tame it. Her manner of dress, so self-consciously fashionable, and the preponderance of jewels draped over her so early in the afternoon suggest both vanity and bad judgment. I knew she would not resist my offer of assistance."

"Do put the wig back on," Wilhelm said. "It rather suits you and I am most fond of Russians, Countess."

Irene returned his kisses but then pushed him away. "There is no time for that now."

Wilhelm watched as she disappeared into her dressing room, returning half an hour later utterly transformed. Something had dulled her rosy complexion, and dark smudges marred the smooth skin under her eyes, making her look tired and drawn. Her chestnut hair, pulled back into a severe and unflattering bun, did not shine. She wore an ill-fitting black gown with a stiffly starched apron tied over it and held in her hand a maid's cap.

"You are to be the maid?" Wilhelm asked, startled, somewhere between shocked and bemused.

"Sigi, please do not say things that will put me off you," Irene said. "I thought you to be in possession of more intelligence than that. The details of our scheme should have been evident to you hours ago."

"I assumed you were going to send your actual maid to her."

"And take the risk that she couldn't locate the letters? Unthinkable. Be a good man, now, and give your Adèle a kiss. She is fast becoming one of my favorite roles. I shall see you later this evening at the ball."

"Will I recognize you?" he asked.

Irene laughed. "That remains to be seen."

⌘

The spectacular glory of Princess Anna Elisabeth Victoria's coiffure would escape no one's notice that night. Irene had employed every skill her years in the theater had taught her, but even so had doubted—more than once—that she could succeed. Yet she had. The smooth mass of braids and curls, woven with flowers and more than a few diamonds, shimmered.

"No crown could be more beautiful, madame," Irene said, her voice, now with a heavy French accent, altered beyond recognition. "My own mistress would—how you say?—desire to change places with you. Is there someone whose attention you seek tonight? He will not be able to resist you. *C'est impossible.*"

"Alas, no, Adèle," the princess said. "My husband is rarely impressed with my appearance. I do not think he sees me at all."

"A lady of your station need not limit her options, *non*? Balls are made for dancing, and I have no doubt your card will be full."

The princess sighed. "Perhaps, but I shall never enjoy dancing as I used to. There is no romance in it for me anymore."

"Then, madame, you must take your memories of romance with you this evening, and think of them while you are on the dance floor. Sometimes recollection is more satisfying than reality. Do whatever you must to bring your feelings back to the fore tonight."

"You are very wise, Adèle," the princess said.

The maid took a step back and examined her work. "Your hair is perfection, madame. If I may, the slightest hint of color . . ." She pulled a small container from her bag, opened it, touched her fingers inside, and daubed the princess's cheeks. "*Oui.* You are ready, and it is still early. What is your favorite place to sit in this house? I shall bring you a glass of champagne there. It is what the countess always has before a ball. She says it fills her with starlight."

When Irene returned to her a quarter of an hour later, in an ornately furnished sitting room, the princess had in her lap a pile of letters wrapped in red ribbon. One she held in her hand; tears glistened in her eyes as she read it.

"I am confident, madame, you will have a most excellent evening," Irene said, handing her the champagne. "Drink up. Your carriage waits."

"I am indebted to you, Adèle, for your services. You may leave me now, but please do thank your mistress for sending you to me. You are a true gem."

Irene gave a little bow and retreated from the room, into the narrow servants' corridor behind a hidden door in the wall. She stood quietly, listening, until she heard a man calling for his wife, and the princess, after a certain amount of shuffling about, leaving the room. After a pause, Irene cracked open the servants' door, and confirming the chamber to be empty, she slipped inside. A quick, well-organized search soon revealed her quarry: the princess had hidden the letters in a small compartment behind a drawer in her writing desk. She started momentarily when the door to the room flung open, but without the slightest hesitation spun around to face the newcomer.

"*Mon dieu,*" she said to the butler. "I had hoped you were your mistress, returning for her forgotten cloak." Adèle held up the satin garment. "I do hope she has not already departed. Will you bring it to her?"

"I must say, Irene, much as I adored the countess—who would not?—and charming though I found Adèle, I prefer you to them both." Wilhelm had called on her before breakfast, as she had instructed. "Dare I hope your mission proved a success?"

"Shame on you if you thought otherwise," she said. "I will not tolerate you doubting me." She handed the stack of letters to him.

"I cannot begin to express my gratitude," he said. "You have saved me from my father's ire."

"There is nothing I would not do for you, Sigi. You have become quite dear to me."

"We must celebrate your triumph."

"It is not yet a triumph," Irene said. "We must wait for her to inform you the letters are missing. She will come to you, feeling guilty at having kept them from you and will warn you that they have fallen into unknown hands. She loved your father and will not want to see him hurt."

A few hours later, in front of his hotel, Wilhelm met the princess, pale with fright, her hair a mess.

"My dear man," she cried. "I am wronged—my letters are gone, and your father's reputation, as well as my own, is now at risk. I have made a most grievous error in judgment and can only beg your forgiveness."

"Have you any idea who might have taken them?" he asked, frowning as Irene had directed him.

"The Countess Xenia Troitskaya sent her maid to me yesterday and I fear now it was a ruse to steal my letters."

"Countess Xenia Troitskaya?" the prince asked. "I am well acquainted with all the Russian aristocrats in Warsaw and had never heard the name before yesterday."

"I did not doubt her for an instant," she said. "I have been such a fool."

"Yes, you have," Wilhelm said, "for it is I who invented the countess with the express purpose of getting the letters back. When you refused to give them to me, I was forced to adopt other methods."

"For hours I have have been consumed with panic, searching for them! How could you let me think some miscreant had taken them?" she asked. "You, sir, are not a gentleman."

"I am gentleman enough to destroy them rather than let either of you be exposed. You should thank me for the kindness, now that you find yourself in the same precarious situation as my father, the king."

"Good morning, Princess Anna Elisabeth Victoria." A wisp of a boy in an ulster bobbed a bow as he passed them in front of the hotel.

"Who is that boy?" the princess asked. "His voice is familiar to me."

"No one of consequence, I am sure," Wilhelm said. "I am afraid I have not time to stand here and comfort you over your loss. Good day, Princess."

"You were the boy?" Wilhelm was standing in front of her in her dressing room, disbelief on his face.

"The evidence is before you, is it not?" Irene said, slipping the ulster from her shoulders. "I could not resist one last disguise."

"I still do not understand why you had me tell her the truth. I would prefer her not to think I had a role in this business."

Irene shrugged. "It would have been cruel to let her spend the rest of her life worrying that the letters might be made public by some unknown thief. She knows you will not compromise your father's reputation, but it was important for her to have experienced the fear of exposure," Irene said. "She was terrified her own husband might learn of the affair. That was the emotion consuming her when she came to you, and it is a feeling she will not soon forget."

"I wish she did not know I was behind the theft."

"She now considers you to be a man with whom one must not trifle."

Wilhelm crossed his arms and frowned. "You frighten me, my dear. It is an emotion I do not often feel. I should not like to find myself on the wrong side of you. I shudder at the thought of what you might do."

"Why ever would you find yourself in such a situation?" She reached for his hand, but he pulled it away and looked down and studied his tall boots. "You know I adore you, Sigi."

"What a queen you would make, Irene. Your wit, your intelligence, your beauty," he said, shaking his head slowly. "Yet it can never be so, can it?"

"Kings can do what they wish."

"Crown princes cannot."

"A crown prince could wait until he became king." Her voice broke, just a bit as she began, for the first time, to doubt him.

"I did love you," he said, his lips in a hard line. "It was a lapse in judgment and must be stopped. Crown princes do not permanently ally themselves with girls from the opera. It simply isn't done."

"I did not ask you to make me your queen." Irene stepped back from him, aghast.

"I cannot risk that someday you might." He turned away from her and started for the door.

"So this is to be our parting?" she asked, blanching. She had not expected the loss of him to cut so close.

"It cannot be any other way. How could I ever trust a woman like you? I have just watched you deceive, with shocking ease, a respectable woman."

"I did it to help you!"

"Someday you might turn on me," he said. "I required your assistance, and you gave it—brilliantly. Now that I know what you are capable of, I must never see you again."

"I did not expect cruelty from you." She spat the words.

"I never thought I would give it, especially to you." He silently contemplated how easily it had come to him; perhaps he ought not to have rejected it as a useful tool. "Yet I do not think anything else capable of so well severing our ties. I will always think fondly of our time together, Irene."

"I shall endeavor to do the same, painful though it will be." She crossed to her dressing table, upon which the cabinet photograph of the two of them stood, and reached for it. He was gone before she could pick it up and hand it to him. Her heart ached as she looked at the image, taken when they had been so very happy. She would have given it to him, if only to save him from the worry his father had felt knowing his letters might be made public at any time. She had misjudged the prince, taken him for a burly sort of good-hearted barbarian rather than a calculating royal concerned only with his narrow bit of the world.

Perhaps it was for the best, her having the picture. Not that she would ever use it against him—it was his character, not hers, that deserved to be thrown into doubt—but this last meeting made her wonder if she might, one day, require the protection it could provide. She would never taunt him with it, never threaten him. But what about him? Would Wilhelm ever lash out against her? If so, it could serve as a weapon of defense.

This, Irene thought, was not the last she would hear from him, this disloyal, ungrateful lout. She would guard the photograph with everything she had. The Crown Prince of Bohemia was not a man to be trusted.

THE SPIRITUALIST

by David Morrell

Again, the nightmare woke him. Again, he couldn't go back to sleep.

As the bells of nearby Westminster Abbey sounded two o'clock, Conan Doyle rose from his bed. Always determined not to waste time, he considered going to the desk in his sitting room to write a few more thousand words, but instead his troubled mood prompted him to dress and go down the stairs. Careful not to wake his housekeeper, he unlocked the door and stepped outside.

A cold mist enveloped shadowy Victoria Street in the heart of metropolitan London. During the day, the rumble and rattle of motor vehicles reverberated off the area's three-story buildings, but at this solitary hour, the only sound was the echo of Conan Doyle's shoes as he reached the pavement and turned to the left, proceeding past dark shops.

Even in the night and the mist, the back of Westminster Abbey dominated, its hulking presence rising over him. He recalled his sense of irony a year earlier when he'd finally found a suitable location for the most important enterprise of his life, noting that it was only a stone's throw from one of England's most revered religious sites. He hadn't spoken with His Grace about their competing views, but he suspected that the archbishop wasn't amused.

A hazy streetlamp revealed the sign above the door: PSYCHIC BOOK SHOP, LIBRARY & MUSEUM. Because a sense of urgency always propelled him, Conan Doyle stretched his long legs to walk the short distance, but of late, those legs—once so strong in rugby, soccer, and cricket—had betrayed him, as had his once-powerful chest, making him pause to catch his breath before he unlocked the door and entered.

A bell rang. During the day, its jangle was welcome, announcing that a rare visitor had arrived, but at night, the bell violated the stillness. Gas lamps would have provided an appropriate moody atmosphere. This was 1926, however. Instead of striking a match and opening a valve, Conan Doyle reached to his left and turned an electrical switch. Two bulbs on each wall provided instant illumination, as did dangling globes in the ceiling. The yellow lights revealed numerous rows of bookshelves, the smell of old and new pages pleasantly filling his nostrils.

He knew their titles without needing to see them: among them, *Letters on Animal Magnetism*, *Footfalls on the Boundary of Another World*, *The Spirit Manifestations*, *Experiments in Thought Transference*, *Phantasms of the Living*, *Minutes of the Society for Psychical Research*, *Survival of Bodily Death*, and—

Brittle rapping startled him. Turning sharply, he saw a constable frowning through a window.

Conan Doyle opened the door.

"Unusual to see you at this late an hour, Sir Arthur." The constable peered into the shop, straining to see its back corners. "Is everything all right?"

"Perfectly. I couldn't sleep, so I decided to come here and catch up on some work." It had been more than four decades since Conan Doyle left Edinburgh, and yet his Scottish burr remained thick.

"You're certain nothing's wrong?" the constable persisted.

"Absolutely. Thank you for your concern."

The constable gave him a troubled nod, seeming baffled about why one of the most revered authors in Great Britain was wasting his time in this strange shop and why he now lived in a small flat just down the street rather than at one of his large country houses.

Only when Conan Doyle closed and locked the door did the constable continue along the misty street, his footsteps receding.

Stillness again enveloped the shop.

Of course, everything was definitely *not* all right, but what troubled Conan Doyle wasn't anything that a constable could correct.

He faced the first display that patrons saw when they entered—not that the shop enjoyed many patrons. Conan Doyle's name was featured prominently above titles that he'd spent much of the past ten years writing but that hardly anyone wanted to read: *The Wanderings of a Spiritualist, The Coming of the Faeries, The Case for Spirit Photography, The New Revelation, The Vital Message,* and *The History of Spiritualism.*

No preposterous fictions here. No supercilious Sherlock Holmes, who solved improbable mysteries about homicidal hounds and trained serpents. No fawning Watson, who was so befuddled that he should never have been allowed to acquire a medical degree. To the contrary, these particular books contained the truth, and yet the world didn't care. Visitors didn't even need to *buy* these books. They could borrow them. It didn't help. Nor did Conan Doyle's exhausting lecture tours throughout the United Kingdom and around the world—to the United States, Canada, France, Germany, South Africa, Australia, and New Zealand. People came to hear him only because they wanted to know why a man whose name was associated with Sherlock Holmes couldn't stop talking about ghosts and faeries.

The floor creaked as Conan Doyle walked toward the rear of the shop. His shoulders were so broad that he needed to shift sideways between rows of bookshelves. He came to murky stairs, their wood protesting as he descended toward the dark basement.

At the bottom, a damp chill greeted him. Emerging from an archway, he turned an electrical switch on a wall. Overhead lights chased the long room's shadows, their glow reflecting off glass cases and framed photographs, creating an otherworldly effect. Some visitors, no matter how skeptical, might have felt uneasy and even fearful about coming down here in the middle of the night, but Conan Doyle felt comforted by the truth before him.

After all, here were photographs of actual ghosts and faeries. Here were the wax gloves of a spirit's hands. Here were a Syrian vase, a Babylonian clay tablet, and a pile of Turkish pennies that had materialized on a séance table. Here were intricate drawings of flowers that someone under the influence of a spirit had impossibly created within seventeen seconds. Here was a brilliant seascape that a woman without any artistic training had painted while under a spirit's influence. Here were pages of automatic writing that mediums had scribbled, responding to questions that loved ones asked and that only the departed could answer correctly.

How can anyone see these proofs, and not be convinced that the dead are capable of communicating with us? Conan Doyle wondered in despair. *I need to try harder, to write more books about the afterlife, to travel to more cities and countries and give more lectures.*

Seeking reassurance, he turned toward a photograph of three faeries next to a waterfall. He was reminded of a painting that his father had—

A creak of footsteps on the stairs surprised him. Had the constable returned to make certain that nothing was amiss? But how would that be possible? The front door was locked. Had someone broken into the shop? To what purpose? If hardly anyone bought or even borrowed the shop's books, why would somebody go to the effort of stealing them as opposed to burglarizing the valuable contents of the garment shop next door?

"Who's there?" he called.

The creak on the wooden stairs became louder as the footsteps neared the bottom.

"Mary, is that you?"

Conan Doyle's daughter—from his first marriage—managed the shop. Perhaps she'd come here in the middle of the night to attend to a pressing detail she'd suddenly remembered.

But in that case, wouldn't she have called out as he himself had, demanding to know who was in the shop?

Conan Doyle stepped backward when a shadow appeared at the bottom of the stairs. The shadow didn't belong to Mary but instead to a tall, thin man emerging from the murky archway.

The man wore an Inverness cape, the grey color of which matched the figure's intense eyes. He was perhaps thirty-five, with an ascetic face, a narrow chin, a slender nose, high cheekbones, and an intelligent forehead that was partially covered by a deerstalker hat.

The basement became damper and colder.

"My dear fellow, you're as pale as if you've seen a ghost," Sherlock Holmes said.

Conan Doyle felt a tight pain in his chest. "If you were indeed a ghost, I'd rejoice."

Holmes surveyed the photographs of faeries, the wax gloves of a spirit, and the pages of automatic writing. "Then look joyous. You murdered me, and yet here I am: proof of what you're looking for."

"Proof?"

"Of life after death."

"I'm still asleep. I never woke from my nightmare. Those fools who send me letters asking for your autograph might think you're real, but—"

"Then how can I be standing here, talking to you? Why are you responding to me?"

"I didn't murder you."

"Perhaps you prefer a more delicate word such as 'killed.'"

"You never died. When you and Moriarty grappled on the ledge, it was only he who plummeted into the Reichenbach Falls."

"But you didn't believe that at the time," Holmes corrected him. "When you wrote 'The Final Problem,' you truly intended to get rid of me. You even bragged to your mother that you'd seen the last of me, even though your mother begged you not to do it."

"You'd become a burden," Conan Doyle protested. "Readers wouldn't let me write about anyone else."

"Ha. You earned a fortune from writing stories about me, and that's a burden? Tell that to my Baker Street Irregulars when those little beggars are desperate for their next meal. Then eight years later, when you needed more money, you suddenly decided I wasn't a burden after all. So you wrote another novel about me, but even then I remained dead, because you had my hound adventure occur years before you killed me. Then a magazine offered you even *more* money to write a story that showed I hadn't actually died at the Reichenbach Falls, so you invented that nonsense about Moriarty falling alone while I escaped to Tibet. Tibet? Is that the best you could think of? Obviously you lacked conviction. You can't fool readers, though. They sensed that something was amiss, that it wasn't really I in those later stories, only someone to whom you gave my name. Certainly I'm not an aged beekeeper. As you can see, I'm still in my thirties. Ghosts don't age."

"Take off that blasted deerstalker hat."

"Readers prefer it."

"I didn't include it in any of my stories about you."

"But Sidney Paget had the inspiration to put it in one of his illustrations of me. Now readers imagine it when they read about me. It's as real as if you'd written it. But if it troubles you . . ."

Holmes removed the deerstalker hat. Now that his forehead was fully exposed, it seemed even more intelligent, his receding hairline emphasizing the height of his brow.

He set the hat on a counter next to a photograph of wispy light in a dark room.

"Ectoplasm?" Holmes asked, referring to a placard in front of the photograph.

"The strongest evidence so far."

"There are various types of evidence. I see that you walked in Hyde Park today, that you're unusually troubled, and that you have limited domestic help," Holmes said.

"Yes, yes. I'm not impressed by your parlor tricks. Remember, I invented them. There are spots of mud on my shoes and my trouser cuffs. The mud has a reddish color that's typical of sections of Hyde Park. The mud would have been removed if I had sufficient domestic help, but at the moment, I have only the assistance of a single housekeeper: Mrs. Hudson."

"Mrs. Hudson is *my* housekeeper," Holmes reminded him.

"A slip of the tongue. Mrs. *Murray*. My housekeeper is named Mrs. Murray."

"Of course. Soon you'll have as addled a memory as you gave to dear old Watson. He can't keep dates or names consistent from one story to the next. He can't even keep straight how many wives he had. Two? Five? I confess that even with my superior powers of deduction, I'm unable to determine the exact number, although it's probably two because you yourself had two. And with regard to my 'parlor tricks,' as you call them, you didn't invent them. You learned them from Dr. Bell at the University of Edinburgh medical school. By the way, you didn't ask me how I knew that you were unusually troubled."

"Obviously because I'm here in the middle of the night."

"I'd have known you were troubled even if we were speaking on Victoria Street at noon. You have a mark on your lower lip, where you've been chewing it."

Conan Doyle raised a hand to his lip, suddenly aware of how tender it felt. "Please leave me alone. Go away and solve a mystery."

"Solving a mystery is precisely what I'm doing."

"I don't understand."

"You, my dear fellow," Holmes said. "*You're* the mystery. This business about ghosts and faeries. People worry that you're delusional."

Conan Doyle stepped forward, clenching his fists. "Never say that to me."

"My apologies. Kindly relax your hands. Although you were once a pugilist, that was many years ago, and if you couldn't walk the short distance to this shop without feeling out of breath, I doubt that an altercation between us would have a successful conclusion for you, especially because I'm an expert in boxing, baritsu, and singlestick fighting. To change the subject, do you recall that Watson climbed the steps at 221B Baker Street many times before I asked him how many steps there were? He couldn't answer the question. Together, he and I climbed the steps while we counted to seventeen. I told Watson, 'You see, but you do not observe.' That's an interesting comment, given that your specialty as a physician involves diseases of the eyes."

"I fail to see the relevance."

Holmes pointed toward the photograph of the faeries at the waterfall. "That photograph was produced by combining two images in what is called a double exposure."

"Prove it," Conan Doyle demanded.

"I cannot unless I have the original two images so that I can demonstrate how the illusion was created."

"Then you don't know for certain. The photograph of ectoplasm that you ridiculed—"

"I did no such thing. I merely implied doubt. Were you at the séance where the ectoplasm appeared?"

"I was."

"Did you see the ectoplasm?"

"I did not. But the medium did and told my photographer to press the shutter on his camera."

"After the plate was removed from the camera and developed, this image appeared?" Holmes asked, pointing.

"Yes."

"Your friend Houdini would perhaps—"

"Mr. Houdini is no longer a friend. He insulted my wife."

"—would perhaps suggest that the medium had prepared a photographic plate beforehand and substituted it for the plate that was in the camera."

"But *our* plate was marked," Conan Doyle emphasized.

"Perhaps an assistant to the medium had the opportunity to examine the photographic plate prior to the séance and apply an identical mark on the plate that was eventually substituted."

"'Perhaps' is not proof."

"Indeed." Holmes reached into a pocket and removed a large, curved pipe.

"I didn't give you a calabash pipe, either," Conan Doyle said disapprovingly.

"But the great actor, William Gillette, used it as a prop when he portrayed me on stage. It looks more dramatic than an ordinary straight pipe. Illustrators took to including it in their depictions of me. Now people imagine it whenever they think of me. It's as real as the deerstalker hat."

Holmes tamped shag tobacco into the bowl of the calabash.

"Do you absolutely need to? There's no ventilation down here," Conan Doyle objected.

"The smoke will cover the odor of the mildew." Holmes prepared to strike a match.

"Stop. These exhibits are delicate. The smoke will damage them."

Holmes sighed. "Very well. But I suspect that the spirits wouldn't mind the aroma. They're probably desperate for a puff now and then."

"That isn't humorous."

"No humor intended. Convince me, my dear fellow. Why did you suddenly believe that there are spirits in an afterlife—spirits who can communicate with us?"

"I don't expect that a man who's obsessed with the surface of things will understand, but my belief wasn't sudden at all. When I set up my medical practice in Southsea, near Portsmouth—"

"Southsea. Aptly named. Almost as far from Edinburgh as it's possible to go and still remain in Great Britain," Holmes noted.

"And your point is?"

"Just an observation. Please continue." Holmes gestured with the unlit pipe. "When you set up your medical practice in Southsea . . ."

"I had a friend there: Henry Ball. Southsea was a bohemian community that enjoyed discussing new ideas. Mediums and séances were a popular topic. Henry and I participated in several attempts to contact the other world—table rapping, automatic writing, and so forth. We decided that since thought transference was essential to communicating with the dead, we'd conduct an experiment. He and I sat back-to-back, with pencils and notepads in our hands. He'd draw something on his pad and concentrate on it. Then I'd try to imagine what he was thinking and draw it. Neither of us had any artist's skill. What we drew were stick figures and geometric shapes. Amazingly I often reproduced what was on Henry's pad, and Henry did the same with regard to shapes that *I* had drawn."

"Fascinating," Holmes said. "In what year did you conduct these experiments?"

"Eighteen eighty-six."

"When you started to write your first novel about me: *A Study in Scarlet.*"

"As a matter of fact, now that I think of it, yes."

"A creative period for you. And what was your marital status at the time?"

"I married my first wife the year before, in eighteen eighty-five." Memories of Louise, of that long-ago innocent time—his fond nickname for her had been Touie—made him pause. He shook his head. "Where are you going with this?"

"I'm merely looking for context." Holmes shrugged and sat in a chair next to a photograph of a ghost's head floating above a man in a doorway. "Kindly continue."

"Because of the successful experiments that Henry and I conducted, we were motivated to go to more séances. What made the difference for me was an evening when a medium spoke in several voices and then wrote frantically on a notepad, referring to me as a healer. But I hadn't been introduced as a physician, so the medium couldn't have known that. Then the medium astonished me by writing a note in which the spirit told me not to read Leigh Hunt's book."

"Why was that astonishing?" Holmes eased back in the chair, crossing his long legs.

"I had a book by Leigh Hunt next to my bed! I was just about to start reading it. How could the medium have possibly known this?"

"Perhaps . . ."

"Perhaps what? Say what you're thinking."

"When you arrived for the séance, did the medium's assistant ask you and your friend to wait in an anteroom?"

"That's the customary procedure."

"Perhaps the medium stood on the other side of a wall and listened to your conversation, learning personal details, repeating them later, claiming to receive this information from a spirit. Did you have any religious convictions that prepared you for your belief in a spirit world?"

"Not at all. I was raised as a Roman Catholic. When I was nine, I was sent to a Jesuit preparatory school and then a Jesuit college. All told, I spent eight years in those schools, but the only afterlife I hoped for was one in which the priests would stop beating me. No, nothing prepared me for my interest in the spirits."

"Nine is an early age for your parents to have sent you away."

"My family life was . . ."

"Yes?"

"It isn't relevant," Conan Doyle said. "My belief in the attempts of spirits to reach us was reinforced in eighteen ninety. I remember vividly that the month was November. I read an item in the *British Medical Journal* about a conference that was about to convene in Berlin. The subject of the conference was new ways to treat tuberculosis."

Holmes gestured, encouraging him to proceed.

"I can't explain the urgency that suddenly compelled me," Conan Doyle said. "All at once, I knew that it was essential for me to go to that conference. I packed a bag and immediately departed for Germany."

"Leaving your wife and your almost two-year-old daughter," Holmes noted.

"That's why my urgency is so difficult to explain," Conan Doyle emphasized. "I had every reason to remain with my family. Earlier that year, I'd studied ophthalmology in Vienna. Then I'd moved my family to London, and suddenly I felt a desperate need to travel yet again, to go to Germany and attend a conference about a disease that wasn't even related to my specialty. My abrupt journey didn't make sense. But I soon understood why I'd felt the urgency."

"Now I'm the one who fails to see the relevance," Holmes said.

"Tuberculosis. Three years later, my first wife was diagnosed with the disease. Isn't it obvious? The spirits compelled me to learn what I could about the latest in treatments. They knew I would soon need that vital information when my wife displayed her terrible symptoms."

"But there might be another explanation," Holmes suggested.

"And what would *that* be?" Conan Doyle asked impatiently.

"You're a physician. Perhaps you subconsciously sensed the early indications of your wife's disease."

"There *weren't* any early indications—none whatsoever! My wife thought nothing of joining me on thirty-mile daily bicycle rides. Her lungs were strong. But then, three years later, in eighteen ninety-three, she became ill."

"Eighteen ninety-three," Holmes said. "Didn't your father die that year?"

"It was a difficult time."

"He was in a mental institution near Edinburgh, I believe."

"I prefer not to discuss my father's illness."

"Alcohol addiction," Holmes said. "I gather that on one occasion, when he couldn't obtain gin or wine or beer, he drank furniture varnish. He sold his clothing in order to buy alcohol. The bed linen. His sketches. Children's toys. Anything. Please, remind me of what your father sketched."

Conan Doyle stood straighter. "I told you I prefer not to discuss my father's illness."

"Were you able to journey to Edinburgh and attend his funeral?"

"Unfortunately, my wife's tuberculosis prevented me."

"And while all this was happening in eighteen ninety-three," Holmes said, "you killed me."

"I didn't kill you! Only Moriarty plunged into the falls! How many times must I explain it?"

"As far as you were concerned, I was dead. Whoever that imposter is in the later stories, it isn't me. But let's move on. It wasn't until fifteen years later, in nineteen eighteen, that you published *The New Revelation* and your readers finally learned about your belief in spiritualism. They were surprised that you'd shifted from an interest in science to mysticism."

"There's nothing mystical about it," Conan Doyle protested. "Twenty years ago, people would have mocked me if I'd said that voices could travel great distances through the air, and yet Marconi's radio accomplished what until recently would have been thought a supernatural occurrence. Science will eventually prove that an afterworld exists just as certainly as *this* world exists."

"Your first spiritualist book coincided with the end of the war."

"Yes, the blasted war." Conan Doyle looked down at the stone floor. "I imagined that the conflict would be noble, that a cleaner, better, stronger nation would come out of it. How wrong I was." His voice faltered. "How far the war was from anything that was noble. So many died, and so brutally. I wasn't prepared."

"One of the dead was your son, Kingsley. Please accept my sympathy," Holmes said.

"He was the second child that Touie and I had," Conan Doyle managed to say. "By then, my relationship with Kingsley wasn't the best. He went to war to defend our nation, of course, but I suspect that he also took risks to prove himself to me. He was wounded at the battle of the Somme. He seemed to be recovering, but then the Spanish Influenza took him down. And my brother, Innis, died in the war. And my brother-in-law, Malcolm. And another brother-in-law . . ." He didn't have the strength to say the name. "And two nephews. And . . . So many of them gone. Surely it couldn't be forever. Surely their souls hadn't merely ceased to exist. At séances, my son contacted me, assuring me that he was contented and that he'd met my brother over there and . . ."

Again, Conan Doyle's voice dropped.

"Perhaps that's when your true conversion to spiritualism occurred, not many years earlier," Holmes suggested. "Could your intense grief have made you want to believe desperately that your son and your brother and all the others weren't truly dead?"

"It was more than my emotions playing tricks on me." Conan Doyle pointed angrily. "Do you see those wax gloves of a spirit's hands?"

"Indeed."

"Prior to a séance, an associate and I prepared a container of heated wax. A dim red light allowed us to see the medium lapse into a trance. Suddenly a spirit's hands plunged into the heated wax. As suddenly, when the hands emerged, they disappeared, leaving these wax gloves on the table. Look at the cuffs on the gloves. They're the size of a man's wrists. If the hands were those of an ordinary person, the gloves couldn't have been removed without being damaged. The only way these gloves could have survived in the perfect way that you see them is if the hands became disembodied."

"Master illusionist that he is, Houdini would perhaps—"

"Don't mention his name."

"—suggest the following: The hands that plunged into the heated wax were those of the medium's assistant. The assistant withdrew his wax-covered hands into the darkness beyond the pale red light, leaving wax gloves that had been prepared in advance."

"You sound exactly like Houdini. But I anticipated his usual smug objection. The gloves couldn't have been prepared in advance. I put an identifying chemical into the wax, and the wax of these gloves contains the same chemical."

"When did you obtain the chemical?"

"The day before the séance."

"If *I* had been the medium's assistant, I'd have observed your activities for a few days before the séance. When you went to the shop to buy the chemical, I'd have followed. When you left the shop, I'd have entered the shop and found a pretense to persuade the shopkeeper to tell me what you'd purchased."

Conan Doyle stared at him. "But you don't know for certain that such a thing happened."

"That is correct."

"Then you haven't disproved the validity of these wax gloves, any more than you disproved the validity of these photographs."

"Granted. Earlier, you said that Houdini insulted your wife."

"My second wife, Jean, is herself a medium. She receives messages from an Oriental spirit named Pheneas. These visitations began five years ago. With her deep honesty, Jean at first resisted the impulses, wondering if perhaps she subconsciously self-willed them. But eventually, through her inspired automatic writing and through a process in which she lapsed into a trance, Jean and I became convinced that the visitations were authentic. Through Pheneas, we received messages from my mother and my brother and our son and all our other dear departed loved ones."

"I gather that Houdini is skeptical about your wife's ability," Holmes said.

"If the wretch had expressed his doubts to me personally, I would have perhaps made allowances! But instead he did it publicly, telling American newspapers—the newspapers, mind you—that my wife's . . . that she's . . . a *fake*! Equally unforgivable, he accused *me* of thinking I was a Messiah come to save mankind through the mysteries of spiritualism. He claimed that I misled the public with teachings that are, to use his words, 'a menace to sanity and health.' I never spoke to him again."

"Understandably," Holmes said.

"Pheneas has been immensely helpful. He warned me that if Jean and I went on a proposed trip to Scandinavia last year, the consequences would have been dire, perhaps a horrible accident. But through Jean, Pheneas approved of a resort in Switzerland for the same vacation. Pheneas also approved of the new country house that I bought for Jean to stay in while I'm here in London, doing what I can to attract people to this shop."

"You mentioned that your mother, brother, son, and other dear departed loved ones visited you through Pheneas. Did that include your first wife?"

"No."

"Doesn't that seem strange?"

"Touie didn't approve of my interest in spiritualism."

"But now your first wife would know that you're right. She ought to be happy to tell you so. What about your father? Was *he* one of the loved ones who visited you from the afterlife?"

"No."

"Doesn't *that* strike you as odd? At one time, didn't your father say that he received messages from the unseen world?"

Conan Doyle didn't reply.

"The sketches that your father drew. What was their subject?" Holmes asked.

"What are you up to?"

"I'm merely attempting to solve a mystery. What was the subject of your father's sketches?"

They regarded each other, neither of them speaking for at least a minute.

"Faeries," Conan Doyle finally said.

"Faeries and phantoms. One of your father's drawings is a self-portrait in which demons swirl around him."

"Alcohol made my father insane. He sketched what his poisoned mind caused him to see."

"Or perhaps . . ."

"Every time you say 'perhaps' . . ."

"Perhaps your father actually did see faeries, demons, and phantoms, so horrifying that he used alcohol to try to stop the visions. Perhaps alcohol didn't cause the visions. It might have been the other way around. Could your father's visions have caused his need for alcohol?"

"But that would mean . . ." Abrupt understanding made Conan Doyle stop.

"I'm only considering every possibility," Holmes explained.

"I want you to leave."

"We haven't finished our conversation."

"Leave. Now. If you don't respect my wishes, we might indeed have the physical altercation that almost happened earlier."

Holmes considered him and nodded. "Very well. The mystery might be better solved by you instead of me. But the clues are all before you."

Holmes stood, put on the deerstalker cap, and walked toward the archway.

"Good night, Sir Arthur."

He climbed the stairs, his tall, thin figure disappearing, the creak of his footsteps becoming fainter.

Silence settled over the museum.

Conan Doyle stared toward the shadowy stairs for a long time. At last he turned toward the photograph of the three faeries next to a waterfall. When he'd last looked at it, he'd been reminded of a sketch that his father had drawn in which faeries lay among blades of grass in a field.

Somehow that recollection had made him imagine a visit from Sherlock Holmes. The intense chill Conan Doyle felt told him that he was in fact here in this basement and not in his bed still enduring a nightmare.

The power of imagination never failed to astonish him: wide-awake trances possessing him, prompting him to envision a lost world of dinosaurs, the White Company of the Hundred Years' War, and . . .

Sherlock Holmes.

"The clues are all before you," Holmes had told him.

Or rather, something in my mind made me imagine that he told me, Conan Doyle thought.

Although he would never have admitted it, his characters often spoke to him. It didn't seem strange to him, but he knew what others would think if he admitted he heard voices. His father had heard voices. "Voices from the unseen world," his father had told people.

And look where his father had ended.

"Perhaps your father actually did see faeries and demons," Holmes had suggested. "Could your father's visions have caused his need for alcohol?"

"But that would mean . . ." Conan Doyle hadn't dared to finish his thought.

What would *it mean?* he asked himself. *That my father was insane? Did my father consume massive quantities of alcohol to drown the faeries and demons he saw?*

Conan Doyle leaned close to the photograph of the faeries. Holmes had said that the photograph consisted of two images combined in a double exposure. It wasn't the first time Conan Doyle had heard that criticism. Skeptics were quick to offer objections that they couldn't prove.

"You see, but you do not observe," Holmes had said.

Conan Doyle leaned even closer toward the photograph. Was there possibly a blur around the fairies? Did they resemble children made to look extremely small?

But if that photograph was fraudulent, then he would need to consider that the photograph of the ghost hovering above the man in the doorway was fraudulent also, and then he would need to consider that the Syrian vase, the Babylonian clay tablet, and the pile of Turkish pennies that had dropped onto a séance table were fraudulent—and the pages of automatic writing, and the ornate drawing of flowers that a medium had somehow completed in seventeen seconds. Certainly Holmes had implied that the wax gloves of a spirit and the photograph of ectoplasm weren't authentic.

But Holmes hadn't been here to imply anything, Conan Doyle forcefully reminded himself. No one had actually been in this basement, sitting in that chair. To believe differently would truly be a sign of madness.

And yet . . .

Why did Holmes emphasize that Southsea, near Portsmouth, is almost as far from Edinburgh as it's possible to go and still remain in Great Britain? Was he suggesting that I felt compelled to put as much distance between my father and myself as I could?

Why did Holmes seem to think it significant that I didn't go to my father's funeral? My father died the same year I killed Holmes. Was he implying that by killing Holmes I was somehow finally ridding myself of my father and my fear that I shared his . . . ?

Stop thinking this way, Conan Doyle warned himself.

But he couldn't stop the voice inside his head.

Did Holmes nod with suspicion when I described all the traveling I did after I was married the first time? Did he seem to think that I suddenly traveled to Germany not because of the tuberculosis conference, but because I wanted to get away from my wife and two-year-old child?

Did he seem to nod with greater suspicion when I described how my second wife was a medium who received messages from the spirit Pheneas about where we should take vacations and whether I should buy another country house for her?

Conan Doyle picked up the framed photograph of the faeries by the waterfall. He made his way to the chair that Holmes had occupied. It troubled him that the cushion felt warm, as though someone had sat in it recently.

He studied the faeries, so innocent, so free of cares.

Did Holmes intend him to conclude that Jean wasn't a medium at all? That she'd taken advantage of his beliefs in order to guide his actions?

Madness, Conan Doyle told himself. *Stop thinking this way. If I believed that Jean was fraudulent, then I'd need to believe that everything in this room was fraudulent, that my* life *was fraudulent.*

He clutched the photograph of the faeries and stared as hard at it as he'd ever stared at anything in his life. He desperately tried to will himself to enter the photograph, to stand with the faeries next to the waterfall whose chill resembled that of this basement. He had a sudden vision that the basement was a crypt and that Holmes was in it, tearing coffins apart, hurling bones into a corner. Bones. Perhaps that's all his dead son and his first wife and his brother and his brother-in-law and his nephews and his mother . . . and his father . . . had become. No. He couldn't believe it.

That would be the true madness.

MRS. HUDSON INVESTIGATES

by Tony Lee and Bevis Musson

Panel 1:

REALLY, MRS HUDSON. I'VE TOLD YOU BEFORE, YOU SIMPLY *CANNOT* REPLACE SHERLOCK HOLMES.

HE'S GONE. WE NEED TO MOVE ON. LET THE POLICE TAKE OVER.

BUT LONDON CAN'T RELY ON THE POLICE, DOCTOR WATSON. THEY NEED A *DETECTIVE*.

AND *GREGSON, LESTRADE,* EVEN *HOPKINS* ARE ONLY ONE STEP ABOVE *YOU*!

Panel 2:

AND WHAT'S *THAT* SUPPOSED TO MEAN?

COME ON - YOU THINK I DIDN'T SEE ALL THOSE '*JOHN WATSON, CRIME DOCTOR*' CARDS? DO YOU *REALLY* BELIEVE YOU CAN REPLACE HIM?

I READ YOUR *STRAND* STORIES, JOHN - AND I WAS THERE FOR THE CASES THEY'RE *LOOSELY* BASED ON.

Panel 3:

AND BEFORE YOU START WAFFLING ON ABOUT THE *ADDRESS,* AND HOW YOU LIVE HERE -

- REMEMBER IT'S *MY* HOUSE. *MY* RULES. AND IF I WANT TO BECOME THE *SECOND GREATEST* DETECTIVE THE WORLD HAS EVER KNOWN?

I WILL.

Panel 4:

ANYWAY, BE A GOOD MAN AND *SOD OFF* - I HAVE A CASE AND I NEED TO START PREPARING.

YOU HAVE... A *CASE?*

THAT'S RIGHT. AND MY *ASSISTANT* WILL BE ARRIVING AT ANY MOMENT --

Panel 5:

OH, I'VE BEEN HERE FOR A WHILE. I'M JUST ANNOYED I DIDN'T BRING *SNACKS* WHILE I WATCHED THE *CABARET.*

IRENE ADLER? YOU'RE WORKING WITH '*THE WOMAN*'?

WELL, *YOU* NAMED ME THAT, BUT WE ALL KNOW *HE* CALLED ME 'THAT #$@$%*! WOMAN'.

HELLO, JOHN.

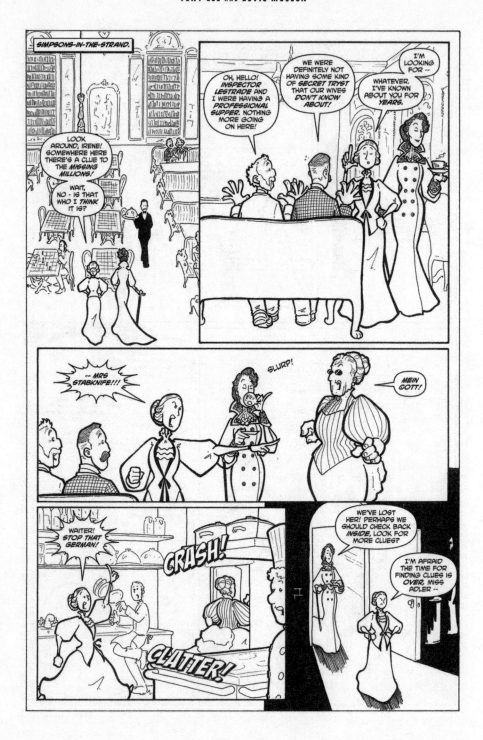

THE ADVENTURE OF
THE DANCING WOMEN

by *Hank Phillippi Ryan*

"It's the end of literacy as we know it," I complained. I leaned back in my swivel chair, plonked my black boots on my desk, and glimpsed the last of the Wednesday sunrise, wisps of pale lavender, still visible behind the coppery foliage of our town's famous beeches. This morning, however, I was lured from our front window and the glorious autumn by the curious email that had pinged onto my computer. I studied it, perplexed. I recognized the sender, but there was no subject line, nor were there words in the message section. The page showed only a colorful jumble of tiny graphic symbols.

"Clearly, the human need for language is threatened, do you not agree? Once we descend into ambiguous shorthand?" I reached for my white mug of oolong, grumbling, not taking my eyes from the screen, then removed my tortoiseshell spectacles, wiped away an annoying speck of dust with my handkerchief, and put the glasses back on. "What, pray tell, does a smiley-face mean? 'I'm only teasing'? Or, 'I'm happy'? Or, 'you win'?"

"You're becoming a curmudgeon at age thirty, girlfriend," Watson warned. She placed her laptop on her desk, flipped the computer open. It trilled into life, and I heard Watson tapping keys as she talked. "By forty you'll be totally ancient."

Watson's not her true name, but it's what we all call her now, for obvious reasons. Though enthusiastic, and learning quickly, Watson is sometimes somewhat cavalier with details. She constantly attempts to engage in conversation and simultaneously work on her computer. I've assured her that cannot be successful, as the human mind is capable of handling only one problem at a time. That problem may be knotty, and require a delicate solution, but step-by-step and total focus, I often have avowed, is the only method with any hope of attaining success.

"Ancient?" I replied. "If by ancient you meant enduring, worthwhile, and eternal, I welcome it, my friend."

I admit I also welcomed Watson's contributions to our still-nascent business. Newly emerged from her criminal justice studies after a black hole of time in Afghanistan (where she helped eliminate the despot she nicknamed the Giant Rat of Kabul), she joined me at Investigative Associates this past summer, thus giving partial veracity to "Associates," since for the previous fifteen months, I had practiced on my own.

Internet-proficient and *semper fi*, Watson's research tends to come from a computer. Mine tends to come from real life. The miracle of the internet has become the grail for local law enforcement, even, cautiously, here in pastoral Norraton. But I use my own brain first. And then books. Not that I don't appreciate the immediacy of a quick Google search. Especially since changes occur so relentlessly these days.

Our little office is the very proof. I rented it seventeen months ago (with a little apartment for me above it) at an agreeably low cost, after its previous incarnation, a tanning salon, went out of business. Prior to that it housed a video rental store, and before that, a twenty-four-hour photo-developing establishment. I hoped our services, the only private detective agency in town, would not so quickly join the ranks of the anachronistic. Two things reassured me. Human nature, for one, and also our fundamental need to understand and solve our problems. A need, it is constantly proved, only intensified by the passage of time.

"You profess to be the expert, Watson," I said, challenging her to translate my email. "What does smiley-face smiley-face heart heart heart puppy-dog mean?"

I swiveled my computer screen so she could see it. But in truth, being more annoyed with emoticons than confused by them, I could not resist offering the answer before Watson could venture her opinion.

"'Thank you for your good work, we are happy you found our missing dog,'" I said, swiveling my screen back into place. "But why not be precise?"

Again, I did not wait for Watson's reply. "Although, I grant you, a smiley-face thank you is preferable to none at all."

"You talk funny," Watson said. "That's why I sometimes don't answer you, just to see what you'll come up with next, you know? All I could think of, back in-country, was to be home again and listen to you talk. It's like being in Masterpiece Theater."

"If we do not protect the precision and clarity of our language," I asked, "who will? Soon we'll be communicating via smiley-faces and little hearts. And won't that be . . . smiley-face?"

The time on Watson's computer dinged seven o'clock, start of our posted office hours. As if on cue, our front door jangled open. I suppose we should employ some more stringent security methods, but our town, Norraton, is small and rural, second-to-last on the 138.1-mile Massachusetts Turnpike that carries commuters and tourists between Boston and New York. Though our town fathers endeavor for economic rebirth, our cases reflect Norraton's placidly suburban milieu—missing relatives or pets, the occasional straying spouse, once a stolen manuscript. Soon after Watson joined me, we'd had a dust-up with a bird-hoarding politician who stashed his pets in the town's decorative lighthouse on the lake at Copper Beach. But that is another story. I—Watson and I— prevailed in all.

I had been away from my hometown for several years, a result of the dearth of employment opportunities for my original profession, fifth-grade geology-geography teacher. But, rock collection in hand, I returned here for the splendor of the Berkshires and their always-surprising terrain. And to pass my P.I. exam.

At first I'd treated my growing interest in detection as a mere hobby. But the search for answers, whether geological or simply logical, never failed to fascinate me. I gave in, changed course, and now cannot think of doing anything else. My father, also a teacher and geologist, had schooled his students and me with his mantra, a maxim of the father of modern geology. Father would hold up a fossil or a newfound specimen of rock and say, "Remember the words of James Hutton: 'The present is key to the past.'"

So in geology, and in the art of detection, my two avocations are similarly grounded. When digging for solutions, one must know where—and how—to look.

"Miss Holmes?" Our visitor stood in the open office doorway, the glare from the morning sunshine creating a momentary silhouette.

He stepped into our office. Raised an eyebrow. "That's your real name?"

And that is why my associate is called Watson. For surely as all Rhodes are Dusty and all Cassidys are Hopalong, if one's name is Holmes, one is inescapably connected with Sherlock. Even though my name is Annabelle.

As for the real Sherlock, Watson reports she has read a few of the classic stories; certainly they are many and beloved. I have not indulged, preferring to create my own adventures. Perhaps I'll write them someday. Or perhaps, in keeping with literary tradition, Watson will.

"May we help you?" Watson replied. With her growing-out military haircut and newly purchased "girl clothes," as she calls them, part of her job is to approach arriving clients and barricade me from the initial contact. That gives me time to assess.

My first assessment: this morning's visitor was dressed like a handsome groom on a wedding cake. Hardly predictable at seven on an October morning. The young man—late twenties, I calculated—held a carryout cup of coffee in a white paper container.

"Annabelle Holmes?" He looked at Watson, then at me, then back at Watson. He appeared to be deciding which of us he sought—the scarecrow in the black jeans, black T-shirt, spectacles, and ponytail, or the short-haired cherub in the flowered skirt.

This bridegroom, or possibly waiter, was clearly flustered: his cheeks were stubbled, dark hair in disarray, bow tie slanted askew. One of the black onyx studs in his shirtfront placket was missing.

"I see you have not rented that evening wear," I said, standing and holding out a welcoming hand. "That you are health conscious. And that you are left-handed." I hid my smile at his wide-eyed response. "I am Annabelle Holmes. How can we be of service, Mr.—Arthur?"

"Health conscious? Left-handed?" The man fairly sputtered in surprise as he shook mine. "And how did you know my name?"

"And I must ask, since you are clearly in . . ." I paused, choosing my word carefully. ". . . distress. Are you missing the bride to your groom?"

"Missing the bride? How did you know?" He blinked at his reflection in the front window. "I see. Yes, I'm Arthur. Arthur Daley. But how did you know *that*?"

I glanced at Watson, who, as always, looked at me for answers. She still has not learned how I analyze small details and how they combine to create larger answers. Sometimes it is not difficult.

"Your name has been written on your coffee cup, sir," I said. "And marked with your health-conscious choice for skim milk."

Watson rolled her eyes. "You kill me," she muttered.

"Your watch is on your right arm, as left-handers prefer," I went on. "As for the attire, your initials are embroidered on your right cuff, meaning that jacket was tailored for you. Now, will you take a seat? Please tell us the reason for your visit."

"Thank you." Mr. Daley sat in the one empty chair in our office, a ladder-backed swivel inherited from the now-shuttered copper mining museum at the end of Lodestar Street. Our local copper industry faded in the late 19th century, but its lore and lure have branded our little town since then. Our sturdy office bookshelves, the pockmarked wood now filled with my favorite textbooks and research materials, were once used in the museum library.

"My partner," Mr. Daley began, "has received a, well, I'm not sure what word I would use. Unusual? Disturbing? Confusing? Series of emails. It might be spam, I suppose, except I think my partner was clearly upset by it."

"Partner?" I imagined many possible clarifications for this imprecise word choice. "Personal? Professional? Or both?"

"Both." Daley swiveled left, then right, then back again, fidgeting. The peevish hinge connecting the seat to the base squeaked in protest. "Wait. I'll show you."

He slid his slim fingers into his jacket pocket, extracted a cell phone in a black plastic case. He tapped a few keys, then paused, waiting. "Before I tell you about the emails, let me play you a video," he said.

I heard a few measures of an old-fashioned tune, one of my favorites, Ella Fitzgerald's version of Cole Porter's "Our Love Is Here to Stay," its distinctive opening minor key instantly recognizable even through the phone's tiny speaker.

Watson approached as Daley held out the screen, and we both leaned in to watch. The music continued, and we saw an empty room with an expanse of wooden floor. One wall was a floor-to-ceiling mirror. Doors in the others might lead to other rooms, or perhaps closets.

"Where's this?" Watson asked.

No explanation was necessary, though, as after the introductory notes, the room was no longer empty. Three couples—Daley and another man in evening clothes, one in an ill-fitting sport coat, and three women wearing flowing ankle-length dresses—whirled into the scene. As the music played, the couples dipped and twirled, dancing an elegant if elementary fox-trot. *Forward forward side close*, I could almost hear the instructions as I watched. I'd been sent to dancing lessons as a young girl. To my mother's delight, I became quite proficient. As my family's fortunes changed, and my attentions were turned elsewhere, my dancing days ended.

Even from this tiny video, I could see that the dancer in our visitor's arms held center stage. She fairly glowed with bliss. I smiled, with a bit of nostalgia, as Arthur Daley dipped her backwards, her toes pointed, her long dark hair almost brushing the dance floor. Then, seemingly with no effort, he swept her back onto her feet and they twirled gracefully away.

"You're a dancer," I said. The camera panned right, revealing a sign on the wall: Anthony Selwyn Harrison Dance Studio. "Or an instructor?"

The music died as our visitor clicked off his cell phone. "Instructor. Harrison had his assistant take this video of my class. It's on the studio website, too."

"Here's the website." Watson had fetched her laptop and held it so I could see.

Located nearby, I noted. The site listed classes, and instructors, as well as job openings and recitals. I could look more closely later, if need be.

"So, Miss Holmes?" Daley gestured at me with his phone. "After the gym where I was a personal trainer closed, the dance studio opened, and I convinced them to let me become a dance instructor. I'm into it now, you know? Even in a small town there's a need for dancing. Weddings, or an anniversary. The prom. Or just a good time. The studio's brand new, but making it. Most students are women, seems like. Some watch old movies on Turner Classics, and want to be swept around the floor in a pretty dress. I teach them, dance with them, give them some—romance."

"Ro—?" I began. This was taking a potentially unsavory turn.

"Oh, no way, not really romance, not like that." He put up both palms, as if to ward off any incorrect assumptions. "But when the music's right, and the skirts twirl, well . . ." He shrugged, envisioning the entirety. "They have fun."

"When you said your partner," I now understood, "you meant your *dance* partner."

"Exactly," he said. "Well, to begin with, anyway. The woman you saw, dancing with me? She's Penelope Moran. She moved back here, a year or so ago. Not to downtown Norraton, but out a mile or two. She's the last of her family, and lives in her parents' old house, they left it to her. It's more like a mansion, really, what they call Stoke Moran. She told me it's been in the family forever, and she's really attached to it. 'All I have left of my history,' she says. Anyway, Penny and I got to know each other in class. We got along great. She started taking lessons twice a week."

His face brightened, and he sat up straighter. "She's—she's good at it, you know? A fast learner, and smart, and . . . well, things developed. A month ago, I asked her to marry me. She said yes."

He glanced at the now-opaque screen of his cell phone. "But now she's—acting strange. Avoiding me. We always tell each other everything, but she's not responding to my calls. She didn't show up for last night's lesson. That's why I'm here."

"Would you email that video to me?" Watson, interrupting, had been watching and listening in silence. She gave her email address, Watson at Holmes dot com, which provides everyone a chuckle. "Best never to have only one copy of anything."

Daley clicked a few buttons, and the dancing men and their partners dipped and whirled through the ether and onto Watson's laptop. In a trice, as she clicked her keyboard, the fox-trot music reprised and the dancers appeared again, their swirl of tulle and glitter now on Watson's much larger screen.

"Better, right?" she said.

"Better." I had to agree. Now I could make out the shabbiness of the ceiling, the smudged mirrors, black streaks from countless soles on the floor.

"Please continue, Mr. Daley," I said, as Watson lowered the sound. "Ms. Moran, recently affianced to you, did not appear for a scheduled lesson? Had you quarreled?"

"No, no. We didn't fight, not at all. So, yeah, when she didn't show up, I was pretty worried. I have a key to the studio, so I stayed later than usual, but she still didn't come. I called, texted, went to her house. Left a note. I went home. No messages. I even checked the hospital. Nothing. I hoped she would call, or something, but she didn't. And then I fell asleep. I couldn't wait to talk to you, that's why I'm still in this getup."

The man blew out a breath, and every one of my instincts whispered "lovesick," though it's not a word we often hear these days. I waited. People tell their stories in their own ways, and that is always instructive. If one is seeking the truth, sometimes it is best to listen.

"Anyway, the weird emails I told you about. Penny's who got them," Mr. Daley eventually went on. He paused, smoothed back a lock of dark hair. "Do I need to fill out a form, hiring you?"

"In due time," I said. "For you still have not explained what you'd like us to do."

"Okay, long story short. After Penny said she'd marry me, it was all pretty great." He stood, began to pace. Not that he had much room to pace in our little office, his long legs taking him past Watson's desk and toward the rear wall in four steps, then back to the swivel chair. "But then, two weeks or so ago? She started behaving strangely. Going off. She missed a class. Then came back as usual. Then missed again. She wouldn't tell me why. I confronted her, you know? Had I done something wrong? If she didn't want to get married, I thought, just say so. I mean . . ."

"She received a series of emails," I prompted.

"Yes, yes, that's the whole point," Daley said. "I'm embarrassed to say I swiped her cell phone when she was asleep. We were at my place, we'd had some wine, and I was pushing her, a little, about why she was unhappy. She insisted there was nothing. But I—well, I got into her mail. I searched to see if anything had arrived around the time she first got upset. I found some . . . strange ones. I couldn't decide whether if I forwarded them to myself she could tell I'd done that—"

Watson looked up from her computer screen. "She could."

"Good thing I didn't, then. Instead I grabbed my own cell and snapped photos." He held up his cell as if to show me. "Want to see one?"

"Will you email it to Watson?" I asked. "And Watson, will you print it out?" Nothing like a good old piece of paper.

Our little printer whirred.

"Could you tell who sent it?" I asked. I stood, as the printer was just out of reach. It ejected one sheet of paper, on which the sender and Ms. Moran's address were clearly apparent. Would this be that simple? No. "It says 'no one at no one dot com.' Did you try to contact them?"

"How could I?" Daley asked. "That'd show I'd taken her phone. And—" He shrugged. "What would I say?"

"Too bad," Watson said, tapping her keyboard. "It's easy enough to create an anonymous email address. Even with that, I might be able to track the sender down, but not without the actual phone."

I studied the page again, frowning. There were no words. Only tiny pictures. An apple. A smiley-face. A heart. Then a sun, a moon, and some wavy lines, like the television meteorologists use to indicate wind.

"Did you ask her about this?"

"How could I?" Mr. Daley said again. "She'd know I looked at her email, something I'd never do. Even though I did. I had to, right?"

"What's done is done," I said. "And we shall go from there." I thought about the emoticons we'd just seen, and the relationship between this heartbroken young dancing instructor and his mysterious—if she was—fiancée.

"An apple. For the teacher, perhaps?" I theorized. "Someone loves the teacher, and wants to marry them, and live happily ever after." I tried to come up with a meaning for the wind. "Somewhere windy?"

"Good one," Watson said. "Or someone named McIntosh, like the apple, you know? Is happy that his heart operation went well, he'll now live through many days and nights unless the wind changes."

"Possible," I replied, simply to be polite. Watson is sometimes cavalier about details. "But we must be wrong, for why could either of those be upsetting to Ms. Moran?"

I picked up a paperweight from my desk. The durable chunk of native granite, a legacy from my father, was speckled with potassium feldspar, quartz, and biotite. A "thinking rock," he called it. I turned its smooth weight in my hand, over, and over, and over. Why do people use symbols instead of words? Sometimes, in emails, to save time. In shorthand, to write more quickly. In the Bayeux Tapestry, or Sistine Chapel, or *Guernica*, to be artistic, or to preserve history. Other times—because they only want specific people to understand their meaning.

"It's a code," I said.

Daley narrowed his eyes. "You think?"

"And Miss Moran obviously understands it. I think we may conclude that the message it sends—whether about apples or true love or a subject we have not considered—is clear to her. Unhappily clear, it seems."

"So? You're the detective." Daley looked hopeful for the first time since he'd walked in. "Can you figure it out?"

"That, I fear, is impossible." I had to admit it. "Even for me."

"But—" His body deflated, and he sank, morose, into the swivel chair. It creaked again in protest.

"There simply aren't sufficient exemplars," I explained, putting down my granite. "A substitution cipher—"

"Where one letter or number stands for a certain letter of the alphabet," Watson interjected. "We used them in the . . . anyway. You were saying."

I cleared my throat. I appreciate Watson's enthusiasm, but when I have the floor, I have the floor. "A substitution cipher, to put it the simplest way, substitutes one thing for a letter. It can be a different letter of the alphabet, or a number, or even a symbol. Some have used stick figures, others foreign alphabets. Random squiggles might be employed, certainly, because such a code only requires the sender and receiver know the system. The most elementary of codes are easily broken, in English at least, by applying the well-understood Etaoin Shrdlu analysis, which proves—"

I noticed Daley exchanging a baffled glance with Watson.

"It has to do with how often a letter is used," I broke off to explain. "In a code, in English at least, the symbol most often present stands for E. The next most commonly used letter is T. And so on, in the order I have mentioned. But in this example, Mr. Daley, there are only six symbols. Far too few to analyze. Using only this, decryption is quite impossible."

"So there's nothing you can do to help?" Daley stood, his fists clenched as he questioned me.

From outside came the sound of a honking horn, as the morning rush hour, such as it is in a tiny New England town, paraded by our front window—a few station wagons, the yellow mini-bus taking children to Louisa May Alcott School, a landscaper's rickety screen-walled truck, clattering with rakes. A gust of wind swirled a sidewalk confetti of autumn-bright fallen leaves. Wind? Someone, or something, would arrive as the wind changes? That prospect certainly changed Ms. Moran's demeanor. And our visitor's life. He seemed to care for his young woman, and worried for their future.

"You spoke of a *series* of emails," I reminded him.

"Oh, right," Daley replied. "So after I found that one, I scrolled around, forward and back—worried she'd discover me any second. There might be some I didn't see, who knows. But I found others, like this one."

He swiped his finger across his cell phone screen, held it up. "It had arrived two hours after the apple smiley-face."

"Send it," Watson said.

"Print it," I said. "The more the better."

As it emerged from the printer, though, I saw it would be no help in our undertaking. Three symbols only, each a man in a blue hat. Police officers, I gathered, from their frowns and tiny gold badges. "Three—"

"Police officers," Daley said. "Doesn't that feel like a threat?"

"Possibly." I paused, considering. "There are, indeed, only three police officers in Norraton. But it's frustratingly ambiguous. And if this is a code, the most used letter, as I said, is E. This cannot mean E."

"One more," Daley said. "It was the last to arrive. That I know of. And it's why I'm here, I guess."

"Email it," Watson said.

"And print." I again pointed to the printer.

The final communication was also unhelpful to our decryption. But helpful, indeed, as to why Ms. Moran was distressed.

"A death's head," I said. "There is nothing ambiguous about that, I fear."

The three of us fell silent. I studied the white stucco swirls on our ceiling, saw how the color deepened in the shadowy corners. The success of a code relies on both parties having the key. Or, like the symbols I had received earlier today from our satisfied dog-recovery client, at least knowing the sender and the context.

Clearly Ms. Moran understood the messages, both context and sender. If she had been as baffled as the three of us, she would certainly have shared her curiosity with her fiancé, not turned secretive and melancholy.

Three coded messages—if that's what they were—with only one repeated character meant my initial idea of the substitution system was probably incorrect. Unless, of course, the clever sender knew that's exactly what anyone with the slightest knowledge of cryptology would predict and created the messages deliberately to foil that notion.

But whatever these messages were meant to convey, Miss Moran understood. Now it fell to me to try—before whatever she feared, or whatever was threatened, took place.

"Penny." Daley shook his head as he pronounced her name, his shoulders slumping, his morose visage a picture of despair, his voice matching. "What good am I as a future husband if she's terrified and I can't even help her? What kind of marriage will we have if she doesn't trust me? Isn't there anything you can do?"

"There is most certainly something I can do," I reassured him. "Indeed. Mr. Daley? If you see any more such messages please contact me. The more symbols we have, the more likely we can decipher the exact meaning of the troubling messages your fiancée is receiving. As for our next move? If schedule permits, we'll begin tonight."

"The game is afoot," Watson said, flapping her laptop closed.

"Afoot?" I repeated. If by "afoot" my partner meant dancing, she was precisely correct.

I hardly recognized myself as I saw my newly minted reflection in the entryway mirror, readying my face and my attitude to leave my apartment and head for our destination. Watson and Arthur Daley were to "meet" me there. Only the three of us would know we were already acquainted.

Parking my Jeep a block away from the Harrison Dance Studio, I walked up Coppersmith Street—the town fathers have a bit of a theme—and entered the studio's redbrick building, a once-desirable address, and clambered up the wooden stairs inside.

Perhaps "clattered" is a better word choice, given the sound my black patent kitten heels made on the uncarpeted steps. The shoes were a gift-with-a-message from my persistent mother, who valiantly tries to make me more socially presentable. "It depends to whom you are planning to present me," I always say in return. Which she never finds amusing.

Tonight I was grateful for the fashionably dance-appropriate shoes. My concomitant efforts with lipstick, hairbrush, and eyeliner were equally appropriate, and proficient as well. I had been in disguise many times before, appearing frazzle-faced as a harried mom, sleek as an undercover cop (what Watson dubbed as meta), and once, to snare a particularly unpleasant spouse, as a hoody-wearing hit man. I'd realized this after-noon, as I prepared for this new adventure by removing my signature eyeglasses, inserting my rarely used contact lenses, and loosening my hair from its ponytail, that I'd never disguised myself as an attractive woman. To me, this felt like a difficult task. Others might disagree. We will leave that for the historians to decide.

Climbing the two flights, illuminated by a row of bare bulbs strug-gling to tempt a few languid moths, I approached the door of the Anthony

Selwyn Harrison Dance Studio. Painted a streaky gold and sporting an elaborate "ASH" logo, the door, the only one in the hallway, was amateurishly decorated with a sprinkle of musical quarter notes in electric blue.

Classes tonight announced a makeshift sign, handwritten and framed in dime store black, affixed to the adjacent wall. *Ballroom 6 and 7 pm*, it read. *All are welcome.*

It was only five now. So I had, if all went as I hoped, plenty of time. The studio's own website had given me the entrée I needed.

The door opened with a feeble creak, and I was inside. Watson and I could not visit Stoke Moran without alerting the owner to our association with Mr. Daley, but we could hope that Penelope Moran would appear as scheduled at tonight's dance class. A first step, at least.

Under the flutter of a weary fluorescent, a twenty-something woman, all curls and pink lipstick, sat behind a computer at a desk that appeared to have been rescued from elsewhere, possibly adopted from a prior tenant. If my present tactic failed, I could simply sign up for a single class. But I'd prefer to work on the inside, and thus be reasonably present for many classes—and the potential sources of information who participated.

"I'm inquiring about your help wanted for the teaching position." I offered my best smile, engaging and confident. "I'm Irene Irvine."

I needed an undercover identity, and assumed no one would recognize the name of my father's teacher, the brilliant Boston geologist.

The receptionist proved me correct. "Resumé?" She held out a beringed hand.

"Of course," I said. "But it's online."

I gave the woman a URL, and she clicked it up and scrolled through. The proficient Watson had rigged up a website for me with impressive speed, showing off the generic stock photos and graphics she'd selected. Technology has made it easier to invent a convincing new identity.

"Ms., um, Hudson?" I read the nameplate on her desk. "I can start right away."

She frowned. At what, I wondered? Surely I had not been here long enough to make an unfavorable impression. She made a dismissive sound and plucked the nameplate from her desk, stashing it in a drawer. "That's left over from the last tenant. I keep forgetting. I'm Della."

I stepped back as Della stood, wobbling on her black stiletto boots for a beat. "Can you fox-trot, waltz, Lindy?" she asked.

"Sure," I said, channeling Watson. "No prob. Cake."

Apparently I had satisfied her, for she started down a narrow corridor, gesturing me to follow. On one side of the hall, the mirrored studio I'd seen on Arthur Daley's video. The other wall, once pale blue but now faded into submission, displayed a single life-sized photograph of a dancer I assumed to be Anthony Selwyn Harrison. Standing in front of an old-fashioned wrought iron street lamp on water-dappled pavement, the man wore toggle-latched galoshes tucked into khaki trousers, and held an open black umbrella in front of his face.

"Singin' in the Rain, I get it," I said, proving my knowledge of the industry. "I can see your boss is a big fan."

"Huh?" We approached a closed door. "Ash?" Della's question was punctuated by her knocks. "It's me. You have a teacher candidate."

Ash, I noted: his initials. The door opened, and behind it, Anthony Selwyn Harrison, I assumed, in black trousers and a black T-shirt, standing behind a cluttered desk, reading his cell phone screen and tentatively sipping pungently-hazelnut-flavored coffee from a carryout cup. *Attractive*, I couldn't help thinking as he ignored me. Cheekbones high, dark hair dramatically long. T-shirt possibly a bit too tight. But then, he was a dancer.

The frayed hem of his trousers told me he'd come upon hard times. The struggling black of his T-shirt bespoke many washings. But he still purchased barista coffee, and his cell phone had the distinctive shape of the expensive new ones.

"I see you just got here," I said, before I could stop myself. "Happy to wait, if you want."

"And you are?" He looked me up and down. From my newly flat-ironed hair to my black cocktail dress (purchased, with much optimism, two New Years Eves ago, but never worn until today) to the kitten heels.

"Irene Irvine," I said, hoping he wasn't conversant in geology.

He shifted his attention to Della, then looked at me again. "Experience?"

"Experience? Sure. Lots. Did Ms.—Della—show you my website?"

"How long have you been dancing?" He went on, half his attention remaining on his cell screen, which piqued my interest. Certainly it was possible that whatever upset Ms. Moran had its center in this dance establishment, where Arthur Daley had met and wooed the young woman—that was my intuition at least. But intuition is the pitfall of investigation. Only facts are my allies.

"How long? Ever since I can remember." Undercover is most successful when you stay near the truth.

"We're down two teachers, and under the gun. Can you start tonight?" Harrison tilted his head, narrowed his eyes. "Hey. How'd you know I just got here?"

I'd hoped he'd forgotten about that. Now I needed to downplay.

"Your coffee." I pointed to the cup he'd set on his paper-strewn desk. "It's still steaming. So, you know." I gestured toward outside, though his office had no window. "Maybe you'd just come from the Starbucks down the block. No biggie."

"Ah," he said. A text pinged onto his phone, and he glanced at it. Clicked it away. "Quite the little observer."

I'm almost six feet tall. *Not that little*, I refrained from saying.

"How about this," he said. "You take the classes tonight. Fox-trot, Lindy, waltz. Del, you'll make it happen? We'll see how it goes. You like us, we like you, we'll negotiate."

Smiley-face! I thought. "I'm in," I said.

I was in the midst of "Stardust," explaining the intricacies of the double-step grapevine crossover to my new partner, when my phone buzzed. Cocktail dresses being what they are, I'd kept my cell in a trim little handbag of leather and silver, worn crossbody over my chest. It had quickly become apparent that this bag was not only valuable to keep the phone near at hand but also to impede my bear of a partner from his persistent attempts to press his tweedy body against mine.

When I first took ballroom lessons, in mandatory white gloves and with Mrs. Gregson's vintage record player scratching out Sinatra, we preteens were required to keep half an arm's distance between us. As with everything else, things changed, and now this Mr. Donovan Brett seemed to think the tuition he'd paid to Anthony Selwyn Harrison Dance Studio gave him permission to paw the instructors.

My phone buzzed again. I knew it was Watson checking in, but I couldn't respond, not now. Not in this guise as a job-seeker. I smiled, executing a clockwise under-hand spin to distract my partner from my vibrating chest. Arthur Daley was scheduled to teach the seven P.M. class, which he'd told us was one of Ms. Moran's scheduled lessons. So far, the elusive fiancée was nowhere to be seen.

As the class continued, six of us circled the floor, our big band music emanating from what appeared to be a Mrs. Gregson-era record player. Anthony Selwyn Harrison himself, changed from phone-obsessed businessman to suave danseur in dinner jacket and shiny shoes, was transforming a sixty-something dance student into a Ginger Rogers, her face beaming as he twirled her in a controlled pirouette.

Was Ginger a suspect? Her manicure indicated care about her appearance, her chic haircut and fashionable dress the wherewithal to afford personal luxury. No wedding ring. Newly divorced? Newly searching? Or maybe a happy and satisfied soul, allowing herself the time to dance. Did she send emails with emoticons?

I guided my partner into the three-point turn, forward forward side-close, positioning myself to get a better look at the other two dancers.

A young couple, he in blue jeans and she in an unflatteringly short skirt, giggled and tripped over each other's feet. One of his hands rested intimately on her curved rear, and she'd flattened herself against his chest in a most un-ballroom-appropriate way. A tiny diamond solitaire attempted to twinkle on her third finger, left hand. Engaged couple practicing for their wedding, it appeared. Emoticon suspects? Possible.

"Forward forward, side close," I said it out loud this time, in my best encouraging voice. Was Mr. Brett—who began telling me within five minutes of our meeting that he'd be delighted to show me the new arrivals on his dealership floor, and that I could drive away happy for nothing down and a mere three hundred dollars a month—the one sending pictograms to Penelope Moran?

"Hey!" Mr. Brett groused. He stopped mid-step, retreated a pace, and glared at me. I'd stumbled, on purpose, to derail his sales pitch.

"Oh, sorry." I twinkled at him. "Happens to all of us, right? The sign of a happy dancer is simply to continue." I raised my arms, returning to partner stance. "The show must go on, right? And a-one."

As the last notes of the Hoagy Carmichael faded away, the six dancers in the room patted soft applause. Anthony Selwyn Harrison was eyeing me, assessing, and I gave him a little half-curtsy.

"Last dance," Harrison announced. "Are we ready to waltz?"

He switched the vinyl record on the turntable, dropped the needle, and after a hiss and a moment of staticky hesitation, the music began.

Irene, someone sang, *good night*. I tossed my head, embracing the irony, and stepped my partner into the one-two-three.

Goodnight Irene? Not quite yet. Not for this Irene, at least. It was almost seven o'clock. Would Penelope Moran come through the door?

Watson, gone continental in a perky beret and clear-glassed spectacles, had arrived as we'd planned, just prior to seven. As the six o'clock students departed, she related, *sotto voce*, how she'd told the receptionist she was new in town, reciting the story we'd concocted—that she'd been invited to a holiday gala some weeks away and hoped to discover a dance school that might help her feel comfortable at the event. And, she'd asked, could she possibly do a trial class?

Della had accepted Watson's one-class-only thirty dollars in cash without further inquiry.

"I'm new around here, too," she reported that Della had said.

Did Della send emoticons?

As the seven o'clock class began, Anthony Selwyn Harrison vanished, likely because no other students arrived. Watson, in her role as trial student, danced with Mr. Daley, and I hovered, a wallflower, pretending to observe. Della had delegated record player duties to me, so for now, the three of us were quite alone—me standing beside the capacious armoire that housed the records, the others dancing. Della or Harrison might return any second, so our pretense had to continue. That is what pretense requires.

At my signal, Watson dashed off, pretending she needed the "ladies' room." I began the Lindy music, as instructed, and stepped into Mr. Daley's arms. If the others came in, he could always explain he was testing me. We were in the process of touch-step touch-step when he confessed he'd just returned from Stoke Moran.

"Her car was there," he reported. "And I think I saw her silhouette through the bay window."

"Did she see you?" I asked. "Did you see anything untoward?"

He shook his head, a tiny bead of perspiration lining one cheek, perhaps not only from the bounce of the Lindy but the stress of his concern. "I don't think she saw me, I stayed in my car. Her car was parked in the driveway. I took a photo."

He ducked us into a two-handed flip turn, and as we settled into the closed position, he held the phone screen so I could see. Stoke Moran was not the British manor house I'd somehow imagined, but a rambling white painted wood farmhouse with an expanse of front porch and winding cobblestone front walkway, flanked by rows of slimly elegant poplars. The lines of the house were not quite architecturally perfect, as if someone had built new additions in haste or frugality, but the patchwork quality of the exterior had a certain charm.

A car was parked in the driveway. Attempting to dance and look simultaneously, I could just make out the license plate. Not that I could run it, since the local police were only begrudgingly helpful to us. Though first-year Officer Jake Lester could be a reliable connection, his veteran colleague, Lieutenant R.T. Moore, was downright obstructionist. But that may be another tale.

"I texted, and emailed, and called," Daley went on as we danced, and he tucked his phone away. "I pretended I was here at the studio, but she didn't answer. I finally texted 'see you in class,' hoping, you know, she'd show up."

But Penelope Moran did not appear.

By the time the class ended, my brain was on overload, my powers of deduction exhausted, and my throbbing feet would never be the same.

Daley left. Watson and I, by previous arrangement in case we had to calculate some action before our departure, met in the bathroom, a tiny white-walled cubicle meant for one. Far as I could tell, no one noticed her going in and me following quickly after.

"Anything?" she asked.

"Possibly," I said. I described how the car salesman had urged me, possibly double entendre, to come 'see a car.' The bride-to-be, who'd been the last person to use the loo following the previous class, had dropped a crumpled wad of mascara-streaked tissues as she hurried away. And I wondered if 'Ginger Rogers' had clung a bit too closely to her suave instructor. There was much afoot at Harrison's, but none of it instantly shed any light on Ms. Moran.

"So we know nothing more than when we started." Watson frowned, tilting her beret in the bathroom's lighted mirror. "Arthur Daley is freaking out, and couldn't even make it through our whole dance without texting and emailing. But Penelope didn't answer."

I twisted my dress into place at the hips, wishing I could trade this unforgiving fabric for the comfort of my usual black trousers.

"So a once social and enthusiastic woman decides to forgo her beloved dance class," I said. I leaned against the white wall, slick tile chilling my bare shoulders. "A once-gregarious heiress decides to keep secrets from her sweetheart."

"Bum *bum*," Watson intoned.

"Beg pardon?" I said.

"Law and order," Watson said.

"Not much of either, I fear." Watson is the only person in the world who baffles me.

My phone buzzed, again. A text. I read the tiny screen.

"It's Daley," I said, my mind fairly racing with possibilities. "We must drive to Stoke Moran at once."

The local firefighters had doused what must have been an infernal conflagration in record time, for by the time Watson and I arrived, some of the smoke that curled from the once-shingled roof of Stoke Moran and puffed into the darkening sky was white. Steam, I knew, not the angry black smoke that signaled the irreparable consumption of whatever the flames touched.

We'd first glimpsed only clouds of black as my Jeep crunched over the last half mile of narrow gravel road leading toward Stoke Moran, the global positioning voice bleating directions that clarified the frantic and misspelled ones Arthur Daley had hastily texted to my cell. The choke of acrid smoke had seeped into our car even before we cleared the final bend, red lights from the local fire department sweeping that now-recognizable stand of poplars bracketing Penelope Moran's two-century-old family estate.

Apple, smiley-face, I thought. Police officer, police officer, police officer. The email emoticons referred to nothing about fire. No houses, no flames, no candles or matches. The moon was out, though, and stars, cobwebbed by the last of the smoke.

Stoke Moran was now a study in chiaroscuro—one half, a stout white wood structure, carefully shuttered and landscaped with gracefully healthy bushes and evergreens. The other half, as dark as its counterpart was white, a charred and blackened crumble that I knew from Arthur Daley's photos had once been the columned front porch, the main entry door, and a pair of slender triple-tall windows.

In the front yard, almost exactly on the line demarking the black and white, a figure I recognized as Arthur Daley. Alone. Firefighters wearing heavy tan turnout gear snaked their hoses into position, one man on his knees aiming his spray of water toward where the front door used to be. Two others stood, stalwart in a wide stance, dowsing the remaining licks of orange flame on the side of the house. The fingers of soot already marked the white walls, like the murky signature of the danger that had come calling.

Water covered us instantly, spray and blowback, and we stood, for a brief moment transfixed, amidst the hiss of the steam and the roar of the pumper, determined voices calling directions to each other as they struggled to beat back the last of the blaze.

The firefighters had won, it appeared. But at what cost? Where was Ms. Moran? How had the fire started? And why?

Was this blaze the threat the emails had so mysteriously contained?

My mother had taught me to prepare for emergency by identifying, in advance, my most precious item, so I could be assured of saving it. Had our Ms. Moran escaped? And if so, had she chosen something to save?

Watson and I ran across the water-soaked grass toward Arthur Daley. I was relieved I'd thrown a sweater over my dress, and allowed one fleeting thought for the delicate patent pumps I still wore. Then I focused on our client.

"Ms. Moran?" I asked him without preface. Watson caught up, a step behind me, and grabbed my arm, almost slipping on the drenched lawn.

"No cars here," Watson said.

Perhaps what Miss Moran saved was herself.

"Not a word," Mr. Daley replied. "And yeah. Her car is gone." His face was lined with soot and rivered with water, or tears. He held his cell phone in one hand, and his attention alternated between its tiny screen and the tragic real-life image in front of us. "We'll never dance again, I'm sure of it."

"You will, of course you will." Watson put a hand on Daley's back, comforting. "Things are never as bad as they seem. Look, there's no ambulance, so the firefighters must not think anyone is inside. And they'll be able to save the house, I bet."

I nodded, agreeing. "Unless they have—" I hesitated, not wishing to add another layer of fear. "Unless they have already transported her?"

Arthur Daley shook his head and waved a hand toward the drenched firefighters, some now coiling their hoses in the fire's endgame. His dinner jacket, the one he'd worn in dance class, glistened with water droplets. "The one in the white hat told me they'd checked inside. No one home, and no trace of anyone," he said. "So where is she?"

A voice broke in. "Annabelle Holmes, of course *you're* here." Officer Jake Lester stomped up to us, in full uniform, soaked and scowling. "Why is it you're always on the scene of disaster?"

"I might say the same for you, Jake," I replied. We have a somewhat contentious relationship, me the only private eye in town, and him the town's newest cop.

"You know anything? About this Penelope Moran?" He pretended to poke me in the arm. "You better tell me, Holmes."

"Never met her," I said, telling the truth. "No, indeed."

As he tramped off to do his policely duties, an ugly thought crossed my mind. What if Ms. Moran had set the fire herself, then disappeared to let it burn? But for what reason? Why would the last surviving member of a venerated family attempt to destroy the last vestiges of her beloved childhood home?

Another ugly thought: had Arthur Daley set it? He'd admitted he was here earlier, although he had texted Ms. Moran that he wasn't—a lie. I tried casting him as the villain of the piece, but only briefly. If he had unsavory designs on Ms. Moran, or her family manse, he would not have reported the cryptic emails to Watson and me.

Which meant either the fire was an accident, or someone capable of sending intimidating emails had made good on their threats.

I thought of the second enigmatic message: Police officer police officer police officer. *If you don't do whatever it is, I shall tell the police*, that pictogram seemed to warn. Tell the police what?

Someone was blackmailing Ms. Moran; I'd thought that from the beginning. Why else send a message that only the receiver can understand? Because if caught, the sender can easily deny the purpose, and no court of law could prove otherwise.

"There is nothing to do but wait," I instructed Arthur Daley over the grumble of a fire truck's throbbing engine. "Go home, Arthur. Let the firefighters finish. If you hear from Ms. Moran, notify me instantly. If not . . . well, sir, let me think. It is what I do best."

There would be no sleep for me. Or Watson either, who insisted on accompanying me back to our offices. We sat side by side, staring out our front window into the glow of the streetlights. Watson poured a brandy, a stout Haut Armagnac given to us by a grateful client, and this night, I joined her. The heady liquor did nothing to salve my fears.

"I'm exhausted," Watson said. "From dancing. And the rest of it. Where's Penelope Moran, do you think?"

I felt, though I would never say it, that we had failed. Failed Mr. Daley, who came to us for answers. And failed Ms. Moran, a graceful young woman we had seen only in a romantic dance, who now had disappeared, her family home in shambles.

"Watson, what are our tangible facts?" I asked. Sometimes it is beneficial to speak a conundrum out loud. I have discovered the subconscious somehow provides answers when the questions become real.

"The emails. Whatever they mean. And Stoke Moran," she added. "I Googled it, by the way. 'Stoke' means 'estate,' did you know that? Built around 1810. I looked up the Morans, too. Seems like they both died twenty-some years ago. I couldn't find a will, though. Penelope Moran would have been—"

"A child," I said. The night seemed especially dark, and our puzzle— along with Ms. Moran's fate—increasingly bleak.

"A series of cryptic emails," I went on, hoping to dispel my melancholy with cogitation. "For which we can endlessly conjure meaning, none of which we can ever prove. A woman in distress, who, though there is no sign of foul play or abduction, now seems to have disappeared. A suspicious fire that almost destroys her family home."

Who what where, I often say to myself. In this case, the "where" was the secluded home of the Morans, left to the only remaining heir, little Penelope. If she were no longer alive, what would happen to the estate?

"He calls her Penny." Watson swirled the dark liquid in her snifter.

Making something out of nothing is a pitfall of our business. When answers are urgently needed, sometimes the range of the search produces incorrect ones. Sometimes our initial responses are wrong.

Apple, smiley-face, heart, I thought. Sun, moon, wind.

"Police officer" was the only pictogram to be repeated. The obstructionist police Lieutenant R.T. Moore? His hand is in all that is unpleasant here in Norraton.

I had tossed my soggy shoes under my desk, and now feared for their restoration. Taking the morning *Times* from my desk, still folded and unread, I ripped away the front page and crumpled it, preparing to stuff the toe of my pumps. Page three of the Wednesday paper was now visible, showing a grainy photo of a group of people. I started, for one of them was Mr. Brett, my "Stardust" partner. TOWN FATHERS SEEK ECONOMIC SOLUTION the headline read. I skimmed it, curious, remembering Mr. Brett's wandering paws. "Just under ten percent of soil in Norraton is potentially . . ." I paused, reading the rest.

Police officer, police officer, police officer, I thought.

Watson's chin had sagged to her chest, her eyes closed, her feet still propped on the low sill of our front window. Peacefully asleep. And let her be so.

Careful not to disturb my colleague, I turned to the bookcase behind me, crouching to face the second shelf from the bottom, the place I kept my geology volumes, as well as the ones I'd inherited. Far less valuable than a rural estate, but all my own modest family could afford to bequeath. I selected one of Father's personal favorites, and opened it. We'd looked at it, together, when Father was still alive and my life had not yet unfolded.

We'd traveled many a rocky pathway together, walking the rolling hills of Norraton, filling our pockets with rocks and our heads with dreams that would never be fulfilled: father and daughter, traveling the world and studying its treasures. One evening, after we'd organized our discoveries on the kitchen table, Father offered me a tattered leather-bound volume, *Final Report on the Geology of Massachusetts*, published in 1841. He'd pointed out the author's name. Hitchcock, just like the master of suspense.

"The earth itself is a mystery, and offers constant surprises," Father had told me. "It is our job to discover the solutions."

I hadn't thought of that in years. Ironic, now, that my current vocation also dealt with mystery. And solutions.

I scanned Hitchcock's table of contents, but it was frustratingly long and, for my purposes, illogical. I flipped to the appendix, which, reliably, was in alphabetical order. Ran one searching finger past the list of A—agate, alabaster, amber, apatite; and past the list of B—basalt, beryl, bloodstone.

Police officer, police officer, police officer. Again, I thought, sometimes our initial responses are wrong.

As the appendix directed me, I turned to page 193.

"Are you ready?" I whispered. It was now almost four A.M. We'd entered the studio using Daley's key. "I hear footsteps coming up the stairs."

"Ready!" Watson whispered back, having taken up her position in the left wall's coat closet.

"Are you ready, Arthur? Careful of the mirrors."

"Ready!" He'd hidden himself behind the armoire housing the record player and collection of vinyl.

"Officer Lester?"

"Yup." Jake was concealed behind the door of the right wall's closet.

If all went as planned, we would soon know whether my deductions were correct. I had the proof we needed close at hand. In Father's bequeathed Hitchcock, on page 193, I'd found "Copper, in Massachusetts."

And on page 194: "Copper, maps of."

The maps revealed the treasure: one seemingly worth arson, and deception, and deadly threats.

Underneath the groomed lawns of Stoke Moran lay a forgotten bonanza—the fabled copper lode of western Massachusetts.

The pictograms had not meant "police officer police officer police officer"—but copper copper copper.

I sent a silent thank you to my departed father, who had once again been my partner.

The footsteps drew closer.

Into the reception area.

Down the corridor.

I ducked into the shadows.

The door to the studio swung open.

"So you have finally come to your senses!" Anthony Selwyn Harrison slammed the door behind him as he entered, and with a dramatic flourish, flipped on the reliably dim overhead lights. "Now that your precious house is gone, you'll have no need for the property. Shall we sign the sales paperwork right now?"

"That's good enough for me!" Lester cried. He sprang from his hiding place and clapped handcuffs on the thunderstruck dance master.

My one reliable ally in law enforcement had agreed, reluctantly, to participate in my trap. I had offered him an arsonist, after all, revealing several convincing bits of evidence, including that Harrison had left the dance studio before the fire started. If I'd called it wrong, Lester would have sneering rights forever. A cop—I smiled at my abbreviation—cannot resist that. Now Officer Lester owed me a drink, which I much looked forward to. I might even wear the black dress. If it ever dried.

"What? What the hell is this? Who are *you*?" Even in handcuffs, Harrison demanded answers. He pointed his chin at me, narrowed his eyes. "Wait a minute—*you*! In the glasses. You're that Irene Irvine! But where's Penny Moran? Only she could know—"

Then he stopped.

"Precisely," I said, pointing at him for punctuation. "Officer Lester, do you have enough?"

"Gotcha, Sherlock," he answered. "And got you, too, buddy."

"You're fired, Irvine!" Harrison, red-faced and fuming, was no longer so handsome.

"It has been my pleasure." I curtsied, briefly, impossible to resist.

"You have the right to remain silent . . ." Officer Lester began.

My initial reaction had been wrong, I thought again as I listened to Jake give the Miranda warning. The messages were not in substitution code. The three cops were shorthand. And the other message? Initials.

Not apple smiley-face heart, but their first letters. A-S-H. Anthony Selwyn Harrison.

Not Sun Moon Wind. But, as events now confirmed, Stoke Moran, Wednesday.

And then the death's head. Unmistakable shorthand. No wonder Ms. Moran had fled in fear.

"Hang on, you morons." Harrison, blustering even after the Miranda, apparently could not fathom the collapse of his scheme. "If Penelope Moran isn't here, then who sent me that email?"

"I did, of course," I said. "My colleague set up our own anonymous email account, and when you saw the pictograms, you assumed, as I intended, they must be from the only other person who understood them. And that Ms. Moran had—after your reprehensible arson of the home she would not sell to you—finally capitulated to your demands."

Orange and kangaroo, the emoticons on my message to Harrison had depicted. Meaning, I hoped, "Okay." I had signed it Pear Moon. Penelope Moran. And then, not in code, the place, time, and date.

"And here you are, arriving exactly as the email proposed," I went on.

"Penelope Moran? I have no idea about her!" Harrison bellowed. "I hardly even know her! Or her idiot boyfriend."

I heard a growl coming from behind the armoire. But for now, I ignored it.

"That's enough from you, sir," Officer Lester interrupted. "Tell it to the judge. And possibly you can also explain arson, extortion, and abduction. But"—Lester gave me a wink—"I doubt it."

The cop and his quarry wrestled out the door, Harrison's protests echoing down the hall. "There's no abduction! I want a lawyer! I have no idea where that woman is!"

"I do," Penelope Moran said, as she stood in the now empty doorway. "That bathroom is really small, Annabelle."

With a whoop I cannot describe, Arthur Daley burst from his hiding place. Watson did, too. It was almost farcical, but Arthur's ardent rush to his beloved's side instead set a joyous mood.

"But how did you—?" Daley looked at me, but briefly, for his eyes were only for his Penelope. "Why did you—?"

"Miss Holmes emailed me," Ms. Moran explained. "Using the same initial code. Look." She held up her phone. "Orange, and kangaroo. And then she explained who she was, and how she understood the code, and how Harrison had found out about the copper lode, and then tried to frighten me into selling Stoke Moran, and how you had come to help, Arthur, and how you loved me, and how everything would be okay. Then she told me the plan."

The rest of whatever she was saying was lost then, muffled by embraces. Watson and I averted our gaze, giving them privacy. Watson sidled up to me, eyes wide.

"That's pretty awesome," she said. "You could put all that in a code? You used pictograms to explain the whole thing—who you were, and the copper, and Harrison, her name, and the plan—all in little pictures? How long did *that* take?"

"No time at all," I replied. "Once I got past the Orange and the Kangaroo, to prove I understood the code, I simply typed the rest in actual words. And then we talked on the phone. In actual English. Imagine that, my friend." I smiled; I could see Watson picturing it. "Someone has to be precise, after all."

"I see you have been at the new studio," I said, eyeing Watson as she returned to our office. A week had passed since the arrest of Mr. Anthony Selwyn Harrison. His suspiciously large bank accounts were now under federal scrutiny, Officer Lester confided, as were the geological maps he'd stolen from the local library. His arson of Penelope's beloved home had been a scheme to convince the terrified woman to leave, and sell him the potentially copper-rich property beneath it—the precious contents of which her parents had died before revealing to her. Except, I mused, through naming her Penny. It was the biggest story Norraton had seen since I'd recovered the Baskervilles' missing dog. (They'd sent me yet another smiley-face email commending me on it.)

"You can't know where I've been!" Watson cried. "There's completely no way. Do I have paint on me from where Della and I redid the hallway color? Or some sort of wax under my fingernails from where we refinished the dance floor?"

Watson is not quite comfortable, yet, with my good-natured teasing. Now that Arthur Daley and Penelope Moran are the new proprietors of Norraton's hottest (and only) dance studio, my many-talented Watson has discovered she has a love not only for dancing but for the mercurial Della, too, and spends many hours in her company.

The others I met on my foray into dance instruction are equally delighted that their dance classes will continue (now-jailed former proprietor notwithstanding). The young couple Elsie and Patrick, whose nuptials we'll attend in a fortnight, the ever-persistent Mr. Brett, and the enigmatically romantic "Ginger Rogers," a widow whose name I now know to be Mrs. Cubitt. I have noticed her dancing with Mr. Brett recently. If it is as romantic as it appears, they may someday be partners of another sort. Or she may soon possess a new car.

"Seriously, Annabelle," Watson said. "How do you know I've been at the studio? I've gotta say, you're pretty amazing."

"I have my moments." I handed Watson a mug of fragrant tea, then pointed to the phone on my desk. "But in this case, Della called me," I said, settling into my chair. "To remind you about dinner."

Watson made a noise, dismissive and admiring at the same time. She wheeled her desk chair to our front window, our favorite place for case postmortems, and propped her feet on the low sill, parallel to mine.

"Anthony Selwyn Harrison, there's a piece of work," she said. "Trolling vulnerable students to bilk them out of money? Must have thought he'd hit the jackpot with Penny Moran—until Arthur Daley came along. And you, of course, Sherlock. He'll never dance again, that's for sure. Score one for the good guys."

A gust of wind swirled up the last of the leaves, briefly plastering a few against our plate glass until they flew off again. The winds had changed here, and so had many lives. I wondered if mine would change as well.

"And thank you," Watson interrupted my thoughts. "I feel like—I have a purpose again. I can make a difference. This is a hell of a lot better than Afghanistan, I can tell you that."

She toasted me with her tea. "And for you? Way better than being a high school geology teacher."

I sighed. Watson is sometimes cavalier with details. Not high school.

"Elementary," I said.

RAFFA

by Anne Perry

It was one of the nicest hotels in London. The dining room was suitably lush, sombre, and filled with the chink of china and the delicate odors of coffee and bacon, but Marcus St. Giles was unimpressed with it. His fame as the current television Sherlock Holmes had accustomed him to such places. He would rather have eaten at a truck stop, and played Hamlet, brilliantly, to a single audience. There was no passion in Sherlock Holmes, not a great deal of complexity that had not already been explored a hundred times.

He was making money, but he had lost enjoyment, purpose. It was all automatic, a caricature more than an art. There was no life in it.

"Please, sir . . ."

He looked up. She was standing a few feet away from him, wide eyes staring at him solemnly. She looked to be about seven or eight years old—a child! A small, thin child with long hair and clothes which did not match.

"You are Sherlock Holmes," she said in little above a whisper.

He drew in his breath to try to explain to her that he was Marcus St. Giles, playing Sherlock Holmes on television. Sherlock Holmes was an imaginary character, not a real person. He never had been real.

But she cut him off. "Please, sir, Mr. Holmes, my mummy has been kidnapped and I need you to help me."

He froze. This was awful. He stared around the dining room to find the child's mother. What on earth was she thinking of to let this . . . urchin . . . wander around alone, and not even properly dressed? But all the diners were busy with their plates of fruit, bacon and eggs, toast. They were all properly English, minding their own business, reading the *Times*, sipping tea.

"Please, Mr. Holmes," she said again. "I saw you on the television, and I've read all your stories. Most of them, anyway. You can help me, can't you?" There was a note of desperation in her voice and she was clinging onto her composure with great difficulty.

He had no children of his own and he had no idea how to deal with her. Was she even old enough to grasp the idea of acting? Pretending to be someone you were not?

"Look . . . what is your name?"

"Sarah," she said with a gulp. Now there were tears in her eyes.

People at the nearby tables looked up. One of them clearly recognized him and drew the attention of her companion.

This was even more awful! He could not be seen to turn away a child in distress.

He pointed to the other chair at his table. "Sit down, Sarah, and tell me what has happened." Was she old enough to drink tea? Should he send the waiter for another cup?

But the waiter had had his attention drawn to the child already and came over to see if he could help.

Seeing him, Sarah stepped closer to Marcus. "Please, Mr. Holmes, you have to help me. I've got to get Raffa, or they'll . . . they'll kill my mummy."

The waiter looked at Sarah, then at Marcus.

"Is the young lady bothering you, Mr. St. Giles? I'll see . . ."

An instant decision must be made. Half the dining room was looking at him now. He could see the headlines—SHERLOCK HOLMES TURNS AWAY A LOST CHILD IN TROUBLE! WHO DOES MARCUS ST. GILES THINK HE IS?

"Thank you," Marcus said firmly. "Sarah is joining me for breakfast. Would you bring her a glass of orange juice, or milk, if she would prefer it?"

"Orange juice, please," she said with a gulp.

The waiter let out his breath with a sigh, and pulled the chair back for her, then helped her bring it forward again. "I'll fetch your orange juice, madam," he said, and left.

There was no turning back now.

"When did you know that your mother had gone?" he asked her gravely.

"When I woke up this morning and she wasn't there," she answered.

"Could she have been in the bathroom?" She was probably at reception now, wondering where on earth her child was.

But Sarah shook her head. She put her hand into her pants pocket and pulled out a piece of paper. Soberly, watching him closely, she passed it across the table to him.

He took it and read it. It was very simple, written in deliberately odd letters, a mixture of upper and lower case, cursive and print.

'Give us the giraffe and your mother will be returned. Fail, and she dies. Leave it in the bedroom and go out. Come back at seven.'

It was not signed.

For a moment he wanted to laugh—but the child was afraid. He had worked with some good child actors, but this was real, one real thing in a world of make-believe.

"I see," he said gravely. "What is this giraffe they want? Do you know? Do you have it?"

She shook her head just a little and her voice was no more than a whisper. "No. Raffa's gone too."

"Raffa?"

"My giraffe."

This was truly awful. Was someone playing the worst kind of practical joke?

"Where did you last see Raffa?"

"I think I left him in the taxi yesterday," she answered.

Somewhere in central London there was a taxi that had not noticed it was carrying a giraffe! Where were the cameras and the laughter? He must play it seriously. It was the only dignified thing to do. Dignified! He had never felt more absurd.

"How did that happen?" he asked, as if it were a reasonable question.

"It was a very long flight and I was sleepy when I got here. All the luggage got mixed up. I was carrying Raffa and I left him behind when I helped Mummy get my stuff out."

Carrying him? Ah: a stuffed animal. Something that made sense.

"Where did you fly from?"

"Kuala Lumpur."

"You're right. It's a very long way indeed. Just you and your mother?" Perhaps it would be tactless to ask where her father was.

"And Raffa," she added.

"How old are you?"

"Nearly nine. I'll be ten before the end of next year." She said it with some pride. Her wide blue eyes did not waver from his. The trust in them was terrifying. Was the real Sherlock Holmes ever faced with . . . but now he was being idiotic. There was no "real" Sherlock Holmes!

"That sounds about right," he agreed. "Why do they want Raffa? Do you know who they are?"

"He's a very nice giraffe, but I love him because I know him. I don't know why anyone else would want him. I've had him for as long as I can remember, and he looks a bit . . . sort of used. I tell him all my secrets, and he listens to me. He really listens, not just pretend, until it's his turn to talk."

He understood exactly what she meant, and it surprised him.

The waiter brought the orange juice and she thanked him solemnly. Marcus glanced at the door, hoping to see a woman looking frantically for her child. But there was just an elderly man with a white moustache and a walking stick.

"Tell me about your journey," he said.

"You're going to help me, aren't you?" Her voice was steadier, filled with hope now.

This was absurd. He had no idea at all how to detect anything. He worked from a script! He wasn't a detective, he was Hamlet, agonizing whether to be—or not! Or Henry V, "once more into the breach," and so on.

She was waiting.

"Yes," he said decisively.

She smiled at him, suddenly, and beautifully.

"So you arrived at the airport yesterday, with your mother, and Raffa?"

"Yes."

"And you took a train in, and then a taxi?"

"Yes."

"In which you accidentally left Raffa?"

"Yes." She took a deep breath. "I'm sorry."

"I'm sure it wasn't on purpose."

She shook her head.

"Then finish your juice, and we will go upstairs and look again to see if your mother has come back, or if someone found Raffa and returned him."

Obediently she drank the juice and put the glass back down.

He signed the bill, and they walked side by side out of the dining room. He wondered for an instant if he should take her hand, she looked so small and alone. But it was not a natural gesture, and she might resent it. Better not to.

They went across the huge foyer and up to the reception desk.

"Good morning, Mr. St. Giles," the clerk said with a touch of awe in his voice. He did not even notice Sarah, who was barely taller than the desk.

"Good morning," Marcus replied. "Perhaps you can help me. My friend, Sarah, has become separated from her mother. Room . . . ?" He looked at Sarah.

She stood up on tiptoe. "Two seventy-three," she replied. "She wasn't in her room when I woke up." She slipped her small, cool hand into Marcus's and held onto him. For the first time he realized just how lost she was, in a strange city halfway around the world from her home, and the only person she knew had vanished. He closed his fingers over hers.

The clerk looked at the register and soon found what he was looking for.

"You're Maria Waterman?" he leaned forward to see Sarah.

"That's my mummy. I'm Sarah Waterman."

She was telling the truth. That was all Marcus had wished to know.

"Have you seen Mrs. Waterman this morning?" he asked the clerk.

"No, sir," the clerk replied. "It appears she is not down yet."

"Thank you," Marcus said quickly. "We must go upstairs and find her." He turned away from the desk, holding Sarah's hand firmly to make sure she was with him.

"Do you have a key?" he asked.

"Yes, but she's not up there," Sarah said with a touch of impatience.

"I believe you," he replied. "But I think it best we don't tell him anything we don't have to."

"Oh! Yes, of course." Her hand tightened over his and she tried to fall into step with him, though she needed two steps to every one of his.

They went up in the elevator in silence. Marcus's mind was racing. What was he going to do if the mother really was not there? His playing Sherlock Holmes had dulled his wits. Sarah had not even questioned that the desk clerk called him St. Giles. Did she just assume it was one of Holmes's aliases?

Please heaven the mother was there, and this was the end of it.

But she was not there. The key worked perfectly. It was an adjoining room and the one bed was slept in, but tidy. A suitcase sat open on the luggage rack. The door to the other room was closed.

Sarah walked over to it and opened it wide. "Mummy?"

There was no answer. She went inside and Marcus followed. The room was in chaos. The bedding was all over the place, cases off the pillows, stuffing tossed haphazardly like the remnants of a snowball fight. Clothes were strewn on every surface. Drawers and cupboards were all open. Two suitcases were turned out. Internal pockets and compartments were out or broken. The door to the bathroom was open, and in no better state.

"She isn't here," Sarah said in a very small voice.

The enormity of it hit Marcus. It was real. This eight-year-old's mother really was gone, maybe violently. She believed he was Sherlock Holmes, and could do something about it. She looked at him now, enormous eyes swimming in tears. She had let go of his hand at the door, and stood totally alone.

He had never felt so utterly helpless. He was not acting. There was no script to give him his lines, no director to tell him where to go or what to do.

"This is very serious," he said quietly. "I think we had better tell the police."

"Aren't you going to help me?" She looked devastated.

"Yes . . . yes, of course I am." What else could he say? "But the police will have technical equipment that I don't. A lot of things have happened since . . ." Conan Doyle was writing, he finished silently. His mind was racing even more. "We should put the 'do not disturb' signs on the doors, both of them. So the evidence is not moved. Then we'll go."

She nodded, too close to tears to speak.

But the desk sergeant recognized Marcus immediately.

"Oh, yes . . . ?" he said when Marcus told him the situation. "And you're Sherlock Holmes, right?" There was a sneer in both his eyes and his voice.

Sarah looked at him. "Yes," she said solemnly. "Mr. Holmes says you are the right people to come to, because even though he's clever, you have technical things that he doesn't."

"Does he, now? So we can do the legwork, and he can take the credit, eh? Go on, kid, beat it. Go and take your wit somewhere else. I wasn't born yesterday."

Sarah looked as if he had slapped her.

Marcus felt real anger boil up inside him, nothing pretend about it.

"What the hell's the matter with you, man?" he said between his teeth. "An eight-year-old child comes to you for help because the only person she knows in the country has disappeared, and you tell her to go away! Who's in charge here?"

The color rose up the desk sergeant's cheeks. "I'm in charge . . . sir! And I won't have some cheap actor coming in here, wasting our time to promote his miserable career. We have real crimes to attend to. Lying to the police and wasting police time is a crime. And if you don't get out of here and stop holding up the line, I'll charge you. How will that look in the newspapers . . . Mr. Holmes?"

Sarah did not move.

"And involving a child in your cheap stunts. That's low, even for one of you." The sergeant peered more closely at Sarah. "I suppose you are a child? You're not some kind of freak, are you?"

Marcus drew in his breath to tell the man what he thought of him; one or two choice phrases came to mind. Then he felt Sarah's hand slide into his, and remembered what this was about. He did not matter; she did.

"I would like your name, Sergeant," he said quietly. "And I would like you to make a note that twenty-five minutes past nine this morning, I brought Sarah Waterman, aged eight, to this station to report that her mother, Maria Waterman, has disappeared, leaving obvious signs of struggle and search in her hotel bedroom. You turned her away as some publicity stunt, and sent her back out into the street again, to fend for herself."

The sergeant was scarlet in the face now. "But I'm not sending her out alone, am I? Mr. Sherlock Holmes! I'm sending her with the most famous detective in the world! What more could I do than that?"

"We can manage without him, can't we?" Sarah asked in a small voice.

"Yes, of course we can," Marcus said firmly, wondering just how big a fool he was making of himself. "Come on." He turned to leave, taking her hand again.

"Damn actors!" the sergeant said between his teeth. "That's the third idiot this month."

"Fourth, if you count the clown who thought he was Superman," the constable replied.

Outside on the pavement Sarah stopped and looked up at Marcus, waiting. How long before the trust in her face turned to doubt, and then fear? What on earth was he to do? Sherlock Holmes was about as real as Hercule Poirot! Why had he not had the sense to tell her that in the first place? He had no idea how to detect anything at all.

She was waiting, the light fading out of her eyes.

"We must begin," he said. "Unfortunately it seems we will have to do it without any technical help, just our brains."

She took a deep breath, and tried a very small smile.

"We will go across the road to the café over there, and you will tell me everything you know. Then we shall proceed accordingly." He took her hand again and walked to the crossing. As soon as they had sat down, he to an appalling cup of tea, she to a dish of ice cream, he began.

"Tell me about Raffa. How big is he? What is he made of? Who gave him to you? And why would anyone want him badly enough to ask for him as ransom for your mother? That is a terrible thing to do!"

She nodded, and answered with solemnity.

"Raffa is about this big." She held one hand about eighteen inches above the table. "But of course half of it is his neck."

"I see. So he is quite big. What is he made of?"

That was harder. "I don't know," she said at last.

"Is he hard or soft? Does he bend?"

She smiled properly this time. "Of course he bends! He's sort of like . . . cloth, on the outside. I don't know what's inside him."

"Good. We are progressing. Who gave him to you?" Please heaven she did not say it was Father Christmas!

"Wayne. I think he's going to marry my mother. But that won't make him my father, will it?"

"Not if you don't want him to be."

"I'm not certain . . ."

"How long ago did he give you Raffa?"

"A long time, when I was too little to remember. But he had him mended last Christmas."

"I see. So in a way he was new again less than a year ago?"

She nodded. "Does that help? Is it a clue?"

"Too soon to say." His mind was racing as to why anyone would want a child's stuffed toy. Was there something hidden inside it? Drugs? Gemstones? Or was it wishing to get the child as well, because she loved the toy? The violence and the thoroughness of the room's search ruled out the possibility of any sort of prank. That was serious, and ugly.

"And you think you left Raffa in the taxi?" How on earth was he going to find one cab, in London? He felt a rising desperation inside himself. He looked at her plate. The ice cream was melting.

"You had better eat that," he said. "I have to think for a while."

"Is it a three pipe problem?" she asked.

"It may be," he answered. "And I haven't got Watson with me, so I am going to have to rely on your help." That was a stupid thing to have said! Now she would think it was her fault if this turned into a disaster.

"Was it a black taxi, or like an ordinary car?"

"A black taxi." She sounded certain.

"Where did you get it? Do you remember?"

"Of course I do. At the railway station."

"Do you know which airport you landed at?"

"Heathrow."

"Then it was Paddington. We are progressing." He felt appallingly guilty for lying to her, building up hope he could not possibly fulfil. He should tell her the truth now: Sherlock Holmes is make-believe! There is no such person!

"Mummy called the company last night, to see if they had found Raffa," she said, watching him intently. "But they didn't say."

A wave of relief welled up inside him. "Excellent! Then we will go back to the hotel and if we ask the right questions, we will be able to trace the call. If we can find Raffa then the people who have taken your mother will find us. Come." He stood up.

"Is the game afoot?" she asked, scrambling to stand up as well.

He found himself smiling at the grown-up reference. "Yes, I rather think it is. Come on."

"Yes, sir," the receptionist said in reply to Marcus's question. "Mrs. Waterman made a call yesterday evening. I have the number on her account. I'll look it up for you."

Sarah was watching Marcus with wide eyes, almost as if the problem were on the brink of solution. If the mother had spoken to the cab company last night, why had she not told her kidnappers the truth, that the giraffe had been left in the cab? Why risk being kidnapped? And above all, why leave Sarah alone? There had to be some other major factor that he did not know.

Maybe the giraffe was not in the taxi? Or maybe it wasn't about him at all. But he must not tell her that. He needed her to be calm and thinking, remembering. He would have no idea what to do with a frightened and weeping child.

Also, he did not want to hurt her.

He thanked the receptionist, took the address of the cab company, and, holding Sarah by the hand, went out to the foyer to find a cab of their own.

As they sat side by side in the back, seat belts fastened, he began to ask her more about herself, her mother, where they lived and how long they were going to stay in England.

Most of it was just talk, to stop her sitting motionless and afraid. From what she said, she had a very nice house, plenty of space, always enough to eat, nice clothes and nice toys. It formed a picture of comfort and innocence. Then why the stolen toy giraffe, the kidnap and ransack of the hotel room? The real Sherlock Holmes would have a major clue by now—but there he was again! There was no "real" Sherlock Holmes. The whole thing was a good storyteller's invention.

"Tell me more about Wayne," he said with a note of desperation. "Do you like him?"

She hesitated. "Mummy likes him." An answer in itself.

"What does he do?"

She stared straight ahead of her at the road jammed with traffic.

"He's some kind of a banker. I asked him, but he said it was too complicated for me to understand. I don't know why he said that. I know what banks are. They look after people's money, and keep it safe. I told him I'm nearly nine, and I understand things, but I don't think he believes me."

"Maybe he's not very good at explaining," he suggested. "Some people aren't."

"My daddy was."

He did not know how to answer.

"What did your daddy do?" He had to think of something, or it would sound as if he did not care.

"He was a diplomat." She said it with pride. "That's how we met Wayne, I think." She sniffed. "He would know what to do. But he's dead."

More to think about. And it made the situation more complicated.

"How long ago was that?" he asked aloud.

"Two years," she answered. "I suppose it's all right for Mummy to marry Wayne now."

"Well if it isn't, I expect she won't do it." The moment the facile words were out of his mouth, he regretted them.

"I don't think I want her to," she said gravely. "We're all right just the two of us."

He had no answer to that at all.

"I suppose he is in Malaysia now?" he asked.

"Yes. This holiday is just for us." She gulped. "When we find Raffa and get Mummy back."

The taxi swung wide around a corner, dodging a motorbike, and Marcus spotted another black taxi with a light blue advertisement on the side. He had seen it before, far closer to the hotel. He saw it again a couple of blocks later, but when they pulled up at the taxi company offices it went on by. Had it been following them? Oh, if only he had a script written for this adventure!

"Do you think they will have found Raffa?" she asked, interrupting his thoughts.

"It's very likely," he replied, pulling his few ideas together. He was used to tension, to being watched with a highly critical eye, at times to carrying the show. Time to be professional. "And it seems they want Raffa very much. Do you know why?"

"No. Why?"

"I think Raffa must have something inside him that is very precious. I will ask if they have him, but I don't think we should take him with us now. We wouldn't want to . . . to lose him before they keep their end of the bargain." He did not want to frighten her, but he could not shake the memory of that blue advertisement.

She nodded, lips tight, fighting not to cry. "They're bad people, aren't they?"

"I think so."

"Are they here?"

"I think they might have followed us." That was another stupid thing to say! It would only frighten her. If that damn policeman had only believed him he wouldn't be in this ridiculous position!

"In the taxi with the blue picture on it," she agreed, still gripping his sleeve.

"You noticed it?" he said with surprise.

She nodded.

"Let's go in." He pushed the door open.

The man behind the counter looked at him curiously. Perhaps a memory stirred, recognizing his face but not recalling from where. It happened now and then, people thought they knew him.

Then the man smiled. "Sherlock Holmes. Right?" He was pleased with himself.

Sarah's face lit up and she nodded vigorously.

Marcus took a deep breath. "I am trying to trace a lost giraffe," he said, knowing he sounded ridiculous. "About eighteen inches high. My friend, Sarah, left him in one of your taxis by mistake. He matters rather a lot. Has he been turned in?"

"Oh, yes. I know the one you mean. If you can just give me Sarah's full name, and the time and route of the taxi, for identification purposes, sir."

"Of course. The journey was from Paddington to the Ritz Hotel, at about seven o'clock yesterday evening. The passengers were Mrs. Maria Waterman, and Sarah."

Sarah nodded, her eyes bright.

The door outside opened and a middle-aged woman came in.

"Please!" Marcus said urgently, "could you just keep the giraffe for the moment? We will return to pick it up later. But it is of the greatest importance that you don't give it to anyone else. Do you understand?"

"Yes, sir." The man glanced at Sarah.

"Please!" she said intently. "Please look after him!"

The clerk looked at Sarah, then at Marcus. "Of course I will," he promised.

Sarah gave him a beautiful smile that lit her whole face. "Thank you."

When they were outside in the street she leaned towards Marcus. "I nearly asked him to tell Raffa we'd be back for him, but he would think I was silly, wouldn't he? I know Raffa's just a . . . a toy."

"The things we love matter, whatever they are," he answered her. "They wouldn't mean the same to anyone else. They keep our dreams and our secrets and never tell anyone, but we always know. If the man had any sense, he'd understand that."

She looked at him unblinkingly. "I think you are a lot nicer for real than you are in the stories that Dr. Watson writes about you."

He felt the warmth rise up inside him. It was absurd. "Actually Watson is a very nice man." He said it instinctively, thinking of Peter Cauliffe, who played the part. Then he thought again. "You know, it might be a good idea if we brought him into this. We could use his help."

She nodded vehemently, but she did not let go of his sleeve.

"Let's get another taxi."

When he had her seat belt fastened, he pulled out his mobile phone and called Peter Cauliffe's number. Please heaven he answered. Marcus was guilty rather often of ignoring calls, but Peter was usually pretty good. He hoped the man would not choose now to demonstrate how annoying it was to be ignored.

It was ringing; Sarah was watching. She couldn't know that this "Watson" was Marcus's own man, and would do whatever he pleased? Peter owed Marcus no favors.

"Hello, Marcus," the voice said at the other end.

"Oh! Watson. Thank God you're there." Marcus rushed on before Peter could hang up, thinking he was playing a practical joke. "Look, I have a rather important matter. Please! My friend, Sarah, she's nearly nine, has a problem of a very grave nature, and needs our help. Don't . . . don't hang up!"

"You'd better be sober, Marcus," Peter said warningly.

"As a judge. Where are you?"

"At my flat. I'm going out to lunch with a friend . . ."

"We'll be there," Marcus cut him off, then leaned forward and gave the taxi driver new directions.

Peter Cauliffe was about the same age as Marcus, but a milder, gentler-looking man.

The thing that made him distinctive was the wit in his face, and the warmth of his expression. Marcus admitted, very occasionally, that he was also the cleverer actor of the two of them, because he could play a wider variety of people. The Watson he played on screen was almost his natural character, perhaps just a little more patient.

Marcus gave Peter a long, steady look, then introduced Sarah Waterman to Dr. Watson, and added, "Sarah is in trouble and has come to us for help. Her mother appears to have been . . . kidnapped and the ransom for her is Sarah's toy giraffe, Raffa. We don't know why, but since they landed from Kuala Lumpur last night, we think there may be something stitched inside him. The threat is quite clear. And she is very alone." He needed Peter to believe him without doubt, and without sowing even more fear in Sarah's mind.

Peter stared at Marcus, noticed his unusual gravity, and perhaps a difference in his manner. A sincerity he rarely carried off set, at least recently.

"Yes," Peter agreed slowly. "It sounds very grave indeed." He looked at Sarah. "We will do all we can to help, Miss Waterman. May I call you Sarah?" He held out his hand.

She took it very solemnly. "How do you do, Dr. Watson."

"The first thing," Marcus went on, "is to get Raffa back from the taxi company, er, Watson." He felt ridiculous calling him "Watson" off set, but he met Peter's eyes very steadily, hoping he would understand, and call him "Holmes." "Will you do that for us . . . ?"

But Sarah pulled on his sleeve. Both men looked down at her.

"They won't give Raffa to Dr. Watson," she reminded him. "You said to give it to no one but you."

Peter raised his eyebrows. "Now what . . . Holmes?"

Marcus knew in a moment of utter certainty that part of Peter was enjoying this. He believed the reality, but he also saw a kind of poetic justice in it.

There was no honorable alternative. "Sarah is quite right. Keep her safe here and I will go back for Raffa."

Sarah gave a little cry of protest.

"I'm sorry," he said gently, looking straight at her. "But this . . . this 'case' is serious. We must get Raffa back before we can do anything else. The police don't believe us. We've no time to waste." He looked back at Peter. "Watson, have you got an attaché case, or some sort of bag I can put Raffa inside? I may be gone a little while. Look after Sarah."

"I have a lunch!"

"Sorry, old chap," Marcus said. "But both Sarah and I think we were followed for a while. They may well be waiting at the taxi company office. I will have to lead them off the trail before I get back here. Don't let anyone in."

Sarah let go of his sleeve, but her eyes were wide and brimming with tears.

What would Holmes have done? Nothing warmhearted, and she must know that. She might well know Holmes better than he did. She needed belief now more than comfort.

"Do whatever Watson says," he told her. "He's looked after me all these years, and saved my neck a few times, as you know. He will look after you. Right, Watson?"

"Surely, Holmes," Peter replied without a flicker.

Marcus left the house and walked quite casually to the taxi stand a quarter of a mile away. There was no one else in the street except a woman walking her dog, and a couple of youths joking with each other. But once he was in the taxi he felt oddly closed in. He asked to be dropped a block away from the office, then wondered if he was actually making himself more vulnerable.

Had he been followed to Peter's house? Would Peter be attacked and Sarah taken while Marcus was away from them? It must be wonderful to be as sure of his own invulnerability as the marvellously fictional Sherlock Holmes! Wasn't he ever afraid? Afraid of pain, of failure, of letting people down? Whatever future scripts said, perhaps he should make him human, frightened and lonely sometimes, full of doubts. Or was that not what people wanted to know? Maybe that was what the drugs were for? Conan Doyle had included that, so the script writers had too, but only rarely.

He was at the taxi company offices. There were several people around, at least four of whom glanced at him as he pulled the door open and went in.

Five minutes later he walked out with the stuffed giraffe in his attaché case, its legs folded up and its neck bent a little. It was a handsome creature, very carefully stitched and with a benign, almost smiling face.

He looked left and right. He recognized no one from five minutes before, but he still declined the taxi that slowed questioningly as he stood on the curb. Instead, he walked a few blocks and stopped a cab at random.

He gave the driver directions, then changed them after half a mile. He watched the numbers of the cars behind him. He saw the same one even after the change of direction. He changed again. Was he safer in a taxi, or walking? Could he find a place where a vehicle could not follow him? Go through a shop and come out on a different street? He stopped at a large department store with three entrances, and went in to mingle with the crowd. Would they expect him to go out at the far side? What if he doubled back and went out the way he came in?

No. Better to cross the street and catch a cab going in the opposite direction. With this traffic, anyone following him could not turn in less than a mile or so.

He arrived at Peter's house without seeing the taxi with the blue advert. Had he imagined it? He was becoming neurotic. What if this giraffe was nothing more than it seemed: a much-loved toy?

Then why ransack a hotel room? And who was Maria Waterman?

He was welcomed with some relief, even though Sarah and Peter seemed to have been getting along rather well, playing dominoes, at which Sarah was surprisingly good. She told Marcus that she had won twice.

Her eyes lit up with pleasure when she saw Raffa and she hugged him tightly before telling him gravely that she was sorry they had to unpick him, but she promised to sew him up again afterwards, and it wouldn't hurt.

"You will be careful, won't you?" she asked a little self-consciously. She knew perfectly well that Raffa was a toy, but they had shared many secrets, and right at the moment, he was the one fixed point in her universe.

"Of course I will," Marcus promised. "And we will stitch him up again straight away."

She nodded, then stood still, biting her lip as she watched Marcus take the nail scissors from Peter and very carefully snip the threads that held Raffa's middle closed.

Gradually he pulled out the tightly packed stuffing. More and more was piled upon the table. There were no packets of powder, no bags of diamonds, nothing but white, fluffy cotton, or kapok.

Sarah was watching him, her fear palpable in the air. Could this be some hideous joke—a warning that next time it would be a living creature, not a toy? He found himself hating these people with an intensity he had not felt in years.

Then his fingers touched something hard. He felt round it. A battery of some kind? It was small and flat, like one of the dominoes they had been playing with.

He looked up at Peter, watching him. Then he pulled it out.

Peter let out a sigh of relief. "That's a flash drive."

"What?"

"A flash drive," Peter repeated. "It can have masses of information on it. You can put entire bookshelves on one of these things. Reams of pictures." He glanced at Sarah. "May we read it, please? I think it is what the men who took your mother are looking for."

She nodded, her eyes never leaving the small piece of plastic.

"Thank you." Peter walked over to his computer and put the flash drive into the slot. He clicked the icon that came up on the screen, and in a few moments, a picture appeared.

It was a still from the classic film, *Casablanca*, black and white, Bergman and Bogart. To Marcus, the perfect movie. With all the millions Hollywood spent these days, all the action, the color, the special effects, no one had ever come close to it. Superb supporting actors, inspired lighting, brilliant sets, great quotes: "Play it, Sam." "In all the gin joints, in all the towns . . ." Even the soundtrack, "As Time Goes By"?

"It doesn't look right," Peter said quietly.

Marcus brought his attention back to the present, and looked more closely. Should there be buttons down the front of Bergman's dress? He had seen the picture scores of times and he did not recall them. Of course, he had always concentrated on her face, the calm lines and the inner turbulence of spirit, but these caught his attention. They never had before.

Experimentally, Peter put the cursor on the top one and clicked. Nothing.

He tried the next one—and to Marcus's amazement, the scene faded and something quite different appeared.

It was one column of names and then several columns of numbers. Some appeared to be dates, and recurred several times, others were in a column headed by the abbreviation for Swiss francs. The second column appeared to contain numbers that were never repeated. The last one was letters and numbers intermixed.

"How'd you do that?" Marcus demanded.

"Remember that friend of mine who coached you on computers?" They'd been doing one of their rare non-Sherlock films together, about a computer hacker. "Well, he's a good friend."

Marcus peered at the screen. "Are those bank accounts?" A hell of a lot more valuable than a giraffe filled with heroin, if the numbers were to be believed. "There's hundreds of millions of pounds worth here."

"And the account passwords." He and Peter stared at each other.

"Is this important?" piped up the child, forgotten at his knee.

"This is very . . . important indeed." He did not want to spell it out in front of Sarah, but for this kind of money there were people who would take a life—any number of lives—without hesitation.

"So we can give it to them? And get Mummy back?"

Marcus looked at Peter, then put his arm around Sarah's shoulders. "Yes."

"We have to give it to them, Sherlock." There was a bitter humor in Peter's voice. "But I think we should make a copy of it first."

"It won't show, will it? I wish we could make it just burn up, as soon as this thing is over."

Peter frowned, his thoughts faraway. "What if we could make it self-destruct, one piece at a time?"

Marcus looked at him. "What are you thinking, Pe—Watson?" he corrected himself at the last minute.

"I can give it to my friend, who will know what to do with it. And he was telling me about a program for a self-destruct, say ten percent at a time, that can be triggered from a distance. When we do that, we stitch it back in Raffa, and give Raffa to them, in return for Maria Waterman. If they want to bargain, or double-cross us in any way, we have a tool to bargain back with. We'll delete it."

"Won't your friend need the flash drive?"

"I'll see if he can set it up just with the copy."

"Good. Then get on with it. When you're finished, Sarah and I will go back to the hotel and wait for them to contact us. Thank you, Pe . . . Watson."

Peter gave him a wry look, but he said nothing more. He went to the telephone and spent a quarter of an hour speaking very quietly to someone he apparently knew well.

Meanwhile Marcus carefully put most of the stuffing back inside Raffa. One thing he had thought to do was save the thread with which he was originally stitched, or more accurately, with which the person had stitched him after the flash drive had been placed inside him. It was very close indeed to the original. Would they look closely enough to notice any difference? It was a linen thread, very strong. They might find which seam had been undone. He should unpick another seam, perhaps a long one, like his neck or leg, and use that to re-stitch the one they would look at.

He explained to Sarah what he was doing, and why, and she nodded again. Raffa was a stuffed toy, and yet he felt almost as if he were poking the needle into a live creature. He did it very carefully, mimicking exactly the depth and distance of the stitches already there.

"You won't hurt him," Sarah said gently. "He doesn't feel, you know." It was difficult for her to say. To her, Raffa was real.

"I know," he answered her, raising his eyes from the stitching for a moment. "But I want it to be exactly like the seam they made, so they won't see the difference."

"Is that why you used the same thread? What about his neck? It will be different."

"I'm hoping they won't look at that so closely, at least to begin with. Later, they will know, because if they don't give your mother back, we will delete . . . rub out . . . part of their flash drive every time they refuse. We just don't want them to know that straight away."

Peter's computer finished the copying, and he took out the tiny slip of plastic and handed it to Marcus, who worked the little thing deep into Raffa's insides. When the giraffe was sewn up again, and he looked exactly as he had before, Marcus said goodbye to Peter.

"You need to take the copy to your friend in . . . wherever he is . . . and let me know if it's gone according to plan." Marcus did not add any more. He wanted Sarah to believe it was all planned for, and safe—that Sherlock Holmes would never fail. It was Marcus St. Giles who needed Peter Cauliffe to know where he was, and have a backup, just in case.

Also it would be better if nothing appeared to have changed since the threat was made. Whoever it was who had taken Maria Waterman knew perfectly well that he was merely an actor who happened to have played the role of Holmes rather well, or at any rate, rather successfully—from somebody else's script.

"We will go into the dining room and have afternoon tea," he said as they walked through the foyer.

"I don't want tea," she replied.

"Neither do I," he agreed. "But we should have it, nevertheless. We need them to know that we are here, and ready to do business. And I would very much rather be where lots of people can see us. It is safer."

"Oh," she said in a very small voice. She grasped onto his sleeve again.

"Do you like chocolate cake?"

"Yes."

"I thought you might. So do I. Not very good for you, but we need a treat, don't you think?"

She nodded.

They found a table and sat Raffa, in the attaché case, on the chair between them. Marcus ordered tea, and two slices of chocolate cake, with icing. He could see that she was frightened. Honestly, he was frightened too. The price of failure in this was infinitely higher than anything he had imagined when he began.

They must talk about something. He could not let her just sit here in silence, trying to pretend she was not terrified, and imagining what might be happening to her mother, and what in the end she would do alone, in a country where she knew no one. The guilt she would feel for failing would destroy her.

What would the real Sherlock Holmes have talked about? Nothing. He did not deal with children, except the Baker Street Irregulars, and they were not well brought-up little girls. They were boys, and street-wise urchins at that.

"Do you like to read?" he asked.

She finished her mouthful of chocolate cake. "Of course I do."

"What's your favorite book?"

"Other than your stories?"

"Other than those, yes."

"A book of poems by Edward Lear. It was my mummy's when she was little. And my granny's before that."

For a moment he was totally lost, then a flash of memory came to his rescue.

"Ah, yes. Lots of limericks. Are there any drawings in your book?"

"Drawings?"

"Yes, of flowers and things."

"No, there are rhymes and stories." She looked puzzled.

He was struggling. He took a piece of paper out of his notebook and a pen, and he drew a picture of Lear's as he remembered it. It was a mock botanical name—"nasty-creature-crawluppia." He made the picture appropriately horrible, then passed it to her.

She took it, and giggled with pleasure. "I've never seen that before. I'd remember."

"He was a real artist, you know, as well as writing nonsense verses. He painted beautiful watercolors of South Africa."

"Really?"

"Yes." He fished for words and recollections of Lear's verses, and recaptured enough to amuse her for quite a while. Some of them she knew and recited with him. The waitress came and Marcus paid the bill.

A few moments later she returned with a receipt—and a note.

Trying to keep his hands steady, Marcus read it. He knew Sarah was watching him almost without blinking.

"They have your mother, and will exchange her for Raffa," he told her. "They are somewhere very close, probably in this room where they can see us, so sit still. Let us keep our composure."

"The game is afoot," she whispered, her eyes locked on his.

"It is indeed. But we must make sure that she is all right before we give them Raffa."

She nodded, just a tiny movement of her head.

He found himself, ridiculously, not wanting to give up the stuffed giraffe. If anything had happened to her mother, it was the only thing she had left of her past life, apart from a few clothes she would soon grow out of.

"We must make sure," he repeated, taking his pen out of his pocket and writing on the note itself. 'We will give you Raffa when we know

Maria Waterman is safe and well.' He gave it to the waitress, along with a couple of one-pound coins, and asked her to return it to the sender. His heart was beating so hard he felt as if his body were shaking with it. His hands were clammy.

"Yes sir," she said obediently, and took it away.

Marcus wanted to say something to Sarah to comfort her, but his mouth was so dry he could barely speak. This was the worst stage fright he had ever had. Of course it was! It wasn't a critical opinion of his performance of a play at stake, it was a woman's life, and a child's happiness.

How strange the world was—everyone around them was sipping tea and talking normally, exactly as if nothing of importance were happening. But perhaps they were making deals that would change fortunes, meeting their illicit lovers, or saying goodbye for the last time.

The note came back. 'Give us Raffa, or we start hurting the mother.'

With a trembling hand, he answered. 'We know what's in it. If you hurt her we will delete the first three names from your list, along with the account numbers. The second time you hurt her, or delay any more, we will take the next three. If you look at the stitching on Raffa, you will see that it has been replaced. This is not an idle threat.'

He passed it back to the waitress. Please God this would work. His mouth was too dry to swallow, and if he took some tea it would choke him.

He looked at the child on the other side of the table.

"Don't worry," he said gently. "What is inside Raffa is worth millions of pounds. They want it very badly. I told them that if they hurt your mother, I will make the flash drive delete a few of the names and numbers they need. Watson is making it so it will do that. He's very clever that way."

She took a deep breath and nodded. Did she believe him?

"Tell me about Wayne," he asked. He realized that it mattered to him that this man who was going to marry her mother was honest and kind. What he did and how much he earned were unimportant; he must be kind to the child, he must like her, as much as if she had been his own.

He asked questions to keep her mind busy, all kinds of questions about the man, but the more she told him, the less did he like what he heard. By the time the waitress approached them again, he was almost as concerned about Wayne as he was about Maria Waterman's safety.

The telephone buzzed against his chest. He fished it out and saw a text from Peter: Mission accomplished. He went light-headed with relief.

Sarah was watching him, looking very pale, her clenched hands on the table.

"Watson's done his part," he told her. "Now we must wait for them to reply. Don't worry, they will. They want what is inside Raffa just as much as we want your mother. And we can destroy it any time we want to."

"Will you destroy it even if we get Mummy back again?"

"Yes, I'm afraid we will have to. They would do a great deal of damage with it."

"Will they know? That you can destroy it?"

"They do now."

She tried to smile, but it did not really work.

He reached across the table and put his hand over hers, just for a moment. It was a very un-Holmes-like thing to have done, but he was not sorry. When she was older, and looked back on this, who would she think he was?

The waitress returned with another note.

Marcus took it and read it almost at a glance. They agreed, naming a restaurant which would be open until at least midnight. They would meet there and exchange the hostage for the ransom. The restaurant was in the theater district. Not good: he might be recognized. He had played in many of them, and his face was known worldwide as Sherlock Holmes. He wrote down the name of an alternative restaurant, less fashionable, where he might pass unnoticed. He tipped the waitress handsomely, and asked her to return with the reply.

He and Sarah waited in silence until it came. It was a jolt, and a relief.

"The game is on," he told her, then looked at what she was wearing. "Do you have other clothes with you? A pretty dress?"

"Yes, in my room."

"Let's put you into that. I will go up with you, and wait in your mother's room while you change. I'm not going to leave you alone." He hoped she would not argue. They had pushed the kidnappers to the limit. They would offer no mercy they did not have to. He could delete everything from the flash drive, but then he would have no bargaining power left. He was bitterly aware of that.

She obeyed without even asking him. She looked very small and frightened. In the rooms, she found the dress and went towards the bathroom.

"Sarah!" he called.

She turned. He could see the fear in her eyes.

"I just want you to be safe," he said without thinking.

"Oh!" She gave a weak smile and her eyes filled with tears.

He could not even imagine how lonely she was, and this evening she was going to have to give away the one stable thing in her life, on the chance of getting her mother back. He would have to find a way to get Raffa back—the real Sherlock Holmes would have. But of course, Holmes would not have cared.

He gave her half an hour, then knocked on the adjoining door.

She opened it straight away, and looked up at him. She had obviously washed her hair. It hung in a shining curtain, and she had on a red dress that in a few months was going to be too small for her. Now it was perfect, plain and simple, and the color made her skin glow.

"You look beautiful," he said seriously. "And red is a good color, bright and brave."

She gave him the best smile she could.

Downstairs the doorman called a taxi for them and they rode through the streets in silence. Raffa was still in the attaché case, which Marcus never let go of. It would have been nice for her to hold him, but dangerous—and perhaps also too emotional.

He thought about talking, and decided against it. She needed a little while to think of what was going to happen. He looked sideways at her once or twice, but if she was aware of him, she gave no sign. Her face was motionless and very solemn.

They arrived at the restaurant, which was brightly lit, people on the footpath stopping to glance at the menus pasted outside. A man and woman passed them and went in, she in a tight, sequined dress.

Marcus took Sarah's hand and held it firmly. This was the very last stage of the transaction and he felt she was desperately vulnerable. He did not even think about whether he was being brave or not. For the first time that he could remember, he was ready to fight if he needed to. But this would not be fists or rapiers, it would more likely be a knife that he did not see coming.

He asked for the table he had reserved, in her name.

"Miss Waterman?" the maître d' said doubtfully.

"Yes," Sarah lifted her chin a little. "That's me."

He was Sherlock Holmes. He did not get emotional, least of all about clients. Villains very occasionally, perhaps.

"Thank you," he said to the maître d', and followed him to the table near the wall where they could see most of the room. They sat down and ordered salad and then a plain omelette. Eating was the last thing on their minds, but they must not appear exceptional.

He looked around the other tables as discreetly as he could, and saw two or three groups that could have been them. He had no idea what Maria Waterman looked like.

"Do you see her?" he asked quietly.

"No. I looked. She's not here yet. She will come, won't she?"

"Yes. They really want the flash drive inside Raffa." He was startled by how calm and certain he sounded. But he was an actor, he often said things he did not mean.

She believed him. He saw it in her eyes, her smile.

He had no idea what the salad was made of. It could have been grass for all he tasted. She was eating too, concentrating on it as if it mattered.

"Hello, Marcus," a sultry voice said at his elbow.

He looked up. "Hello, Lettie. How are you?" Of all the times for the damned woman to turn up. He saw Sarah's dismay.

"I'm fine, darling. You look fearfully solemn . . ."

His mind raced for a way to get rid of her.

"This is a working dinner, Lettie. I'll call you next week some time."

Lettie was startled. Sarah looked up and down her elegant, rather thin figure and its emerald green dress. Clearly she did not approve. Lettie gazed around, searching for the cameras she expected, but did not see them.

Marcus gave Sarah a bright smile. "We should pick up again at the top of the page." He hoped she would understand that he meant the remark for Lettie. The actress made a sound, then turned and stalked away.

"Was she someone else you helped, Mr. Holmes?" Sarah asked.

"She wants me to. But there is nothing else until this one is solved and you and your mother are safe again. This is perhaps the biggest case I have ever dealt with."

"Bigger than *The Hound of the Baskervilles*?" she asked, her eyes wide.

"Oh yes." He knew all the cases by heart. Here was something to talk about, to take her mind off the waiting. "Don't forget, the poor dog was not actually supernatural at all."

"Or *The Musgrave Ritual*?"

"Definitely. There is far more money involved, but more importantly, lives."

"*The Speckled Band*?"

He answered more questions but all he could think of was Maria Waterman, and the men who were holding her.

"There she is!" Sarah said urgently.

He froze. "Where?"

"Behind you, over your shoulder. Left . . . no, right," she answered.

"Are you sure it's her? Absolutely sure?"

"Yes."

"Can you walk over and make certain it is your mother, and that she is all right, not hurt or sick?" It was a lot to ask.

"Yes." She had hesitated only a moment, almost too short a time to be certain it was a hesitation at all.

"I'll keep Raffa." He wrote another short note: 'A straight swap. Meet in the middle.' "Are you sure?" he asked Sarah again.

She stood up, took the note out of his hand, and without looking at him again, set out across the floor. He swivelled around and watched her, his heart thumping so hard he was sure he actually shook.

She reached the table and looked long and hard at her mother. One glance at the woman, and Marcus knew beyond doubt that she had to be Maria Waterman, and she was terrified for her child. This had to work!

Sarah put the note on the table and one of the two men picked it up and read it. He turned to the other and said something. The other man nodded. He spoke to Sarah, but he was looking beyond her, straight at Marcus and the attaché case. Then in one moment he rose to his feet and moved towards Sarah. He had only just touched her shoulder when she shot forward and bumped into a waitress carrying two bowls of soup. They clattered to the floor. Another waitress jumped to help, and Sarah slipped between them to run back to Marcus, throwing herself against him. Instinctively he held her for a moment, far more tightly than he had intended to.

Then he let her go. He opened the attaché case and took Raffa out. He held the giraffe tightly in one hand, and his mobile phone in the other. He flicked it open, and deleted one file. He returned the telephone to his pocket and held up his hand, one finger pointed. He shook his head.

"One gone," he mouthed, and the man's face told him that he had understood.

Suddenly, Sarah snatched Raffa out of his hand and started off across the restaurant towards her mother and the two men. When she got there, she said something to her mother, who rose very slowly to her feet.

Sarah hugged Raffa tightly, and said something to him, then she passed him over to the man. She and her mother walked across the floor and stopped next to Marcus.

It was done. Maria was safe.

The two men rose to their feet and started to walk away, pulling the stuffing out of Raffa as they went. In a moment, they had the flash drive—but they still carried the giraffe, dangling by one leg.

Sarah shook free of her mother's hand and began to go after them.

"No!" Maria called out, her voice sharp with fear. "They'll . . ."

Near the door, the two men stopped: a large party, a dozen or more guests, was coming in—and behind them, a pair of uniformed police.

The men instantly stopped. One of them spotted a doorway, and pushed his partner towards it. Marcus knew, however, that it was not a side entrance, but led towards the roof garden—and, an external stairway down again.

Sarah was on their heels.

"Stay here!" Marcus said to Maria grimly. "Stay where people can see you. If you come you'll be a hostage again. That's an order! Do you understand?"

"Get her back," she pleaded.

"Stay here and I will!" Another wild promise he could only try to keep.

He dodged across the floor through the milling guests, sending one man crashing into a chair, but Marcus did not pause. He had to get Sarah before one of the men grabbed her.

Through the door, he saw the men near the top of the empty flight of stairs. The child was close on their heels.

"Sarah!" Marcus shouted as loudly as he could. "Stop!"

"They've got Raffa!" she called back to him. "It's not right!"

It wasn't right. Why couldn't the bastards drop the toy? They were getting away with it, escaping. He charged up the flight, taking the steps two at a time. One of the men made a grab at Sarah, but she jerked sideways, and Marcus was only five steps away. The man changed his mind and raced after his partner.

Sarah went straight after him, quicker than Marcus would have believed. He increased his speed, but she was always two steps beyond his reach.

They went clattering up the next flight, and then the last one. The first man flung the door open onto the roof, the second man right behind him.

Sarah went straight after Raffa.

Marcus reached the door just as the second man lunged for Sarah, catching her wrist.

Marcus hit him with all his weight. He had never hit anyone so hard in his life. He felt bone crack under his fist, and the shock up his arm. The man collapsed to the ground. Was he foxing? Just in case he was, Marcus picked him up and hit him again.

Sarah had fallen, and was sitting up slowly. In the glare of the city lights she looked small and crushed.

Where was the other man? He was standing near the gate to the emergency stairway, Raffa in his hand, swinging him as if about to let him fly into space.

Sarah climbed to her feet, her eyes on Raffa.

"No!" Sarah shouted desperately. "Wayne! Don't!" She took a shaky step towards him.

This was *Wayne*? Marcus lost his temper completely. The betrayal was total and unforgivable. He charged at Wayne, who had turned to wrestle with the gate's latch, and hit Wayne with all the impetus of a man with

Sherlock Holmes's considerable height. Wayne smashed into the iron gate, dropping the giraffe as he staggered backwards, the breath knocked out of him. But before Marcus could seize him, the man's heels caught on a tile and he stumbled towards the edge of the roof.

For a moment he teetered.

Marcus grabbed Sarah, blocking her view so she would not see her mother's lover go over.

There was a long, thin wail, then silence. Marcus and Sarah stood, listening to the cries of passersby rise up from below. He bent, and picked up the limp toy giraffe, now minus a good deal of his stuffing. Beside it lay the scrap of plastic at the heart of everything. He pocketed the flash drive, and brushed some of the dust off Raffa. Very gently, he laid the child's friend in her arms.

"He can be mended," Marcus said. This time it was not a wild hope: he really did know how to do that. "It won't be difficult at all. And I think we should wipe away everything on the flash drive anyway, just in case."

There were sirens in the street below, and the maître d' was standing in the doorway to the stairs down, Maria Waterman beside him.

Sarah looked up at Marcus. "Thank you," she said gravely. "Not that I was afraid, Mr. Holmes. I was sure you would get Mummy and Raffa back, and make it all right." She gave him a slow, sweet smile.

He had not been sure—had never been less sure of anything in his life. But the child had just given him the most stellar review he'd ever received.

"It was you who got Raffa back," he pointed out.

Now her smile was radiant. "Maybe I'll be a detective when I grow up. I'll come and find you . . ."

"I'll be here," he promised. He would be. Sherlock Holmes would always be, because he would be needed.

THE CROWN JEWEL AFFAIR

by Michael Scott

I forget things.

Today is a blur, yesterday is lost in fog and the day before that gone completely.

The calendar on the wall tells me it is October, 1980, and the nurses have drawn a red circle on the 13th, which is my birthday. I was born in the year of our Lord, 1880, so this year I will turn one hundred. It is an incomprehensible age. When I am asked to what I attribute my good health, I have no real answer. I ate all the wrong foods: white bread and sugar, red meat and little fruit. However, in my favor, I rarely drank and never touched opium, hashish nor laudanum, because I never wanted to lose control. I have seen, too often, what happened to women who lost control. I never smoked cigarettes, but not for health reasons; when I was growing up, a lady never smoked.

Though my recent past is gone and faded, the further back I go, the clearer the images and memories become. When I scroll back through the years, the fog of memory clears and I remember who I was, and what I was.

Today, the nurses call me Miss Lundy and the young doctors rather familiarly call me Katherine. They ask about the past, and if I remember the Wars—First and Second—or rationing, and they wonder if I was in Dublin for the Easter Rising? And I do, I remember it all and yes I was in the city for that terrible week in 1916.

But I prefer to remember the city before the Irish revolutionaries and the British army fought in the streets and changed it forever. I lived there during its heyday, when it was beautiful, elegant, and cultured, the second capital of the Empire . . . though, like most cities, there was another side to it: diseased and pox-ridden, with one of the highest child mortality rates in Europe, home to the first venereal diseases hospital in the world.

Society knew me as Katherine Lundy, a widow—though, in truth, I had never married. By day, I was a society hostess, elegant, refined, and reserved, but like the city, I too had a dark side. When night fell, I became Madam Kitten, sometimes called The Whoremistress—though never to my face. I ran one of the most exclusive brothels in the city and my tentacles ran deep into Dublin's underworld.

What a time that was!

I may not be able to remember yesterday, but I do remember the woman I was half a century and more ago, the life I lived and the man I loved. He was a policeman and it was a crime which brought us together. He believed I had stolen the Irish Crown Jewels.

Katherine Lundy woke at five minutes before noon. Even if she had only been to bed with the dawn, she would open her eyes just before the city trembled with the sound of the noon-day bells. In a city divided by religion, the bells simply marked midday for the Protestant and Church of Ireland Dubliners, but for the majority Catholic faithful, they were a call to prayer.

Absently counting down the peals, Katherine sat up in bed and settled back on the pillows. On cue, as the last of the chimes faded, there was a discreet tap on the bedroom door. Katherine started to smile as Tilly Cusack appeared, carrying a tray with tea, toast, and the morning papers.

"Why do I employ maids, when you insist on bringing me tea every morning . . ." Katherine began and then stopped. The flame-haired, red-cheeked woman was followed by a large shaven-headed man whose thick ears and twisted nose suggested a former career as a boxer. Katherine's smile faded: she could count on the fingers of one hand the number of times Mickey Woods had stood in her private chambers. "Good morning, Mickey."

"Good morning, ma'am, though technically," he added, "it's more of an afternoon." The huge man stood at the foot of the bed and twirled a grease-shined bowler hat in his hands as Tilly poured tea from a solid silver service into almost transparent china.

"I take it we have a problem," Katherine said finally.

"A situation," Mickey said in a whisper. In his youth, a jezail bullet had damaged his larynx during the Battle of Maiwand, rendering him incapable of raising his voice.

Tilly perched on the end of the bed. On other mornings, she would quickly run through the events of the previous night in the score of houses owned and controlled by Madam Kitten: the number of guests, the amount of food, drink, laudanum, and opium consumed, the most popular girls and boys—and, the all-important profit at the end of the night. Tilly would also report if the services of Mickey, or one of the twenty men under his command, had been called upon.

"Well, it cannot be too bad," Katherine said, "at least you've not killed someone tonight."

"Not tonight," he rasped. "How did you know?"

"You're still wearing your work clothes and boots. And there's no blood on them. You've not washed your hands, and your knuckles are not bruised."

The big man looked down at his hands and grinned. "Could have used a shillelagh," he suggested. He carried a short length of iron-hard blackthorn tucked into his belt.

"You like using your hands, Mickey." Katherine looked from Mickey to Tilly. "Problem with one of the girls . . . or guests?"

"No. All in all, a quiet night," Tilly said, with just the hint of her Cockney upbringing audible under a flat Dublin accent.

"So, there is no problem, but there is a situation?" Katherine said.

"There's been a robbery," Mickey whispered.

Katherine's lace nightdress slipped off one shoulder. "Were we robbed?" she asked quickly, a touch of disbelief in her voice.

Tilly and Mickey shook their heads.

"A client . . . a girl?"

"No," Tilly said, a broad smile curling her lips. "No one would dare."

"Enough with the teasing . . ."

"The Crown Jewels," Mickey rasped. "Someone's only gone and nicked the Irish Crown Jewels."

Katherine started to smile at the thought, but then it faded as she worked through the ramifications. "Who did it? Anyone we know?"

Mickey shook his head. "I shook down everyone this morning. They all deny it and you know none of them would even think about lying to me. This is not a local crew. And none of the fences have been offered the stones."

"This will be bad for business," Katherine said slowly. "Very, very bad. The king was due to wear those jewels next month when he came over from London."

"He's already taken a personal interest in the case," Mickey said. "My sources tell me that Scotland Yard is sending an Inspector Kane to investigate. He's got a fearsome reputation."

"The police will be after every fence and jewel thief in the city. Sooner or later one of them will mention me."

"No secret that Madam Kitten likes her jewelry," Tilly said, "and will pay a good price for them."

Katherine sat back into the pillows and drew her knees up to her chest, then wrapped her arms around her shins and dropped her chin onto her kneecaps. In that moment, she looked at least a decade younger than her twenty-seven years. "You know I've often thought about snatching them," she said softly. She glanced over at Mickey. "We looked into it a couple of years ago."

"We did. Would have been a piece of piss, too."

"Why didn't you?" Tilly wondered.

"I have nicer pieces—certainly much more valuable pieces—although the thought of wearing the Crown Jewels of Ireland really appealed to me. But I knew that something like this would put us under a spotlight." She smiled, and her entire face lit up. "And we do prefer the shadows."

Mickey suddenly turned and padded silently across the room, then snatched the door open to reveal a startled-looking housemaid, with her hand raised to knock. She ignored the huge man and looked across to the woman in the bed. "Begging your pardon ma'am, but you've a visitor."

Katherine and Tilly looked at one another. Visitors to the four-story house on Gloucester Street were strictly by appointment, and always under cover of darkness.

"He asked for Madam Kitten by name," the housemaid said a little breathlessly.

"And did he give you a name in return?" Katherine asked.

The housemaid handed a card to Mickey, who carried it over to Katherine. She turned it over in her hands. "Unexceptional paper." She brought it to her nose and breathed in. "No smell of tobacco or snuff and just a hint of carbolic soap. God, I hope it's not one of the Legion of Mary again!" The staunchly Catholic organization had recently moved into the brothel-lined street and begun a campaign to save the fallen women. Katherine held the card up and tilted it to the light. *"Dermot Corcoran, Esq.,"* she read. "A rather conventional font on medium paper stock. Interesting: there is neither title nor address." She turned it over. "Ah. Our visitor has added something in a neat copperplate hand. *Insp. DMP.*"

Mickey started. "Inspector, Dublin Metropolitan Police."

"One of ours?" Katherine asked.

Tilly shook her head. "No one by that name on our payroll."

Katherine looked at the maid. "And he asked for me by name?"

"He did, ma'am. I gave him all the usual excuses, but he simply stepped into the Morning Room and said he'd wait."

"Did he come in a cab?" Mickey asked.

"I looked," the maid said, "but there was no one waiting outside."

Katherine nodded and threw back the covers. "Tell Mr. Corcoran that Madam Kitten will see him shortly. Offer him tea and the morning papers." The maid bobbed a quick curtsey and disappeared.

Katherine stood by the side of the bed and peered through the lace curtains. Her bedroom was at the rear of the house with an uninspiring view across the backs of the neighboring gardens to the streets beyond. "A visit from a police inspector on the morning the jewels are stolen: that's not a coincidence."

Tilly and Mickey nodded in agreement.

"Mickey, check the area. Make sure we're not about to be raided. Tilly, find out what you can about this Inspector Corcoran." She looked over the small ormolu clock on the marble mantelpiece. "Let him wait awhile. I will see him in an hour."

She would make him wait, he knew that. An hour, maybe an hour and a half, but she would see him: her curiosity would ensure that. Ignoring the morning papers, Dermot Corcoran sipped tea from a wafer-thin china cup, sitting in a room that would not have looked out of place in any of the great houses in Merrion Square—not that he had actually sat in one of those drawing rooms. Lowly police inspectors did not investigate the crimes of the wealthy. The furniture was new and in good taste, showing no wear, the heavy flocked wallpaper was unmarked and the carpet pristine. Even though the room evidently saw no use, a low fire crackled in the grate and he was sure if he ran his finger across the white marble mantelpiece, he would find no trace of ash or dust. Curiously, no art hung on the wall, and the trinkets on the occasional tables and mantelpiece were surprisingly tawdry. Crudely painted figurines, pieces of glass and pottery: they looked like gifts a child would bring back from a journey. But as far as he knew, there were no children in this house.

Dermot Corcoran stood and peered through fine lace curtains onto the street. Georgian houses lined both sides of Gloucester Street. At the top of the street, when it curved onto the main thoroughfare of Sackville Street, the houses retained all of their former glory and elegance, but as the street dipped, so too did the quality, until the once-grand houses at the bottom of the street were little better than slums. And every house was a brothel. Some, like Madam Kitten's, were the flash houses, catering to the wealthy, where the very finest food, wines, and opiates were available, along with exquisite and guaranteed disease-free girls. The houses at the very bottom of the street and in the surrounding warren of alleyways and lanes were the kips and stews, where the alcohol was watered if you were lucky and poisonous if you were not. There, girls and boys were bought for pennies and a tryst—a knee-trembler—might last only a few minutes.

This once-elegant street was now the cancer at the heart of Dublin, the second city of the British Empire. Crime, perversion, and disease were rampant and it was ruled by a series of terrifying women: Bella Cohen, Mrs. Mack, Long Liz, and, of course, the mysterious Madam Kitten. All of Dublin, from the Viceroy in the Park to the urchin on the wharves, knew her name, but no one knew the woman. He knew a little more than most, and none of what he knew made sense. She was an enigma.

The door behind him opened and he turned, expecting the maid, but a huge shaven-headed middle-aged man stepped into the room. Dermot knew him by reputation: this was Mickey—never Michael—Woods. Former soldier, former boxer, and now Madam Kitten's Bully. Her enforcer. The big man closed the door, folded his arms, and lay back against it, then slowly looked the police inspector up and down.

Dermot felt his heart quicken.

Mickey's voice was a terrifying whisper. "I'm to check you for weapons—guns, knives, sticks."

The young inspector started to shake his head.

"No one gets to see the Madam without being checked out," Mickey continued, "and if I find they're carrying anything they shouldn't be, then they don't get to see the Madam. Plus, they get their legs broken," he added with a gap-toothed smile.

Dermot Corcoran drew himself up to his full height and shrugged out of his wool jacket. "I assure you I am unarmed." He was pleased that his voice remained steady. "This is a courtesy call," he said, turning in a complete circle.

Suddenly Mickey was towering over him, and Dermot found his eyes on a level with the man's scarred throat. "No disrespect," the bully whispered, "but I've found that coppers often lie." With quick practiced movements, he ran his hands across Dermot's arms, around his chest and then up and down both sides of his legs. Satisfied, he stepped back, picked up the inspector's discarded coat, and checked the pockets before holding it by the shoulders for the younger man to slip into. "Madam Kitten will see you now," he said. He stepped back to open the door, and a woman stepped into the room.

Dermot Corcoran was expecting an old crone: most of the women who ran the Dublin brothels were ex-working girls who wore their life of dissipation and excess on their faces and bodies, but he was shocked to discover that the figure in the doorway was tall and slender, elegant in a high-necked, long-sleeved widow's black traced with hundreds of pearls around the throat and sleeves. Her face was concealed behind a thick black lace veil.

"Thank you Mickey."

There was a second surprise when she spoke. He was expecting to hear a Dublin accent roughened by the rasp of whiskey and cigarettes; instead the voice was elegant, educated, and English.

"I'll be outside," the big man whispered, glaring at the inspector.

Madam laid a black gloved hand on the bully's arm. "I am sure I will be perfectly safe with the inspector. If one cannot trust the police, then who can be trusted?"

Katherine Lundy perched on the edge of a high back Chippendale. "Please sit, Inspector. Or would you prefer 'Mister'?"

"Either. Miss . . . Misses . . . Madam. What do I call you?" The young man returned to his chair and sank back into it, then pulled himself forward when he discovered that the woman was looking down on him.

"Madam Kitten will suffice." Katherine folded her hands in her lap, resting them lightly atop a black clutch bag. It held a silver-plated, pearl-handled Derringer, and the back of the bag was slit to allow her to pull the gun free without opening the purse. "How may I help you, Inspector?"

Dermot opened his mouth to reply, but Katherine held up her right hand.

"And is this an official or an unofficial call?"

He hesitated just a fraction too long.

"Unofficial then," she said evenly. "I gathered as much since you did not arrive in a police wagon, or even by public cab. That suggested you did not wish to leave a record of this visit. And since I can see dried red mud on your shoes, and the eternal road works on Marlborough Street are of that distinctive color, then I must conclude that you walked."

Dermot glanced down at his highly polished shoes; there was a rim of hard red dirt on the soles. "You are very perceptive."

"It comes with my unusual profession. My sex are naturally observant, but women in my business need to be even more so. It keeps us alive."

"I take it you've had me checked out in the hour I was waiting?"

Katherine nodded, silk whispering across her face. "Of course. We would not be meeting if you had not passed muster."

"Then you will know that I take no bribes and am not in the pocket of any of the madams on this street. I am a good police officer, with a tolerable arrest record."

"You specialize in smuggling and contraband. And yet you have come about the theft of the Crown Jewels." She saw his blink of surprise. "Come, come, Inspector: what else could bring you here this afternoon? It is the talk of the city. But surely, jewelry thefts are outside your remit?"

"Yes . . . and no," he said.

Katherine cocked her head to one side. "Which is it?"

"It is a little outside my specialty, but every available officer has been tasked with finding the jewels. The king is sailing into Kingstown in a few weeks. He is due to wear the jewels when he invests some Irish knights. They must be found before then . . . and I want to find those jewels," he added vehemently.

"You must be desperate indeed to come to me. Why is that, I wonder?" she asked, and then, beneath the veil, she smiled. "You are a brilliant police officer—you must be to have reached the rank of inspector while still not yet thirty. Your accent is Dublin and is neither refined nor overeducated, so you do not come from money or have a sponsor within the force."

The inspector blinked in surprise and then nodded. "I have made my own way."

"And you are a Catholic in a predominantly Protestant and Masonic organization."

The inspector straightened. "Your researchers have been busy."

"Not so. I saw the impression of a silver crucifix beneath your shirt when you sat forward. You are not yet engaged but there is a young woman in your life. And before you can ask for her hand, you need to advance in your career."

Corcoran sat back, startled. "No one in the force knows that I am seeing a young lady; that cannot be in my file."

"The skin on your upper lip is a lighter shade than the rest of your flesh, suggesting that you had worn a mustache for a very long time. The only reason a gentleman shaves off his mustache is if a lady requests it. And only a man in love would do so."

Color flooded the inspector's cheeks and he raised his thumb and index finger to smooth down the nonexistent mustaches. "You are correct. There was a mustache and there is a lady. She thought the mustache made me look old . . . and it reminded her of her father."

"It might also have left a rash upon her skin," Katherine added gently.

The inspector blinked in surprise. "I did not think of that."

"Your lady friend did. You might think about asking her how she knew that a beard could cause a rash. That sort of knowledge only comes with experience."

Katherine watched the thought flicker behind his eyes and a quick tracery of emotions ran across his face. It appeared that the young inspector was already suspicious about his lady friend.

"Thank you for your insights, Madam Kitten. I will consider them carefully. And you are once again correct: I am a Catholic in a Protestant force. I have reached my present position at least a decade too early. And now I have nowhere to go. But if I were to solve this case, then it would bring my name to the attention of my superiors and even the king himself. My advancement would be guaranteed, and my lady friend's father could not refuse me when I ask for her hand."

"And you believe I stole the jewels?" Katherine asked bluntly.

Dermot blinked in surprise. "You are the obvious suspect."

"Not that obvious if only you have come to that conclusion."

"I suspected that you had paid off the others."

"Slipping a constable a few shillings or a free ride with the girl of his choice is very different to what you are suggesting, which is bribery on an industrial scale. And, may I remind you, the jewels are both ugly and really not that valuable: Brazilian stones, rose diamonds, some emeralds, rubies, and enamel. Recently valued at just over thirty thousand pounds and worth a lot less than that if they were broken apart for the individual stones.

Allow me to be definitive, Inspector: I did not take the jewels. You have my word upon it—though I am sure that the word of a woman like me carries no weight." She watched color touch his cheeks again and wondered why.

"I understand that not all women who enter your business do so voluntarily . . ."

"None," she snapped. "This life is not only the last resort, it is often the only resort. At least I can offer the women in my employ a roof over their heads, clean food and water, medical care and protection." Her gloved hand waved in the direction of the street. "Practically every house in this street and those adjoining are brothels; we give employment to hundreds of girls, but there are many hundreds more on the streets who do not have the protection of a house. And why? Because the Government in Whitehall allows us to exist. It needs us."

The inspector started to shake his head. "I cannot believe—"

"Mr. Corcoran, there are more whores in this city than in London and Manchester combined. That is because we are a garrison city, a port city. We have English regiments training in the Royal Barracks and on the Curragh, and the quays are busy with British warships and merchantmen from around the world. All those soldiers and sailors are looking for relief. It is much easier to contain them in this triangle of streets than to have them wander the city, or have the working girls mixing with the women of quality."

The inspector sat back in the chair and licked suddenly dry lips. "I never thought . . ."

Katherine's laugh was bitter. "Our existence suits the establishment. They may rail against us in Parliament or from the pulpit, but they come here in the evening. Would you be shocked to learn that when our present king was undergoing his military training in this city, he often visited these houses? Do you want me to show you the presents he left the girls, or the receipts he signed?"

Dermot shook his head.

"I am many things, Inspector: a madam, a thief, a liar, but I am not a hypocrite. If you have done any research on me, then you will know that my word is my bond."

He nodded. "I heard you were to be trusted."

Beneath the veil, Katherine smiled. "And what else did you hear?"

"I heard that you have few enemies—"

"I am sure there are a few."

"—few enemies left alive," he finished.

Katherine stood and crossed to the window. Through the fine lace curtains, she watched the scattering of people—mostly women and children—moving up and down the quiet street. An occasional carriage or dray moved down the dung-scattered cobbles. When darkness fell, everything would change. The street would be lined with carriages with blacked-out crests and all the houses would be ablaze with lights. "What will the police do?" she asked suddenly.

Dermot heaved out of the low chair and joined the veiled woman at the window. Standing so close to her, he could almost make out her features through the lace. Her eyes, he decided, were bright green. "Given that this area is the heart of crime in the city, I would imagine that they will flood the streets with officers. They will go house to house, interviewing everyone. There will be arrests; men like Mickey have form. He will be taken in for questioning. Doesn't matter who you've paid off, this crime is too big, too public. The police will need to be seen to be doing something."

"And how long will that last?" she asked.

"Until the jewels are found, or the public loses interest. At the very least until after the king leaves."

"It will close down everything for weeks."

"It will."

Katherine waved a gloved hand at the street. "And how will the women earn their living for those weeks? Who will pay the rent or feed their starving children? There will be evictions and deaths."

The police inspector clasped his hands behind his back. "I never thought of that," he admitted.

"And do you know something, Inspector? No one will care. Women and children will die in these streets because the king's baubles were taken."

"I will take my leave of you, Madam Kitten," Dermot said suddenly. "And let me thank you. You have given me a proper reason to find the jewels. Something more important that my own rather petty ambition. You have my word that I will do my utmost to find those jewels." Stepping back, he bowed quickly—an old-fashioned, almost courtly gesture.

Madam Kitten spun around to look at him. And then, slowly and deliberately, she raised the veil off her face and looked at him with bright, grass-green eyes.

Caught off-guard, the inspector's mouth opened and closed wordlessly. Madam Kitten would never be called beautiful, but she was handsome. "Thank you, Inspector," she said very softly, laying a gloved hand on his arm. Color flooded his cheeks. "Mickey," she said, not raising her voice.

The door opened and the huge man filled it, an ugly twist of blackthorn stick in his hands. He stopped in surprise when he saw the couple standing together with the woman's veil pushed back off her face.

"Mickey, bring around the carriage, we need to take Inspector Corcoran back to the Castle."

"I can walk."

"I am going with you."

Both men looked at her in surprise.

"And you will return here at eight o'clock this evening."

The inspector blinked in surprise. "I will?"

"You will," she said simply.

"Why?"

"Because I will tell you then who stole the jewels."

Hopelessly confused, Dermot looked from the woman to Mickey and then back again. "You will? Why? How?"

"Because you set a thief to catch a thief," she said, spinning away in a cloud of delicate lavender perfume. "Give me thirty minutes and I will join you. Remember: eight o'clock, Inspector. Mickey will meet you at the corner of Marlborough Street and bring you in the back way. A man like you should not be seen visiting a house like this."

"A man like me: a policeman?"

"A good man," she called over her shoulder.

Dermot Corcoran looked at Mickey. "I've never been called a good man before."

"I'll wager you've never met a woman like Madam Kitten before either."

❖

Tilly Cusack sat on the edge of the bed and watched Katherine dress. "And if I was to tell you that I think this is a very bad idea . . ."

"I would listen to you and then ignore you."

"Can I at least come with you?" Tilly's Cockney accent was more pronounced now, a sure indication that she was concerned.

"No. I don't think someone like me can be seen in the company of an older woman!"

"Bitch!" Tilly grinned.

Katherine spun around and spread her arms. "What do you think?"

Tilly looked her up and down. "I think you look like an apprentice clerk."

Katherine was dressed in a slightly shabby man's black suit. The cuffs on the coat and the hem on the trousers were a little long, to help disguise her wrists and ankles. Tilly had helped her bind down her breasts with gauze bandages, and a slightly overlarge shirt and waistcoat lent bulk to her slender figure. Her hair was wrapped in a tight coil on top of her head and concealed beneath a cap. A hint of five o'clock shadow on her cheeks and chin, cotton balls in her mouth, and wire-framed glasses with plain glass completed the disguise.

"Now let's see how good this get-up is," Katherine said, linking her arm through Tilly's.

Arm-in-arm, the women descended the stairs and peered into the sitting room. "Now there's something you don't see every day," Katherine murmured. The inspector and Mickey were deep in conversation over the remains of tea and biscuits.

"Bet he's telling you his war stories," Tilly said loudly. "His days in the Sixty-sixth Foot." Moving over to Mickey's shoulder, she ran her hand across the scar on his throat.

He reached up and squeezed her fingers. "Lucky to be here," he whispered. "The surgeon saved my life."

Dermot Corcoran stood and stared at the young man standing in the doorway. He frowned. "I'm usually good with names and faces," he said. "I believe we've met . . ."

"Aye, we've met," Katherine said in a masculine rasp, and then added in her own voice, "not more than thirty minutes ago, in this very room."

Once again, Dermot's mouth opened and closed, but no sound came out. Katherine looked at Tilly and Mickey. "Told you it would work."

"What is troubling you, Inspector? You've barely said a word."

The couple sat facing one another in an elegant black brougham which swayed down Sackville Street.

He shrugged. "I am not entirely sure what to say. It has been a morning of revelations. I believe I may be in shock."

"The theft of the jewels must have been a shock," she agreed with a slight smile.

Dermot grinned. "In truth, I don't care about the jewels. I was thinking more of the other surprises the day has had to offer . . ." He pulled out a battered pocket watch. "And it is not yet two o'clock."

"The day is not yet over," Madam Kitten smiled.

"And the biggest surprise of all was you."

Color touched the woman's cheeks. Surprised by the emotion, she dipped her head and focused on the cap in her hands. "Ah, the disguise . . . well, it's a useful way to be able to move through the city."

"The disguise was a shock—not a surprise—but no, I was more surprised that you would offer to help."

"The sooner we get this cleared up, the sooner my world will return to normal, and those who need to can get back to earning a living."

The inspector shook his head. "That's not what I was talking about."

"You thought I would be older: a wizened harridan."

"I've heard the stories."

"So did I. Most of them I put out myself."

"Why?" he wondered.

"We all wear masks, Inspector: by necessity, by circumstances, or by choice. The face you reveal to your fellow police officers, for example, is not the same face you show to the young lady in your life. The face you show to your superiors is not the face you would use with a criminal."

He nodded. "So Madam Kitten is an invention created to frighten and intimidate."

"All the other madams in Dublin are harridans and shrews, ex-working girls. So, Madam Kitten should be cut from the same cloth. It is something people expect, and once they get what they expect, they will not look any deeper."

The carriage lurched across sunken tram lines and the ambient sound changed. Katherine peered beyond the blind. They had entered the court-yard of Dublin Castle. The cobbled square was swarming with police, most of them concentrated around the imposing facade of the circular Bedford Tower. The carriage halted and Mickey slid back the panel in the roof and peered down. "End of the road. Place is alive with coppers." He winked at Dermot. "I'm guessing that a few will know me and it might not be good for you to be seen in my company."

"Good thinking, Mickey," Madam Kitten said, fixing the cap on her head and tucking in any stray hairs. She looked at Dermot. "How do I look?"

"Like a man," he grinned.

Mickey swung the carriage to a halt close to one wall and jumped down to open the door on that side. No one would be able to see who exited the carriage. He took her hand and helped her down. She squeezed his fingers. "I know," she said. "You were about to tell me to be careful."

"I was," he admitted. "If there's a problem and anything . . . happens," he said carefully, "just sit tight: we'll come and get you."

"I know you will. But I can look after myself."

Mickey didn't quite manage to disguise the look of disbelief on his face.

Dermot Corcoran climbed out of the carriage, blinking in the after-noon sunlight. Mickey's hand fell on his shoulders, fingers biting not quite painfully. "I'd be upset if anything were to happen to the Madam," he said.

"So would I," Dermot said, surprising them both.

"Mickey," Katherine said. "Wait for me in the street outside; I will be back within the hour. Inspector, I will see you at eight." Then, shoving her hands in her pockets and dipping her head, she strode across the cobbled courtyard, weaving her way through the assembled police officers.

"It has been a pleasure meeting you." Dermot stretched out his hand. Surprised, the big man took it. "And you were right," the inspector added, looking across the courtyard, but not finding Katherine in the mass of people. "I've never met a woman like Madam Kitten before."

⬥

At precisely eight o'clock, Dermot Corcoran stepped into Madam Kitten's private drawing room. Mickey clapped him on his shoulder and pulled the door closed.

Madam Kitten and Tilly Cusack sat on either side of a small circular card table, playing two-handed patience. Katherine was in her widow's black, but without the veil, while Tilly was wearing a spectacularly low-cut gown which had gone out of fashion a decade previously. Katherine looked up, green eyes glittering in the low gaslight, and smiled. "Why, Inspector, you look quite pink."

Tilly slapped down her cards and then wordlessly scooped half a dozen buttons from the center of the table, then twisted in her chair to look at the policeman. "Goodness me, I do believe he is blushing," she said, almost wistfully. Turning back to Katherine, she asked, "Can you remember the last time someone blushed in this house?"

"Mickey led me in through the kitchen," Dermot said. "Some women were having their supper. None of them were wearing clothes," he added. "Well, some were almost wearing clothes."

"Tilly, get Mr. Corcoran a drink. I don't think he's seen that much naked female flesh before."

"I haven't," he admitted. "Oh, and I don't drink alcohol," he added, just as Tilly was about to pour a brandy.

"I'll get you a hot chocolate," Tilly said. She stopped before the inspector, enveloping him in lavender, and looked him up and down. "A policeman who doesn't drink and blushes more often than any man I have ever met. Have you ever been in a brothel before?" she wondered.

"Never," he admitted.

She looked at him with something like awe. "Are you sure you're a real policeman?"

"Don't tease, Tilly," Katherine said. "Get the inspector his hot chocolate and I will have a coffee. Inspector, come sit with me by the fire." She moved away from the card table and took a deep wing-backed leather chair set at an angle to the glowing fire. Dermot settled into the facing chair.

"I know there's really no need of a fire in the middle of summer," Katherine said quietly, "but I love the light, don't you?"

"I do. But I usually don't light a fire in July."

"Why not?"

"By the time I'm finished for the day and get back to Drumcondra, where I live, it's close to nine and too late to light one. And, I couldn't afford it on my salary."

Katherine sat back into the chair, until she was almost lost in shadow. Firelight danced red and golden in her eyes. "If it is difficult for you to survive on your salary, then how will your young lady cope? Would you be able to tell her not to light a fire, to scrimp and save her pennies? She is obviously used to better things?"

"She is, and yes, it will be difficult."

"You can see how so many of your colleagues begin the slide into taking little donations to supplement their wage."

"I don't judge them. I did, when I was a lot younger, but no more. They do what they have to survive. But it certainly makes my job harder," he added.

Tilly returned with two cups on a silver tray. The room immediately filled with the odor of hot chocolate and rich coffee.

Katherine lifted the coffee off the tray. "Tilly, lower the lights and make sure we're not disturbed. We do not want a repetition of last week's adventure."

"I've two men on the stairs and another outside the door."

"What happened last week?" Dermot asked when Tilly had left. "Or is that an impertinent question?"

Katherine smiled. "A young man somehow found his way into this room. He presumed I was one of the girls and made a very crude suggestion."

Dermot sipped the chocolate. "What happened?"

"I shot him."

The inspector sat bolt upright. "You shot him!"

"A flesh wound in the thigh only, I assure you."

"I didn't see any reports of a shooting in your file."

Katherine laughed. "Oh, it is not in my file."

"You sound confident."

"I have a copy delivered to me every week."

Dermot wrapped both hands around the cup and sipped. "Somehow that does not surprise me."

Katherine brought the coffee cup to her lips to hide her smile. "What did you discover today?"

"Nothing," he said. "Nobody knows anything. The last time the jewels were seen was on the eleventh of June, when Sir Arthur Vicars showed them to some visiting librarian. What is extraordinary, however, is how casually he is taking it. It is almost as if he expects the stones to turn up."

"I believe he does," she said enigmatically, and waved away his next question. "Suspects?" she asked.

"No one. Everyone associated with the jewels are gentlemen of impeccable character."

Katherine laughed softly. She raised her chin slightly to the noise from the rooms above. "This house is filled with gentlemen of impeccable character."

"I did discover something odd—amusing too."

"Tell me."

"When the jewels were moved into the Bedford Tower four years ago, a special strong room was constructed. An impregnable Radcliffe and Horner safe was purchased to hold the jewels." Dermot started to smile. "The only problem was that when the safe arrived, it was discovered that the door to the strong room was too narrow to admit it. So the safe was temporarily moved to the library. It's been there ever since."

"Who holds the keys to the safe?" Katherine asked.

"There are two keys. Both are in the possession of Sir Arthur Vicars." He stopped and sipped the chocolate. "Perhaps a duplicate key . . ."

Katherine shook her head. "Mickey checked with all the locksmiths today. No one has been approached to make a duplicate. What does that tell us?" she asked.

"That one of the original keys was used."

She nodded. "So someone close to Sir Arthur."

"Or Sir Arthur himself."

Katherine shook her head. "He has too much to lose: pension, reputation, position."

"Then I am at a loss. Perhaps it is a joke?"

Katherine remained silent.

"You do not think so?"

"I spoke with the cleaning lady, Mrs. Farrell, today."

Dermot sat back in the chair. "I did not know there was a cleaning lady. No one has mentioned her before."

Katherine's smile was humorless. "Servants and children are always the invisible observers. It would be a mistake to ignore their testimony."

Dermot nodded.

"Mrs. Farrell finishes early in the morning. Last Wednesday, when she turned up for work, she discovered the door to the entrance to the tower unlocked and open. And then again, last Saturday, she arrived to find the door to the library ajar."

"And did she report it?" He pulled out a notebook and flipped through the pages. "There is no record of it."

"She told Mr. Stivey, the messenger, and he, in turn, reported it directly to Vicars."

"But why didn't Vicars report it?"

"You must ask Sir Arthur that. I also spoke with Mr. Stivey. He told me that Vicars took the news with some equanimity and was apparently unperturbed."

"How odd."

Dermot sipped his chocolate, watching Katherine's eyes over the rim of his cup. Finally, he sighed. "Your two-hour investigation has discovered more than the rest of the DMP. Do you know who stole the jewels?"

"I can tell you that Sir Arthur Vicars shares a house with Francis Shackleton, younger brother of the arctic explorer."

"I knew that. I've seen Shackleton. A rather vain and foppish young man."

"Who happens to have accrued some spectacular debts to some unfortunately unforgiving people." Katherine's face appeared out of the gloom. "The IOUs are on the floor beside your chair."

Dermot put down his cup and picked up the scraps of paper, turning them to the firelight. "How did you get these?"

"I bought them for a percentage of their worth."

"Why would you do that?"

"Oh, Inspector, remember who I am and what I am. Leverage is always useful. Now, see who has guaranteed the notes."

Dermot turned over the page. "Vicars!" He looked at Katherine. "Vicars guarantees Shackleton's debt. But how could he afford that on his salary?"

"He could not," she said simply. "He asked a friend of his, Frank Goldney, to take on the debt, which he did."

"What a tangled mess . . ."

"There is another twist. I am presuming that you did not know that Shackleton is an intimate of Lord Haddo."

The inspector sat bolt upright. "The son of the Viceroy?"

"The same."

"And when you say 'intimate . . .'" he asked cautiously.

"Both gentlemen are also very close to the Duke of Argyll, who has a fondness for guardsmen."

"Guardsmen?"

"Guardsmen."

"How did you discover all this?"

"Why, by listening, Inspector. People do love to gossip. The Castle is abuzz with stories of Vicars and his entourage of handsome young men. Did you know that they frequent some of the flash houses at the bottom of the street—those which cater solely to men? And that they sometimes dress in women's clothing and . . . wear the jewels as part of their costumes?"

"Oh God!" Dermot leaned forward and put his head in his hands.

"And that the jewels have disappeared before, when the boys accidentally forgot them at one of their parties?"

Dermot sat back into the chair. "You have been busy. And, let me say that you seem to be enjoying yourself."

Katherine nodded. "One in my position is rarely given an opportunity to exercise her abilities, although I have spent my entire life watching and listening. It makes me quite suited to the role of detective, don't you think?"

"What should I do?" he asked suddenly.

"This is a scandal, and scandals destroy careers. If you identify the thief, then you earn the enmity of him and his friends. If you continue to investigate you will bring yourself to their attention and even if you make no accusation, then your career is destroyed."

"So what should I do?" he asked again.

"Do nothing. The jewels will either mysteriously turn up, or they will not."

"But the police will still descend on these streets and close your businesses. This morning you spoke about children starving . . ."

Katherine leaned forward, firelight turning her face golden. Her smile was feral. "About an hour ago a letter was delivered to both the Viceroy and the head of the Dublin Metropolitan Police outlining some of the facts of the case. There will be no real investigation, I assure you; the scandal would involve the crown, and Edward now works hard to distance himself from the excesses of his youth. I am sorry that you will not get that promotion, however. Your future fiancée will be disappointed."

"There will be other cases," he said. "And I have waited this long to propose; another few months will not make any real difference."

"Women do not like to wait, Inspector. Propose. If she loves you, then she will say yes, in spite of your circumstances."

"And if she says no?"

"If she loves you she will say yes," Katherine said softly.

Finishing his hot chocolate, he stood. "I will take my leave of you. All in all, it has been quite the day."

Katherine rose and stretched out her hand. Dermot bowed over it. "Thank you for your help, Madam Kitten."

"Katherine. Call me Katherine."

"Will I see you again, Katherine?"

"I have no doubts about it."

Dermot Corcoran paused with his hand on the door handle and turned to face the woman lost in the shadows. "You never did say who stole the jewels . . ."

"Inspector. Follow the money. And then, when you have eliminated the impossible, whatever remains, however improbable . . ."

". . . must be the truth."

◈

The jewels never did turn up and, as I predicted, the scandal destroyed careers. Inspector Kane came over from Scotland Yard, investigated and discovered the culprit. His report was never published, then mysteriously disappeared.

Vicars went to his grave convinced that Shackleton had stolen the jewels. He openly accused him, even going so far to include the accusation in his Last Will and Testament. I know that Shackleton was exonerated by the investigating Royal Commission, despite some strong evidence that if he was not involved, then he knew who had stolen the jewels. But Shackleton had friends in very high places and his brother, Ernest, was about to embark on his Nimrod Expedition to Antarctica. Vicars lost his position, his pension, and ultimately his life, when he was shot on the lawn of his home by the IRA in 1921.

Years later, I learned that Shackleton had been charged with fraud and spent some time in prison in England. When he was discharged, he changed his name and disappeared.

No one ever looked too closely at Goldney, the man who had rather recklessly guaranteed Shackleton's debts. He went on to become the Mayor of Canterbury. When he died a decade after the theft, amongst his possessions was discovered a cache of items he purloined over the years from the various offices and positions he had held.

Perhaps the last word belongs to Vicars, a distant cousin of Sir Arthur Conan Doyle, who told a Daily Express *reporter: "The detectives might well say that it is an affair for a Sherlock Holmes to investigate."*

UNDERSTUDY IN SCARLET

by Hallie Ephron

It's not an open casting call, Angela Cassano realizes as she takes in the emptiness of director Glenn Lancaster's outer office. The gloomy space, on the second floor over storefronts on Santa Monica in Beverly Hills, has rough stucco walls painted off-white. The furnishings are chrome and ebony and black leather, and the stale air smells faintly of cigar. Her appointment was at two. At three she's still waiting for Lancaster to emerge from his inner sanctum.

"They want you," her agent had said when he called, sounding as surprised as she was that a remake of *A Scandal in Bohemia* was afoot, this time as a major motion picture. Same director, same actor as Sherlock Holmes, and they wanted her to read for the role she played twenty-five years ago: Irene Adler, the one woman who outsmarted the great detective.

Was she interested? Of course she was. The only gig she's got lined up is summer stock in Ojai playing Martha in *Who's Afraid of Virginia Woolf?* But she's also more than a bit wary. She and Lancaster didn't part on the best of terms, not after she refused to sleep with him—something he seemed to think was his due for casting her in his movie. Bygones, she hopes. Because if he were holding a grudge, why would he be calling her agent?

The office suite hasn't changed much since she was here last. The door to a small inner office stands open, and Angela has a dim memory of Lancaster's bookkeeper working in the now-empty room, his desk piled high with computer printouts. The receptionist, who is studiously avoiding eye contact, could be the same one Angela had to get past years ago. The woman's chin sags and her hair is more salt than pepper.

Angela sits up, straightening her shoulders, fluffing her hair, and bunching a bit more cleavage into the deep V-neck of her top. She crosses her legs and tugs at the hem of her pencil skirt.

Last night she got out the old script and put on a slinky red silk gown like the one that she wore in the film. She practiced her lines, watching herself in the mirror. Then practiced again with her eyes closed. She could feel Irene Adler spring back to life inside her.

She's capable of far more nuance than when she first played the part, though reviewers were kind. The *LA Times* critic called that performance, her first in a starring role, "luminous" and "dangerous."

She's still luminous. Still dangerous. And at forty-five, far more suited to the role of the retired opera singer whose torrid love affair with the Crown Prince of Bohemia—captured in a compromising photograph— threatens to derail that Royal's impending marriage.

Her best line in *Scandal* is the painfully grammatically correct, "I love and am loved by a better man than he." She can deliver it sad and brooding. Or defiant. Or proud. Or secretive. She can even make the statement sound self-deluding if that's what they want. Or start one way and end another.

Anthony Fox, the actor who played Sherlock opposite her Irene, is reprising his role in the remake, too. Even way back then, he was on the downhill side of a semi-distinguished acting career. The *Times* reviewer called his performance "solid." After *Scandal* he found himself showered with cameos in films like *Scream IV* and *The Muppet Mystery*. Not the Royal Shakespeare, but it was a living. On top of which he had points on

the back end of *Scandal,* which Angela did not. That's turned out to be
the gift that keeps giving.

Because who could have predicted that their *Scandal* would develop
a cult following? At classic film festivals, Angela's Irene Adler is nearly
as recognizable as Carrie Fisher's Princess Leia. Fans come to midnight
showings dressed in character and intone famous lines like "To Sherlock
Holmes she was always *the* woman." They boo and throw popcorn at
the screen when the king dismisses his former lover as "a well-known
adventuress."

At last the door to Lancaster's inner office opens. "Angela!" The man
himself emerges. He doesn't look half bad. Black T-shirt tucked into jeans,
sockless loafers, his shaved head gleaming. That weird scruffy beard is
new. He bounds over to her with the intensity of a much younger man.

"Darling!" he says. "There you are." He bends down and, pure reflex,
she crosses her arms over her chest as she leans in for what turns out to
be a perfectly innocent air kiss. He whispers, "There's someone I need
you to meet."

Coming out of the office behind Lancaster is a young woman. A tiny
sprite, pale and ethereal as a ghost, she's got to be a natural blonde. Her
tight blue jeans are artfully ripped like the ones that cost hundreds. She's
carrying an enormous pumpkin-colored bag, its straps too long and floppy
to be a real Birkin.

"Angela, this is Ruby Lake," Lancaster says.

"Miss Cassano!" Ruby says, holding back, shy. "I'm such a fan girl.
I've seen you in this movie a gajillion times. I just hope I can be as good."
Angela doesn't get time to consider what that means because the girl, she's
barely out of her teens if she's a day, adds, "And I adored *Wallflower.*"

Angela is taken aback. She stands. "You saw it?"

"At Sundance. It was great. Really terrific."

"Thank you so much," Angela says, and she means it. *Wallflower*
was a low-budget film that she wrote and directed, and when it got into
Sundance a few years ago Angela thought maybe, just maybe she'd break
into Tinseltown's most exclusive boys' club. But despite rave reviews, the
film didn't get picked up. No opportunities to direct more motion pictures
came flooding her way.

Angela can count on two hands the number of people she knows who've actually seen her movie. She can tell from Lancaster's blank expression that he's not one of them.

"I'm so looking forward to working with you," Ruby says. "I can use all the help I can get."

Help? It's not until then, as Angela registers the look of undisguised pity that the receptionist is sending her way, that the penny drops and Angela's stomach goes queasy.

"Won't Ruby make a splendid Irene Adler?" Lancaster says, standing back and appraising his prize. Confirming the worst.

Angela's face burns with humiliation and her insides feel thick. How is she supposed to respond? She wills her face to go expressionless. She's an actress. She can handle this.

Lancaster turns to Angela. "And of course, you'll make a fabulous Mrs. Hudson. One for the ages."

She swallows the lump in her throat. From infamous *femme fatale* to iconic landlady who, in the script, doesn't even get a name. The thought should have cracked her up but instead it's put her on the verge of tears.

"I'm so delighted to meet you," she says to Ruby, forcing a smile and extending her hand. She imagines that Ruby is her sister's daughter Gracie, an adorable precocious six-year-old. But the person Ruby actually reminds her of is Angela herself, twenty-five years ago. Beautiful, sexy, ambitious, more than a little insecure, and just nineteen when she walked out of this same office with the role of Irene Adler. She hopes Ruby can handle Lancaster's advances, since the old dog's undoubtedly up to his usual tricks.

Angela wants to kill her agent. Deliberately ambiguous, that's what he was. Knew he had to be in order to get her to show up for this. But really, what had Angela been smoking that made her think Lancaster would still yearn for the smoldering sexuality and timeless beauty that only Angela Cassano could bring to the role? It's no secret that Hollywood considers any woman a day over forty far too old to play opposite a man who's pushing seventy. Only British leading ladies are allowed to age.

"See you," Ruby says, waving as she backs into the hall. Angela wants to follow her out, but the bitter truth is she needs the work. So she follows Lancaster into his office and takes a seat across his massive desk.

The walls are hung with movie memorabilia. A neon sign that reads BATES MOTEL NO VACANCY. A bowler hat like the one Malcolm Mac-Dowell wore in *A Clockwork Orange*. A rack of five flintlock pistols that would have been at home on the *Bounty*. She also recognizes a full-length portrait of herself as Irene Adler. It's a 25-year-old prop from the original *Scandal in Bohemia*.

"You were fabulous," Lancaster says, following her gaze to the portrait.

I know. "And now you want me for Mrs. Hudson?" Is he being deliberately cruel or can he be that clueless?

"Of course I want you. And not just for Mrs. Hudson. I also want you to be our stand-in for Ruby."

"Stand-in." She tries to say it without sneering.

"You know the plot. You know the character. You'll be perfect, and you'll be able to mentor Ruby on her performance. After all, you set the gold standard."

What he wants her to do is smile. Bask in praise from on high. What she wants to do is scream. Tell him to take his gold standard and . . .

She takes a cleansing breath and waits. She hears the voice of her first acting coach: *Don't rush to fill a silence.*

"I'm prepared to pay you well. Very well," Lancaster says. She says nothing. He holds up a finger. "Supporting player." A second finger. "Stand-in." He balls his fist. "More for any time you need to step in for her."

Step in for her? "Why would I need to do that?"

"She's"—he looks for the word—"inexperienced. She's done some commercials and worked a season on *Mean Girls*." Angela's never watched it. "This is her first major film role."

"Talented?"

"Very. But learning the ropes. Having you there will be a godsend. If she needs advice. Shaping. And you'll be there to pick up the slack if she should have to take a sick day."

Actors don't get sick days during a movie shoot. Not unless they're dying. "What, she has a drinking problem?"

Lancaster shakes his head.

"Drugs?"

He scoffs.

"Neurotic?"

He raises his eyebrows, allowing that might be the case. "She's green. And she can be"—he gazes past Angela—"volatile."

It sounds weird. Why would Lancaster hire a drama queen for a role she's not ready to play? It's not as if there's a shortage of talent in this town. But it's his movie, he can do whatever the hell he pleases, which apparently includes casting Angela Cassano as Mrs. Hudson.

It's hardly the "comeback" she envisioned. As she recalls, Mrs. Hudson has three scenes, and mostly they involve serving tea. Angela can't be luminous or dangerous. She can only be old.

As Ruby's stand-in, Angela will have to be on the set much more, moving through Irene Adler's motions while the lights and camera setups are tweaked. But no screen time. The only up-side is the extra she'll be paid, which better be considerable.

Lancaster is sitting forward, waiting for her to respond. Sensing her advantage, Angela leans back in her chair and waits. His chair creaks as he leans back, too, tenting his fingers over his stomach. Light gleams off his head.

From outside she hears the beep-beeping of a truck backing up. A phone rings in the outer office.

"How much?" she says.

He winks and claps his hands together. "That's what I've always liked about you, Angie. No bullshit."

Two months later, the movie begins shooting. Day one, Angela arrives early. A makeup artist who introduced herself as Briana is stippling Angela's face with liquid latex aging makeup when Ruby arrives. She's wearing a short dungaree skirt with a frayed hem and a T-shirt the same orange as the fake Birkin. The cell phone she's clutching is encrusted with red rhinestones. *Branding.* It's all Angela can do to keep from rolling her eyes.

"I'm super nervous," Ruby says, dropping her phone in the purse. "That hair," she says, studying the Irene Adler wig of wild auburn curls that's waiting patiently on a blank-faced, Styrofoam head. "Looks like I'm playing a Wookie."

Angela laughs. Briana squeezes her shoulder and says, "Don't make me have to start over with this. You can talk but try not to move your mouth."

With Ruby watching, Briana finishes with Angela's face. The aging makeup is extraordinarily natural. When Briana pins on Mrs. Hudson's granny wig, it's scary. *Picture of Dorian Gray* scary. She's going on camera looking like this? If she's lucky, no one will recognize her, because there's no way she can make this part into a bravura turn.

"I'm so nervous," Ruby says. "Seriously, I hope I don't forget my lines."

Last night Angela studied the new script, learning her lines for the scenes scheduled to film today. Mrs. Hudson has exactly two. "But Mr. Holmes, you have to eat something!" and "Dr. Watson, just look at you, half-soaked to the skin!" Preferably not delivered through clenched teeth.

She's learned Ruby's lines in her first scene, too, all eight of them. Ruby also gets to fire a gun at burglars and emote like crazy. If Angela were directing the film, the drama of that opening would take place in Ruby's face.

"You'll be fine," Angela says.

"You think?" Ruby's eyes go wide and her lower lip trembles as she kneads her hands. Overacting could get to be a habit.

Angela smiles, feeling her face pull. *Mentor her,* she recalls Lancaster's instructions, reminding herself of the reason why, for once, she's being paid well above scale. "You do improv, right? Make the words your own." This is a safe bet because it's unlikely that Lancaster has read the script all that carefully himself. He calls himself a *big picture* kind of picture maker.

"Really? Is that, like, okay?"

"Just remember, Irene Adler is It-*AL*-ian. Or that's her schtick, though she was born in New Jersey. *Donna fatale.* Eez all about affect." Angela gives a hand flourish.

Ruby gives her an odd look, and Angela realizes she's the one who's overacting now. Actresses may be self-obsessed, but even young ones are rarely stupid.

"The lines are the easy part," Angela says. "Emote, but don't lose yourself. Think about the conflict. Holmes wants to uncover, to reveal.

Irene is the enigma who refuses to yield her secrets. She's proud. Her goal . . . is to hide."

"Hide." Ruby nods, apparently mesmerized, though the advice couldn't be more basic. "Something she can't afford for anyone to find out." She adds, as if to herself, "Or promised not to tell."

Angela stands and Ruby takes her seat at the mirror. Briana snaps open a fresh cloth and drapes it over Ruby.

"Go out there and knock 'em dead," Angela says, gazing at her own reflection in the mirror, indulging for a moment in the fantasy that she'll go onto the set, rip off her Mrs. Hudson wig and makeup, and take over as Irene Adler.

"Just watch me," Ruby says, her face animated with inner light and a yearning tinged with sadness. The camera is going to love her.

On the soundstage forty minutes later, Angela sits next to Anthony Fox, who's made up as Sherlock with a few days' worth of grizzle on his face and wearing a rumpled silk dinner jacket. In his first scene he's supposed to be wasted, bored out of his skull with no puzzle to harness his prodigious intellect. Members of the crew in baseball caps, their muscles bulging under *de rigueur* tight black T-shirts, upend Victorian furniture and adjust brocade drapes in the drawing room set. Taunting Angela from over the fireplace is the painting of her as Irene Adler, the prop from the earlier movie.

Cameras move in position. Technicians tinker with the lights.

"Where the hell's *the girl*?" Lancaster directs the question at Angela.

"I'll go check," Angela says. She's happy to be doing something other than waiting. She makes her way to the exit, carefully stepping over cables that crisscross the concrete floor of the soundstage. Her neck itches from the high starched-lace collar and she's sweating under padding that thickens her chest. The latex makeup makes her face feel as if she's got her head stuck in a surgical glove.

As she nears the dressing room door, she hears Ruby's plaintive voice. "Why is this happening?" And, "Oh . . . my . . . God."

Angela knocks gently. "Ruby?"

From the other side of the door, sobbing.

"Ruby, they're ready for you."

"Nooooo." A heartrending cry.

Angela pushes the door open. Ruby is sitting in the chair, facing the mirror, her hands covering her face. She's wearing the wig, a ton of Medusa curls.

"What is it? What's wrong?" Angela says.

Peering at Angela through her fingers, Ruby says, "I want to die." She lowers her hands. Her face is swollen and covered with bumpy red blotches. Her eyelids are puffy. She takes a tissue, blows her nose, and leans into the mirror, running her index finger across her cheekbone.

"Oh, honey," Angela says, crouching beside her. "You're having an allergic reaction. That's all."

"That's all?" Ruby's voice is a wail.

"I'll be right back," Angela says and rushes off to find a gofer to fetch some Benadryl and hydrocortisone cream. When she returns, minutes later, Lancaster and actors and crew members are crowded around Ruby. The group goes silent and they all turn to face Angela.

Angela breaks open the Benadryl, shakes out a tablet, and offers it to Ruby. Ruby stares at it. Then at Lancaster. Lancaster takes the pill and the container and eyes the label. He nods and passes the pill to Ruby. Then he offers Ruby a bottle of water.

Ruby puts the pill in her mouth and then tilts back her head and swallows some water. But a moment later she drops the bottle, choking and sputtering.

Angela picks up the bottle. Half of it has spilled on the floor. She sniffs at the open neck. The smell is familiar, medicinal. Vodka?

Lancaster takes it from her and sniffs, too. Takes a tiny taste. "Jesus Christ."

"Wasn't that *your* water?" Ruby asks Angela. "And that cream Briana used on my face. It's got your name on it." Sure enough, there's a jar of face cream with CASSANO written in black marker on its tape label. "You left it for me, with a note."

"Me? I most certainly did not—" Angela starts.

"The note was right here." Ruby looks around but she doesn't come up with one.

"And that," Angela says, pointing to the jar, "is not mine. Here's what I use." She picks up her own makeup bag and forages for her own cleanser. Realizing even as she's showing it to everyone that it proves nothing.

Ruby looks betrayed. Lancaster furious. And for a moment Angela flashes back to high school when she played Elizabeth Proctor, unfairly accused of witchcraft in *The Crucible. There be a thousand names, why does she call mine?*

"You need to go home," Lancaster says to Ruby. "Take care of yourself and we'll pick it up tomorrow, first thing." He turns to Angela. "You go home, too. I don't know what's up here. Truly, I'm stumped." He shakes his head. "Everyone else, back to work."

That evening, Angela is sitting in her kitchen, picking at takeout sushi. Ruby hadn't even looked her in the eye earlier as they'd both gotten their things together and left the building. Word of what had happened must have traveled because everyone she encountered, including the security officer at the studio gate, gave her the stink eye. She doesn't blame them. She gets how bad it looks. Log line: a jealous harridan, about to be eclipsed in her own best role, sabotages her young rival. If it were a movie, it would be called *All About Eve: Payback.*

But really, what audience would buy it? Itching cream? Spiked Evian? If Angela were going to sandbag another actor she'd be far more creative. For heavens sake, that jar of skin cream had her name on it. An obvious setup.

But if Angela didn't do it, then who did? And to what end?

She's volatile. That's what Lancaster said about Ruby. Was that code for paranoid? Manipulative? Psychotic?

Just watch me. Ruby said that just before Angela left the dressing room.

Did Ruby ink Angela's name on that jar of cleansing cream and plant it in the dressing room herself? Spike the water and then wait until she was surrounded by witnesses to drink from it? Was that allergic reaction a sham? Angela saw the blotchy red patches and the swelling with her own eyes, but modern makeup could be extraordinarily realistic.

Angela finds herself smiling. If so, then BRAVA! Brilliant performance. Ruby Lake is one hell of an actress. But why would she go to all that trouble?

One possible answer: to get Angela booted off the film. Angela has no idea why Ruby would be determined to do that, but Angela's not about to let it happen.

The next morning, Angela arrives on the soundstage early, ignoring the disdain broadcast her way by actors and crew members. Even her buddy, Anthony Fox, gives her a stiff chilly smile. Only Lancaster greets her warmly.

Ruby shows up minutes before Lancaster is ready to run through the opening scene. If there's any residual blotchiness or swelling, her makeup covers it. She seems so tiny under all that hair.

Ruby and the actor playing her manservant huddle with Lancaster, then take their places behind the closed drawing room door. The burglars crouch among the upended furniture. They begin to rehearse the scene.

Lancaster pronounces the first run-through "not bad." He adjusts the camera positions. Tells the burglars to raise their knives higher so the blades catch the light. Asks Ruby to lean in and wait a few beats before she fires. He takes the pistol and demonstrates.

Angela is impressed. It's not exactly the way she would block the scene but it works.

They run through the scene again and again. Each time Ruby's performance gets better, her look more doe-eyed and vulnerable as, after the burglars leave, she lowers the gun and resolve drains from her face.

Finally Lancaster shouts, "Last looks." The actors leave the set to get their hair and makeup touched up. Angela and the other stand-ins take over for the final blocking. It will be a tricky scene to light because it has to be dark in the drawing room and yet light enough to see Irene's gown, her gun, and most of all her emotional transformation. The manservant behind her has to be visible, too, not in her shadow, as well as the disarray of the room and the burglars' knives.

As Angela walks onto the set, a production assistant hands her the prop pistol that looks like an antique flintlock but feels like a toy. She and the actor standing in for the manservant take their places behind the drawing room's closed door.

"Action." She hears Lancaster start the run-through. The two burglar stand-ins scuffle. Angela throws open the door and steps into the drawing room. Lancaster motions her further in. Mentally she marks the spot.

The burglars hold out their knives. Technicians adjust the lights. Angela holds the smooth wooden grip of the pistol in two hands and aims above their heads. More lighting tweaks.

"Fire," Lancaster says, standing behind the cameraman and watching a video monitor.

Angela thumbs back the hammer and pulls the trigger. Even though the gun is loaded with blanks, the sound is huge. The pistol bucks in her hand and the grip turns warm as smoke wafts from it.

The lights brighten and one of the cameras lifts. "Fire again," Lancaster says.

After a few more pistol shots and lighting adjustments, they run through the entire scene with dialogue. By the time they're done, Angela's ears are ringing. She barely hears the shout, "In five."

Angela explains to Ruby the blocking changes and shows her the new mark where she's supposed to stand and fire the gun and how high to raise it. Briana straightens Ruby's wig, arranges a few stray curls around her pale face, and squeezes her into the plunging neckline of her red gown.

Ruby goes to wait behind the closed door and Angela takes a seat to watch the first take. The lights go down throughout the soundstage. Lights dim on the set, too. A fluorescent light, shaped like the moon, glows through the curtains.

"Quiet!" Lancaster shouts and his own moon face rises behind the camera boom in the darkened soundstage. "Action!"

Everyone and everything is in place. A production assistant holds a clapperboard in front of a camera, the time stamp a digital readout. Angela can't help it. A chill runs down her back. *Let the magic begin.*

The burglars scuffle. Angela is astonished by how tall Ruby seems when she makes her entrance as Irene Adler, all heaving bosom and steely calm. With those enormous dark eyes, the girl is one big emoji. But she's got a presence that makes it hard to take your eyes off her.

Ruby has the gun raised, pointing it at the burglars. It wobbles in Ruby's grip, and Angela can feel the heft, even though she knows it's not heavy at all. Light glints off the shaft as Ruby motions with it.

That's when Angela realizes that the gun is larger than the prop they used in rehearsal. It looks like it's got a metal grip, and it's not just the lighting. It's a different gun.

She glances toward the camera as the question flashes through her brain: After all that work getting the lighting and camera focus just right, why would they switch guns? The answer: they wouldn't.

At that same moment, she realizes that Glenn Lancaster is not in position beside the camera. She doesn't see him at all, not until she spots him in the shadows, half-hidden behind the cameraman.

Angela looks back at the set. It feels as if time slows down as the burglars brandish knives. As Ruby raises the nose of the gun. In a moment she'll fire the pistol that's not the prop they used for rehearsal.

Before Angela even registers the thought, she's on her feet, bolting onto the set. She knocks the gun from Ruby's hand. It hits the ground and goes off, filling the air with smoke and an acrid smell. There's a long pause as the gunshot echoes in the soundstage.

Belatedly, Lancaster screams, "Cut!"

He comes out from behind the camera. "What the hell?" Gazes at Ruby sitting on the floor, looking completely bewildered. At the pistol, or what's left of it, lying smoking on the floor nearby. He lunges for the gun but Angela gets there first. It's hot. She uses the hem of her skirt to protect her hand as she picks it up.

Lancaster looks around, assessing his audience. Then glares at Angela. "What are you up to now? Give me that."

"You want this?" She holds out the gun for everyone to see that the barrel is ripped open. "I think Ruby might like to have a look at it first. Someone booby-trapped it."

"Someone?" Lancaster draws himself up and puffs out his chest. "The only other person outside of props who handled that gun is you."

It's what Angela expects him to say. "You know as well as I do, this isn't the gun we used in rehearsal." She wonders why the prop assistant didn't flag it. "Couldn't you feel the difference?" she asks Ruby.

Ruby's mouth opens but at first no words come out. "Actually, I did. It felt cold and heavier."

"It's a different gun," Angela says. She peers closely at a bit of what looks like a nugget of hard plastic stuck inside the exploded barrel. "And it looks as if someone jammed it with—"

"Probably latex," Lancaster says. Now everyone turns and stares at him. Because how could he know that from twenty feet away? Latex hadn't even occurred to Angela and she's looking right at it.

Lancaster continues, "A gun loaded with blanks can kill you if it's been jammed with—"

"Aging makeup?" Angela finishes the thought. "The stuff that makes me look old?"

"Old*er*." Lancaster nods, but it's an uneasy nod. Maybe he's starting to realize he's overplayed his hand. Tipped over into caricature.

Angela says, "There's only one person who behaved as if he knew something was about to go wrong before it did. Just one person who moved well out of the way before Ruby fired the gun." Angela scans the faces of the actors and camera operators and crew. "Surely I'm not the only one who noticed."

No one steps forward. And why would they? All eyes had been on Ruby. A herd of orangutans could have sauntered across the soundstage and no one would have noticed when Lancaster crept away.

"Bastard!" Ruby screams. She's a red blur as she throws herself at Lancaster, clawing at his face. It takes both of the burglars and an electrician to pull her off. She struggles and finally shakes them loose. In a cold, clear voice, she says, "My father trusted you and you betrayed him. Again."

In the uneasy silence that follows, Angela can feel the polarity in the room reverse. Lancaster has become the focal point.

"Who's your father?" Angela asks.

Before Ruby can answer, Lancaster raises both arms and says, "That's enough. Clear the set." When no one moves, he bellows, "Now!"

Moments later, it's just Ruby and Angela and Lancaster on the soundstage.

"My father was Ralph Lago," Ruby says, her soft voice echoing in the vast empty space. "He"—Ruby tips her head in Lancaster's direction—"and my father were long-time business partners."

Of course Angela's heard the name. Seen Lago's picture in the paper, a Hollywood accountant who committed suicide a few months ago after he was convicted of embezzling studio funds. Now she realizes that Lago must have been the man she saw years ago, working surrounded by computer printouts in the small office next to Lancaster's. Angela had assumed he was Lancaster's bookkeeper.

"You were best friends." As Ruby spits out the words, Lancaster recoils. "Dad padded production charges so you could skim profits. When you realized you were being investigated, you got my dad to take the rap. God forbid the great director should face charges."

Lancaster doesn't contradict her.

Ruby takes a deep breath and wipes away a tear. "Just hours before he killed himself, Dad told me you'd promised to give me this part. But you couldn't even do that for him, could you? You've got someone else you've promised the part, haven't you? I can only imagine what she's got on you."

Lancaster just hangs there, staring at the floor and looking deflated. No wonder he needed Angela. Not only to play Mrs. Hudson and stand in for Irene Adler and mentor an inexperienced performer, but also to play an aging actress desperate enough to kill off her rival. How convenient it would have been for him, disposing of both Ruby and Angela with a single blank.

Eight months later, the new *Scandal in Bohemia* opens in Westwood Village at the Fox Theatre. Strobes light up the crowd gathered beneath its phallic Art Deco tower and a searchlight arcs across the sky. Ruby and Angela arrive together in a black limo.

Ruby steps out, resplendent in a red, off-the-shoulders gown with a flowing cape. Angela follows in a black-silk tuxedo jacket over a long skirt slit up to her thigh. She looks down, trying to slow time as the pointy toes of her black stilettos hit the red carpet. She lifts her gaze to the marquee.

WORLD PREMIERE TONIGHT

Yes! She gives a mental fist pump.

Anthony Fox, starring in the film as Sherlock Holmes, comes over to them. He's every inch the dashing elder statesman in his tux. He and Angela pose for photographs, standing on either side of Ruby.

A young reporter—his press pass says he writes for *Variety*—draws Angela aside. "Ms. Cassano, 'Scandal in Bohemia' marks your transition from actor to filmmaker. At what point in your career did it hit you that you wanted to make this big career move?"

"I'd been thinking about directing films for quite a while," she says, not bothering to correct him, to say that this isn't the first film she's directed. It's a better story if it is. "When this opportunity literally fell into my lap, how could I pass it up?"

Fell into my lap is a bit of an overstatement, but Glenn Lancaster took defeat more gracefully than Ruby or Angela expected. In return for their silence about the lethal prop pistol and Lancaster's part in the embezzlement scheme, Ruby got to play the lead she'd been promised and Angela took over as director. Angela let Lancaster know that she'd stashed the cassette with footage from that disastrous first take in a safe-deposit box. She's taking her cue from Irene Adler, who tells Sherlock Holmes that she's keeping the compromising photograph "to preserve a weapon which will always secure me from any steps which he might take in the future."

The reporter gives Angela an earnest look. "As a female director—"

"Just 'director,'" she says, cutting him off. "You don't say 'female reporter,' or 'female postal worker.'"

The reporter colors. Licks his lips. "I understand you're finished shooting a sequel and starting something new? Can you tell me more?"

Angela luxuriates in the question. Over the reporter's shoulder she sees Ruby surrounded by photographers. Anthony Fox is trying to edge into the limelight. Unnoticed, Glenn Lancaster moves quickly through the crowd, making his way into the theater. There are no photo ops for executive producers. Angela feels sorry for the beautiful young woman on his arm. She looks familiar, and after a moment Angela realizes she might have been one of the production assistants that worked on *Scandal*. In charge of props? Possibly.

The lights in the theater lobby are flashing and ushers are shooing people inside. Angela answers the reporter's question and a few more before excusing herself. She hurries inside and takes her seat next to Ruby.

The house lights go down. The theater reverberates with music as the movie starts. There, among the opening credits, is Angela's production company: Adventuress Films LLC. The logo is the red outline of two women, both wearing slinky low-cut gowns. Their arms are linked.

MARTIN X

by Gary Phillips

The dean of black empowerment lay dead on the worn throw rug. A ragged bullet hole violated Professor Lincoln Barrow's wrinkled forehead. He was dressed in slacks and slippers, a ratty robe splayed open over an athletic T-shirt covering his pot belly. Near his outstretched hand was the spilled cup of tea he'd been holding. The stuff had soaked into the rug, the cup and saucer amazingly unbroken though the summation was he'd dropped to the floor instantly after being shot.

"That was part of a set C.L.R. James had given him," said the beefier of the two men who stood looking down at the body. He meant the fine china items on the floor. "He mentioned it to me once," he added, as if that meant the murdered man had shared a confidence.

The one he told this to was also over six feet. He had shoulders like a linebacker, thick Fu Manchu mustache, modest sideburns, and hair flattened on top and close-cropped at the sides, what they called a "fade" in uptown barbershops. John "Dock" Watson turned from the body and began inspecting the spacious room—chamber, he supposed it would be called in the *Post*. Two walls were composed of tall built-in bookshelves. On those packed shelves were numerous first and rare editions, from W.E.B. DuBois' *The Soul of Black Folk* to *Capital* by Karl Marx and a personally signed copy of *I am not Spock* by the actor Leonard Nimoy.

Watson knew one of the late leader's guilty pleasures was being a science fiction fan. He could imagine a future when all were free to pursue their hopes and dreams. But now his resourceful intellect had been stilled, his inspiring voice silenced to inspire no more. Replacing the biography, his roaming gaze indicated nothing on the shelves had been disturbed—but Watson knew better than to believe such. He knew at some point it might mean all the books would have to be taken down and the surfaces behind them studied carefully for a hole, possibly hidden among the wood grain—or even a hole that had been recently patched from the other side. He quickly took in the rest of the great man's private library and study. There weren't many framed photos or plaques on the walls, though what there were of them chronicled the stalwarts of the domestic and international freedom struggle. An animated Fidel Castro, intense Malcolm X, and the good Doctor sitting around a table when Castro had stayed at the Hotel Teresa in Harlem, the time he came to speak at the U.N. Grace Lee Boggs accepting an award from the doctor-professor at some ceremony, and a grainy shot taken of him marching with farm workers, in the lead alongside organizers Delores Huerta and Cesar Chavez in California's agricultural-rich Central Valley.

There were rectangular windows high up on the walls, and Watson stood on a footstool the deceased man had also used. Though he was taller than Barrow had been, Watson couldn't reach the windows over the bookshelves.

"There must be some sort of extension he used," he said to the other man.

"Here it is." He began to reach for a length of slim pole with a catch on the end of it leaning against the dead man's desk.

"Don't touch it," Watson said, looking over his shoulder.

"But it would be normal for our prints to be in here."

"I know, but you're going to tell the cops everything the way it happened—only, leave me out."

"Right on."

Watson moved the footstool about, standing on it and studying each window. The room was a basement construction and the windows let out onto the sidewalk. They were barred on the inside and as far as he could tell, each was latched in place.

"The heat ain't gonna like it I busted in the door," said the good-sized Tony "Squelch" Waller.

"You were doing your job."

"If I was doing my job, Dr. Barrow would be alive."

Watson smiled grimly. "Don't beat yourself up, brother. This was his sanctum sanctorum."

"Meaning what?"

"Meaning this is where he went to be alone, to get away from the masses to read and contemplate, or to work on his writing. It wasn't unusual for him to be holed up days on end."

"But they got to him, Dock," Squelch Waller said, strain and worry contorting his mild features. "What the hell we gonna do, man?"

Watson crouched down, studying the doorjamb, faceplate, and lock mechanisms. The door locked from the inside but it wasn't a sophisticated piece of equipment, no doubt once upon a time bought at the neighborhood hardware store. The door wasn't that heavy either, but solid wood, dating back to the thirties was his guess. The door chain had also been in place when Waller used his shoulder and a fire axe to get in.

"You walked with Dr. Barrow here two days ago?" Watson asked.

"Yes," Waller answered. "We'd been at the meeting planning the anti-apartheid teach-in and we stopped at the store to get him some groceries. I carried his bags back here and left him in good shape." A faraway look settled his face.

"And Martin called him earlier this morning? Here in his library?" There was an adjacent back room to the study that had a cot, hot plate, and mini-refrigerator.

"Said he'd been calling off and on since last night. He'd sent some-body to his apartment and he wasn't there. That's why our folks started to get worried."

Watson again examined the locks, looking for signs of tampering. "Then you get called because you were last seen with him."

"So I came around, knowing Doctor Barrow was always up early like. I knocked and knocked but got no answer." He gestured with his hands. "Him being up there in age, I figured it was best to get in here and see to him."

Watson removed his Minox mini-camera from his jean jacket pocket. He was clicking away as he talked and walked around the space. "We play this like it lays out, Squelch, at least as far as the fuzz is concerned." He paused at the desk, examining the papers and letters on the desktop. Before he'd entered the room, he'd put on his lambskin gloves. Watson sifted through the material. He snapped pictures of the various sheets of paper and letters as well.

"Did you call me using this phone?" Watson asked, pointing at the rotary sitting on a corner of the desk.

"Hell no, went around the corner and two blocks up and called you from one of the followers. Sister Mable. She's an early riser too." It was just edging toward six in the morning.

"She gonna get rattled in case the cops question her?"

Waller shook his massive head side to side. "Man, she been around since the Palmer raids. She's stand-up before they invented the word."

"Solid. I'm out of here. Call Sid and tell him what you found. Tell him everything but me being here. Then he can call the law and be here with you when they arrive so they don't jack you around."

"Okay." Waller rubbed the back of his neck. "What are you gonna tell Martin?"

Watson was at the broken-in door which, according to the big man, had been locked and bolted from the inside when he got here. "What he's going to already know. It's going to be on him to keep a lid on things . . . if he can."

"Yeah," the other man drawled, "that might be a big if, soul brother."

"You ain't never lied." Watson nodded curtly and left. He ascended the concrete steps to the kitchen in the rear of Francine's Southern Cantonese

Style Café. There was one person already there, a cook who was busy chopping onions, celery, and peppers and sautéing the vegetables in a wok as big around as a radar dish. As the savory aroma from the mix filled Watson's nose, he exited by a side door onto a narrow passageway that was surprisingly trash free. At the open end of this he checked the quiet street and then walked briskly along Amsterdam Avenue away from the crime scene.

A bleary-eyed afro-Latina no more than twenty-three, dressed in a waist jacket with a dirty fake fur collar, jean shorts, torn fishnet stockings, and scuffed Chuck Taylor All-Stars, weaved on the sidewalk. A half-smoked Kool cigarette dangled from a corner of her slack mouth, miraculously not dropping to the pavement. She was heading in the opposite direction and veered into Watson's path as he strode past. They bumped shoulders and she rocked back on her heels, giving him a crooked grin.

"Hey, Stagolee, what's your hurry, baby? Shit," she said, wiping her nose with the side of her hand. She looked him up and down. "Huh, for a quick twenty I'll polish your knob till steam blows out of those big ears of yours." She giggled, barely able to keep herself upright.

He frowned pityingly at the junkie, briefly considering giving her money but knowing she would only use it getting her next fix. He moved on. She watched him go, a bemused set to her now closed mouth. The thin cigarette smoke trailed upward past her face and unkempt hair.

By one o'clock that same day, there were more than three thousand people gathered before the Gothic and Tudor Revival designed Abyssinian Baptist Church on 138th Street. A small stage with a podium had been placed on the sidewalk, and though a rally permit hadn't been secured, given such short notice, the police had been advised by the mayor's office not to interfere but to be on alert. The compact man now on the stage leafed through his notes, then contemplatively removed his fedora and placed it on the podium.

The blackout last year, happening at the same time the city's economy went into the toilet, then the ongoing hunt for the Son of Sam, and the resulting looting, firebombings, and rioting, had pushed the city to its limits. Now more than twelve months on, with no relief in the temperature during the sweltering summer, Martin Collins, former pimp and drug dealer Newark Red, now known as Martin X, stood between order and chaos—depending on what he said today. No one had a clue what that would be from this civil rights leader, this firebrand who'd been the target of FBI director J. Edgar Hoover's considerable dirty tricks counter-intelligence efforts.

Martin X paused, gazing at his audience. He again looked out on the throng of expectant faces, mostly black, some whites not including the police, and a smattering of Puerto Ricans and Chinese Americans he was pleased to see.

"Brothers and sisters, friends and allies," he began, several micro-phones taped in place before him. Various television news crews were covering the presentation, more than one news van close to the stage. Several cameramen were stationed about with their bulky video cameras harnessed to their bodies and porta-packs like an astro-naut's oxygen tank strapped to their backs. There were also several others still using 16mm film cameras and didn't have to be tethered to control panels. Cables of various gauges were strewn everywhere, leading back to news vans double- and triple-parked up and down the packed street. Agile radio reporters, mobile with their light-weight microphones plugged into cassette decks, easily eddied through the crowd as well.

"This is a troubling day for us, for the movement." A palpable wave surged through the crowd. "Our beloved Doctor Professor Lincoln Mills Barrow has been cut down savagely, cowardly." As one of the uniformed police who stood about tensed at these words, Martin X paused and gazed at his audience.

"That it was murder is obvious. That this heinous act is meant to dis-hearten and subvert the long march we have been on is all too evident as well. Like the bombing of those innocent children in their church in Birmingham and the kidnapping and brutal murders of Schwerner, Goodman, and Chaney in Philadelphia, Mississippi, fear and terror are the twin instruments of repression visited upon us," he continued, his voice rising in accordance to the import of his words. "These forces are out to deter our inevitable and irrevocable advance to freedom and equality. But we will not be dissuaded, we will not be intimidated nor stopped. No sir. Not today, not tomorrow, not any day."

Applause and yells of support went up from the gathered. Martin X gripped the podium on either side, rocking the thing slightly. "I stand today before this magnificent house of worship not to implore the powers that be to bring our beloved Lincoln Barrows's murderers to ground. No, I say this city, this state, has no choice but to drag these villains into the light and wherever the truth lies as to who put the gunman in motion, so be it."

"Tell it," several exclaimed loudly as the murmuring grew. More than one police officer tightened his grip on their sheathed nightstick, wiping the tip of their tongues across dry lips.

"There is no choice but accountability in this regard," Martin X declared, sweat prominent on his brow. "Too long have we peacefully demanded justice for the wrongs waylaid against us, and too long have we had to grin and bear it."

There was more clapping and whoops of approval. Dock Watson scanned faces, cops and civilians, as he stood behind Martin X, but not on the small stage. Oddly, situations like this didn't cause him to have flashbacks to this or that firefight he'd been in, going on a decade ago. Rather, he found himself centered, his heart rate and pulse slowed, errant sounds as distinct to him as glass bursting in slow motion, so he heard the tinkling of each shard. Off to one side he zeroed in on a cameraman who had just tilted his device upward. What the hell?

Watson craned his head around. "Dammit," he muttered, looking for his short-barreled .44 revolver in its rig under his jean jacket.

"Then we must not wait any longer," bellowed a figure from the roof of the church. He was dressed in a colorful dashiki and black pants. But this wasn't just some rogue rabble rouser suddenly piggybacking on Martin X's thunder. People gasped as word spread through the crowd like sub-atomic particles: the man up there looked like the recently murdered Lincoln Barrow. "We must show the system we can't be fooled," the figure shouted. "There must be retribution in blood."

As if in reply, gunfire exploded from the WZIX news van near the stage. But Dock Watson was already in motion. He tackled Martin X as bullets splintered the podium into firewood. A round nicked the back of his calf as the two men landed hard on the sidewalk. All around him people were panicking and there was the squealing of tires and the continued thudding of gunfire as the news van tore away, a police car roaring after it in pursuit.

"You okay?" Watson demanded.

"Yes, yes I think I'm fine, John," said the civil rights leader. He was shaken but not coming unglued.

"Rasheed, Elliot—get Martin inside the church," he told two of the security team. They rushed to the man as Watson was up and running.

The news van bounced off the side of a double-parked station wagon, tearing loose the vehicle's front bumper. The van's back doors banged open and a machine gun on a tripod streamed gunfire in all directions. Bullets peppered the chasing police car's windshield. Blinded, the wounded driver crashed into a junk cart. A discarded toilet on the cart skidded along the sidewalk while sections of copper pipe and loose girly magazines flew through the air.

A man on a Triumph motorcycle zoomed into view. He adeptly weaved and maneuvered in such a way that the machine gun, operating by a pre-set electrical-mechanical device, shot impotently at the rider. As the weapon swung left, he went right and vice versa. Dock Watson was running and, when possible, given the density, jumping from car rooftop to rooftop in pursuit as well. The news van rounded a corner and bore down on two movers carrying a couch out of an apartment to their truck. The two cursed, dropped the couch, and scrambled for safety. The van slammed into the couch then fishtailed into a lamppost on the sidewalk. This was in front of Peoples Clinic No. 3.

Snapped loose from its moorings, the lamppost's live wires snaked and sizzled about on the street. The Triumph circled the corner, and the rider intentionally laid it down in a flurry of sparks. The motorcycle slid under the rear of the van, the ruined machine wrapping around the rear axle, immobilizing the vehicle. Gas spurted from the Triumph's gas tank onto the roadway. The rider had rolled when his bike went down. Now he was up and running toward the van. He flung open the driver's door.

"I didn't have a choice!" the cameraman at the wheel of the van pleaded.

"I know," the motorcycle rider said. He had a hawk-like nose and combed-back black hair longish to the nape of his neck, and his grey probing eyes seemed to take everything in at once. "Let's get out of here before this thing goes up."

"I can't," the other man said, worry in his voice. "He told me I had to drive until I couldn't drive any more. And if I was stopped I couldn't leave the driver's seat. I had to be—" he choked off as his voice became garbled with emotion.

"Until you were dead," the stranger finished. "I assure you, your wife and young daughter are safe. No harm will come to them."

The driver gaped at the other man. Who was he? Did he know about the calm man on the other end of the telephone who'd threatened his family? Was he working for this man? Was he the criminal who had set all this in motion?

"If he tells you your wife and kid are okay, they are, man," said Dock Watson as he came up, tucking his piece away.

"John," said the motorcycle rider.

"Holmes," Watson nodded curtly.

"Get your goddamn hands up," a command rang out.

Ringed about them were police officers, sidearms drawn and pointing at the three. Others were using their wooden nightsticks to push the live wires away from the spreading gas as sirens announced the approach of patrol cars and the fire department. Those who'd been gathered for the Martin X presentation milled about too.

"Y'all be cool now," one said. "Brother Watson and them white fellas got their hands up, and ain't nobody about to make no sudden moves, ya hear?"

"We got eyes on you," said another. He'd brought his Christmas present, a Super 8 movie camera, to film Martin X and had the thing on.

The officers, white and black, were keenly aware that on the heels of an assassination attempt, following the morning's murder of Dr. Barrow, it would only take one wrong word or crack of the nightstick to set off a riot. The three men walked slowly to the curb under the gaze of hundreds of pairs of eyes. They were patted down. Watson told the officers he was armed, and his gun was taken. From the one he called Holmes a folding knife of unusual design was removed, as was a sort of baton of maple, a short round stick in a scabbard strapped to his calf. The trio were then handcuffed and each hauled off to the 32nd Precinct in separate cars.

Dock Watson was interrogated by two detectives, one black, the other white.

"You were in 'Nam," said the black one, Murphy, consulting an open file folder that Watson figured included a photocopy of his New York State–issued private investigator license.

"I was," said the former staff sergeant.

"Huh," Murphy muttered, leafing through a few pages, noting Watson's citations and the redacted classified portions of his record.

"You are on retainer with the Freedom Now Coalition?" the white one, O'Malley, asked.

"I am." He felt no need to elaborate. It had been Watson's experience that, like on the witness stand, answer only what you were asked when talking with a member of law enforcement.

"And you at times handle security for Martin Collins, called Martin X by you . . . by some people."

"I do. And I'm licensed to carry the firearm you confiscated from me."

He was asked more than once what he'd seen leading up to the supposed appearance of Barrow's ghost on the roof of the church. He told them what he'd witnessed, including that he didn't believe in reincarnation and the good doctor didn't own a dashiki. The second time he asked, "Your men find the dashiki that was probably left behind? Betchu when the lab finishes their tests, they'll find theatrical makeup on it."

Both cops gave him a baleful look. He was here to answer their questions, not pose them—and certainly not advance his theories.

After an hour or so elapsed, the white cop, who'd been leaning in a corner while the other one sat across from Watson, yawned and said, "Gonna get a little air, Kev, be right back."

He walked out. When he came back after a few minutes, he tapped his partner on the shoulder and they both left. Watson remained as he was, sitting at the metal table, his hands relaxed on it. The black one had been sipping coffee from a cup emblazoned with the distinctive blue and white amphora design. The table was a dull industrial green, as was the linoleum, which had been trafficked to streaks of black smudges in several sections. The walls were dirty beige and the acoustic ceiling tile buckled in places with water stains. The coffee cooled near him. The door opened again. Watson heard fingers tick-tacking away on an electric typewriter in the adjoining hallway. The door closed again as a man entered.

"You're looking fit, Dock."

"It's been awhile, James."

James Moriarty, crisp in a three-piece suit and tie, strode to the table with his hand out. Watson half rose and shook it. They both sat, Moriarty clasping his long fingers before him. "I suppose it goes without saying that the mayor's office has a keen interest in getting a handle on this situation."

Watson measured his response. "I imagine you have a theory or two."

Moriarty, whose hair was prematurely white, scratched at an ear lobe. "As you do."

Watson shrugged a shoulder. "I'd picked up some rumblings from the streets. I was leaning toward whoever had taken over from Nicky Barnes." Leroy "Nicky" Barnes had been a drug lord given to ostentatious tastes. His being on the cover of the *New York Times Magazine* had prompted President Jimmy Carter to pressure the Drug Enforcement Administration to get Barnes. He was incensed that someone like Barnes should be seen as a twisted image of emulation. Barnes had been arrested and jailed last year.

"The East Harlem Purple Gang is supposed to have stepped into the void and been supplying his lieutenants," Watson continued.

"But you dismissed this notion?"

"As we both know, dope men don't go out of their way to be clever in rubbing out an opponent. Why all the rigmarole with the locked room bit and what have you? Sure, Professor Barrow made speeches decrying the parasitic pusherman but he also denounced plenty of others preying on the black community."

"Including his allegations of the CIA being involved in flying heroin out of the Golden Triangle for profit and geo-political reasons," Moriarty offered, stern-faced.

"He wasn't the only one stating that," Watson observed.

"Agreed." Moriarty steepled his fingers. "Martin X has been making something of a campaign of unmasking the true players in this insidious enterprise, often noting poppies do not grow in the ghetto. Could be too Dr. Barrow uncovered a bombshell, proof of some local connection."

"You're not trying to have me chase my tail, are you, James?"

Moriarty smiled, spreading his hands apart. "Our friend says all avenues must be explored."

"Speaking of which, are you getting him sprung too?"

Moriarty said, "He was gone by the time I got here. Possibly his brother had something to do with that. Still, you're free to go too, Dock."

Watson wondered if Holmes had examined Barrow's library. "The driver of the news van, his story check out?"

Moriarty nodded. "Seems he got a call at the station this morning as he was getting ready to cover the Martin X speech. The voice on the other end told him they had his wife and daughter. A woman comes on the line, sobbing, calling his name, and is then cut off. He naturally assumed it was his wife."

"The voice was faked?"

"Apparently. Wife and daughter were safe. But he was told not to try and call home or their throats would be slit." He paused, taking in the other man. "At the time, what would you have done? He drives off in the van with the reporter, then makes a stop as he was told to do. The reporter is knocked out and the remote-controlled machine gun quickly installed in the rear by two masked men with portable power tools."

Watson absorbed this. "That's some heavy planning and access to resources involved."

Moriarty concurred.

Weighing the import of that, Watson said, "Can you get me a copy of the autopsy results on Professor Barrow? And if I get in a bind, can I drop your name?"

Both men rose. "Of course—this is in the service of justice. The mayor wanted me to emphasize what you already know: the city's on edge. Satisfactory answers need to be forthcoming tout de suite, my friend."

"I heard that," Watson said.

They shook hands again, then Moriarty handed Watson a card with a handwritten phone number on it. From his coat's inner pocket he also took out a device the size of a hip flask, though thicker. It was made of black plastic with a readout screen.

"This is a pager. You call that number on the card and your phone number will appear on the screen," he said. "Only two other people have my pager number, so I'll know an unfamiliar one is from you."

Watson knew one of those people was the mayor. As they walked out, he asked about the second person. "How is Irene?"

"She's well, I'll tell her you said hello."

"Cool."

The detective's hunting and pecking on the electric typewriter filled the silence as the two departed.

As the cooks prepared food for the evening crush, Dock Watson snapped on his penlight at the entrance to Professor Barrow's library. Late afternoon light filtered in from the high windows but there were pockets of gloom as well. He held the tight beam steady on the broken chain guard. In particular he examined where the base had been screwed to the side of the door. His gloved fingers touched the gouged wood and he made a sound in his throat. The light went out. After leaving the library, he found a payphone and called Moriarty's pager.

Two nights later, Sherlock Holmes entered the back area of the second floor of Club 99 trailing Jerry "Little Fish" Genero. Holmes was dressed in a colorful Rayon knit shirt and disco-style bell bottom slacks high up on his trim waist. His shirt was open several buttons and a gold chain sparkled on his tanned chest. The nude form of a golden woman hung from the chain. Her nipples were sparkling zircons.

"You let me do the talking, Terry," Genero said.

"Sure thing, Little Fish," Holmes said as Terry Ritchie, affecting a Cockney accent by way of a transplant living in New Jersey for several years.

The two came to a closed double door, a good-sized individual standing guard before it. He wore a Pierre Cardin suit sans tie, collar up, shoulder pads like the prow of a boat. His neck was thick and corded and led to a thicket of chest hair.

"Gotta search you," he said. "Protocol," he added, as if he were building his vocabulary one new word a day.

They submitted. As the guard's large hands expertly probed Holmes's wiry frame, the door opened and out stepped three women of varying ethnicities in shimmering garments that clung to their model-perfect bodies. Two of them, a blonde and a raven-haired one, carried their high heels in their hands and they laughed like wayward school girls returning from a ditch party. The third had flakes of coke residue under her nostrils. They eyed the two newcomers and departed along the red velvet lined hallway.

Little Fish snickered. "That 'Rican chick with the great ass was sending you all kinds of signals." He shook his head admiringly.

"Yeah," said "Terry," feigning nonchalance. "But I got my mind on business."

"I hear you."

"Okay," the bodyguard said and opened one of the doors behind him. The two stepped through into the private room, somber via indirect lighting. Inside were large plush chairs, each with a side table upon which were leftover cartons of Chinese take-out, champagne, and the telling remains of white powder dusting a razor blade on a hand mirror. A pair of lacy woman's underwear lay on the floor beside the foot of one of the seated men. He had a pleasant face, like a junior college professor with a full schedule and a new sports car. Akin to the other two in the room, he regarded the visitors with a contained reserve.

"We got plenty of chicken lo mein left," said a standing man, working a fingernail between his side teeth. "Shit's good." He wore a baby blue suit over a darker blue shirt with a flared collar.

"We got something better than that," Little Fish said.

"You the Limey," declared the other seated man. He had a beard and scratched at his crotch.

"That's me, china plate."

"Huh?"

"It's a slang thing from where he comes," Little Fish interjected.

The one in the baby blue suit came forward from where he'd been before a Patrick Nagel print on the wall. "Now that introductions have been made, like the man said."

"This better not be about some bullshit," the beard said as he produced an ostentatious Sig Sauer and placed it lovingly on the end table near his hand. His fingers were like stuffed sausage links, and the little finger and the one next to it bore rings. "That goes for you too, Little Fish. You being the one that vouched for this dude."

"It's primo," Little Fish said, keeping the edge out of his voice.

Holmes held up his hands like a conjurer showing his audience they were empty in preparation for the closing trick. He slowly lowered his right hand and passed it before the large buckle on his belt. In relief on it a couple was engaged in the act of 69 lovemaking. Now the false front of the buckle was in his hand and in the hollow of it was a compact amount of white powder wrapped in plastic. He handed the heroin to the man in baby blue. This one, the leader of the crew, examined it for a moment and handed it over to the pleasant-faced man.

He in turn slit open the packet and put some power on the end of his blade. From beside his chair he picked up a small metal case. Setting it on an end table he opened the case to reveal a small testing kit. Holding a glass test-tube-like container aloft, he tapped the powder into it and added dollops of reagents from two eye-dropper bottles. He closed the tube, shook it, then held it up to look at its purple color. Whistling his satisfaction, he passed the tube to the standing man.

"Well, hell, gentlemen, you weren't pulling our legs."

Little Fish said, "No we wasn't."

"Fifteen keys, eighty percent pure," Holmes said, knowing the boss in blue had already calculated the millions they'd make once the product was "stepped on"—diluted for street sales.

Particulars were worked out on price and delivery. Holmes and Little Fish left.

"Tomorrow we're in clover," Little Fish said as they entered back into the bustling dance floor area. The DJ was spinning an Alicia Bridges tune, "I Love the Night Life."

Holmes grinned broadly. "Swimming in tons, son."

Little Fish was damn near giddy. "What you said."

As they headed for the exit they passed a section of the bar. Sitting there was the blonde who'd been upstairs. She sipped a martini while a man with a massive mound of dark hair was trying to talk her up. She put her icy blues on Holmes over the rim of her glass, and reached out to touch his arm. Leaning in close, she whispered, "Did you see my panties up there?"

"Why I believe I did." He took her hand and, pausing no more than the tick of a clock's sweep hand, bent and kissed it. "Maybe I can help you with finding another pair."

Her bedroom eyes could pin a man's stomach to his spine. "I believe you can."

Little Fish didn't have to be hit with a two by four to take the hint. "I don't know what you got, Terry, but I'm sure gonna buy me some. See you tomorrow when we said, right? Get our thing down before showtime."

"Right you are," Holmes answered, his attention on the woman. Big hair mumbled a curse and ambled away.

It wasn't too long before Holmes and the woman entered her modest apartment in the east forties. They were backlit by light in the hallway as they kissed and grabbed at each other in the open doorway. The bearded man tip-toed from the shadows of the apartment's front room, a set of nunchuks in his hand. Being a fan of Hong Kong kung fu movies, he'd taken a few lessons on how to handle the instrument. He raised the weapon over his head, spinning one of its blunt ends to strike Holmes.

Squelch Waller left the Five Note bar in Harlem and, after a cab ride, got out on a quiet block in Queens. He looked up and down the dark street and then went up the steps to a nondescript row house. He tapped his knuckles on the screen door. The porch light came on. The door's peephole swung inward and the front door opened thereafter. Waller entered and the door closed. Dock Watson witnessed this from the LTD he had parked up the street on the opposite side.

❖

Sherlock Holmes shoved the woman away, twisting his body, taking a glancing blow from the nunchuk on his shoulder. He winced and, finishing his pivot, delivered an uppercut to his attacker's jaw. The bearded man rocked back but employed his weapon again as he did so. Holmes went low, the stick missing his head. He whipped his leg around and upended the kung fu fan.

The man went down hard on his back. "Get his ass," he blared. The bearded man began to rise and Holmes rammed stiffened fingers under his heart, momentarily stunning him as he held onto the man.

The blonde produced a small-caliber automatic from a garter holster on her inner thigh. For Sherlock Holmes, the world's only consulting detective, had not only smelled the gun oil on her hand when he'd kissed it in the bar, he'd felt the weapon while pretending—or at least, semi-pretending—to be lost in lust. He tensed for the bullet to strike him, but she hesitated.

Holmes shoved the bearded man into her. The gun went off impotently, plaster falling onto his hair as he snatched up the nunchuks and expertly used them to disarm her. Holmes retrieved the gun and leveled it on the two.

"Now, let's chat about the Council, shall we?" he said.

Glaring at him, a false eyelash askew, she said, "Go to hell."

Holmes smiled wickedly.

❖

On the front page of the *Amsterdam News*, a black weekly, a story ran. The article alleged that Tony "Squelch" Waller was an FBI informant, and had been one for a number of years. It was further alleged he'd first been pressed into this role by a combination of factors, including an assault charge from a picket line incident in Brooklyn. The piece went on to say that he'd been confronted by a high-placed member of the Freedom Now Coalition and had confessed his sins. Waller was said to have disappeared to parts unknown.

"You noted the marks where the base of the door's chain guard had been," Holmes said to Dock Watson.

"I'm sure you saw those the first time you were in the library," Watson responded. Reviewing the photos he'd taken in Barrow's library, he'd finally noticed the gouges and returned for a second look. Once he surmised the chain lock had been pried off with a flat head screwdriver, and not broken away as Waller claimed, he began tailing the man.

The two sat at a table in Francine's Southern Cantonese Style Café having lunch. Harlem was electric with the discussion about Waller and the implications of that.

"The professor must have found out Waller was a snitch and Waller killed him, terrified he'd be exposed," Watson said.

Holmes sipped his tea, saying nothing.

"But then again," Watson added, "that meant Martin had to speak out to calm things down. So was he the real target all along? The Peoples Clinics sponsored by the FNC have been effective in battling the drug scourge. Then there was the voice on the phone making the cameraman drive the van away. The imposter on the roof not being found. The two masked men who planted the remote-controlled machine gun in the van." He sat back. "But your brother and MI6 didn't send you here about what us poor ole' black folks are up to, now did he?"

"Not precisely, Watson. But as it happened, the Council, this entity that arose from the remains of the infrastructure Nicky Barnes created before he was put away, now that was of interest."

Watson considered his companion's words. "Using dope money to fund other activities."

"Yes, sadly, heroin and cocaine addictions yield millions in broken lives and shattered families, and dollars and pounds." Holmes had also mentioned the woman had hesitated shooting him the other night as no doubt her orders were to take him alive until they could beat out of him where his supposed cache of heroin was hidden.

Watson tapped the table. "The exchequer was caught up in some kind of hooker and blow scandal earlier this year."

"Tip of the iceberg and all that. But I'm heartened to see you keep up on news from your once-adopted environs."

After mustering out of the service, Watson had landed in London, like a number of ex-pats. That was where he'd met Holmes and where later, both of them pursued Irene Adler.

"How deep are the tentacles of this Council, Holmes? Into the American halls of power. The CIA for instance?"

Holmes took a forkful of fried noodles. "I honestly don't know, John. I do know there's a hidden hand at work. A, shall we say, an international Napoleon of Crime who is moving the pieces around. Was it the mayor's current fixer who told you about the FBI operations house where you trailed Waller?"

"Yes, but come on, Holmes, we both have reasons to dislike him, but are you suggesting he's this mastermind? Then why tell me about the FBI pad and blow up the operation?"

Holmes gestured. "You asked him about the house because a man like him, a man who moves back and forth on both sides of the Atlantic, who has a hand in American and British politics and circles of influence, would know such things. Your suspicions would be raised if he didn't produce an address."

Watson cut off a piece of his smothered steak with fried rice on the side. "That fine pretend junkie chick, she's one of your Irregulars isn't she?"

"Indeed," Holmes confirmed. "She and I were shadowing Martin X's rally as we surmised some chicanery might be in the offing. When the imposter appeared on the roof as a distraction, and seeing you had Mr. X safe, I went after the van." Holmes sampled his rib tips.

At that moment in an Upper East Side penthouse, U.N. Special Ambassador Irene Adler was also sipping tea. The dark haired, sharp-featured woman was in her dressing gown, looking out the large window. Moriarty came up behind her. He slipped an arm around her waist and nuzzled her fragrant neck.

"I'm going to miss you," he said.

"No more than I'll miss you." She turned and raised her head to kiss him.

Back at Francine's, Holmes paid the bill and they walked outside.

"What if this Napoleon of yours was a woman?" Watson said.

His lunch companion slowly nodded his head. "You might have something there. . . . Dock."

"See you around, Holmes."

"Indeed."

As Dock Watson walked away, he idly put a hand in his jean jacket pocket. There was an object in there and he took it out. In his hand was a fortune cookie. He frowned, concluding Holmes must have surreptitiously slipped it on him. Watson cracked the cookie open and read the fortune.

The game's afoot, the message read.

He chuckled and ate the bits.

THE PAINTED SMILE

by *William Kent Krueger*

He was an odd child to begin with. After he received the book as a Christmas present, things only got worse. Eventually his aunt was beside herself and sought my help.

I have an office in Saint Paul, in a building that was grand about the time Dillinger was big news. It's long been in need of a facelift. One of the things I like about it is that I can see the Mississippi River from my window. Another is that I can afford the rent.

Although she'd called ahead and had explained the situation, when she brought in the boy, I was still surprised. He was small, even for a ten-year-old. But his eyes were sharp and quick, darting like bees around the room, taking in everything. I welcomed the woman and her nephew, shook their hands, and we sat in the comfortable easy chairs I use during my sessions.

"So, Oliver," I said. "I'm very curious about your costume."

"My name is Sherlock. And this is not a costume."

"Your aunt has told me that your birth certificate reads Oliver Wendell Holmes. You were named after the great Supreme Court justice."

"I prefer Sherlock."

"All right. For now. Tell me about your attire. That hat is pretty striking, and your cape as well. Tweed, yes? How did you manage to come by them?"

"I made them myself."

I looked to his aunt.

She nodded. "He taught himself to use my sewing machine. And he does a fine stitch by hand, too."

In our initial phone conversation, she'd told me her nephew had been tested in school and had demonstrated an IQ of 170. I'm generally leery of quantifications of this kind, but it was clear the boy was gifted.

"When did you become Sherlock Holmes?"

"I've always been Sherlock Holmes. I just didn't realize it until I received the volume of Conan Doyle at Christmas."

"Always?"

"Just as you've always been Watson."

"But I'm not. You know that. My name is simply Watt."

"Are you not the son of Watt, therefore Watt's son?"

"Clever," I admitted with a smile.

"I'm not crazy, Watson," he said quite calmly. "Not delusional. I'm well aware that Sherlock Holmes is a literary fiction. I'm simply the mental and emotional incarnation of that fictional construct, the confirmation that the literary may sometimes, indeed, reflect a concrete reality. The name Sherlock feels suited to me. But all this is something my aunt has difficulty accepting. I understand."

"You get made fun of," his aunt said to him, a situation that clearly caused her distress. "The other kids at school pick on you. Doesn't that bother you?"

"I'm the object of ridicule because they're not comfortable with who they are. They work hard at creating just the right image, and I threaten that. It's the same with adults. If you weren't so insecure in your own circumstances, Aunt Louise, you would see me for who I am instead of who you want me to be."

"That's a rather harsh judgment, Oliver," I said.

"Sherlock," he reminded me. "And I would say the same about you, Watson."

"Oh?"

"Your office is on the third floor of a building that houses enterprises of a less than robust nature. Your shelves are full of books on psychology that haven't been read in a good long while. You spend a lot of time sitting at your desk and staring at the river, wishing that instead of becoming a child psychologist you'd gone to sea. You've recently separated from your wife. Or perhaps divorced. And you'd like desperately to find a woman who understands you."

"I beg your pardon?"

"The building speaks for itself," he explained. "The dust on your shelves is evidence that you seldom reference your reference materials. You've arranged your office so that the best view—the river—is in front of you, and only a very dedicated individual wouldn't be constantly seduced by that wistful scene. Your walls are filled with photographs and paintings of great ships at sea. Your left ring finger still bears a strip of skin much paler than the area around it, indicating that, until very recently, you wore a wedding band. And in your wastebasket is the latest issue of *City Pages* folded to the personal ads section."

Though I was shaken by the accuracy of his observations, I did my best not to show it. From that point on, I conducted a fairly standard intake interview. The boy's parents were deceased, killed two years earlier when their car slid off an icy road while they were returning from a New Year's Eve party. His parents had both been successful attorneys.

At the end, I spoke with his aunt alone. I told her I thought I could help the boy, but that it might take some time. She agreed to bring him back for sessions twice a week.

I walked her out of my office to where the boy sat waiting in the hallway. I explained what his aunt and I had decided. He didn't seem upset in the least. I bid them goodbye, and the woman started away. But the boy held back and, before catching up with his aunt, whispered something to me in a grave voice.

I returned to my office and stood at the window, looking down at the street, watching them get into the woman's old sedan and drive away. The whole time, the final words the boy had spoken to me ran through my head: *One thing you should know, Watson. Moriarty is here.*

I'm a bit of a dreamer. That's why my wife left me. Well, one of the reasons. And so, truthfully, I was inclined to be sympathetic toward Oliver Holmes, who, like me, and despite his protestations to the contrary, was someone wanting to be someone else. I found myself looking forward to our next visit three days later. When Oliver showed up, his aunt simply dropped him off, saying she would be back in an hour. She had errands to run.

We sat in my office, and I asked how his days had gone since I last saw him.

He cut to the chase. "I've been worried about Moriarty."

"Tell me about him."

"You know who he is, Watson."

"I've read my Conan Doyle," I said.

"Then you understand the evil he's capable of."

"Is this really Moriarty or another instance of some kind of, what did you call it? 'A concrete reflection of a literary reality'?"

"Moriarty is not the source of all evil, Watson. But his malicious intent here is quite real."

"So he's up to something?"

"What a stupid question, Watson. Of course he's up to something. The real question is what?"

"You've seen him, then?"

"Of course."

"Can you describe him to me?"

"I've never seen him except in disguise."

"If he was in disguise and you've never seen him otherwise, how do you know it was him?"

"A wolf may don sheep's clothing, but he still behaves like a wolf."

I sat back and considered the boy.

"Do you play chess?" I finally asked.

"Of course. Since I was four."

"Care to play a game?"

"On my aunt's nickel? Isn't that a bit unfair to her, Watson?"

"Tell you what. I give every client one free session. We'll count this as your free one."

He shrugged, a very boy-like gesture, and I went to a cabinet and brought out my chess set.

"Carved alabaster," he said, clearly impressed. "Roman motif."

"I take my chess seriously."

We set up the board and played for half an hour to a stalemate. I was impressed with how well he conducted himself. I'm no slouch, and he kept me on my toes. Mostly, however, it afforded me an opportunity to observe his thinking. He was aggressive, too much so, I thought. He didn't consider his defense as carefully as he should have in order to anticipate the danger inherent in some of his bolder moves. He was smart, beyond smart, but he was still a child. I could tell it irritated him that he didn't win.

"Tell me more about Moriarty," I said.

"I believe he killed my parents." It was an astounding statement, but he spoke it as a simple truth.

"Your aunt told me they died in an automobile accident."

"Moriarty was behind it."

"To what end?"

"I don't know. Ever since I realized he was here, I've been observing him. I haven't quite deciphered the pattern of his actions."

"Observing him how?"

"How does one normally observe, Watson? I've been following him."

This alarmed me, though I tried not to show it. His brashness, if what he told me was true, was the kind of heedless aggression I'd seen in his chess play. Though I didn't believe in Moriarty, whatever the boy was up to wasn't healthy.

A knock at the door ended our session. His aunt entered the office.

"Could I speak with you alone?" I asked.

"I'm in a bit of a hurry," she said. "Perhaps next time. Come on, Oliver. We've got to run."

When they'd gone, I was left with a profound sense of uneasiness. Whatever was going on, I couldn't help thinking that the boy was heading somewhere dangerous, dangerous to him and perhaps to others. Frankly, I wasn't sure what to do except bide my time until our next visit.

⊲◇⊳

"Would you care to see him, Watson?" the boy asked. "Moriarty."

His aunt had dropped him at the door to the building, and he'd come up alone. He'd insisted on a chess rematch, and while we'd played I'd probed him more about his obsession with that fictional villain.

"I'd like that," I said.

"Meet me at six this evening at the corner of Seventh and Randolph."

"I beg your pardon?"

"Do you want to see Moriarty or not?"

"I do."

"Then meet me."

"I'll have to discuss this with your aunt."

"No."

"Oliver—"

"Sherlock, damn you!"

"Oliver," I replied firmly, "there are lines I won't cross. I can't connive with you behind your aunt's back."

"I'll make a deal with you, Watson," the boy said, having calmed himself. "Meet me tonight, this one time. If you're not convinced that there's danger afoot and that Moriarty is the source, I won't insist anymore that you call me Sherlock."

I considered his proposal and decided there was nothing to lose. I certainly didn't believe in Moriarty, and so this might be a way to crack through the boy's wall of resistance.

"Six," I agreed.

He was there to meet me and got into my car when I pulled to the curb. He directed me a couple of blocks away to an apartment building in a working-class section with a view of the old brewery. We parked well back from the entrance, sandwiched inconspicuously between two other cars.

"What exactly are we watching for?" I asked.

"At six-fifteen, you'll see."

I talked with him while we waited, asked him about his aunt.

"She's a bit dull," he said. "Not like my mom or dad were. She feels trapped, but I believe she does her best."

"Trapped?"

"In her life, in her marriage."

"She's married?" This was a piece of new information. His aunt had said nothing during the intake interview, and the boy had been silent on the subject until now.

"Of course. I assumed you saw the ring." He frowned at me. "Really, Watson, you need to pay closer attention to the details."

"Tell me about your uncle."

"He drives a semi truck. He's gone most days of the week, but usually makes it home for the weekends. It's better when he's not around. He's got a mean streak in him." He glanced at his watch. "She should be coming out any minute now."

There she was, right on time, pushing out the front door of the apartment building at six-fifteen sharp. She crossed the street and got into the old sedan I'd seen her driving before.

"Follow her," the boy said.

I pulled out and stayed behind her for the next ten minutes.

"Now watch," the boy said. "This is where it gets interesting."

The street ran past a large entertainment center called Palladium Pizza. On the big sign out front was a neon Ferris wheel and below that a lit marquee that proclaimed: FOOD, FUN, AND GAMES FOR THE WHOLE FAMILY. The parking lot was quite full. The place was clearly a popular enterprise. The boy's aunt pulled into the lot and parked. I pulled in, too, but stayed well away. She left the sedan, glanced at her watch, then stood looking expectantly toward the double glass doors of the establishment.

Lo and behold, a clown appeared. He wore a big red wig and his nose was tipped with a little red ball. His clothes were a ridiculous burlesque of elegant evening wear, complete with a large fake flower on his lapel that I was certain shot water. The shoes on his feet were a dozen sizes too big. His mouth was elongated with red face paint into a perpetual and, I thought, rather frightening grin. He approached the woman. To my amazement, they kissed.

"Who's that?" I asked. But no sooner had I spoken than the light dawned. "Moriarty."

The boy gave a single, solemn nod. "Moriarty."

They walked arm in arm to a van at the other end of the parking lot. The vehicle was decorated with brightly colored balloon decals, and floating among them were the words "Marco, the Magnificent: Magic and Buffoonery for All Ages." They got in, the van pulled onto the street, and it quickly disappeared amid the traffic.

"Your aunt is having an affair with a clown?"

"With Moriarty," the boy said.

"Your uncle doesn't know?"

"Clueless."

"Okay," I said. "If this is Moriarty, what's he up to?"

"That's the question, isn't it, Watson? I hope to have an answer soon."

He continued to stare down the street where his aunt and the clown had gone.

"Did you see his face? The painted smile? Such a grotesque mockery of good will." His eyes narrowed in a determined way and he said grimly, "Pure Moriarty."

When his aunt dropped him off for his next session, I caught her before she rushed away and asked to speak with her privately a moment. She seemed a bit put out, but stepped into my office while Oliver waited outside.

"You're seeing someone," I said.

She was clearly startled. "What do you mean?"

"Marco the Magnificent."

"How—" she started, then her eyes shifted to the office door. "Oliver." She looked at me again, and I could see that she was trying to decide on a course of action. She finally settled on what seemed to me the truth.

"I don't love my husband anymore. Morrie makes me feel special. Makes me feel young. Makes me laugh."

"Morrie? That's his name?"

"Morris Peterson."

"When did Morrie enter your life?"

"A while ago."

"Could you be more specific?"

"Just before Christmas."

"About the time you gave Oliver the volume of Conan Doyle stories. Look, I believe your nephew is threatened by Morrie. He's lost his parents. I think he might be afraid of losing you, too. You're all the family he has now."

"He's never said anything."

"You're having an affair. What could he say? But it comes out in this fantasy of his that he's Sherlock Holmes. He uses it to justify his feeling of being threatened. And also, I believe, as a way of trying to have some control over the situation."

She looked again at the door, beyond which her nephew sat, a lonely, orphaned boy dressed in a deerstalker hat and matching cape. I saw the pain in her eyes. But I went on, laying it all out for her.

"Although your nephew claims to understand that he is not, in fact, Sherlock Holmes, I think that deep down he really believes he is. He's not just emulating that literary creation, he sees himself as the flesh-and-blood incarnation. He can rationalize it all he wants, but he's not acting truly rational."

"And I'm responsible?"

"No. Or at least, not entirely. But your current situation certainly isn't helping."

"So you're saying I have to break it off with Morrie? That will fix Oliver?"

"It's not a question of fixing. Oliver's not a broken machine. He's simply a child, brilliant but lost."

She looked truly lost herself, and I could tell that pushing her at this point would do no good.

"Take some time to think it over," I advised. "But not too long. In the meantime, I'll work with Oliver and do what I can to help him face the truth of the situation."

"He can't tell my husband," she said, and now her eyes bloomed with fear. "He would kill me."

"I'll talk to him," I promised.

When she'd gone, I called the boy into my office and we sat together.

I said, "Moriarty isn't his real name, you know. His name is Morris Peterson."

"That's simply an alias," the boy said. "He's using a name similar to his own. A common ploy. Look, Watson, I know the true nature of his interest now."

I thought I had a pretty good idea of the true nature of his interest myself. The boy's aunt was a woman desperate for attention. She wanted to feel loved, young, special. And she would probably do almost anything to please the man who made her feel that way. Even a clown.

"You know, of course, about sexual attraction, Oliver."

"Sherlock," he said in an icy tone. "My name is Sherlock." He took a moment to settle himself, then said, "Of course, I know that sex is a part of his attraction. Will you just listen to me for a moment, Watson? Let me explain everything to you."

"You?" I said evenly, after he'd laid it all out for me. "He's after you?"

"I present a threat to him. And a challenge. I'm the only person alive who is his intellectual equal and moral opposite."

"And you believe he wants to do you harm?"

"Not just harm, Watson. He wants me dead."

And there it was, the full manifestation of his delusion. Against my best judgment, I'd come to care about the boy, and this paranoia troubled me greatly.

"I can see that you don't believe me," Oliver said. "Just listen to me for a moment, Watson. Moriarty is, in fact, a fugitive on the run. He has warrants for his arrest in California, Oregon, and Colorado. Any other common criminal would have been taken into custody, but Moriarty is not your common criminal."

"Warrants for what?"

"Theft, fraud, and one for a particularly nasty incident in Denver."

"How do you know this?"

"Because of the greatest boon to the modern detective, Watson. The Internet. You know the game of poker?"

"Of course."

"An experienced poker player watches for what's called a tell, an unconscious gesture that gives another player away in the heat of betting. Moriarty has a tell."

"And what would that be?"

"The clown costume. It's an unusual disguise, to say the least. But it's clearly one he's comfortable with. I merely did an Internet search for crimes that involved clowns. I came across a case in California several years ago. A clown who called himself Professor Perplexing. He traveled with a small circus as one of their sideshow offerings. He entertained the children with his clown antics and their parents by appearing to read their minds. He also managed to read their credit cards and charged up a hefty sum. He skipped just ahead of the police. According to the circus folks, Professor Perplexing's real name was Martin Petters.

"The next case I found was in Portland. A clown working for a non-profit called Smile A Day. The organization provided entertainment for nursing homes and senior residential facilities. In addition to offering the old people a few laughs, he offered to invest their savings. Again, he left town just before the police caught up with him. The non-profit reported his name was Mark Patterson.

"Finally Denver. A little over a year ago. A man working for a service that provided entertainment at children's parties was accused of molesting a child during one of these parties. He vanished immediately thereafter. His name, according to the service, was Milton Parks."

"That's quite a leap from Denver to the Twin Cities."

"There's one more connection, Watson. Moriarty, or Parks, as he was calling himself then, was involved with a widow. Before he fled town, he'd stolen much of the money she'd received from her husband's life insurance." Oliver counted off on his fingers. "M. Petters. M. Patterson. M. Parks. And now Morris Peterson. All Moriarty."

"I still don't understand why he would want you dead."

"The insurance money that came from my parents' deaths is quite a tidy sum—over a million dollars. My aunt isn't just my legal guardian.

In the event of my death, she inherits the money. If Moriarty gets rid of me, he not only eliminates his greatest foe, but all that money becomes available to him."

"There's your uncle," I said. "He's an obstacle."

"If she doesn't divorce him, I suspect Moriarty will find a way to deal with him, too."

"Why would a villain as brilliant as Moriarty stoop to such petty crimes? Even a million dollars, I imagine, would be a paltry sum in his view. If he is Moriarty, why hasn't he set his sights on grander schemes?"

Young Holmes seemed not at all perplexed by the question. "I've wondered that myself, Watson. But I believe he's simply been biding his time."

"Until what?"

"Until he could get to me. When I'm out of the way, who's to stop him from whatever grander design he has in mind? Something needs to be done about Moriarty, Watson, and soon."

I realized the boy's delusional behavior had taken a sudden, more troubling turn. "You wouldn't act on this belief, would you?"

"I already have, my dear fellow."

Alarm bells went off.

"What have you done, Oliver?"

He gave me an exasperated look and wouldn't reply.

"Sherlock," I said. "What have you done?"

"I've simply set the wheels in motion, Watson. Moriarty's own inertia will carry him to his just end."

"Indulge me. What exactly do you mean?"

"Reichenbach Falls," the boy said.

"Where Holmes and Moriarty struggle?"

"More importantly, where Moriarty falls to his death."

"But Holmes falls to his death there, too."

The boy arched an eyebrow. "Does he?"

"There is no Reichenbach Falls in Minnesota."

"No, Watson, there is not." He gave me a smile, but so tinged with sadness that it nearly broke my heart.

Our time was up, and a knock came at the door. I desperately wanted to speak with the boy's aunt alone, but when I opened up, a man stood there. Big, bearded, wearing a ball cap with PETERBILT across the crown. He looked quite put out. "I've come for my nephew."

"Uncle Walter?" the boy said at my back. "Where's Aunt Louise?"

"She's too upset to drive. So I'm here to get you."

"What's wrong?" I asked.

"Family business," Uncle Walter said to me, much on the surly side. "Come on, Ollie. Let's go."

I knelt at the door and looked into the boy's face. "Promise me you won't do anything until I've had a chance to talk to your aunt."

"It's too late, Watson. The great mechanism of fate has been set in motion." He put a hand on my shoulder. "It's all right, dear friend. I can take care of this."

I was overcome with a deep concern for the boy. I knew that despite his intellect—or maybe because of it—he was living a profound delusion, one that seemed more and more to promise harm to himself and to another.

Because I had a session immediately afterward, it was quite a while before I could sit down uninterrupted at my computer. I conducted an Internet search, in the same way that I imagined young Holmes had. It took me no time at all to find the story he'd referenced in our session about one Milton Parks, still wanted in Denver, Colorado, on a charge of fraud stemming from the scamming of a widowed woman and also a charge of child molestation. I found a picture of him, in the clown costume he'd worn while working at children's parties, a costume very similar to the one I'd seen Morris Peterson wearing. I could find no photograph showing me what he looked like without face paint and ridiculous clothing. In short order, I also found the other incidents the boy had referenced in Portland and California. But still no photographs of what Moriarty looked like beneath the face paint.

And that's when I caught myself. I'd begun to think of the clown as Moriarty.

I drove to the building where Oliver lived with his aunt and uncle. I buzzed their apartment. A moment later I heard the gruff voice of Uncle Walter through the speaker in the entryway.

"I need to speak with Oliver's aunt," I said.

"It'll have to wait."

"It's rather important," I said. "It's about Oliver's safety."

"A little late for that," he said.

"I beg your pardon."

"Ollie's gone. Run away looks like."

Reichenbach Falls. There was nothing like that in the Twin Cities or anywhere near. But there was a rather famous waterfall in a park across the river in Minneapolis: Minnehaha Falls. It was a thin prospect, but the only one I had.

It was nearing dark when I arrived at the park, and I was greeted with an amazing sight. Near the falls stood a pavilion with a bustling restaurant and outdoor patio. The pavilion was surrounded by tall trees, and on the grass between the trees a multitude of colorful tents had been set up. A huge banner strung between two of the trees declared SOUTH MINNEAPOLIS NEIGHBORHOOD CIRCUS. Temporary floodlights lit the scene. Carnival music blared. On a little stage, a man in a jester's costume was juggling swords. A tightrope hung a few feet off the ground, and a young woman dressed as a ballerina and carrying a parasol balanced precariously on the line. In front of the tents, local hawkers called to the milling crowd to come inside and see the wonders of two-headed snakes and dogs who did tricks and yogis who could turn themselves into pretzels. There were games of all kinds, and the air was redolent with the smell of cotton candy and mini-donuts, and children ran to and fro trailing balloons on long strings. And everywhere there were clowns.

I made my way among the confusion of bodies to the bridge above Minnehaha Creek and its waterfall. We'd had a wet spring. The creek was full, and the water swept in a roaring torrent over the edge of the falls. Laughing children half-climbed the stone walls that edged the bridge. Their parents called harsh warnings to them or pulled them back. The bridge was lit with glaring streetlamps that had come on with the dark, and the people on it cast shadows so that it seemed as if the bridge was populated by two species, one of flesh and the other of black silhouettes.

I couldn't see Oliver anywhere, nor could I see a clown that looked like the one I'd seen coming from Palladium Pizza. But I knew Moriarty had used different costumes in the past, so God only knew how he might have been dressed that night. I searched desperately, overwhelmed with a mounting sense of dread.

A scream shot like a rocket above the chaos of sounds around me. It came from the other end of the bridge. The scream of a child. I turned and pushed through the crowd in that direction. Another scream, and my heart raced as the crowd parted before me. I came at last to a place where a little boy stood near a clown who knelt with a huge boa constrictor draped over his shoulders.

"He won't bite," the clown assured the boy. "But he might swallow you."

The clown leaned nearer, with the snake's head in his hand. The boy screamed again and danced back, but it was clear he was delighted.

The crowd had formed a little circle and was focused on the boy and the snake. That's when I caught sight of Oliver Wendell Holmes. He was standing off the bridge, in the shadows next to a tree near the edge of the chasm where the creek ran and fell fifty feet to the rocks below. He wore the deerstalker hat and the cape of his own making. He was alone, and I was washed in a great relief.

Then, from behind the tree next to Holmes, the clown emerged, with that grotesque grin painted on his face, that cruel mockery of good intent.

"Oliver!" I cried.

But at that same moment, the boy near the snake screamed again, and the crowd roared with laughter and gave their applause, and my desperate cry was lost.

I watched helplessly as the clown reached out and little Holmes turned suddenly to face him. The clown grasped the boy and shoved him toward the edge of the precipice. Oliver in turn grabbed the clown, and in the next instant, my heart broke as I watched them tumble together over the edge of the precipice.

"Oliver!" I cried again, though I knew it was hopeless. Absolutely hopeless.

I shoved my way across the bridge and off the path to the tree where the boy and the clown had fallen. I knelt, leaned over the edge, and looked down at the bottom of the chasm. The streetlamps on the bridge lit the scene below with a raw glare, and I saw the body of the clown sprawled on the rocks where the water crashed and ran on. But I saw no sign of Oliver.

"I could use a hand, Watson."

The voice startled me. In disbelief, I stared below where young Holmes hung upside down, flat against the chasm wall, his right ankle secured with a rope that, as I followed it, I could see was tied to the base of the tree. I drew him up quickly. When I'd pulled him to safety, I couldn't help myself. I took him firmly into my arms and hugged him dearly.

"Please, Watson, a little decorum," Holmes whispered into my ear.

"I took his number off my aunt's cell phone and called him," the boy explained to me as we stood on the bridge with the rest of the crowd and watched the body being dealt with below. We'd talked with several policemen already and were waiting for a detective who was supposed to arrive soon to take our official statements.

"I told him I knew who he was and that I wanted to meet him here, and that if he didn't come I would tell my aunt exactly who he was, and I would inform the police as well."

"You knew about this neighborhood circus?"

He looked at me with disappointment. "I never do anything without knowing everything in advance. I was certain Moriarty would feel quite comfortable in this setting. Bold and, I speculated, reckless."

"Why didn't he just skip town?"

"Because I'm Holmes and he was Moriarty. Just as I thought, he couldn't resist the confrontation. A simple push, that was all he thought it would take. But because I'd anticipated his move and held to him, my own weight carried him over the edge along with me."

"Except that you had the rope around your ankle."

"Yes."

"Why didn't you just talk to the police?"

"He was a clever fellow. He slipped them in California and Portland and Denver. There was no reason to believe he couldn't slip them here. No, Watson, this was something I had to take care of myself."

The detective finally arrived, a tall fellow in an ill-fitting brown suit. "We've called your aunt and uncle," he informed the boy. "When they get here, we'll all sit down together and talk."

"May I stay with him?" I asked.

"For now," the detective agreed.

I looked at Holmes. The crowd had cleared away from him but still stared, as if he was just another of the oddities of the evening. He was a lonely boy, with no friends. But I thought he needed one. Didn't everybody, even the most brilliant and solitary among us?

"When this is all over, I'll still expect to see you in my office on Thursday," I said, then added with a gentle and genuine smile, "my dear Sherlock."

THE FIRST MRS. COULTER

by *Catriona McPherson*

Miss Cordelia Grant did not mourn the world of damp dressing rooms, damper lodgings, and Sunday travel in a third-class railway carriage. True, her current role—lady's maid to Mrs. Gilver—was performed on a smaller stage than that of even the lowliest provincial theater and her cast of one worked hard at thwarting most of her best ideas when it came to costume but still she thought herself lucky. There were men marching for work, women queuing for bread and soup, and her parents' little acting company was reduced to church halls and social clubs. Miss Grant was accordingly grateful for her settled home, steady wage, and security.

Sometimes, however, the quiet comforts of rural Perthshire in wintertime failed to satisfy appetites formed during a theatrical childhood and Miss Grant's efforts to supplement those comforts only made her chafe the more.

Today was typical. *Moriarty*, wheeled out during the matinee at La Scala, had riled up all her lusts like a stiff wind in a pile of leaves, and reading "The Adventure of The Veiled Lodger" in a back issue of the *Strand* on the way home had worsened matters—for, where the picture was silly and melodramatic, the story was clever and thrilling and left Miss Grant longing for clients to visit *her*, to pour their agonies into *her* willing ear, to gasp in astonishment when *she* deduced all.

She would, she decided, put in some practice right here on the Perth to Pitlochry omnibus, just in case. Reading was making her feel rather sick anyway.

There was precious little to see out of the window now the town was behind them, so she scrutinized her fellow passengers and, being a lady's maid, it was their clothes that drew her eye: the nap of a felt hat that knew careful brushing though of average quality; the tiny holes along a hem hinting that a skirt had been taken up to get more wear from it after the fashion changed; the crisp fit across the shoulders on the bespoke coat of a Dunkeld solicitor, and the stretched seams and bunched gussets on the ready-made coat of the butcher who sat beside him.

Rolled brims, covered buttons, invisible darns; all were of note to Miss Grant. She was so intent on a beautiful lace handkerchief—needle-made, corners turned without a pucker, rosettes point-ironed so their petals were cupped, not flattened by pressing—that she had been looking at it for several minutes before she realized it was held to a weeping face. She withdrew her gaze.

That was Mrs. Coulter, she thought, and looked back again out of the corner of her eye. Yes indeed, that was Mrs. Edward Coulter.

Edward Ernest Coulter was an architect, but he married well, took up residence at Benachally Castle, and lived there quietly. It was the talk of the county when all of a sudden FOR SALE signs went up at the gate lodge and the Coulters removed themselves to a semi-detached sandstone villa where Mrs. Coulter gave piano lessons by the hour. *Mr.* Coulter was only fifty at the move but if he had done any more architecting, Miss Grant had not seen him at it.

Now there she was, erstwhile chatelaine of Benachally, sitting on a bus in a gabardine mackintosh that was green with age and thin with washing, her woollen stockings drooping at her ankles, her shoes scuffed pale and snub-nosed from wear. She was poor-looking even for a piano teacher and she was still weeping when Miss Grant pulled the cord and climbed down.

Drysdale the chauffeur had the dog cart waiting at Gilverton's gates and had brought a hot bottle for Miss Grant to hug while he trundled her up the drive. As she tucked the blanket more cozily about her knees, she thought what a long cold walk it would be from the bus stop to the sandstone villa in that thin mackintosh, and how the chill of the road would seep through those worn-down shoes. How shameful then that, although her heart sank as the cart slowed by the back door, it did not sink for poor Mrs. Coulter but for poor Miss Grant, who could ape the great detective with her skills of observation but would surely never get the chance to try the rest of it: investigation, revelation, and glory.

Her sinking heart would have soared had she known how soon that chance would come.

Young Lorna was at Gilverton for tea, installed in the kitchen, sighing fit to blow out the fire and complaining. Miss Grant tutted. Lorna was a head housemaid at the age of twenty, in a household with no butler, no housekeeper, no children, and not even a mistress yet. In other words, Liberty Hall.

"It's as dull as church," she was saying. "There's nothing to do."

"You said he had you clearing the attics," said Miss Grant. *He* was Donald Gilver, elder son of her own mistress, Benachally's third owner in ten years, lately set up there to grow barley and kill pheasants and generally stay out of trouble until it was time to marry.

"The attics are clear!" said Lorna. "All except some filthy dirty trunks from ages back that I'm not touching."

"Send them on to the Wilsons," said Miss Grant. She was beginning to drowse, what with the fire, the tea, and the two warm scones she had eaten.

"They're from long before the *Wilsons*!" said Lorna. "Ancient old things. E. E. C. are the initials on them."

Miss Grant snapped awake. "They must be the Coulters'," she said. "Trunks? Clothes, you mean? Any jewel cases? Strongboxes? Anything of that kind?"

"Why would you care?" said Lorna, in her pert way. Ordinarily Miss Grant would have drawn herself up at such cheek but right at that moment she barely heard the girl. She was plotting.

Friday found her first in the library, looking up COULTER in the Post Office Directory, and then in Pitlochry on a trim enough street of nice enough houses—unless you had been used to a castle, anyway—lifting a glistening brass knocker and rehearsing her spiel.

The maid who answered was neat and smart in a blue serge day-dress with shoes mystifyingly better-heeled and polished than Mrs. Coulter's own. The explanation was not long in coming.

"Bonnethill," said the maid. "Behind the wee barber."

"Ah," said Miss Grant. "I see."

For while Pitlochry is too small a town to have an unsavory district, at a push Bonnethill would do. Certainly coats would grow thin there and soles wear through. Miss Grant rang the bell at a faded blue door up a narrow stairway and it opened to reveal Mrs. Coulter, the Hon. Miss Elizabeth Larbert as was, standing there.

"Can I help you?" the woman said, with no spark of recognition in her tired eyes, either from the bus or from the Benachally years. She was wiping reddened hands on the front of her apron.

"I'm hoping I can help you, Mrs. Coulter."

"I'm not interested." She began to close the door.

"I'm not selling things," said Miss Grant quickly. "I'm from Gilverton. I think I've found something that belongs to you. Or to your husband anyway."

"Some*thing*?" said Mrs. Coulter.

"At Benachally," said Miss Grant.

"Not some*one*?" said Mrs. Coulter. She slumped a little against the jamb, saying: "No of course not. That would be far too good to be true."

"Possessions of your husband's, in the attics," Miss Grant went on, puzzling away all the while at the other woman's curious words. "Trunks they are. I wondered if I might have them delivered to you. There could be something in them of some . . . interest to the family."

Mrs. Coulter saw through the nicety and gave a single huff of unhappy laughter.

"They are nothing to do with the family," she said. She gave a look over her shoulder and lowered her voice. "Just burn them or do what you will."

"And if what I decide to do is sort through them and sell what I can? Can I bring you the money?"

Mrs. Coulter gazed at her for the time it took to breathe in and out twice without hurrying. Then she blinked.

"From Gilverton?" she said. "Are you one of the servants?" There was a little tremor in her voice as the ghost of her old self looked at her current self and wondered whether to laugh or cry.

"What happened?" said Miss Grant. "What on earth *happened* to you?"

Mrs. Coulter's shoulders dropped so completely that the straps of her apron might have slipped off them.

"You can't come in," she said. "My—" Again she lowered her voice. "My husband is resting and my children will be back from school soon. But there's a tea-counter at the back of the bakers."

"Let me buy you a cup," said Miss Grant. "And you tell me all about it."

It was excellent tea: blistering hot, the color of teak when the milk went in, and fragrant too. Proper leaves, Miss Grant concluded, not those sweepings in little sacks that were enjoying such a vogue. Mrs. Coulter got a bit of color in her thin cheeks as she sipped. By the time she was halfway down the first cup she was ready to begin.

"My husband," she said, "was married once before. Briefly. I didn't tell my parents. It was hard enough . . ." Miss Grant nodded. It certainly would have been, trying to sell an architect of all things to Sir Stephen and Lady Larbert. Better than a doctor, at least, since he would not hand Lady Larbert into a carriage with hands that had just left off examining a rash, but an architect was not a gentleman and their daughter was a lady.

"He was young," Mrs. Coulter went on. "And he had his head turned. It was in New York. She was very glamorous by all accounts." Mrs. Coulter's voice dropped a little. "She was a soubrette."

Miss Grant leaned forward to hear better. "A socialite?"

"Good Lord! Hardly," said Mrs. Coulter. She laughed again as she had before—but this time, perhaps there was a little amusement in it. "She was quite outside society. Quite outside. What I mean is, she was theatrical." Miss Grant would hardly tremble at that and, emboldened by such a calm reception, Mrs. Coulter went on. "Burlesque, actually." Miss Grant did have to work just a little to keep her eyebrows straight then, but she managed, and so Mrs. Coulter, after swallowing a strengthening mouthful of tea, finished with: "A hoochie-coochie girl by the name of Za-Za-Zita."

"Heavens."

"He was a stage-door Johnnie and no bones about it. He saved her."

"Good for him," said Miss Grant. "From what?"

"Oh, she was in with a very rough crowd. Down in a part of New York called the Bowery or the Battery or some such outlandish place. She was mixed up with a jewel thief and if Edward—my husband—if my husband had not swept her away she might have ended up in some rather hot water. I sometimes think, uncharitably perhaps, that she used him."

"I wouldn't wonder."

"His family cut him off."

"I wouldn't wonder about that either," said Miss Grant, trying to imagine a hoochie-coochie-dancing daughter-in-law being introduced to whatever blameless merchant or banker had been Mr. Coulter's father. "And am I right in thinking that the marriage was not a success? She left him?"

"The marriage wasn't even a marriage!" said Mrs. Coulter. "Yes, she left him. As soon as he'd got her out of New York, out of America, she abandoned him."

"And divorced him?" said Miss Grant. For surely not even Sir Stephen and Lady Larbert would care about an indiscretion that left a man a widower.

"She had no grounds!" cried Mrs. Coulter. "My husband is as loyal as the day is long."

"Too loyal to divorce *her*?" asked Miss Grant.

"He could have," Mrs. Coulter said. "He had photographs of her in her costumes; he had the costumes themselves. Any judge in the land could see a woman like that would never be faithful."

"They can be sticklers for hard evidence," said Miss Grant, thinking of Brighton boarding houses and what good livings there are for indiscreet chambermaids.

"And besides, he didn't need to," Mrs. Coulter said.

"She died?"

The woman had the strangest look on her face, Miss Grant thought to herself. She dabbed her lips and folded her little napkin before she spoke again.

"She may have died for all we know. But what I meant was that he had no need to divorce her. He applied for annulment." Miss Grant waited a moment or two but Mrs. Coulter said nothing, so she prompted her.

"On the grounds that . . ."

"Yes." Mrs. Coulter did not blush and did not hang her head. On the contrary, she put her chin in the air and stared down her nose at Miss Grant, daring her to speak.

Miss Grant was always one for a dare. "And the same judge who'd never believe she was faithful refused to believe she was chaste?" she said. "Dear me."

"We had both been so sure it was a mere technicality!" Mrs. Coulter said. "We had already told my parents we were engaged. We couldn't find the words to describe our difficulty. So we went ahead with the wedding."

"Dear me," said Miss Grant again. Then, as all the ramifications arrived in her brain together, she said in quick succession: "But that—So you're—The children—" before she managed to press her lips closed again.

"We are married in the eyes of God and in our own two hearts," Mrs. Coulter said.

"Well good then," said Miss Grant, thinking that two hearts and the eyes of God were all very well but did not explain weeping on an omnibus or living behind a barber's.

"Money, however, has become a problem," Mrs. Coulter conceded. "As I said, my husband was cut off when he married . . ."

"Za-Za-Zita," Miss Grant supplied.

"But I had a settlement, a very generous portion, from my father. All was well until my sister, whom I turned to for help and comfort, to still my troubled thoughts, betrayed me. My own sister. And do you know why?"

"Because your portion was a wedge cut from the same pie as hers?" Miss Grant guessed, making the other woman blink. The Hon. Miss Elizabeth had gone from castle to villa to rooms without becoming inured, it seemed, to plain speaking.

"My mother, while she lived, gave me a little income from her own," said Mrs. Coulter. "But when she died, even that money stopped. My father warned my husband not to try to get work: "worming his way in to the homes of respectable men by passing himself off as one of them." I shall never forget those ugly words! And every penny that was meant for my children is gone."

"Gone?" said Miss Grant.

"Gone to my sister. My father could reverse it if he cared to. I went to him just days ago and begged him again. My older son is finishing school. He should be going to Oxford. I *begged* him. But he just sat there glaring at me, telling me that when *his* father set the terms the words were mere formalities."

"What words?" asked Miss Grant gently.

"Legitimate issue," whispered Mrs. Coulter. "I begged. I told him we were desperate. That my husband was very foolish, but nothing more. He was bedazzled by her. She was a temptress and a trickster and she has ruined all our lives."

With that she stood, put her chair neatly under the table, said good-bye and walked away, leaving Miss Grant a-quiver.

She had not met many Americans in her life and none of them burlesque dancers, but those she *had* come across were dazzling. There had been that one, years ago now, not long after she had arrived here. He was walking along the road, just walking along the road, swinging a carpet bag and singing a music-hall song at the top of his lungs, his voice as rich as treacle. His hair had been like raven's feathers, his skin like milk, and his teeth when he smiled at her had glittered in the sunshine.

"Are you lost?" she had asked him.

"Nope," he had replied and kept walking.

If a single American man in ordinary clothes in a country lane could set the heart of Delia Grant fluttering and stay in her dreams for weeks afterwards, she could not imagine what a soubrette from the Bowery might do when seen across the footlights by a Perthshire architect far from home.

Neither could she easily imagine what a soubrette from the Bowery might *wear*. The thought of her clothes, just sitting there in the attics at Benachally, called to Miss Grant with a siren song. Clothes to make a judge grant a divorce, she thought. Clothes in which to dance a hoochie-coochie.

"I've come to sort those trunks in your attics, Lorna," she said casually, sweeping into the Benachally kitchen the next afternoon. Lorna exchanged a glance with the cook, who shrugged. "There might be some very interesting . . ." Thankfully, the door to the passageway closed behind her before she was forced to finish this sentence, and she went on her way.

They were easily found. Most of the attics were still empty, only a year or so after Master Donald had moved in; swept and bare, they echoed her footsteps back to her, but in one corner, under the eaves, at the farthest point from the stairs, the humped shapes of two steamer trunks lay waiting.

"She was no pixie," Miss Grant said to herself, presently. The first trunk held hatboxes, shoe bags, and glove cases and, when she tried one of the hats on, what was supposed to be a flirty little concoction in the pillbox style fell down around her ears and looked like nothing so much as Bo-Peep's bonnet. The gloves—red satin, black lace, kid dyed a shade of pink unknown to both nature and fashion—were as large as pruning gauntlets. And when it came to the shoes, Miss Grant began to pity poor Zita and wonder if perhaps she was a comedy act and not a glamour girl after all.

For the shoes were quite simply enormous. They were beautifully made, hand-stitched, with fine leather soles, and even the silver tips of the high heels glittered with lacquer, but all the hand-stitching in the world could not change the fact that Zita had feet like loaves.

Hard upon that thought, though, came another. If she was as large as it seemed and if her dresses were the same quality as her incidentals then there would be plenty of cloth to make it worth unpicking them.

Feeling the thrill of the chase—for she loved a bargain—and relishing the prospect of having a frock admired and saying very airily, "It's

American, of course—New York," Miss Grant turned to the second trunk and began rummaging.

The dress she held up did not disappoint her. It was amethyst silk, true silk, generous across the back, even if the waist was as waspish as the fashions of the day had demanded, and from the length of it Za-Za-Zita must have been almost six feet tall. It seemed to be decent cloth, too, from the weight as she held it high. Eagerly, she turned the seam to look at the finish. She rubbed the material between her fingers and found herself frowning.

"Hmph," she said. "Flimsy. Weight's in the lining." Miss Grant had not been above helping a cheap dress hang better with a sturdy lining, in her younger days.

And yet, when she subjected the lining to the same scrutiny, it appeared to be finest lawn. The weight, she now saw, was all in the bodice and such a weight, so oddly placed, that her fanciful mind immediately leapt to jewels. Jewels, or banknotes, or shares in a goldmine, stitched in and left there.

The explanation, of course, was far more humdrum. Za-Za-Zita had not been blessed with womanly lines. Her bodice was heavy because into it she had sewn a pair of little pockets stuffed with . . . Miss Grant palpated one of them and tried to determine what that odd yet familiar substance might be . . . sawdust! There were bags of sawdust sewn in behind the boning of this amethyst dress. And the emerald satin gown underneath it in the trunk, and the pink and yellow bombazine frock which was surely the partner of the pillbox. Miss Grant laid it aside and reached for the next one, but her fingers touched paper instead of cloth. Paper rolled into a scroll and tied with a ribbon.

She took it over to the little sky-light window to read it there.

There was something written on the outside of the scroll in a pretty, feminine hand. Miss Grant squinted at it in the dying light.

"Dearest Edward, you are free. With my undying gratitude for your chivalry, Z."

What could it be? Miss Grant asked herself. Divorce papers? A suicide note? An annulment? How could Zita simply set her husband free? Carefully, she pulled on one end of the bow and let the loosened ribbon drop to the floor.

It was not a letter, she saw as she unrolled the crackling paper. Not legal papers. It was something much, much more exciting. Something so exotic and undreamed of that Miss Grant could scarcely believe it was real. She had seen them in the pictures but she had never imagined she would hold one in her hands.

It was a WANTED poster. A drawing of a scowling face with $100 REWARD printed in red ink underneath. Miss Grant's heart thrilled at the sight of those penetrating eyes as it had seldom thrilled in all her years.

"This must be the jewel thief she was in with," she said to herself. And then she grew very still as an idea rolled towards her and washed over her, head to toe, unstoppable.

She had *seldom* thrilled at the sight of a stranger's face, but not never. Once before she had seen those eyes, when they were smiling. And the hair had been clean and soft and had looked like raven's feathers on a milk-white brow. It was him. It was her American stranger. She had watched him walking away down the lane, into his future, leaving his past behind, and leaving Edward Coulter his freedom—if he had only looked in this trunk and seen it there.

Years of shame and misery, thought Miss Grant. A ruined career, a broken family, and a sister who was about to get the shock of her rotten, greedy little life.

"I'm using your telephone," she announced to Lorna and the cook, putting her head round the kitchen door. "I don't suppose they're on the phone at Bonnethill, but it's worth trying. If not, I'll ring Drysdale to take me to Pitlochry in the cart."

For that poor weeping woman should not spend another wretched minute before hearing the news that *she* was the first Mrs. Coulter after all.

THE CASE OF THE SPECKLED TROUT

by Deborah Crombie

My name is Sherry Watson. It's a crap name, Sherry, I know. But what can you do? It's not like I had a say in the matter. My parents, to give them credit, were trying to do the right thing—a sentimental gesture I wondered if they were sorry for after.

They named me after my godfather, who is—or was, before he vanished a year ago—a famous detective. All I have to say is it's a good thing I wasn't a boy, or I would really have something to be pissed off with him about. Actually, he's responsible for a lot of things I should be pissed off about, my godfather, not the least of which was me standing in a freezing Scottish kitchen, up to my elbows in fish guts.

My godfather has a history of vanishing, so it wasn't a big deal in the beginning. But the months went by with no word, no calls, no dropping in unexpectedly for dinner, then Mum and Dad getting more and more stony-faced and changing the subject whenever I asked about him. It was my last year at school and I was expecting at least the encouraging text now and again. I know my godfather supposedly doesn't like women, but he never treated me like one. Like a girl, I mean. He helped with my science projects, quizzed me on my history, corrected my grammar—even in my texts. (Very annoying, I can tell you.)

Then, nothing. No congratulations when I aced my exams. Not a whisper when I got accepted at Cambridge to read medicine. Mum and Dad took me out to dinner to celebrate that and my eighteenth birthday, at the Ivy. Dad must have booked months ahead, and they were both so fish-out-of-water, it was simply embarrassing. Daniel Craig was there and they actually nudged each other when they saw him. I could have died. But the worst thing was that *he* wasn't there. He'd never missed a birthday. We all knew it and that thought was like the spectre at the feast, if you don't mind me waxing poetic.

The next day, Dad called me into his study. He wore his most solemn, doctor-about-to-give-bad-news-in-the-consulting-room look. He sat down in his leather chair with a sigh and said, "Sherry, darling. I think we have to accept that this time he may really be gone. You know he does dangerous things." He cleared his throat. "You have an exciting time ahead of you, your own life. We all have our own lives, good ones. We'll be fine."

"No," I said. "I don't believe it." Meaning, a) I didn't believe he was gone, and b) I certainly didn't think we'd be fine. And I stomped out. Because there'd been something in my dad's eyes I didn't want to see, something more than sadness. Being pissed off was the only way I could not keep seeing it, over and over.

The next day there was a card in the post. Addressed to me, it had a photo of a gray stone house on the back. There was type as well, in a bright yellow that stood out against the purple heather in the photo's background. Some stupid advert, I thought, and almost threw it in the bin. But something made me give it a closer look.

YOUR GAP YEAR DREAM JOB it read. CONTACT BURNS HOUSE NOW FOR THE OPPORTUNITY OF A LIFETIME.

Really? I crumpled it. Then, a thought stopped me. I smoothed it out and reread it. The only contact information was an email address;

burnsgapyear.co.uk. Weird. Seeing as how I was bound to be at the bottom of anyone's mailing list, I texted some friends from my year. No one else had a card. Weirder.

A quick Internet search turned up a website for a Burns House in Aberdeenshire, Scotland—an upscale hunting lodge. So I shot off an email to the address on the card.

Two weeks later I was on the train to Scotland. My parents were happy enough that I was doing something useful before I started volunteering at a local hospital for my gap year experience. (Dad insisted that I find out whether I could cope with the sight of blood, even though I reminded him repeatedly of how cool I'd been the time my godfather had a little accident while testing various knife blades for incision patterns.) In fact, I think Mum and Dad were more than happy not to have me moping round the house for the entire summer.

I'd never been north of the Border, so as the train gathered speed out of Edinburgh's Waverly Station I looked out the window with interest. I'd never seen so much green. We climbed, through hills and glens and bits of forest, until at last the train hissed to a stop in the little Highland town of Aviemore. The train station looked like a transplanted Swiss chalet, but the mud-splattered Land Rover in the station parking lot looked as Scottish as things come. So did the big, bearded man in oiled jacket and wellies leaning against it. He gave a nod when he saw me and strolled across the parking lot. For a moment, I wondered how he'd recognized me, but then I remembered I'd sent a photo with my application.

"Giles," he said, lifting my pack as if it was filled with candy floss instead of work boots and Aran knit sweaters. "Giles Burns." The glance he gave me was critical and he did not seem inclined to conversation.

We set off, first along a winding, green-cloaked river, then up and across the most desolate moorland I'd ever seen. It was fit for the Hound, I thought with a shiver.

I dared to interrupt Mr. Burns's silence. "Um, what exactly will I be doing at the lodge?" My contract had read "domestic assistant."

"A bit of cooking and scrubbing, and skinning, I should think," he added. "Whatever the wife needs."

"Skinning?" I said. It came out a squeak.

This time he threw me an amused glance and I saw the glint of white teeth in the beard. "It is a hunting lodge, lassie. We occasionally pot rabbits for our suppers."

That shut me up. While I was trying to decide whether I had sold myself into Dickensian slavery—or was destined to be a Scottish Jane Eyre, stuck on the moor with a dour master and a mad wife—the road ran downhill and we were again in the land of green glens and burbling streams. In the distance, the hills were a patchwork of gold and black, as if a giant quilt had been thrown over the land. I'd read that they burned the heather to encourage the grouse but I'd never imagined it looked like that.

Giles swung us off into a smaller track and soon, round the trees, the house I'd seen on the postcard came into view. The sun was slanting low across the land and the lamps were just coming on in the house. The Land Rover's tires scrunched on the gravel drive and a moment later the front door swung wide and the mistress of the house came out to greet us.

Morag Burns was tall, red-headed, and as chatty as her husband was taciturn. She was also quite pregnant. "I thought I could do with a bit extra help this season," she explained as her husband carried in my bag. "For obvious reasons." She grinned and patted her belly. "None of the locals are willing to live in so we enlisted an agency to find someone. We thought your medical training would be useful."

"I haven't actually had any yet," I said hurriedly, trying to avert my eyes from her bulge.

Morag laughed. "Don't worry. I'm not due until the end of August. It's just that we assumed anyone wanting to be a doctor would have a good head on her shoulders. And you were highly recommended."

That gave me pause. I mumbled responses as she took me into the house and gave me a tour. My head swam with tartan. It was everywhere, in shades of red and green. Carpet, wallpaper, over-stuffed armchairs. But somehow it all worked and the effect was cozy, aided by the just-lit fires in the fireplaces.

"There are six guest bedrooms," Morag explained. "All en suite. At the moment we just have a couple of Dutch gentlemen, but from Sunday we're fully booked until the end of the grouse season. We do breakfasts but dinners are only by special arrangement. The local girls come in to help when there's a big shooting party, but otherwise it will just be you and me."

I gulped.

Morag must have seen my expression because she gave me an encouraging pat on the back. "You'll be fine."

And I was. My room was in the attic, but it wasn't Spartan. I even had my own bathroom. We soon settled into a routine. I got thin, and fit, and really good at washing up and setting tables and airing linens, and at cleaning trout and salmon. The venison, thank God, went to a local processor, as I don't think I'd have managed that.

I got used to the sound of the stalking parties' guns booming in the hills, and to red hands, and to the fact that what Scots called "a nice day" barely got me out of my down waistcoat.

When I needed a break from the kitchen, I communed with the fish prints that lined the central hall on the ground floor. They were Victorian, Morag said, hand-colored and intricately drawn. I loved the delicate play of colors in the salmon's scales and the cheerful polka dots on the big brown trout. Their fins seemed almost to quiver as they stared back at me with their flat, luminous eyes.

"You're a funny girl," Morag said, coming into the hall one day and catching me gazing at them.

I shrugged. "My godfather always told me to pay attention to detail. And they have personalities, don't you think?"

Morag stood for a moment, hand pressing into the small of her back. "Old Spot, there"—she nodded at the brown trout—"seems to have an opinion about something." There came the now-familiar crunch of gravel as the Land Rover pulled into the drive and we went back to work.

I'd soon begun to see that the guests were wealthy. We generally booked week-long stays, but we had one guest who had reserved for the remainder of the summer. Thirty-something and ordinary looking, with short brown hair and wire-rimmed glasses, he was from some Balkan country whose name I never managed to pronounce. Unlike some of the guests, Stefan was friendly and always seemed to have time for a chat.

He was a civil servant, he said, in his slightly accented Received English, interested in learning ways his country could increase tourist revenue.

He spent most of his days going out with Giles, almost as if he was an assistant, but I noticed that Giles treated him with a deference he didn't extend to even the poshest of the other guests.

Stefan was standing in the drive one afternoon when I went out to ask him if he wanted to join us for dinner. His back to me, he seemed to be gazing at the distant moors, where if you looked just right you could see the first faint blush of purple from the heather. Summer was moving on.

"Stefan," I called, but he didn't turn. "Stefan," I said again, but he stood unmoving, his hands in his pockets. It was only when my footsteps crackled on the gravel as I crossed the drive that he turned, a startled look on his face.

"Oh, Sherry, I didn't hear you." He quickly rearranged his face into his usual affable expression.

I delivered Morag's invitation and started to go back to the house. Then I turned and blurted the thought that had come into my head. "Your name isn't really Stefan, is it? That's why you didn't hear me."

"Ach, I was merely daydreaming," he protested, shaking his head. Then something in his face relaxed and he sighed. "No, you are right, Miss Sherry. It is not. But please don't say anything to anyone."

"But Morag and Giles—"

"Oh, your employers know who I am, but they have promised discretion. You see, I try to do some things for my country that will help people, and there are those who don't like that. Or like me." He gave a ghost of a smile. "So better I be Stefan for a while."

"Mum's the word." I nodded solemnly, all the while a little thrill tingled up my spine. Maybe I was here for something besides cleaning and washing up, after all.

After that I worked even harder at noticing details. I made it my business to know everyone on the estate, from the white-haired, burly gamekeeper to the tall, thin beekeeper, who was spending the summer in a little hut on the hillside that the Scots called a *bothy*. There was a tenant in the distant estate cottage as well, an ex-military bloke called Trevor. He looked a soldier, with his flat cap and neat little moustache, and his enormous Irish wolfhound was always at his side.

We were only a few miles from Balmoral as the crow flies, and as July rolled into August, we began to see black cars on the road that ran past the lodge.

"Security," Giles growled into his beard when I asked him. "Advance teams for the bigwigs who'll be arriving for the shooting parties at Balmoral."

Stefan grew quieter, abstracted, and spent more and more time poring over papers he kept locked in a briefcase in his room.

Well, I could put two and two together, couldn't I? Stefan was here for more than learning about estate management, and his summer-long visit had something to do with the August parties at Balmoral. I tried to keep an eye on him as much as I could, but then the Glorious Twelfth arrived and we were absolutely bonkers with work. We had two weeks of parties with only men, and they wanted packed lunches for the shooting and the fishing, as well as full-course dinners most nights.

Morag was as big as a house by this time and looked exhausted, so I tried to take up slack in the kitchen where I could. Cooking, it turned out, was only chemistry.

Then we had a break. Two cancellations, two pleasant couples, and a single woman in Room 6. She was an actress and her name was Amanda.

The two wives were tweedy types, as big on sport as their husbands, so were out during the day, but Amanda spent more time around the lodge. She said she was *resting* and had thought a holiday in the fresh air would do her good.

Amanda was anything but tweedy. She wore Burberry and Prada and chattered about hairstyles and nail polish and celebrities, the sort of thing I'd found desperately boring at school. But I found I didn't mind, really. When I told her she looked familiar, she said I'd probably seen her in a coffee advert on the TV or in some horror movies. "Bit parts," she added with a shrug. "But they pay the bills."

They must, I thought, for her to have booked a week at Burns House.

She went out with the shooting parties and seemed chuffed with her braces of birds, but fishing, she said, was really her thing. But then the rain set in, coming down in sheets for three solid days. The guests were bored and Morag kept me busy organizing charades and board games and helping with special treats in the kitchen.

"I thought it wasn't supposed to rain in August," said Amanda, popping her blond head in the kitchen door. The kitchen was supposed to be off-limits to guests, but Morag seemed to welcome the female company, too.

"It doesn't, usually. But this is Scotland. There are no guarantees." Morag wiped a floury hand across her brow.

Amanda came all the way in and wandered about the room, stopping to admire the array of bottles and jars of spices and vinegars on the shelves of the big dresser. Then she spied the picnic hamper. "Ooh, what fun," she said, folding back the top. "That's what I'll do when the rain stops. I'll take a fishing picnic and invite Stefan. Will you make us something nice, Morag? Maybe a game pie? With cold salads, and a tart?"

I turned away so she wouldn't see me frown. Stefan had been very chatty with her over the last couple of days and he had lost that worried air. I felt a little disappointed in him. It seemed even a serious man was easily distracted by a fragile-looking woman who made him feel important. And Amanda, I'd decided, was older than she'd first looked. I could see the fine lines at the corners of her eyes, even with her always perfectly applied makeup.

I snapped at Stefan the next time he spoke to me and he looked surprisingly hurt, but I'd begun to wonder just what sort of a bloke Stefan really was. Had he told me the truth about why he was spending the summer at Burns House? Or did he have a more nefarious purpose?

The next day dawned fair and the sky was a rain-washed, brilliant blue. The fields around the lodge were emerald, and on the moors the rain had brought out the heather in glowing, purple swaths.

"You know it will be muddy by the river?" Giles warned at breakfast when Amanda proposed her fishing picnic.

"I'm prepared." She held out a foot clad in a pink designer wellie.

"I'll take you down to the Avon in the Land Rover," Giles said, but he didn't sound happy about it, and neither was I. "Make certain you're wearing bright colors. There will be guns out today."

I met Amanda coming out of the kitchen as I was going in. "Just checking out the picnic basket," she said with a smile. "Giles says he'll put it in the Land Rover with the fishing stuff."

I was blocking her way, but I was feeling contrary, so instead of letting her by I nodded at one of the prints. They were my friends now, those old freckled fish. "Going to land a big one, are you?" More fish guts for me, I thought.

"Mmm, I hope so," said Amanda. "I adore trout."

I stepped back and she swept past, wellies squeaking on the tiles.

I followed her out. Stefan waved at me from the Land Rover. He looked like an excited child going on an adventure.

I watched them pull away, all the while thinking furiously. Was I paranoid? Or really and truly mad? But if I was right . . . Going back to the kitchen, I told Morag I had to run an errand. Then, my message duly delivered to the gamekeeper, I tried to concentrate on scrubbing the breakfast things and starting lunch.

A half-hour later, I heard Giles come back. He called to Morag that he was going up the fields to check on the shooting party and a minute later I heard the Land Rover drive off again.

I couldn't stand it any longer. "Go have a lie down," I told Morag, who was looking decidedly peaky. "I'll finish the lunch prep."

"Right. Thank you, Sherry." She gave me a quick hug. "You're a gem."

I felt guilty for deceiving her, but as soon as I heard the bedroom door close on the upper floor, I was out the front door like a shot. I knew the spot where Giles had left Amanda and Stefan. The river ran wide and shallow over a stone bed, then dropped into a deep pool where the trout liked to lurk, snapping for flies, real or false, on the surface.

I could make it, I thought. I ran across the field and down into the woods, glad now for all the stair-climbing and bed-making and scrubbing. When I came to the river I followed it downstream. It was running high and fast. There was nothing merry about the water rushing over the rocks today.

There was a flash of color through the trees—the bright picnic oilcloth, laid out on the high little ledge of grass above what before the heavy rains had been a pool, but was now just a wider place in the torrent. But where were they?

Then I saw them. Stefan, dutifully dressed in his red anorak and his waders, stood at the water's edge, rod in hand. He was explaining something to Amanda, but I couldn't hear him over the rush of the water. She nodded and patted his shoulder, as if encouraging him to demonstrate.

Stefan turned and cast his line over the pool in a beautiful shining arc. Then Amanda gave him a hard shove in the middle of the back.

Stefan twisted as he fell, the rod flying from his hand. His eyes and mouth were round with surprise, then the water closed over his face. He came up sputtering and shouting, but the current was strong and his waders were instantly filled. I could see he was being pulled towards the sharp fall at the end of the pool.

Amanda stood and watched.

I started to shout, then froze. Surprise was the only thing I had on my side. I ran towards her, hoping the rush of the water would cover the sound of my boots, hoping she would stay focused on Stefan and not turn around. Some small part of my brain wondered just how I was going to get him out even if I could knock her in, but there was no time for a better plan.

A deep woof rang out over the sound of the river. On the other side of the pool appeared Trevor, the military bloke, wolfhound at his side. Then, below me, two shadows raced out of the woods. Men, wearing camouflage. I skidded to a stop.

Amanda heard—or sensed—them, spinning round, her hand going to the pocket of her anorak. But the men were on her and in a flash her hands were cuffed behind her back.

Trevor had a rope coiled in his hands and as he reached the pool he spun it out across the water. As Stefan caught it, Trevor wrapped his end round a tree trunk and knotted it. Then Trevor reeled Stefan in, just like a bloody big fish.

There were more shouts as Giles and the gamekeeper came crashing through the woods. But things were all in hand. After a moment of spit and fury, Amanda had gone quiet, but I made certain her captors were keeping a close eye on her.

The gamekeeper gave me a wink. "All sorted, then?" he asked.

"Thanks to you," I said. I'd caught him just as he was leaving to take the shooting party up on the moor.

He'd listened to me, then given me an assessing glance before nodding and agreeing to take my message. "Why didn't you think I was bonkers?" I asked.

"Trevor there told me to keep an eye on you," he answered.

Once we'd convoyed back to the lodge, Amanda bundled off in a military jeep and Stefan sent off for a hot bath, Trevor invited me up to his cottage for a cup of tea. Morag, still looking shocked, had waved me off my kitchen tasks.

"What gave her away?" he asked, when we were settled at his pine table with steaming mugs. He looked younger without the flat cap, but I was still getting used to the fact that his eyes were now brown rather than blue, and that there was something very odd about the shape of his nose and chin.

"Besides the fact that I didn't like her?" I heard him give an appreciative snort into his tea. "She said she was an angler. But she said fishing *stuff* instead of *tackle*. And"—I thought back to my spotted friends—"when I showed her the fish prints in the house, I pointed right at a big old salmon and she said she loved trout. Any real angler would know a salmon from a brown trout."

The dog, snoring beside Trevor on the flagged floor, lifted an ear and thumped his tail, then went back to sleep.

"She's a professional," said my godfather. "Improvising when she saw an opportunity. They will have sent her in because they thought Stefan would be vulnerable to a pretty face. But she should have done a better job on her homework."

"But why Stefan? Or whatever his name is?"

"*Stefan*"—he put emphasis on the name—"has a meeting at Balmoral next week. It's important that he keep it."

"Important enough that you disappeared for a year? Without telling anyone where you were?" I meant him to know I was still mad.

"The balance of power in Eastern Europe may depend on decisions Stefan makes. And on who supports him."

He didn't apologize for worrying us. He never did.

"Okay," I said. "I get it. But why the post card? Why get me here?"

He shrugged. "I thought you might be bored. And I missed your birthday." Sipping his tea, he added, "Just how did you discover me, by the way? I thought the disguise was pretty good."

"You were the only one who never spoke to me."

"Yes, well. I couldn't very well, could I? The voice is the hardest thing to change. But I think we should talk about what you are really going to do in your gap year."

I stared at him. Then I grinned. I couldn't help it. But turnabout was fair play. Looking at my watch, I said, "Could we have this conversation tomorrow? I have a date."

"A date?" He couldn't have looked more shocked if I'd said I had two heads.

"Yes. A date. With the beekeeper. His name is Malcolm, as I'm sure you know. He's on his summer break from university, and he's quite hot."

"Oh. Ahem, I see . . ." Never had I seen my godfather at such a loss for words. "Well, good job today, Sher—"

"Don't," I said, giving him my sweetest smile. "You know how I feel about the name."

THE ADVENTURE OF THE EMPTY GRAVE

by Jonathan Maberry

It was in the spring of 1894 that I experienced an encounter so strange and enigmatic that only now, many years later, I am committing it to paper. Had I shared this matter to anyone but a few confidents among the police I would surely have been called, at best, a liar, or at worst a madman. Perhaps now the world is ready for it.

It had been three years to the day since this world lost its champion and I my best friend. Surely you have read the many accounts in the papers, and perhaps my own feeble attempt at prose wherein I described the titanic and fateful battle between Professor James Moriarty and Mr. Sherlock Holmes.

As had become my habit on a Sunday, I sat in the cemetery on an iron bench and contemplated the many adventures I was fortunate enough to share with Holmes. Some of those have been committed to paper and thus shared with the public, while others remain unwritten and untold—a few because they revolve so heavily around the person of Sherlock Holmes that I do not have the heart to write them out, and others because I know that Holmes did not want them told. Perhaps he might have agreed in time, but he did not feel that the world was ready to shine a torch into some of the darkest and strangest corners of our world.

I occasionally brought the notes to some of those unwritten papers with me when I came to sit on my bench near the empty grave. It is perhaps a foolish and overly sentimental thing, and a case can be made that grief has to some degree unfastened the hinges of my reason, but I took comfort in being there, reviewing case notes as Holmes and I had done in our chairs on opposite sides of an evening fire. I would read through the notes I had made in pocket diaries, or on any stray sheet of foolscap that came to hand while we were engaged in the hunt. Some of those pages were smeared with ash, others with rainwater, spilled wine—even blood. And so it took some effort to decode my hasty and obscured notes, and in doing so I was with my friend again, and we were on the case.

On a particular Sunday morning I was deeply immersed in a set of extensive notes on a matter Holmes and I had left unfinished. He often had more than one matter in hand, and would advance each a little at a time when one of his experiments yielded reliable results, or the reply to a telegraph arrived, or information came from his network of spies. Even I, his closest friend and confidant, had but an inkling of all of the many problems which occupied Sherlock Holmes. More than once he would tell me that he had solved a crime about which I had no idea he was even considering, and we would while away an evening with wine and pipes while he recounted the details. Many times he would lay out the facts but withhold the solution, then challenge me to properly assess them and deduce the likely outcome. I pride myself on saying that more than a few times I was indeed able to come to the right conclusion, and in such instances Holmes would favor me with a smug smile, and I knew that he took pride in my ability to make sense of it all. And that is fair enough, for was our friendship not in many ways an apprenticeship wherein he attempted to school me on the finer points of observation and investigation? If I was a slow apprentice, in my own defense I say that any student may appear a dullard when the teacher is so exceptional.

Most often, I admit, even when he laid out the facts for me, there was some element, often an apparently trifling detail, that I dismissed and yet which proved crucial. In one such case it was the way rose petals had settled on the surface of spilled wine; in another the paucity of blowflies was the key. At times like those, I felt like a feckless and inexperienced knight seated next to Lancelot at the table.

Thinking about Holmes on that particular Sunday morning created an ache in my chest. Sometimes his absence is most keenly felt. Not merely because of the case notes in hand, but because of the flowers that lay on the green grass of the empty grave.

It was not unusual for someone to lay flowers on the grave of so great a man as Holmes. It was far more uncommon to find no bouquet or token, for there were very many people whose lives he touched. However the usual tribute is a clutch of hothouse flowers tied with ribbon and laid with a degree of ceremony before the marble headstone. Not so on this occasion. This morning, as on one or two other mornings over the last few months, I found a handful of wildflowers thrown haphazardly across the grass. They were of a kind I felt I should know but could not name. White petals surrounding anthers of a singular bright blue.

I bent to gather the flowers and did my best to arrange them into an acceptable bundle, but I am no artist with such things and the result was clumsy and inelegant. Even so, I placed the bouquet on the grass and stood for a moment with my fingers lightly touching the cold marble. Then, with a heavy sigh I turned, intending to reclaim my seat on the bench—only to discover that not only was a new occupant ensconced on my very seat, but he held my sheaf of case notes.

"Sir," I cried as I hurried over, feeling quite cross and at the same time violated, for those papers were very precious and private, "those belong to me."

The man looked up from the topmost paper and I perceived that he was a very elderly gentleman, perhaps eighty or even older. His wizened features were deeply lined and beneath his top hat a few thin wisps of snow-white hair escaped. His mustache was equally white but precisely trimmed. His smoke-grey topcoat was of excellent cut, though perhaps a few years out of step with current fashion. His eyes, however, were striking and the sheer force of them slowed me in my tracks and made my tirade falter before it had truly begun. They were like the eyes of a great predator bird, a peregrine or eagle. Very dark and intensely sharp.

"Dear sir," he said, his accent clearly French and his voice surprisingly firm for so old a person, "I am most heartily sorry for such a bold intrusion. I merely caught these sheets as they began to blow away."

While this may have been true, it did not explain why he had clearly begun to read those errant pages. My anger overmastered my surprise and I thrust out a hand for them. The old Frenchman surrendered them at once and even gave me a small bow of the head as he did so. I hope that I did not snatch them from him or clutch them petulantly to my breast, but I fear that any witness—had there been any—might have judged me harshly.

The Frenchman gave me a small smile in which I perceived no trace of genuine embarrassment for his *faux pas*. Instead, he half-rose, and moved a few feet sideways to allow me room to reclaim my own seat. He had a cane with a silver head fashioned in the shape of a leaping trout, and he placed both of his hands upon it.

I considered stuffing my papers into the Gladstone case in which I'd brought them, squeezed in among the powders and instruments of my trade, but I did not. Instead I turned and sat down, the papers on my lap. I was intensely aware of his scrutiny as I did so.

"You are a medical man, I perceive," said he.

I looked at him coldly. "If your comment is intended as a joke, sir, it is in poor taste."

"A joke . . . ?" he replied, eyebrows rising. "I do not understand."

"You are in this place," I said irritably, "and have only this moment finished rifling my personal pages. The conclusion is obvious and the joke offensive."

The Frenchman shook his head. "I have offended you, sir, but without intent. And I make no joke, not here and never in the presence of one who is troubled with grief both old and recent."

"Enough," I cried. "Even a person of venerable age should be mindful of manners."

He placed his palm flat over his heart. "How am I being rude, monsieur?"

"You know who I am and yet pretend to deduce things about me in an imitation of a great man. That is—"

"—not what I am doing," said the Frenchman. "Please, sir, calm yourself."

"Then explain your comments."

He folded his hands in his lap. "Which comments require an explanation, monsieur?"

"You claim to know that I grieve."

"You are in a cemetery," said the old man.

"Many people come here who are not torn by grief," I said. "It is a quiet place."

"You gathered the flowers on that grave and stood touching the headstone. The former is something a casual visitor would leave to the groundskeeper, and the latter suggests an intimate connection with the person who is presumed to be buried there."

"We will come back to that," I growled. "If you do not know who I am then what do you know of my recent grief?"

"I know that you lost someone very dear to you. Not a brother or sister, not parents and not a child." He cocked his head for a moment, then nodded as if agreeing with his own thoughts. "You're a new widower, of that I am reasonably certain."

I felt my face turn to stone. "It was in the newspapers."

"Perhaps it was," said he, "but not in Paris, and I am recently come here from there. Too recently to have read about your wife's death. And, before we proceed, let me offer my sincerest condolences."

I mumbled a barely civil reply. "How are you so sure that it is my wife who was lost?"

"It is written all over you."

"It is not," I snapped.

"Forgive me, monsieur, but it is." He drew a breath and considered a moment longer. He looked wearied by his years, but there was a spark of something in his eyes as he began to speak. "It is an exceptionally chilly May this year and you are wearing the greatcoat you wore this past winter. The coat is an obvious favorite of yours, as it shows extensive wear. It is quite weather-stained, however there is a band on the arm that is slightly less faded. It is the size and placement equal to a mourning band. Had the death been that of a colleague or acquaintance it would not have been worn so long, but the difference in weathering speaks to an extended use. A beloved family member seems likely."

"You said it was my wife," I said tightly. "Not a parent or a child. Surely an extended period of grief would be appropriate in either case."

"It would, but the weathering is not the only telltale sign. The polish of your shoes is professional, clearly done by a bootblack who was once a military man. He even uses the same brushes—or, the same type of brush—with which he was familiar during service. A wife would use one of the commercial brushes that are popular on the market, but the density of bristles would be different. Commercial brushes are softer, and there is a different quality to the ink used in the polish. No, you have had to go out to have your shoes tended to."

"Many men frequent bootblacks," I said, "and there are countless veterans in that trade."

"There are," he conceded, "but it is one point. Allow me to finish, yes? Returning to your coat, it has been brushed by an indifferent hand. The strokes are brisk to the point of harshness but they are not thorough. There are fragments of leaf debris from trees not found in this green park. I see two types of decorative oaks of the kind that are more common in the courtyards of public buildings. Such trees grow near Scotland Yard, among other places."

I said nothing, but I could feel my hands clutching slowly into fists.

"Your hat is similarly brushed, and I do not believe a wife would allow a husband to venture forth in such a state. I could go on and mention the state of your cuffs and the fact that one of the threads that had been used to secure the mourning band in place still lingers on your sleeve, but I will relent. No, monsieur, it is your wife who has left us, and again I offer my condolences on your loss, Doctor."

"How do you know that I am a doctor?"

He nodded toward the Gladstone. "That alone is suggestive. However, there are three small stains upon the back of your right shirt cuff which I perceive are iodine. As the stains are faded to different degrees it suggests that you have used the antiseptic with some frequency over a period of days. Few people outside of the medical profession would carry such stains upon their clothes. The fact that you have not changed your shirt in that time is also suggestive, and reinforces my deduction that you are a widower. You have no wife to attend to you and you seldom return to the house you shared with her, likely because of the pain it inflicts. Such a man in such a state might well bury himself in his professional duties, going day upon day without pausing to refresh and change clothes. You have, however, shaved recently, which is something that can be done in your own surgery or at a club, so you are not so deep into despair that you have abandoned all pride. That and the removal of your mourning band tell me that enough time has passed that you are beginning—but are not far into—a period of recovery from grief. "

"You toy with me, sir," I said, rising sharply to my feet. "You pretend to deduce these things when in fact you already know who I am and what I have lost."

"I know these things now," he said, "but I swear that I did not know it until a minute ago—of this I can assure you, Doctor Watson."

"My name was on my papers," I protested, but he shook his head.

"I saw only the topmost page on which was what I took to be a personal letter on common foolscap. I did not read past the first two lines, which appeared to continue an account of a murdered chimney sweep."

On that score he was correct, as I now remembered. The case files I had been reviewing concerned an odd matter involving a poisoned Christmas gift and a missing soot brush. Holmes had solved the case but had asked me to withhold its publication as there were elements that would compromise a noted and much admired opera soprano. I opened my bag and studied the page to verify that no one—neither I nor Holmes—was named therein. There were no names at all on that page, nor on the next, and there had not been enough time for the old man to have read further. I closed the bag and resumed my place on the bench.

"If you know who I am," I said, my anger back on its leash, "then you know whose grave this is."

"I do," said he. "That is the headstone erected on the empty grave of the late Mr. Sherlock Holmes of Baker Street."

"It is."

"Just so. However, it did not immediately tell me who you were. Your identity, monsieur, became apparent as I observed you, your belongings, and heard you speak. The rest—the sad news of your wife's passing—were facts about which I was entirely ignorant prior to our meeting. Deductions of that kind are child's play, and if my playing such a game has offended you, once more I apologize. Sadly, it would not be the first time I have been accused of being inhuman in my interactions with people. A failing in some views, though I hold a contrary opinion."

I did not rise to the challenge of that statement and instead demanded of him his name. The old man braced his hands on the bench and, with great apparent effort, pushed himself to a standing position. He was not particularly tall or imposing, and would not have been so even if he was a younger man, but there was something compelling about him none-theless. He carried a weight of authority with him, which I have seldom encountered before except in my late friend, his brother, Mycroft, and a select few notables.

"Doctor Watson," he said in a formal tone, "allow me to properly intro-duce myself. I am Le Chevalier C. Auguste Dupin, late of Paris, and it is my pleasure to make your acquaintance."

To say that I was flummoxed would be to understate my reaction. Once more I felt my anger rise. Had he not been old and frail, I would have thrashed him roundly and kicked him like a dog. He could no doubt see the anger on my face, for my cheeks burned with heat. His dark eyes twinkled with amusement and it took a very great effort of will not to spew at him the bilious words that formed on my tongue.

He nodded and sat down. "Yes, I see that I have done my credibility no service by admitting the truth of my identity."

"Auguste Dupin does *not* exist," I snapped. "He is entirely a product of fiction."

"Do I appear to you to be a thing composed of nothing but ink and paper? Am I a dream, Doctor, or do you assert that I am nothing but the product of the fevered imagination of a drunken fool of an American writer? And a *dead* writer at that?"

"Of course not."

"Nor a ghost met by ill chance in a graveyard?" He smiled and tipped his hat to the golden sun. "Though a strange and singular phantom would I be, were I capable of haunting you on so bright a day."

"Neither phantom nor fiction," I said, "but a man who has either taken leave of his senses, or who possesses a brand of humor that is both crude and ill-considered."

"Neither of those things, I assure you," he said. "My name is Dupin and if M. Poe has convinced the world that he created me out of whole cloth, then that is to the best."

"In what possible way?"

"You are no doubt familiar with the lurid tales penned by the late Poe?"

"'The Murders in the Rue Morgue,'" I said irritably, "and two or three others."

"Two," the old man corrected. "Badly written fantasies at best."

"Come now, sir, this joke has gone far enough, and is in the poorest taste."

"It is no joke, Doctor," he said.

"You claim that you are a detective, then?"

He bristled. "I do not. Nor do I appreciate that label. I am a gentleman from a good family and am proud to be a member of the *Ordre national de la Légion d'honneur.* Only a cad and scoundrel would claim such an honor falsely, and it is one thing in life I do not take lightly."

"But Dupin was a fictional character!" I cried. "Everyone knows this."

"Do they?"

"Sherlock Holmes and I have discussed Dupin on many occasions, as each of us had read the *fiction* in which that character appears." I recalled quite vividly the conversation I had with Holmes on this very topic when we first met. When I observed that his methods called to mind

Poe's *Dupin*, Holmes said, with some asperity, *'No doubt you think you are complimenting me in comparing me to Dupin. Now in my opinion, Dupin was a very inferior fellow. That trick of his of breaking in on his friends' thoughts with an apropos remark after a quarter of an hour's silence is really very showy and superficial. He had some analytical genius, no doubt; but he was by no means such a phenomenon as Poe appeared to imagine.'*

I did not recount my friend's words, but instead restated that Auguste Dupin was conjured entirely from the imagination of a writer of fiction and had no other reality.

"Is Holmes an equally literary phantom?" countered the old man.

"Holmes is—*was*—a real person and I had the very great honor to serve as his biographer," I said indignantly. "Or at least I attempted to do so, though I admit to my own shortcomings as a writer."

"No," he said, "you are quite an acceptable writer, although I will go as far as to say that it is clear you do not fully grasp the subtleties of either the deductive or inductive process of observation, analysis, and assessment. For my part, however, I was briefly acquainted with M. Poe when I was much younger, though he was more closely associated with a dear friend of mine. I fear my friend—who bears some great similarities to you, I will admit—was wont to share intimacies. Drink, you know. A fine fellow in his way, but he had no head for wine. Not after the second bottle. He and Poe beguiled many an evening in salons, and it was there, I learned later, that my friend shared the details of some . . . er, *matters* . . . with which I was involved."

"You mean the matter of the stolen letter, the grotesque situation with the ape, and the woman found floating in the river?" I said, and I could feel my anger transforming by slow degrees into astonishment, even fascination.

"Indeed," said Dupin—for now I was coming to think of him as that person in truth. "Though if you have read those fictions—I cannot in truth credit them as objective accounts—then you will be aware that M. Poe tended to embellish in favor of hyperbole and dramatic flair. He could not be chased away from superlatives, the scoundrel. He would err on the side of style—God help us—when a cold, unemphatic statement of the bare facts would have been both more accurate and more exciting to the intellectual mind."

I said nothing. Holmes had many times criticized me for much the same faults.

"If you are who you say you are," I said, "how is it that you are here, in this cemetery and on a bench beside this grave?"

He smiled again, but this time there was a guarded, even mysterious, quality to it. "I was drawn here."

"Drawn by what? Or by whom?"

He reached into his pocket and withdrew an envelope, tapped it thoughtfully against his chin for a moment, then handed it to me. I accepted it and noted that the paper was remarkably crisp and expensive, but of a kind unknown to me. It was addressed to M. C.A. Dupin in the Faubourg Saint Germain, a section of Paris known for expensive townhouses of the *hôtel particulier* variety. The envelope was unsealed. At Dupin's encouragement I opened it and removed a folded sheet of onionskin, and discovered that a flower had been enclosed within the page. It was a delicate but faded specimen of a dried flower, with white petals with slender green filaments and anthers of a startling blue. I gaped at the flower, for had I not gathered up a handful of the same blossoms only moments ago? Dupin watched me as I stood, walked over to the grave, and knelt to compare the dried example with its freshly cut cousins.

I glanced at him. "What flower is this? What does it mean, that it was both sent to you and scattered on Holmes's grave?"

"It is very curious," he said. "What do you make of it?"

"Nothing," I confessed as I returned and reclaimed my seat. "It is a flower and nothing more."

"You do not recognize the variety?"

"Not at all. It seems familiar," I said, "but I am no botanist. Perhaps a flower seller might know."

"I have consulted several," said Dupin. "Eight, to be precise, and only the eighth was able to identify this flower, but barely so. He recommended that I pursue the matter further with a learned professor of botany at the *Institut de France*, which of course I did. The professor was able to identify it, but only after consulting several books. There was only a single example of it in his cases, the flower is so rare. He remarked that it was unusual for such a thing to be found anywhere in Paris, and I have since confirmed that it us utterly unknown here in London except to botanists at the Royal Society."

"And yet I have seen it," I cried, "and in bloom, though I cannot for the life of me recall where it was."

His eyes pierced me with their intensity. "Can you not, Doctor?"

"No. I seldom take particular note of flowers. The odd rose or carnation, perhaps, but . . ."

Dupin was shaking his head in obvious disapproval. "Take a moment before you decide that you have never taken note of this flower before. What can you tell about it by pure observation?"

I suppressed a sigh. Dupin clearly possessed some of the same intellectual qualities as my late friend, but he also had a fair few of the less appealing habits that apparently are part and parcel. Superiority and condescension, not the least.

"It is similar to a common edelweiss," I said slowly. "That much is obvious, for that flower is common in the better flower shops, but it is also unlike one."

"How so?"

"It is smaller and far more delicate than that flower. And the colors do not quite match any example I've seen."

"Very good. It is indeed a species of *Leontopodium alpinum*," he agreed, "but it is a very rare subspecies. The professor at the *Institut* says that this particular flower grows only in one place on Earth."

"And where is that?"

Dupin looked mildly surprised. "You truly do not know?"

"I confess that I am unable to connect this flower with my memory of where I saw it. Perhaps it was in a book."

"Or," he said, "perhaps you were emotionally distraught at the time."

I bristled. "If you are suggesting, sir, that this flower was presented to me as a token of sympathy when my wife—"

Dupin held up a hand to stop my outburst. "No, no, not at all. Dear me, I seem unable to do anything but offend you. If I were a younger man I daresay you would attempt to thrash me for this and other perceived slights."

"I made no such threat," I said at once.

"No, but you cannot say that it did not occur to you, at least as a wistful lament that my age and infirmity stand between you and a burst of violence that would, at least, make you feel better in the moment."

"You are being rude, sir."

"I am often perceived as such, Doctor, but surely you of all people can recognize that a statement made based on observation, insight, and logical supposition stands apart from—and perhaps above—the niceties of common conversation. Your many accounts of the investigations of your late friend build a case in support of my point. Even Poe was keen enough to perceive that much."

I said nothing, not trusting my voice.

Dupin offered another small bow. "Nevertheless, Doctor Watson, allow me once more to apologize. I intended no reference to your late wife. No, monsieur, not at all. My intention was only to provoke thought and memory, not pain."

"Then perhaps," I said tightly, "such a process might benefit from more straightforward statements rather than cryptic questions or obscure remarks."

He laughed. "*Mon dieu*, doctor, but you remind me of an old friend, long passed, who often said as much to me. And I will confess that to a logician in a world of those who do not prize rational and informed analysis, a sense of drama is perhaps inevitable. An ugly and even cheap habit, to be sure, but I never claimed to be a saint among men. Nor, I suspect, did your late friend, Mr. Sherlock Holmes. His love of drama was well known. Were his death faked and he alive, I would not put it past him to break the grassy sod upon his grave and spring forth with a dramatic flair. And the world who, through your writings, came to adore him, would think it all a fine performance worthy of ovation."

"What a vile thing to say!"

"Would you claim that Holmes never fooled you in some cruel way if it served his love of the dramatic revelation? How would you feel if a conductor on a train or a beggar on the street suddenly revealed himself to be none other than your friend, not dead but quite alive? Would that not be in keeping with M. Holmes's theatricality?"

"There were limits," I said, "even for him."

"Indeed," said Dupin diffidently. "Perhaps I am in error."

"I believe you are, sir."

"Then you will have another apology from me."

"No," I snapped, "I don't want another apology. What I want is an answer to your riddle about the edelweiss."

"Ah."

"You say I should know this particular species of that flower. Tell me your thoughts on that, because a graveyard is an ill place for a child's guessing game."

He rose again and bent carefully to pick up one of the flowers from the bouquet on the grave, then came back and held it up so that we could both see it. I joined him.

"First," he said, "I will tell you a bit of history."

"More drama?"

He shrugged in the way Frenchmen do, the kind that allows for so many interpretations. "Context will encourage understanding."

"Go ahead then, but please be quick about it." I said it with bad grace, not feeling that this strange gentleman deserved more than the shallowest civility, his many apologies notwithstanding.

"There is an organization operating through Europe," he said as he took my arm and led me back to the bench. "A criminal organization that is as subtle as it is vast. It has operatives by the hundred, though I doubt that many of them know they are part of something larger than their own local gang. From the basest petty street thief to the most sophisticated stock swindler, the underworld of Europe has been sewn like threads into a tapestry of corruption, evil, and criminality. The replacement of priceless art with brilliant forgeries in the Louvre is but one example. The sale of stolen military secrets in Russia and England has been attributed to spies working for foreign governments, but those spies are actually under the employ of this organization of which I speak. Jewel thefts and quiet murders, apparent suicides and arson, intimidation and blackmail . . . these are all the tools of this empire." He cut me a shrewd look. "I can see by your expression that you know something of which I speak."

"No . . ." I began but did not pursue what would have been a lie. Dupin nodded.

"You think I am mistaken, perhaps?"

"The organization to which you refer was the creation of Professor James Moriarty," I said, "and he is dead."

"He is," agreed Dupin. "Though his body was never found. Nor was, I believe, that of Mr. Holmes. Both men smashed upon cruel rocks and whisked away by an unforgiving river."

"That is what happened," said I. "And with the death of Moriarty, so came the fall of his criminal empire."

"Ah, if that were only true," said the old man. "You know firsthand that there have been serious attacks on the credibility of M. Holmes since his death, just as I presume you are aware that these attacks have been made by friends and—some say—relatives of the late professor."

"Impugning a dead man's good name is the act of a coward," I said, "but that hardly suggests that Moriarty's confederates are behind it."

"You're saying they're not?"

"Oh, they are, but it is not because they want to defend the memory of a man they claim was cruelly wronged by M. Holmes. No, hardly that. By deflating the importance of what Holmes achieved, they reduce the veracity of his claim that Moriarty was anything more than an eccentric academic. I believe you suspected this, which is why, after two years of silence, you chose to publish an account of the last battle between your friend and his great enemy."

I nodded. "As you say. But to my point about Moriarty being—as Holmes put it—the Napoleon of crime, has not criminal behavior dropped significantly since Moriarty's fall?"

"In England? Mm, perhaps it would appear so, from a certain distance. Arrests have, to be sure. *Obvious* crime has changed in frequency. But, Doctor, the death of Professor Moriarty has not resulted in the destruction of his empire."

"It has."

"It could *not* have," insisted Dupin, "because Moriarty was not the emperor of crime that your late friend suggested. He was formidable, make no mistake, and had he lived he might well have risen to become the true king of kings to the world of crime. A strong case can be made for that, though not an unbreakable one. After all, Moriarty became *known*, did he not? M. Holmes discovered his name and was able to provoke him so thoroughly that in the end, the professor was trapped into believing that there was nowhere left to turn except direct physical attack. Alas, M. Holmes rose to this challenge and they fought like animals on a cliff, and in their folly plunged to their deaths."

We sat for a moment with the heaviness of his words weighing upon us. I wanted to argue, to defend Holmes's rash action in descending to barbarity when his intellect had always been his keenest weapon. Even now, three years since that horrible moment, I could not understand why he did it in that way. He robbed the world of himself and of all the good he could do.

Finally, I cleared my throat and said, "Holmes sacrificed his life to protect the world from Moriarty."

"He did," agreed Dupin, "but the matter has greatly disturbed me, for the way in which it played out offends logic. Having read your account I know that it offends you, too."

"For someone who has never met Sherlock Holmes or Professor Moriarty you profess to know much about them and their motives."

Dupin nodded. "It is my particular, ah, *method* to try and open a door into the head of a person in order to try and think as they think. It is a kind of subjective analysis overseen by logical process, do you follow?"

"I believe so." And I did, because I had read about it in Poe's stories—and seen examples of it with Holmes. To understand a criminal, or at times a victim, he needed to tune his thoughts to what he supposed theirs must have been. I said as much to Dupin and he nodded.

"Very good, Doctor, and well put. You are a remarkable fellow and perhaps do not give yourself enough credit in your accounts of M. Holmes's investigations." He patted his thighs with his palms. "As for Messieurs Holmes and Moriarty . . . their actions trouble me *because* they are out of keeping with who they were. Moriarty was, at least in terms of his dominance of crime here in England, a Napoleon of sorts. Holmes was, inarguably, an intellect of the first order. If you have not exaggerated his powers—and I believe the contrary to be the case—one might say he was a Da Vinci. Ahead of his time, and energetic enough to make sure that he did not squander his gifts. For my part, Doctor, I confess that I have been content to allow the police to consult occasionally with me, but I seldom went in active pursuit of a case. My family was once wealthy and we fell upon hard times, and perhaps I suffer from a kind of familial ennui. I have my skills, but I have always lacked the energy to find new battles in which to test them."

I immediately thought of Mycroft Holmes, who Sherlock said suffered from a similar kind of lassitude.

"Unlike me, M. Holmes appeared to believe that he had some obligation to oppose villainy. Perhaps it began as a hobby, something to satisfy a mind that needed some problem upon which to chew, but I do not think so. Was he not already studying the science of criminality in its many forms when first you made his acquaintance? Medicine, surgery, anatomy, chemistry, and more? His natural gift of intelligence may explain the curiosity he had for knowledge, but it cannot explain the depth and breadth of the specific fields of knowledge to which he became addicted."

I almost flinched at that last word but managed to keep it off my face. "What is your point?"

"Holmes was not born to a study of crime," said Dupin, "but instead *made* it his particular field of expertise. It is possible that he will influence the next generations of actual police detection, should they actually begin to study his methods. They should. Some are poking at it even now."

I nodded. That was true enough. Since we met, in 1881, I had seen some Scotland Yard detectives attempt to employ Holmes's method of evidence collection and analysis. Not to great degrees of success, but the influence was there to be seen.

"That M. Holmes was making inroads into the *local* empire of Professor Moriarty is evident. But there was a greater battle to be fought and surely Holmes was aware of it. The larger—the *true*—empire of crime is still out there. I cannot and will not believe that Sherlock Holmes was unaware of it, or indifferent to it."

"And if he was?"

"Then why throw his life away in a senseless battle? Why die to remove a rook or bishop from the board when the other side still has so many pieces? Why leave the ruling pieces in play?" He shook his head. "No,

Doctor, M. Holmes's death as it appears spits upon logic. It offends M. Holmes's own methods. He would not sacrifice himself when there is so much work still to be done."

"He did it to save others," I said. "There were threats made—"

"Doctor, please," said Dupin. "Although you believe Holmes to be sentimental toward you and a few others, he was a general in the midst of a great war. When the stakes are this high then what are a few lives?" He paused. "Oh dear, I can see that I am being offensive once more."

"Continue with your argument," I said, my words squeezed from a tight throat.

He sighed. "It would have been much smarter, much more in keeping with the subtlety and vision of a man like Holmes, to simply put a bullet in Moriarty's head. No, don't yell, Doctor, I am being practical. This is war of which we speak, and although there are not vast armies marching under banners or cannons firing, have no doubt that nations could fall. The lives of many thousands of innocents are at risk. Knowing this, what would it be to a general to kill an enemy who has vowed to continue doing great harm? Would you, a former soldier, eschew taking such a shot if you knew it would have saved the life of your friend? Could you sit there and tell me with a hand raised to all that you believe, that you would not fire a bullet into the heart of a monster who would willingly kill the helpless and innocent? Yes, of course you would, because even though you are a doctor sworn to protect life you are also a practical man of the world. Wars happen and wars need to be fought."

"Perhaps," I said softly.

"The war rages on, Doctor," he said, and he sounded sad. "If I were a younger man I might even shake off my laziness and step onto the field. I daresay I might have struck a blow or two—yes sir, I may have."

"Perhaps," I said again. A bit unkindly.

He half turned. "This war of which I speak is not entirely concerned with stealing paintings and swindling the stock market. Men like Moriarty have bigger ambitions, and it is not an exaggeration to say that they, or their trusted agents, stand in the shadows of thrones. They have the ear of kings and presidents, and this is a process that has been grinding forward for many years. Decades without a doubt, and perhaps centuries.

But the cunning! In Canada there is a man named Simon Newcomb who is revered, like Moriarty, as a mathematician, but he is every bit the secret and nefarious manipulator of criminality as the professor. Adam Worth of Germany is a colleague of his, and Duke Yurivich of Russia, and Bellini of Florence."

"I don't know those names."

"You would not because they do not choose to be known. That I know them is significant because I have paid attention."

"I thought you said you don't get involved, that you lack energy for this kind of thing?"

"Oh, this is a recent burst of energy that has come too little and, I fear, too late. I have made some discreet inquiries and drawn inferences from information I have obtained, but what can I do? I'm an old man cursed with a curious mind and a change of heart that has come too late in my own game."

"Then, forgive me, but why are we having this conversation?" I demanded.

"Because wars are fought by the young, Doctor, and you are much younger than I."

"I am not a detective."

"Nor was I. That word did not exist when I began assisting the police with a few of their more *outré* cases. But what does that matter? You assist the police even now, and it would surprise me if they did not expect from you some of the same methods and observations for which M. Holmes has become so famous."

"I do not pretend to be his equal," I protested, "not even by a tenth or hundredth."

He flapped a hand to dismiss that. "I make no such accusation. My point is that you are involved in this war, Doctor, and I merely wanted to provide some useful intelligence. Listen to me when I tell you that the war is ongoing, and it is much larger and more extensive than you know."

"So you say," I said, still stubbornly fixed on my belief that Holmes sacrificed himself to remove the enemy general from the field.

He raised the flower. "So says this, Doctor Watson."

"It is a flower. What of it?"

"One was sent to me when it became obvious in some quarters that I was asking the wrong kind of questions to certain persons."

"Meaning what? That it is a threat?"

"A warning more than a threat," he said. "Or . . . perhaps it is even a challenge." He moved his fingers so that the stem rolled between them and the flower twirled. Because he stood at the edge of the shadows thrown by an elm tree, the tips of each petal moved in and out of darkness only to return to the light again. "I told you that this is a subspecies of *Leontopodium alpinum*, but I did not give you its full and complete scientific name."

"Which is?"

He looked into the heart of the flower. "*Leontopodium alpinum Reichenbachium.*"

"I beg your pardon . . . ?" I gasped.

"Yes," said Dupin, "it is a delicate flower that grows in meadows and along streams that feed the Reichenbach Falls of Switzerland." He raised his eyes to study me. "I see that you remember now where it was you last saw this singular bloom. You would have taken particular note of it only in passing, for there are many mountain flowers in that region of the world, but it grows along the banks of the river. And as a friend of the late M. Holmes, there is no doubt at all that you scoured the riverbanks for miles in hopes of finding your friend."

"Yes," I said weakly. "But what does it *mean*? Who would put these flowers here, on an empty grave? And to what end?"

"Those are indeed the correct questions," said Dupin. "Who indeed, and why?"

"You think it is a warning from these other criminals?" I demanded. "From confederates of Moriarty?"

"Perhaps," he said.

"That makes no sense," I said. "It calls attention to their existence, even if in a vague way. How does that benefit them?"

"Maybe it does not. Surely M. Holmes had secret friends and allies, some of whom you know and some you do not. Perhaps this is a message from *them*."

"What kind of message? After all, a flower was sent to you."

"And how suggestive that is," he said.

"In what way?"

He spread his hands. "Are we not having this conversation? Have we not discovered that we are also players on the same chessboard?"

"If that's what we are," I said cautiously.

"I prefer to think we are," he said. "Though it makes me wonder if similar flowers have been sent to other addresses and inspired other encounters and conversations. Who knows? It is a large and interesting world."

"It does not explain who sent them," I protested, "or who laid this bouquet on my friend's grave."

"Do you call it that?" he asked. "Was it a bouquet you discovered?"

"A scattered one," I said. "I collected them and laid them as you see."

"And ruined evidence in the process, no doubt," he said, once more sighing.

"What evidence? They are flowers."

"They are pieces of a puzzle, Dr. Watson. You see them as a whole, but perhaps they were not brought here by one person, but by many. Perhaps there has been a whole procession of people drawn here to this empty grave, each one following a clue whose connection is obvious."

"It was not obvious to me. I received no flower."

"No, of course not. If this was a message by someone who understood M. Holmes, then surely they would have understood you as well. Your devotion to your friend is well known, and surely you would come to visit his grave. A simple observation of your habits would establish that."

"Perhaps," I said grudgingly, taking his point. "So naturally I would find the flowers."

"As you have."

"Again I say, to what end? Why would someone take such elaborate pains to make so obscure a statement?"

Dupin sniffed the flower, smiled sadly, crossed the grass, and, with some effort and a flicker of arthritic pain, bent to place it on the green grass of the quiet, empty grave. Then he held out his hand for the dried one he had received via the post. I gave it to him and Dupin placed it next to the others. I took his arm and helped him straighten. For an old and infirm man, his arm was solid and muscular, suggestive of a great deal of wiry strength in his youth. He took his arm back as if uncomfortable with a younger person supporting him, and then stood for a long moment, rubbing the handle of his cane with the ball of his thumb, a thoughtful expression on his face.

"This world is cold and vicious so much of the time," he said at length, "and it is easy to fall out of love with it. But . . . if an old and frequently rude man may be permitted to give advice to a friend who has many years left ahead of him . . . ?"

I nodded.

"Do not lose hope," said Dupin.

"In what? Hope for winning the war? You paint it as an impossible fight."

"Oh, no," he said quickly, "the war cannot *be* won. It can only be fought. It needs to be fought, and with intelligence and energy. It needs to be fought with bright minds, strong arms, and good hearts. But that is not the hope to which I refer."

I stood. "Then what, sir, for I confess that your meaning is still as obscure to me now as it was when first you spoke."

"What I mean, dear doctor, is that you should not believe that you are alone in this fight. There are other players on the board, and unlike chess, there are no inflexible rules. Who knows? A piece once removed from the board may yet be played."

"Riddles to the last," I said.

He gave another Gallic shrug. "Perhaps. Time, like distance, often provides clarity to understanding." He paused and cocked his head. "Tell me, Doctor, do you believe in ghosts?"

"Not as such, no."

He smiled and there was an enigmatic twinkle in his eye. "Neither do I."

With that he tipped his hat and, leaning heavily on his cane, walked away along the crooked path in the old cemetery.

I returned to the bench and sat for some time in the quiet of the cemetery. No one else accosted me. I will admit that my thoughts were scattered and dark, for much of what Dupin told me was deeply troubling. A war? A plague of master criminals, uniting to form a secret empire across the globe? It was appalling. And it made me feel the loss of my friend so very deeply. How could he leave us when his powers and wisdom were so badly required?

Grief warred with despair and anger in me, and I bent and placed my head in my hands as the sun moved behind the elm tree and covered me in shadows.

Then, later, when I had composed myself, I retrieved my case, stood, took a last lingering look at the small flowers, then turned and made my way out of that place.

One singular thing happened on my way to the street. Near the entrance of the cemetery was another bench and what I saw upon it made me stop and stare. There, folded neatly, was a greatcoat of smoke-colored cloth and a battered top hat. Against the edge of the bench, standing at an angle, was a walking stick with a slender silver head shaped like a leaping trout. I turned, alarmed, thinking that the old man had taken leave of his senses and left his belongings behind, but the cemetery was quite empty. When I accosted passersby on the street, no one admitted to having seen an old man fitting Dupin's description. The newsboy on the corner looked at me as if I was mad.

I returned to the cemetery to check the coat pockets for some clues and found nothing. No cigarette case, no calling cards, no ticket stubs for a train. Nothing at all.

I lingered there at the edge of the cemetery until darkness began to fall and was not able to find a clue. So I gathered the items and flagged down a cab to take me to Scotland Yard, where I shared them and my strange story with Inspector Gregson.

"Someone has been playing a prank on you, I'm afraid," he said.

"Impossible. I spoke with the man. Go and see if those flowers are not there."

He doubted me, but he sent a constable. While we waited he sent a series of telegrams to his colleagues in Paris. After hours of my fretting and feeling like a fool, Gregson and I sat in his office with the coat, hat, and stick upon his desk. The constable had returned with the loose bunch of flowers. The responses from Paris had all been in agreement on one point. There was no one named Le Chevalier C. Auguste Dupin in the Faubourg Saint Germain in Paris, and no one of that name had ever lived among the townhouses of the *hôtel particulier* variety. The Paris police were not at all amused by Gregson's inquiries and accused the detective of playing a poor joke.

We sat and stared at each other.

"What are we to make of it?" he asked me.

"I have no idea," I confessed. "Do you believe me?"

He gestured to the clothes. "I have known you too long to believe that you are a prankster, Doctor. And we have these."

We sat and wrangled over it for hours, but we got nowhere. Our final conclusion was that I had been the victim of a particularly elaborate and cruel joke. I felt like a fool, and in low spirits I left his office and headed to my empty house.

It was only when I reached my own door that the last and strangest thing occurred, for there, tucked into the knocker of my front door, was yet another example of that strange, delicate, and enigmatic flower, *Leontopodium alpinum Reichenbachium*.

There was no note and I was left to interpret it however I would like. I nearly crushed the cursed blossom and snatched it up to do that very thing, but in the act of commission I paused and then relented. Instead I bore it inside with me and put it in a teacup of water. My mail had been delivered and I sorted through the various bills, notices, letters, and magazines in an attempt to distract my troubled mind. There, half buried by the detritus delivered by the postman, was a small envelope addressed in a familiar hand. I opened it quickly to confirm that Mycroft Holmes had sent it and it was an invitation to attend a lecture at a club in the city. I frowned, for it was not Mycroft's custom to seek out my company. Nor was I in the habit of attending any events with him, lectures on travel the least of all. The invitation had been to hear of the recent travels of a Norwegian by name of Sigerson.

Mycroft's addendum to the advertisement was a hastily scrawled, "You might find this of particular interest."

He was wrong. I did not, and I threw the invitation onto my desk and promptly forgot about it. Full dark had come upon the city and I retired to my sitting room with a cold piece of meat pie and a tall bottle of whiskey. I built a fire and placed the teacup with the flower on a table so that I could see it in the firelight.

What did it mean?

Who was the man who pretended to be Auguste Dupin?

In hopes of discovering some clue to my mystery I read again "The Murders in the Rue Morgue" as well as the other two Dupin stories from a book I purchased that evening from a tiny bookshop at the corner of Church Street. However if there were answers to be found in Poe's writing it was beyond the reach of my perception. So, I closed my eyes and thought of Sherlock Holmes, dead these three years. Gone with so much left undone. Gone, with so much wreckage left behind. The recent murder of the Honourable Ronald Adair was but the latest of the matters which I feared the police were mishandling and which Holmes would have attacked with great zeal and singular insight.

"Why have you left me here to do this alone?" I asked aloud. As if he could hear me. As if his ghost would even care.

In the silence, I drank my whiskey and watched the firelight trace the edges of the flower.

The house around me felt as dark and immense as the night.

LIMITED RESOURCES

by Denise Mina

Three hundred alcoholics clinging to a rock. That's what our neighbors call our island. It's only partly true. There is drinking, there's no getting away from that, and we can be a bit wild, but the good side of island life is how close we are. People here look after each other. If you're a native, like me and Margie, your fates are forever intertwined. We support each other, an insult to one is an insult to all, one person's win is everyone's win. Outsiders are outside. Incomers, well, that depends on the person. Shirley is an incomer.

We are the northern-most habitable island in the UK. Maps show us in a wee box in the corner, an addendum to the main map, because they'd have to show miles and miles of sea to include us. We are a meeting place for two seas and an ocean: the North Atlantic, the Norwegian Sea, and the North Sea. It's windy. You know where you live is quite extreme when people visit on a dare.

They arrived on New Year's Eve. Three of them. Head to foot in all-weather clothing, driving from the ferry with a Range Rover full of equipment. They walked into the baker's shop when it was full of us locals. Everything shuts down for three days when the year turns and we were all giggly and excited. They looked like spacemen. You could hardly see a patch of skin on them. Hoods up, hands double-gloved, trouser legs tucked into £300 all-weather boots.

I want to point out that Shirley is not a witch. She's not psychic either, whatever the older ones say. She's odd, but there's room for that here.

Shirley likes being alone and she likes room to think. Those are good reasons for living here. She's writing a book about why DNA evidence is wrong. She says it's an art, not a science. Results may come from a lab but they still need subjective interpretation. Good science doesn't require interpretation; it's a series of observations leading to irrefutable conclusions. She doesn't like leaps of logic. To be frank, that's as much as I listened to—it's dry stuff. Anyway, she came from Glasgow but she fits in perfectly here. There's room for odd here.

At first people thought she was psychic. Shirley knew exactly what you had just been up to. She'd say she was "in purdah," wherever that is, somewhere in her house I think, writing for weeks. She'd see no one and then she would meet you, out on a hill, walking past her garden, and she'd ask you weird psychic questions: Who drained your septic tank? How did your Golden Labrador die? She knew things.

Margie said she was following everyone on Facebook, but no one posts about draining a septic tank. Anyway, some of the stuff she knew had just happened two minutes before. Margie and I cornered her in town and made her explain. Shirley said it was elementary: Jonny O smelled of septic tank and pipe cleaner, fresh, and had red hands from the cold and clothes that smelled of washing powder. Kelly was covered in short blond hairs. They were on her shoulder and all down her back. She's small, the dog is big, so it must have been asleep or unconscious. Her eyes were red. She loves that dog. If the dog was unconscious, Kelly wouldn't be out for an aimless walk. Reasoned deduction. Can you go away now please?

It isn't witchcraft. Shirley's witchcraft is that she can take all of that in with one glance. It's overwhelming, she says, so much info at all times. That's why she needs to be alone so much.

I was in Margie's baker's shop when they walked in. It was busy that day because of the holiday. The door tinkled and silence fell as it shut behind them. They were tall and looked alien compared to the rest of us, a gaggle of small women in anoraks and woolly hats.

Margie looked at them and asked innocently, "Has there been an anthrax attack?"

We all laughed—not unkindly, just because spirits were high. We don't really do open confrontation here. There are other ways.

They didn't laugh. The leader ordered Margie: "Give me three loaves and the rest of your pancakes."

Everyone stopped laughing. Disapproval crackled in the air.

It was very rude, both the way he said it and what he'd said. We're an island. Resources are limited. You're only allowed as many pancakes as there are people in your party, Margie's rule. She says, otherwise it's anarchy, people queuing before the bakery is open and all sorts of madness.

Margie didn't confront it straight on. That's not her way. She changed the subject.

"What are you fine gentlemen doing here?" It was clear that she was annoyed, though.

"Camping," he said and dropped, and I do mean dropped, a shower of pound coins onto the counter. "A loaf and the pancakes."

Not even a please. Margie glared at the money and then at him. He looked back at her. They had a bit of a silent standoff.

"We're here for New Year's Eve." One of the other ones had spoken. He was smiling around the room as if asking us to stop hating him. "We want to be the first to sign the new visitor's book."

Ah, the famous Saxa Vord Visitors' Book. Saxa Vord was a radar station until satellites made it redundant. They shut it down. Now it is an extreme campsite of international renown. People use their visitors' book signature as an avatar on Twitter. They would blog about how rough it is in their extreme sports club or whatever. This was the most extreme day of the year. They couldn't have been less interested in us or our rules about pancakes.

"We call it Yules here," Margie told him. "That's Norwegian for 'New Year.'"

Margie was being friendly. Saying this to a visitor normally leads to a discussion about how close we are to Norway or about the Viking history of the place. Conversations with outsiders have a course, like a river, and she was inviting them to follow her down the course of this one to a softer bank. But they didn't take it. The first man spoke again.

"Yeah, the loaf and the pancakes."

Margie was furious now, which was bad because everyone knows she has a temper. She went to prison for killing her husband. It's not a secret. I used to go visit her. We stick together here.

Looking straight at him, she laid her forearm on the counter and swept all the coins onto the floor. They bounced and rolled around our assembled feet. "Get out."

We all watched the men leave in silence. They didn't even pick up the money. It was a bit much.

I ran after them. I thought they deserved an explanation. I told them, you know, all the shops will be shut for three days. You can't just roll into town and buy everything up, d'you see what I mean? They seemed quite interested in that but the rude one said, you know what, to hell with it, we're not coming back to this shit-hole. We'll be gone by tomorrow. Then they climbed up into their all-terrain Range Rover and sped off to the headland.

They were right. They were gone the next day.

Margie and I were out for our "Yule day yomp" and ended up at Saxa Vord. I heard her shout: "Oh God, no!"

We stood looking over at the cliff top, the bitter north wind stinging our faces. There was no one in sight. The tent was gone. Their Range Rover was still there, one door jammed open and stuff strewn all over the ground. The heavy chassis was rocking in the wind.

We hurried over, buffeted one way and another. The wind caught my hood, shoving me in a staggering little circle. Margie caught my arm and we looked at each other. We both knew they were all dead. Margie looked at me, frightened and sad. I cupped her face to comfort her. She didn't want to go over to the car, she wanted to turn back but I made her come with me to make sure.

We got there, finally, and they were gone. The grass was flattened in a rectangle right on the headland. Tent pegs lay on their sides like sharpened metal question marks. A length of rope was trailing on the ground under the car, whipped hither and thither by the wind, tied to the door handle as if they'd used it as a winch. Anyone seeing it could well imagine those men staggering around in their specialist clothes, unable to see, tying off the rope and lowering it down to the companion who had slipped onto a ledge, clinging on for dear life. Margie was shaking her head and asked, why didn't they tie the rope to the axle? Why the door? It made no sense.

On the way back we passed the sunken radar bunker. If they'd had any sense they would have sought shelter in it. We slipped in and saw the brand new visitors' book. They had all signed it and written, "Here for midnight 2015! Happy Yule!"

I groaned inwardly at that.

We went home to phone and tell everyone. Then the cops came from the neighboring island. Two incomers, both transferred up here from Glasgow. They asked after Shirley. They knew her from there. Said she had worked with them before.

They went off to see the campsite. They were there for a while. They came back with Shirley: they'd picked her up on the way back. Awkward, they said, to bring it up but they'd heard on the ferry that there was an argument in the bakery yesterday when Margie refused to sell them pancakes?

"No," I corrected, "Margie refused to sell them all of the pancakes. That was the point. They wanted to clear the bakery out of pancakes and leave none for the rest of us. That's not on."

"I see," said the one policeman thoughtfully. "Thing is, we looked in the car and found three pancakes on the back seat. It seemed strange."

I suggested that the pancakes could have come from elsewhere. They seemed quite selfish, those men. Maybe they already had pancakes before they came into the bakery and were just being really greedy?

No one answered, but Margie looked uncomfortable. They took out a phone and showed her a photograph of the pancakes in situ. Yes, she said, they did look like her pancakes. She makes them big and half an inch deep. They left to go back and see the scene again and took Shirley with them. She might have something to add, they said. Margie sat crying in the front room.

An island is a self-selecting community, and that attracts a lot of oddities. People move here without really knowing anything about it. If an incomer mentions getting away from the rat race you know they won't last. Give them one winter. They've usually argued with everyone, wherever they were before, and think other people are the problem. It takes coming here for them to realize that they're the problem. We get cast in this uncomfortable psycho-drama every so often. When anyone comes here you wonder why. You wonder what their motive is. Not me though. I'm from here, as is Margie. Shirley isn't, but we know she's here for peace and quiet. And now the police are taking her to Saxa Vord and that's the opposite of peace and quiet.

I like Shirley. I was a bit worried about her. That's why I followed them.

Up across the hills and heaths, over the headland and down into the shallow valley, I followed the cops in my car. The wind was pulling and shoving my old Mini. It's built for a city and not this exposed rock on the very edge of the Arctic Sea. It was already getting dark, still only early afternoon but the night glowered on the horizon, the sea clawing viciously at the cliffs. I drove with my lights off. No point in giving them a rear view warning.

Just before the Vorde there's a small cove in the hillside. I parked there and watched, keeping low.

The cop car had stopped on the cusp of the hill. The lights went out. I could see the three of them silhouetted in the windows, chatting for a while in the twilight. The doors opened, front and back, and they all got out. Shirley put her flashlight on first. She was watching the ground, her waxed Inverness Cape flapping in the frantic wind. She went into the radar bunker first. When she came out her shoulders were slumped. She walked slowly along the path to the Range Rover. The flashlight flicked up, catching the rope whipping under the wheels. She followed the ground markings to the tent pegs and the flat rectangle of grass. She brought her flashlight up to the ground beyond it, at the edge of the cliff. I knew she could read it all. I think I started blushing.

The vicious wind bullied her sideways, her cape snapped around her face, and, as she lifted her hands to push it down, she saw me.

"Get her!" she shouted.

I didn't run. There's nowhere to run on an island.

It seemed to take the police officers a long time to get to me, but I stood still, waiting, my hands out to the side. They walked us all back over to their car and we got in. They asked Shirley to explain, the way Margie and I had asked her about the Golden Lab and the septic tank. She looked at them and told them what had happened step by step. It was uncanny.

I arrived after midnight: she knew this because the visitors' book had been signed. I crept around the headland so that the camping men wouldn't see me, tied the rope to the door handle, and left the door open. I set the rope on the ground and covered it with leaves. Then I held the rope and waited in the dark, watching the warm lights flickering in the tent. Shirley pointed to the flattened thicket. "She waited there. Didn't you, Alison?"

She's so smart. It's weird how clever she is. It must be exhausting.

"I did," I said. I was looking at where the Range Rover was fading into the darkness, and I told them, the visitors were only here for one night. I knew they wouldn't unpack completely, they were bound to come out for something they'd left in the car. I described how the wind changed direction, carrying the sound of the men singing towards me. How I'd crouched, rain lashing my cheeks, thinking about selfishness and anarchy and the island. I was cold, I told them, so cold that my teeth went numb when I smiled, thinking about what I would do.

I told them how I saw the light change as the tent door was unzipped. A man crept out and turned back to zip it up before making his way to the car.

After a minute, Shirley opened her door, and the rest of us followed her over to where it had happened.

"Look," said Shirley, pointing her flashlight at the ground. "His footsteps come this way, and then there's a flattened patch on the ground.

She yanked the rope and the open door slammed into him, knocking him on his back."

I was nodding now, yes, that's right, Shirley, he was out cold. I dragged him, unconscious, all the way to the cliff edge and rolled him over. The policemen didn't look as if they believed us so Shirley traced my steps for them with the beam of the flashlight. One cop's hand tightened on my arm.

I rolled the man over and he went head first, over the edge into the jagged dark, onto the knife-edge cliffs. The hungry sea swallowed him.

Shirley told them what happened next: "Then she pulled the pegs out and rolled the tent over the cliff with the men inside."

The cops looked at me, horrified, imagining themselves in the dark tent, blind and terrified, being shoved over the edge. The ground was damp and soft. It wasn't difficult. When I lifted the edge of the ground sheet at first the men were annoyed, they thought it was their friend playing a joke. I felt their anger change to panic as they realized that I wasn't their friend.

One of the cops looked as if he might cry. He stared at me and asked, "Why?"

I just shrugged. I think maybe I was sort of smiling but I didn't find it funny, I was just smiling a bit. Remembering: They weren't even from here and they were rude, and if you buy all the pancakes there will be anarchy.

He tried again, "Did you put the pancakes in the car so we would think it was Margie?"

I didn't answer that either. I couldn't answer that. You can't explain that to incomers. The other cop tried to make sense of it. "Why did you try to make it look like Margie? She's your friend, isn't she?"

Shirley looked at me, her eyes open a little too wide. She seemed excited. "Did you think Margie could make it all right, Alison?" I just smiled, but my heart was hammering. And then she said: "You've done it before, haven't you?"

Well, I was angry then. I shouted at her, "Shirley! That has to be witch-craft. How could you possibly know Margie took the blame?"

Shirley's voice dropped so low, the wind almost took it away. "Why did she do that?"

Well, I was just burbling by then. I said, "Margie told me, she said, 'Killing a friend's husband is bad, Alison, but if I say I killed my own husband, people will always suppose he did something. We can tell them that, Alison, and I'll get two years.'"

Shirley was standing back from the cops, she was shaking her head softly, warning me, but I wouldn't be told what to do. I shouted again, "Margie said, 'If we tell them you came to the house in one of your moods, your odd moods, and just hid and jumped out and killed him, they'll put you away forever, Alison. They'll never let you out!' But you can't know that, Shirley, not from Margie crying and footsteps and visitors' books and pancakes! How can you know all that?"

Shirley's eyes were wide and shining. The bitter wind shrieked as it pulled at her cape.

"Alison," said Shirley quietly, "I didn't."

THE ADVENTURE OF THE EXTRAORDINARY RENDITION

by Cory Doctorow

Holmes buzzed me into his mansion flat above Baker Street Station without a word, as was his custom, but the human subconscious is a curious instrument. It can detect minute signals so fine that the conscious mind would dismiss them as trivialities. My subconscious picked up on some cue—the presence of a full stop in his text, perhaps: "Watson, I must see you at once." Or perhaps he held down the door admission buzzer for an infinitesimence longer than was customary.

I endured unaccountable nerves on the ride up in the lift, whose smell reminded me as ever of Changi airport, hinting at both luxury and industry. Or perhaps I felt no nerves at all—I may be fooled by one of my memory's many expert lies, its seamless insertion of the present-day's facts into my recollections of the past. That easy facility with untruth is the reason for empiricism. No one, not even the storied Sherlock Holmes himself, can claim to have perfect recollection. It's a matter of neuroanatomy. Why would your brain waste its precious, finite neurons on precise recall of the crunch of this morning's toast when there are matters of real import that it must also store and track?

I had barely touched the polished brass knocker on flat 221 when the handle turned and the door flew open. I caught a momentary glimpse of Holmes's aquiline features in the light from the hallway sconce before he turned on his heel and stalked back into the gloom of his vestibule, the tails of his mouse-colored dressing-gown swirling behind him as he disappeared into his study. I followed him, resisting the temptation to switch on a light to guide me through the long, dark corridor.

The remains of a fire were in the grate, and its homey smell warred with the actinic stink of stale tobacco smoke and the gamy smell of Holmes himself, who was overdue for a shower. He was in a bad way.

"Watson, grateful as I am for your chronicles of my little 'adventures,' it is sometimes the case that I cannot recognize myself in their annals." He gestured around him and I saw, in the half-light, a number of the first editions I had gifted to him, fluttering with Post-it tabs stuck to their pages. "Moreover, some days I wish I could be that literary creation of yours with all his glittering intellect and cool reason, rather than the imperfection you see before you."

It was not the first time I'd seen my friend in the midst of a visit by the black dog. Seeing that man—yes, that creature of glittering intellect and cool reason—so affected never failed to shake me. This was certainly the most serious episode I'd witnessed—if, that is, my memory is not tricking me with its penchant for drama again. His hands, normally so steady and sure, shook visibly as he put match to pipe and exhaled a cloud of choking smoke to hover in the yellow fog staining the ceiling and the books on the highest cases.

"Holmes, whatever it is, you know I'll help in any way I can."

He glared fiercely, then looked away. "It's Mycroft," he said.

I knew better than to say anything, so I waited.

"It's not anything so crass as sibling rivalry. Mycroft is my superior in abductive reasoning and I admit it freely and without rancor. His prodigious gifts come at the expense of his physical abilities." I repressed a smile. The Holmes brothers were a binary set, with Holmes as the vertical, whip-thin 1, and Mycroft as a perfectly round 0 in all directions. Holmes, for all his cerebral nature, possessed an animal strength and was a fearsome boxer, all vibrating reflex and devastating "scientific" technique. Mycroft might have been one of the most important men in Whitehall, but he would have been hard-pressed to fight off a stroppy schoolboy, let alone some of the villains Sherlock had laid out in the deadly back-ways of London.

"If my brother and I have fallen out, it is over principle, not pettiness." He clenched his hands. "I am aware that insisting one's grievance is not personal is often a sure indicator that it is *absolutely* personal, but I assure you that in my case, it is true."

"I don't doubt it, Holmes, but perhaps it would help if you filled me in on the nature of your dispute?"

Abruptly, he levered himself out of his chair and crossed to stand at the drawn curtains. He seemed to be listening for something, head cocked, eyes burning fiercely into the middle-distance. Then, as if he'd heard it, he walked back to me and stood close enough that I could smell the stale sweat and tobacco again. His hand darted to my jacket pocket and came out holding my phone. He wedged it deliberately into the crack between the cushion and chair.

"Give me a moment to change into walking clothes, would you?" he said, his voice projecting just a little louder than was normal. He left the room then, and I tapped my coat-pocket where my phone had been, bewildered at my friend's behavior, which was odd even by his extraordinary standards.

I contemplated digging into the cushions to retrieve my phone—my practice partners were covering the emergency calls, but it wasn't unusual for me to get an urgent page all the same. Private practice meant that I was liberated from the tyranny of the NHS's endless "accountability" audits and fearsome paperwork, but I was delivered into the impatient attentions of the Harley Street clientele, who expected to be ministered to (and fawned over) as customers first and patients second.

My fingers were just on its corner when Holmes bounded in again, dressed in his usual grey man mufti; Primark loafers, nondescript charcoal slacks, canary shirt with a calculated wilt at the collar, blue tie with a sloppy knot. He covered it with a suit-jacket that looked to all appearances like something bought three for eighty pounds at an end-of-season closeout at a discounter's. As I watched, he underwent his customary, remarkable transformation, his body language and habits of facial expression shifting in a thousand minute ways, somehow disguising his extraordinary height, his patrician features, his harrowing gaze. He was now so utterly forgettable—a sales-clerk in a mobile phone shop; a security guard on a construction site; even a canvasser trying to get passers-by to sign up for the RSPCA—that he could blend in anywhere in the UK. I'd seen him do the trick innumerable times, with and without props, but it never failed to thrill.

"Holmes—" I began, and he stopped me with a hand, and his burning stare emerged from his disguise. *Not now, Watson*, he said, without words. We took our leave from the Baker Street mansion flats, blending in with the crowds streaming out of the train-station. He led me down the Marylebone Road and then into the back-streets where the perpetual King's Cross/St Pancras building sites were, ringed with faded wooden billboards. The groaning of heavy machinery blended with the belching thunder of trucks' diesel engines and the tooting of black cabs fighting their way around the snarl.

Holmes fitted a bluetooth earpiece and spoke into it. It took me a moment to realize he was speaking to me. "You understand why we're here?"

"I believe I do." I spoke at a normal tone, and kept my gaze ahead. The earpiece was on the other side, leaving Holmes's near ear unplugged. "You believe that we are under surveillance, and given the mention of Mycroft, I presume you believe that this surveillance is being conducted by one of the security services."

He cocked his head in perfect pantomime of someone listening to an interlocutor in an earpiece, then said, "Precisely. Watson, you are an apt pupil. I have said on more than one occasion that Mycroft *is* the British government, the analyst without portfolio who knows the secrets from every branch, who serves to synthesize that raw intelligence into what the spying classes call 'actionable.'"

We turned the corner and dodged two builders in high-visibility clothing, smoking and scowling at their phones. Holmes neither lowered his tone nor paused, as either of those things would have excited suspicion.

"Naturally, as those agencies have commanded more ministerial attention, more freedom of action, and more strings-free allocations with which to practice their dark arts, Mycroft's star has only risen. As keen a reasoner as my brother is, he is not impervious to certain common human failings, such as the fallacy that if one does good, then whatever one does in the service of that good cannot be bad."

I turned this over in my mind for a moment before getting its sense. "He's defending his turf."

"That is a very genteel way of putting it. A more accurate, if less charitable characterization would be that he's building a little empire through a tangle of favor-trading, generous procurements, and, when all else fails, character assassination."

I thought of the elder Holmes, corpulent, with deep-sunk eyes and protruding brow. He could be stern and even impatient, but— "Holmes, I can't believe that your brother would—"

"Whether you believe it or not is irrelevant, James." He only called me by the old pet name of my departed Mary when he was really in knots. My breath quickened. "For it's true. Ah, here we are."

"Here" turned out to be a shuttered cabinet-maker's workshop, its old-fashioned, hand-painted sign faded to near illegibility. Holmes produced a key from a pocket and smoothly unlocked the heavy padlock to let us both in, fingers going quickly to a new-looking alarm panel to one side of the door and tapping in a code.

"Had an estate agent show me around last week," he said. "Snapped a quick photo of the key and made my own, and of course it was trivial to watch her fingers on the keypad. This place was in one family for over a century, but their building was sold out from under them and now they've gone bust. The new freeholder is waiting for planning permission to build a high-rise and only considering the shortest of leases."

The lights came on, revealing a sad scene of an old family firm gone to ash in the property wars, work-tables and tools worn by the passing of generations of skilled hands. Holmes perched on a workbench next to a cast-iron vise with a huge steel lever. He puffed his pipe alight and bade me sit in the only chair, a broken ladderback thing with a tapestry cushion that emitted a puff of ancient dust when I settled.

"I was deep in my researches when the young man knocked. I may have been a little short with him, for he was apologetic as I led him into my study and sat him by the fire. I told him that no apologies were necessary. I have, after all, hung out my shingle—I've no business snapping at prospective clients who interrupt my day."

Holmes spoke in his normal tones, the raconteur's humblebrag, without any hint of the nervousness I'd detected in him from the moment I'd stepped through his door. We might have been in his study ourselves.

"I knew straightaway that he was a soldier, military intelligence, and recently suspended. I could see that he was a newly single man, strong-willed, and trying to give up cigarettes. I don't get many visitors from the signals intelligence side of the world, and my heart quickened at the thought of a spot of real intrigue for a change."

"I understand that you are a man who can keep confidences, Mr. Holmes."

"I have held STRAP 3 clearance on nine separate occasions, though at the moment I hold no clearances whatsoever. Nevertheless, you may be assured that Her Majesty's Government has given me its imprimatur as to my discretion."

My visitor barked a humorless laugh then. "Here stands before you proof that HMG is no judge of character."

"I had assumed as much. You've brought me a document, I expect."

He looked abashed, then defiant. "Yes, indeed I have," and he drew this from his pocket and thrust it upon me.

Holmes drew a neatly folded sheet of A4 from his inside pocket and passed it to me. I unfolded it and studied it.

"Apart from the UK TOP SECRET STRAP 1 COMINT markings at the top, I can make neither head nor tail," I admitted.

"It's rather specialized," Holmes said. "But it might help if I told you that this document, headed 'HIMR. Data Mining Research Problem Book,' relates to malware implantation by GCHQ."

"I know that malware is the latest in a series of names for computer viruses, and I suppose that 'malware implantation' is the practice of infecting your adversaries with malicious computer code."

"Quite so. You may have heard, furthermore, of EDGEHILL, the TOP SECRET STRAP 1 program whose existence was revealed in one of the Snowden documents?"

"It rings a bell, but to be honest, I got a sort of fatigue from the Snowden news—it was all so technical, and so dismal."

"Tedium and dismalness are powerful weapons—far more powerful than secrecy in many cases. Any bit of business that can be made sufficiently tedious and over-complexified naturally repels public attention and all but the most diligent of investigators. Think of the allegedly public hearings that demand their attendees sit through seven or eight hours of monotonic formalities before the main business is tabled—or of the lengthy, tedious documents our friends in Brussels and Westminster are so fond of. If you want to do something genuinely evil, it is best for you that it also be fantastically dull."

"Well, this document certainly qualifies." I passed it back.

"Only because you can't see through the lines. EDGEHILL—and its American cousin at the NSA, BULLRUN—is, quite simply, a sabotage program. Its mission is to introduce or discover programmer errors in everyday software in computers, mobile devices, network switches, and firmware—the nebulous code that has crept into everything from insulin pumps to automobiles to thermostats—and weaponize them. All code will have errors for the same reason that all books, no matter how carefully edited, have typos, and those errors are discoverable by anyone who puts his mind to it. Even you, John."

"I sincerely doubt it."

"Nonsense. A nine-year-old girl discovered a critical flaw in the iPhone operating system not so many years ago. The systems have not grown less complex and error-prone since then—the only thing that's changed is the stakes, which keep getting higher. The latest towers erected by our offshore friends in the formerly unfashionable parts of London rely upon tuned seismic dampers whose firmware is no more or less robust than the iPhone I made you leave under a cushion in my flat. The human errors in our skyscrapers and pacemakers are festering because the jolly lads in signals intelligence want to be able to turn your phone into a roving wiretap."

"You make it sound terribly irresponsible."

"That's a rather mild way of putting it. But of course, we're discussing the *unintended* consequences of all this business, and my visitor had come about the *intended* consequences: malware implantation. Watson, allow me to draw your attention to the very bottom of the deceptively dull document in your hand."

I read: "Could anyone take action on it without our agreement; e.g. could we be enabling the US to conduct a detention op which we would not consider permissible?" A cold grue ran down my spine.

Holmes nodded sharply and took the paper back from me. "I see from your color and demeanor that you've alighted upon the key phrase, 'detention op.' I apologize for the discomfort this thought brings to mind, but I assure you it is germane to our present predicament."

My hands were shaking. Feigning a chill, I stuck them under my armpits, wrapping myself in a hug. My service in Afghanistan had left many scars, and not all of them showed. But the deepest one, the one that sometimes had me sitting bolt upright in the dead of night, screaming whilst tears coursed down my cheeks, could be triggered by those two words: *detention op*. I did not sign up to be an Army doctor expecting a pleasant enlistment. What I saw in Kandahar, though, was beyond my worst imaginings.

"Take your time." There was a rare and gentle note in my companion's voice. It made me ashamed of my weakness.

I cleared my throat, clasped my hands in my lap. "I'm fine, Holmes. Do go on."

After a significant look that left me even more ashamed, he did. "I said to my visitor, 'I presume that you are here to discuss something related to this very last point?' For as you no doubt perceived, Watson, the page there is wrinkled and has been smoothed again, as though a thumb had been driven into it by someone holding it tightly there."

I nodded, not trusting my voice.

Holmes continued his tale.

"I had done many of these insertions," the man said, looking away from my eyes. "And the checklist had been something of a joke. Of course we knew that we could break something critical and tip off an alert systems administrator. Likewise, it was obvious that exposure would cause diplomatic embarrassment and could compromise our relationships with the tech companies who turned a blind eye to what we were doing. As to this last one, the business about detention ops, well, we always joked that the NSA was inside our decision loop, which is how the fourth-gen warfare types talk about leaks. Christ knows, we spent enough time trying to get inside *their* decision loop. The special relationship is all well and good, but at the end of the day, they're them and we're us and there's plenty of room in that hyphen between Anglo and American.

"But the truth was, there was always a chance the Americans would act on our intel in a way that would make us all want to hide our faces. Don't get me wrong, Mr. Holmes, we're no paragons of virtue. I've read the files on Sami al-Saadi and his wife, I know that we were in on that, supervising Gaddafi's torturers. I don't like that. But since the Troubles ended, we've done our evil retail, and the Americans deal wholesale. Whole airfleets devoted to ferrying people to torture camps that're more like torture cities.

"Have you ever read an intercept from a jihadi chat room, Mr. Holmes?"

"Not recently." He gave me a look to check if I was joking. I let him know I wasn't.

"The kids don't have much by way of operational security. Loads of 'em use the same chat software they use with their mates, all in the clear, all ingested and indexed on Xkeyscore. Reading the intercepts is like being forced to listen to teenagers gossiping on a crowded bus: dirty jokes about mullahs whose dicks are so short they break their nose when they walk

327

into a wall with a stiffie; trash talk about who's real hard jihadi, who's a jihobbyist, complaints about their parents and lovesick notes about their girlfriends and boyfriends, and loads of flirting. It's no different to what we talked about when I was a boy, all bravado and rubbish."

"When you were a boy, you presumably didn't talk about the necessity of wiping out all the kaffirs and establishing a caliphate, though."

"Fair point. Plenty of times, though, we fantasized about blowing up the old Comprehensive, especially come exams, and some of my mates would honestly have left a pipe-bomb under the stands when their teams were playing their arch-rivals, if they thought they'd have got away with it. Reading those transcripts, all I can think is, 'There but for the grace of God . . .'

"But they're them and I'm me, and maybe one of 'em will get some truly bad ideas in his foolish head, and if I can catch him before then—" My visitor broke off then, staring at the fire. He opened and shut his mouth several times, clearly unable to find the words.

I gave him a moment and then prompted, "But you found something?"

He returned from whatever distant mental plain he'd been slogging over. "They wanted a big corpus to do information cascade analysis on. Part of a research project with one of the big unis, I won't say which, but you can guess, I'm sure. They'd done a new rev on the stream analysis, they were able to detect a single user across multiple streams and signals from the upstream intercepts—I mean to say, they could tell which clicks and messages on the fiber-taps came from a given user, even if he was switching computers or IP addresses—they had a new tool for linking mobile data-streams to intercepts from laptops, which gives us location. They were marking it for long-term retention, indefinite retention, really.

"I—"

Here the fellow had to stop and look away again, and it was plain that he was reliving some difficult issue that he'd wrestled with his conscience over. "I was in charge of reviewing the truthed social graphs, sanity-checking the way that the algorithm believed their chain of command went against what I could see in the intercepts. But the reality is that those intercepts came from teenagers in a chat room. They didn't have a chain of command—what the algorithm fingered as a command structure was really just the fact that some of them were better at arguing than others. One supposed lieutenant in the bunch was really the best comedian, the one who told the jokes they all repeated. To the algorithm, though, it looked like a command structure: subject emits a comm, timing shows that the comm cascades through an inner circle—his mates—to a wider circle. To a half-smart computer, this teenager in Leeds looked like Osama Junior.

"I told them, of course. These were children with some bad ideas and too much braggadocio. Wannabes. If they were guilty of something, it was of being idiots. But for the researchers, this was even more exciting. The fact that their algorithm had detected an information cascade where there was no actual command structure meant that it had found a *latent* structure. It was like they set out knowing what they were going to find, and then whatever they found, they twisted until it fit their expectations.

"Once we have the command structures all mapped out, everything becomes maths. You have a chart, neat circles and arrows pointing at each other, showing the information cascade. Who can argue with math? Numbers don't lie. Having figured out their command structures from their chat rooms, we were able to map them over to their mobile communications, using the session identifiers the algorithm worked out.

"These twerps were half-smart, just enough to be properly stupid. They'd bought burner phones from newsagents with prepaid SIMs and they only used them to call each other. People who try that sort of thing, they just don't understand how data-mining works. When I've got a visualization of all the calls in a country, they're mostly clustered in the middle, all tangled up with one another. You might call your mum and your girlfriend regular, might call a taxi company or the office a few times a week, make the odd call to a takeaway. Just looking at the vis, it's really obvious what sort of number any number is: there's the 'pizza nodes,' connected to hundreds of other nodes, obviously takeaways or minicabs. There's TKs—telephone kiosks, which is what we call payphones—they've got their own signature pattern: lots of overseas calls, calls to hotels, maybe a women's shelter or A&E, the kinds of calls you make when you don't have a mobile phone of your own.

"It makes detecting anomalies dead easy. If a group of people converge on a site, turn off their phones, wait an hour and then turn 'em on again, well, that shows up. You don't have to even be looking for that pattern. Just graph call activity, that sort of thing jumps straight out at you. Might as well go to your secret meeting with a brass band and a banner marked UP TO NO GOOD.

"So think of the network graph now, all these nodes, most with a few lines going in and out, some pizza nodes with millions coming in and none going out, some TKs with loads going out and none coming in. And over here, off to the edge, where you couldn't possibly miss it, all on its own, a fairy ring of six nodes, connected to each other and no one else. Practically a bullseye.

"You don't *need* to be looking for that pattern to spot it, but the lads from the uni and their GCHQ minders, they knew all about that pattern. Soon as they saw one that the persistence algorithm mapped onto the same accounts we'd seen in the chat rooms, they started to look at its information cascades. Those mapped right onto the cascade analysis from the chat intercepts, same flows, perfect. Course they did—because the kid who told the best jokes was the most sociable of the lot, he was the one who called the others when they weren't in the chat, desperate for a natter."

I stopped him. "Thinking of your example of a group of phones that converge on a single location and all switch off together," I said. "What about a group of friends who have a pact to turn off their phones whilst at dinner, to avoid distraction and interruption?"

He nodded. "Happens. It's rare, but 'course, not as rare as your actual terrorists. Our policy is, hard drives are cheap, add 'em all to long-term retention, have a human being look at their comms later and see whether we caught some dolphins in the tuna-net."

"I see."

"We have their 'command structure,' we have their secret phone numbers, so the next step is to have a little listen, which isn't very hard, as I'm sure you can appreciate, Mr. Holmes."

"I make it a policy never to say anything over a telephone that I would regret seeing on the cover of the *Times* the next morning."

"A good policy, though one that I think I might have a hard time keeping myself," I said, thinking of the number of times my poor Mary and I had indulged ourselves in a little playful, romantic talk when no one could hear.

"Watson, if you find yourself tempted to have a breathy conversation with a ladyfriend over your mobile, I suggest you cool your ardor by contemplating the number of my brother's young and impressionable associates who doubtlessly personally review every call you make. You've met my brother on a few occasions. Imagine what sort of man he would surround himself with."

I shuddered. I had no interest in women at that time, and memory of Mary was so fresh and painful that I couldn't conceive of a time when that interest would return. But I had cherished the memories of those silly, loving, personal calls, times when it had felt like we were truly ourselves, letting the pretense fall away and showing each other the truth behind our habitual masks. The thought that those calls had been recorded, that someone might have listened in on them—"just to check" and make sure that we weren't up to no good . . . It cast those cherished memories in a new light. I wouldn't ever be able to think of them in the same way again.

I was sure that Holmes had intuited my train of thought. He always could read me at a glance. He held my eye for a long moment and I sensed his sympathy. Somehow that made it worse.

My guest (Holmes went on) began to pace, though I don't think he realized he was doing it, so far away in memory was he.

"The problem for the brain-boys was that these kids never said anything on their secret phones of any kind of interest. It was just a continuation of their online chat: talking trash, telling jokes, making fun of whoever wasn't on the call. I wasn't surprised, of course. I'd been reading their chat logs for months. They were just idiot kids. But for the spooks, this was just proof that they were doing their evil work using their apps.

Damned if they do and if they didn't: since it was all dirty jokes and messin' on the voice chat, the bad stuff had to be in text.

"These boys were playing secret agent. They bought their burner phones following a recipe they found online and the next step in the recipe was to download custom ROMs that only used encrypted filesystems and encrypted messaging and wouldn't talk to the Google Play store or any other app store whose apps weren't secure from the ground up. That meant that all their mobile comms were a black box to the smart boys."

"I imagine that's where your checklist came in, then?"

He grimaced. "Yeah. That OS they were using was good, and it updated itself all the time, trying to keep itself up to date as new bugs were discovered. But we knew that the NSA's Tailored Access Operations group had some exploits for it that we could implant through their mobile carrier, which was a BT Mobile reseller, which meant they were running on EE's network, which meant we could go in through T-Mobile. The NSA's well inside of Deutsche Telekom. By man-in-the-middling their traffic, we could push an update that was signed by a certificate in their root of trust, one that Symantec had made before the Certificate Transparency days, that let us impersonate one of the trusted app vendors. From there, we owned their phones: took their mics and cameras, took their keystrokes, took all their comms."

"I suppose you discovered that they were actually plotting some heinous act of terror?"

My visitor startled, then began to pace again. "How did you know?"

"I know it because you told me. You came here, you handed me that extraordinary document. You would not have been here had the whole thing ended there. I can only infer that you exfiltrated data from their phones that caused our American cousins to take some rather rash action."

He dropped down on my sofa and put his face in his hands. "Thing was, it was just larking. I could tell. I'd been there. One of these boys had cousins in Pakistan who'd send him all sorts of bad ideas, talk to him about his jihad. It was the sort of thing that they could natter about endlessly; the things they'd do, when they worked themselves up to it. I'd done the same, you understand, when I was that age—played at Jason Bourne, tried to figure out the perfect crime.

"They'd found their target, couple of US servicemen who'd had the bad sense to commute from the embassy to their places in the East End in uniform, passing through Liverpool Street Station every day. I suppose you know the station, Mr. Holmes, it's practically a Call of Duty level, all those balconies and escalators and crisscrossing rail and tube lines. I can't tell you how much time my friends and I spent planning assaults on places like that. That's the thing, I *recognized* myself in them. I knew what they were about.

"We must have been terrors when we were boys. The things we planned. The bombs. The carnage. We'd spend hours—days—debating the very best shrapnel—what would rip in a way that would make wounds that you couldn't suture closed. We'd try and top each other, like kids telling horror stories to each other around the fire. But I know for an iron-clad *fact* that my best friend Lawrence went faint at the sight of actual blood.

"The exploit we used to own their phones was American. It came from the NSA, from the Tailored Access Operations group. We had our own stuff, but the NSA were, you know, *prolific*. We have a toolbox; they've got a whole DIY store.

"Do you know what's meant by third-party collection?"

"Of course."

❖

"Well, I don't, Holmes."

"Watson, you need to read your papers more closely. First- and second-party collection is data hoovered up by GCHQ and NSA and the Five Eyes, the so-called second parties. Third parties are all other collaborating nations that GCHQ and the NSA have partnerships with. Fourth-party collection is data that one security service takes by stealth from another security service. There's fifth-party collection—one security service hacks another security service that's hacked a third—and sixth-party collection and so forth and so on. Wheels within wheels."

"That all seems somehow perverse," I said.

"But it's undeniably efficient. Why stalk your own prey when you can merely eat some other predator's dinner out from under his nose, without him ever knowing it?"

My visitor spoke of third-party collection, and I saw immediately where this was going. "They saw what you saw, in the lads' communications. They read what you read."

"They did. Worse luck: they read what we *wrote*, what the analysts above my paygrade concluded about these idiot children, and then—"

Here he rattled that paper again.

"I see," I said. "What, I wonder, do you suppose I might do for you at this juncture?"

"It's life in prison if I go public, Mr. Holmes. These kids, their parents are in the long-term Xkeyscore retention, all their communications, and they're frantic. I read their emails to their relatives and each other, and I can only think of how I'd feel if *my* son had gone missing without a trace. These parents, they're thinking that their kids have been snatched by paedos and are getting the *Daily Mail* front-page treatment. The truth, if they knew it, might terrify them even more. Far as I can work out, the NSA sent them to a CIA black site, the kind of place you wouldn't wish on your worst enemy. The kind of place you build for *revenge*, not for intelligence.

"It's life in prison for me, or worse. But I can't sit by and let this happen. I have this checklist and it told me that my job was to consider this very eventuality, and I did, and it came to pass anyway, and as far as I'm concerned, I have to do something now or I'm just as culpable as anyone. So I've come to you, Mr. Holmes, because before I go to prison for the rest of my life, before I deprive my own sons of their dad, forever, I want to know if there's something I'm missing, some other way I can do the right thing here. Because I was brought up right, Mr. Holmes, and that means I don't believe that my kids' right to their father trumps those parents' rights to *their* sons."

"What an extraordinary fellow," I said. Holmes was never one for the storyteller's flourish, but he had an eidetic memory for dialog, and I knew he was giving it word for word—beat for beat and tone for tone.

It was as if I was in the room with the tormented soul. The hair on my neck sprang up.

❖

"'Leave it with me,' I told him, and showed him out. When I returned to my study, I found that I was curiously reluctant to do what I knew I must do. I found myself delaying. Smoking a pipe. Tidying my notebooks. Cleaning up my cross-references. Finally, I could delay no further and I went down to the station taxi stand and had a black cab take me to Mycroft."

"Mycroft!"

"Of course. When it comes to signals intelligence, my dear brother sits at the center of a global web, a point of contact between MI5, MI6, GCHQ, and the highest ministers and civil servants in Whitehall. Nothing happens but that he knows about it. Including, it seemed, my visitor."

❖

"Sherlock," he said to me, once I had been ushered into his presence, "as unfortunate as this is, there's really nothing to be done."

The boom years since the 9/11 attacks have not been kind to my brother, I'm afraid. As his methodology has come into vogue and his power in the security services has grown, he has found himself at more unavoidable state dinners, more booze-ups at a military contractor's expense, more high-level interagency junkets in exotic locales. Hawai'i seems a favorite with his set, and I've heard him complain more than once about the inevitable pig-roast and luau.

Always heavy, but now he has grown corpulent. Always grim, but now he has grown stern and impatient. Watson, my brother and I were never close, but I have always said that he was my superior in his ability to reason. The most disturbing change to come over my brother in the past fifteen years is in that keen reasoner's faculty. By dint of circumstance and pressure, he has developed the kind of arrogant blindness he once loathed in others—a capacity for self-deception, or rather, self-justification, when it comes to excusing the sort of surveillance he oversees and the consequences of it.

"There is something obvious that can be done," I told him. "Simply tell the Americans to let those boys go. Apologize. Investigate the circumstances that led to this regrettable error and see to it that it doesn't happen again. If you care about excellence, about making the country secure, you should be just as concerned with learning from your failures as you are with building on your successes."

"What makes you say that this is a failure?"

"Oh, that's simple. These boys are a false positive. They lack both the wit and the savagery to be a threat to the nation. At most, they are a threat to themselves."

"And what of it? Are these six fools worth jeopardizing the entire war on terror, the special relationship, the very practices at the heart of our signals intelligence operation?"

"Yes," I said.

My brother colored, and I watched as that great mind of his went to work mastering his passions. "I'm afraid you don't know what you're talking about. It comes of being too close to the trees, too far from the forest. Human intelligence is fine as it goes, but when you conduct your investigations retail, you miss the patterns that we find in the wholesale end of things."

"When one conducts one's affairs at the retail level," I told him, "one must attend to the individual, human stories and costs that vanish when considered from the remove of algorithmic analysis of great mountains of data."

He sighed and made a show of being put upon by his brother. I expect that there are Whitehall mandarins who quake in their boots at such a sigh from such a personage. I, of course, stood my ground and ignored his theatrics.

"Come now," I said. "There's nothing to discuss, really. One way or another, the truth will out. That young man will not sit on his hands, whether or not I offer him a safer route to his disclosure. It's not in his nature."

"And it is not in mine to have my hand forced by some junior intelligence officer with a case of the collywobbles." Mycroft's voice was cold. "Sherlock, your client is hardly an innocent lamb. There are many things about his life that he would rather not have come out, and I assure you they would come out." He made a show of checking his watch. "He's already been told as much, and I'm certain that you'll be hearing from him shortly to let you know that your services are no longer required."

Now I confess it was my turn to wrestle with my passions. But I mastered them, and I fancy I did a better job of it than Mycroft had.

"And me?"

He laughed. "You will not betray a client's confidence. Once he cries off, your work is done. Done it is. Sherlock, I have another appointment in a few moments. Is there anything further we need to discuss?"

I took my leave, and you have found me now in a fury and a conundrum, confronting my own future, and that of my brother, and of the way that I failed my client, who trusted me. For as you've seen, I kept my erstwhile client's bit of paper, and the names of the boys he feared so much for, and have made inquiries with a lady of the press of whom I have a long and fruitful acquaintance. The press, Watson, is a most valuable institution, if you only know how to use it. I have been most careful, but as I have said on more than one occasion, my brother Mycroft has the finer mind of the two of us."

He filled his pipe and struck a match. There was a sound at the door.

"I fancy that's him now," he said and puffed at his pipe. Someone who did not know him as well as I did may have missed the tremor in his hand as he shook the match out.

The door opened. Mycroft Holmes's face was almost green in the bright light that lit it like the moon.

"You brought Watson into it," he said, sighing.

"I'm afraid I did," Holmes said. "He's always been so diligent when it came to telling my story."

"He is a veteran, and has sworn an oath," Mycroft said, stepping inside, speaking with the air of a merchant weighing an unknown quantity in his scales.

"He is a friend," Holmes said. "Sorry, James."

"Quite all right," I said, and looked at Mycroft. "What's it to be, then?" I was—and am—proud of how steady my voice was, though my heart trembled.

"That is to be seen," he said, and then the police came in behind him.

ABOUT THE CONTRIBUTORS

TASHA ALEXANDER first discovered Sherlock Holmes when she was ten years old and stumbled upon the stories when making her way systematically through the stacks in the South Bend Public Library. She immediately read them all twice and was entirely convinced Holmes was an actual person. She is the *New York Times* bestselling author of the Lady Emily Series and, when walking in Baker Street, still feels a twinge of regret that Holmes was fictional (or so she understands). Find her at www.tashaalexander.com.

DANA CAMERON's relationship with Sherlock Holmes has always been tempestuous. She went from being terrified out of her wits by "The Speckled Band," to consuming the canon as a teenager living in London, to currently being obsessed with Mycroft Holmes (she is a founding member of the Diogenes Club of Washington, D.C., a scion of the Baker Street Irregulars). Dana writes fiction inspired by her career as an archaeologist; in addition to six Emma Fielding mystery novels and three "Fangborn" urban fantasy adventures, she has written more than twenty short stories (including the Sherlockian pastiche, "The Curious Case of Miss Amelia

Vernet"). Several of those stories feature colonial tavern-owner Anna Hoyt, who has a small role in "Where There Is Honey." Dana's work has won multiple Anthony, Agatha, and Macavity Awards, and has been short-listed for the prestigious Edgar® Award; in 2016, she became a member of The Baker Street Irregulars, with the investiture "The Giant Rat of Sumatra." Learn more about her at www.danacameron.com.

JOHN CONNOLLY's first exposure to Sherlock Holmes came in the form of Saturday afternoon TV screenings by the BBC of the Basil Rathbone-Nigel Bruce adaptations, and these have inevitably colored his view of Holmes and Watson ever since. He finds committed Sherlockians mildly perturbing, which may explain the nature of his contribution. He is the author of more than twenty novels and collections of short stories, including the Charlie Parker series and *The Book of Lost Things*, and finds the possibility of the Caxton Private Lending Library's existence strangely consoling. Visit him at www.johnconnollybooks.com.

New York Times bestselling author DEBORAH CROMBIE is a Texan who writes crime novels set in Britain. Her Duncan Kincaid/Gemma James series has received numerous awards and is published to international acclaim. Crombie lives in North Texas with her husband, German shepherds, and cats, and divides her time between Texas and Britain. Her seventeenth Kincaid/James novel, *Garden of Lamentations*, will be published by William Morrow in 2016. She blames her lifetime affliction with Anglophilia on an early introduction to the world of Sherlock Holmes and Dr. John Watson. Find her at www.deborahcrombie.com.

CORY DOCTOROW (www.craphound.com) is a science fiction author, activist, journalist, and blogger—the co-editor of Boing Boing (www.boingboing.net) and the author of the YA graphic novel *In Real Life*, the nonfiction business book *Information Doesn't Want to Be Free*, and young adult novels like *Homeland*, *Pirate Cinema*, and *Little Brother* and novels for adults like *Rapture of the Nerds* and *Makers*. He works for the Electronic Frontier Foundation and co-founded the UK Open Rights Group. Born in Toronto, Canada, he now lives in Los Angeles.

HALLIE EPHRON is the daughter of Hollywood screenwriters, so her first encounters with the Sherlock Holmes Canon were through movies. It was only natural that she set "Understudy in Scarlet" on a movie set. Hallie is a *New York Times* bestselling author of suspense novels. Her latest, *Night Night, Sleep Tight*, received a starred *PW* review: "Old Hollywood glamour, scandals, and lies infuse this captivating thriller." Her books have been finalists for Edgar®, Anthony, and Mary Higgins Clark awards, and her *Never Tell a Lie* was made into a Lifetime Movie Network movie. She is an award-winning book reviewer for the *Boston Globe*. Find her at www.hallieephron.com.

MEG GARDINER grew up watching Basil Rathbone play Sherlock Holmes. But she only came to appreciate the great detective after moving from California to London and reading *The Hound of the Baskervilles* when her children were assigned it in elementary school. The kids had to grab the book from her hands. She's been a Holmes fan ever since. Meg is the author of twelve thrillers that have been bestsellers in the U.S. and internationally and have been translated into more than twenty languages. *China Lake* won the 2009 Edgar® Award for Best Paperback Original. *The Dirty Secrets Club* was chosen one of the Top Ten Thrillers of 2008 by Amazon. *The Nightmare Thief* won the 2012 Audie Award for Thriller/Suspense Audiobook of the Year. Her current novel, *Phantom Instinct*, was chosen one of *O, The Oprah Magazine*'s "Best Books of Summer." She lives in Austin, Texas. Visit her at www.meggardiner.com.

LAURIE R. KING is the *New York Times* bestselling author of the Mary Russell-Sherlock Holmes stories, beginning with *The Beekeeper's Apprentice* (one of the IMBA's 100 Best Crime Novels of the Century). She has won or been nominated for an alphabet of prizes from Agatha to Wolfe, been Guest of Honor at several crime conventions, and is probably the only writer to have received both an Edgar® Award and an honorary doctorate in theology. She was inducted into the Baker Street Irregulars in 2010, as "The Red Circle." Find her at www.LaurieRKing.com.

LESLIE S. KLINGER is the *New York Times* bestselling editor of the Edgar®-winning *The New Annotated Sherlock Holmes* and the multi-award-winning ten-volume *Sherlock Holmes Reference Library*. He also co-edited, with Laurie R. King, the anthologies *A Study in Sherlock* and the Anthony-winning *In the Company of Sherlock Holmes*. He became hooked on the Sherlock Holmes Canon while he was attending law school, desperate for some non-law reading. He freely admits that even more than the stories, the footnotes of *The Annotated Sherlock Holmes* by William S. Baring-Gould were his primary interest. He also writes about other geeky subjects, such as Dracula, H. P. Lovecraft, and Frankenstein and has edited two anthologies of horror stories. Klinger was inducted into the Baker Street Irregulars in 1999 as "The Abbey Grange." Find him at www.lesliesklinger.com.

Probably like many of his generation, WILLIAM KENT KRUEGER came to Sherlock Holmes via Hollywood. Those atmospheric black and white gems cranked out in the thirties and forties guided him to the classic original texts and he was, of course, hooked on Sir Arthur Conan Doyle. Nevertheless, for him, Basil Rathbone will always be the image of that greatest of detectives and the bumbling, mumbling Nigel Bruce will always be Watson. Krueger writes the *New York Times* bestselling Cork O'Connor mystery series, which is set in Minnesota's great Northwoods. His novel *Ordinary Grace* received the Edgar® Award for Best Novel in 2014.

As a child, TONY LEE was a reluctant reader and therefore never read any of the Sherlock Holmes novels, only ever reading of Holmes's exploits in a special issue of DC comics *Batman*. That was until he saw Jeremy Brett's portrayal of *Sherlock Holmes* on TV in 1984. Following this, he devoured every one of Holmes's adventures, in the process discovering a joy for reading that he has never lost. Now a #1 *New York Times* bestselling writer of comics, books, TV, and film, Tony has written for the world of Sherlock Holmes in both audio (*The Confessions of Dorian Gray: Ghosts of Christmas Past*) and comic form (his series of *Baker Street Irregulars* Graphic Novels were so popular, they were even made into a US stage play), but hopes more than anything to write something one day that redeems the poor, misunderstood and maligned Professor Moriarty. He can be found at www.tonylee.co.uk.

JONATHAN MABERRY is a *New York Times* bestselling novelist, five-time Bram Stoker Award® winner, and comic book writer. He has been a longtime fan of Sherlock Holmes and wrote a Holmes story, "The Adventure of the Greenbrier Ghost," which is based on the only case in American legal history where the testimony of a ghost was introduced in court and led to the conviction of a murderer. Jonathan has also performed in regional theater in several one-act dramatizations of Holmes stories, playing Mycroft Holmes, James Moriarty, and Charles Augustus Milverton. He writes the Joe Ledger thrillers, the Rot & Ruin series, the Nightsiders series, the Dead of Night series, as well as standalone novels in multiple genres. His comic book works include, among others, *Captain America, Bad Blood, Rot & Ruin, V-Wars*, and others. He is the editor of many anthologies, including *The X-Files, Scary Out There, Out of Tune*, and *V-Wars*. His books *Extinction Machine* and *V-Wars* are in development for TV, and *Rot & Ruin* is in development as a series of feature films. He is the founder of the Writers Coffeehouse, and the co-founder of The Liars Club. Prior to becoming a full-time novelist, Jonathan spent twenty-five years as a magazine feature writer, martial arts instructor, and playwright. Visit him at www.jonathanmaberry.com.

Growing up in Edinburgh, CATRIONA MCPHERSON had Holmes, Watson, Conan Doyle, Deacon Brodie, Burke, Hare, Jekyll, and Hyde hopelessly muddled until she read her way to clarity in her teens. When she started writing her own fiction she was drawn back into their world, not so much for the gaslight and cobblestones as for the secrets and the shame. Edinburgh, rigidly respectable on the surface, is a great place for secret shame. She has written ten novels in a historical series set in Scotland, featuring private detective Dandy Gilver, which *The Guardian* calls "quietly subversive." They have won Agatha, Macavity and Bruce Alexander awards and been shortlisted for a CWA dagger. Recently, she began a strand of contemporary standalones and has won two Anthony awards for these as well as being an Edgar® finalist for *The Day She Died*. Her latest is *The Child Garden*. You can find her at www.catrionamcpherson.com.

DENISE MINA has long been slightly obsessed by Joseph Bell, Doyle's inspiration for the character of Sherlock Holmes. She studied and lives in

Glasgow, a hop, skip and a jump from Edinburgh Medical School, where Bell taught his systematic reasoned deductions to Doyle himself. When not being a tedious pedant herself, she is the author of seven graphic novels, including the DC Comics adaptation of Stieg Larsson's "Millennium Trilogy." In her spare time she is the author of thirteen novels. Her first, *Garnethill*, won the CWA John Creasy Award for Best First Novel and the Spirit of Scotland Award. She is the author of the Paddy Meehan series, the second of which, *The Dead Hour*, was short listed for the Edgar®. The Paddy Meehan books have been brilliantly adapted for BBC Drama starring Peter Capaldi and David Morrissy. The Alex Morrow Series began with *Still Midnight* and includes the multi-award-winning *End of the Wasp Season* as well as her current book, *Blood Salt Water*. If you can bear to find out any more, her web site is www.denisemina.com. She whitters on Twitter at @DameDeniseMina.

DAVID MORRELL can't remember a time when Sherlock Holmes wasn't part of his imaginative DNA. Writing "The Spiritualist" gave him a wonderful impetus to re-read the Holmes Canon and re-enter the dizzying Great Game. A former literature professor at the University of Iowa, Morrell created the character of Rambo in his debut novel, *First Blood*. His numerous *New York Times* bestsellers include the classic spy novel *The Brotherhood of the Rose*, the basis for the only TV mini-series to be broadcast after a Super Bowl. An Edgar® and Anthony finalist, a Nero and Macavity winner, Morrell is a recipient of three Bram Stoker Awards® and the Thriller Master award from the International Thriller Writers organization. His latest novels are the Victorian mystery/thrillers *Murder as a Fine Art* and *Inspector of the Dead*. Visit him at www.davidmorrell.net.

BEVIS MUSSON claims that he never heard of Sherlock Holmes before drawing *Mrs. Hudson Investigates*, which probably explains a lot—although he seems to know a lot about *Basil The Great Mouse Detective*. He hopes that he got all the details and references correct but is sure that no one will think anything out of place. He is the artist on *Knight & Dragon* from Improper Books and is the writer and artist of *The Dead Queen Detectives*. His one wish in life would be that people stop getting

him to draw stories that have horses in them. Find out more at www
.bevismusson.deviantart.com/.

ANNE PERRY has published over eighty books. Fifty-three of them
feature either Inspector Thomas Pitt, first of Bow Street, then of Special
Branch, or Commander William Monk, lately of the Thames River
Police. They, plus several short stories, are all mysteries set in Victorian
London, and so it is hardly surprising that she was influenced by
Sherlock Holmes and Dr. Watson. The invitation to join in this
collection was irresistible. Her story "Raffa" is dedicated to her friend
Kira Gangi. Visit her at www.anneperry.co.uk/books.

Still on GARY PHILLIPS's shelf is a book his aunt gave him decades ago
called *Conan Doyle Stories: Six Notable Adventures of Sherlock Holmes*,
Platt & Munk, Publishers. At nine or ten he read *A Study in Scarlet* and
was hooked. Further cementing his fascination with the character, Phillips
fondly recalls those Sunday afternoons in high school when he and his
dad would watch the Rathbone-Bruce interpretations on Channel 9. Other
recent work includes "The Two Falcons" in the *Highway Kind, Stories of
Cars and Crime*, and a second Decimator Smith story in *Black Pulp II*,
and comics miniseries for Hard Case Crime and DC Comics. Please drop
by his website at www.gdphillips.com for further goings-on.

HANK PHILLIPPI RYAN's parents tell the story of the Black Hole of Time,
when their eldest daughter disappeared into the hayloft of the barn behind
their home. Turned out thirteen-year-old Hank had settled in to read the
entire volume of the Christopher Morley edition of *The Complete Sherlock Holmes*. Afterward, briefly, she communicated only in the code she
learned in "The Adventure of the Dancing Men." She also vowed to become
a detective herself, solving crimes and catching bad guys. Hank kept
her vow, in her own way, and is now the winner of thirty-three Emmy®
Awards for investigative reporting at Boston's NBC affiliate, where she is
still on the air. After adding fiction to her resume, Ryan, author of eight
mystery novels, has won five Agatha Awards, two Anthony Awards, two
Macavitys, and, for *The Other Woman*, the Mary Higgins Clark Award.

Her newest novel, *What You See*, which national reviewers have called "superbly entertaining" and "a perfect thriller," is a *Library Journal* Best of 2015. Though she no longer writes in code, Hank has actually read a portion of Edward Hitchcock's 1841 tome *Final Report on the Geology of Massachusetts*, but only enough to matter. Visit her at www.hankphil lippiryan.com.

MICHAEL SCOTT is the *New York Times* bestselling author of *The Secrets of the Immortal Nicholas Flamel*. Published in thirty-seven countries and twenty-five languages, he is one of Ireland's most successful and prolific authors, with over one hundred titles to his credit. He grew up in a book-filled house where nothing was off-limits—except the very top shelf which held his father's almost complete collection of *Strand Magazines*. However, a chair on top of a table gave him access to the world of Holmes and Watson. He got so caught up in reading *The Hound of the Baskervilles* that he fell off the chair and broke his wrist. Luckily, the magazine was unharmed. Later, a long career as an antiquarian bookseller allowed him to add to the collection, though it is still not quite complete. He spent the best part of a decade researching the events surrounding the theft of the Irish Crown Jewels. Conan Doyle himself borrowed elements from the story for "The Adventure of the Bruce-Partington Plans." All the revelations in the short story are based on fact because truth is always stranger than fiction. His website is www.dillonscott.com.

ACKNOWLEDGMENTS

Our thanks to Don Maass for his astute advice regarding the contract for this book. Special thanks to Claiborne Hancock, Iris Blasi, Maria Fernandez, and Christine Van Bree of Pegasus Books for all their hard work to make this happen and for their belief in an audience for short stories.

We were fortunate to win both the Anthony and the Silver Falchion awards for "Best Anthology" for the previous book in this series, *In the Company of Sherlock Holmes: Tales Inspired by the Holmes Canon*, and we're very grateful to the readers who voted for those awards. However, we both know very well that the real credit for those awards goes to our amazing friends and contributors, Laura Caldwell, Michael Connelly, Jeffery Deaver, Michael Dirda, Harlan Ellison, Cornelia Funke, Andrew Grant, Denise Hamilton, Nancy Holder, John Lescroart, Sara Paretsky, John Reppion & Leah Moore, Michael Sims, and Gahan Wilson, whose stories shone. The friends who contributed to our first volume, *A Study in Sherlock: Stories Inspired by the Sherlock Holmes Canon* (Random House), Alan Bradley, Tony Broadbent, Jan Burke, Lionel Chetwynd, Lee Child, Colin Cotterill, Neil Gaiman, Laura Lippman, Gayle Lynds & John Sheldon, Philip & Jerry Margolin, Margaret Maron, Thomas Perry, S. J. Rozan, Dana Stabenow, Charles Todd, and Jacqueline Winspear, got the idea started and were enthusiastic cheerleaders for succeeding volumes. Thanks also to Kate Miciak of Random House for her early support, as well as Barbara Peters and Rob Rosenwald of Poisoned Pen Press and Otto Penzler of Mysterious Books.

Finally, endless gratitude to those who work hard behind the scenes on all of our books and on whose constant support we depend: Zoë Elkaim and Sharon Klinger.